VOWS MADE IN WINE

Oliver de Lacey had no time for love. He pursued pleasure with relentless fervor. Then one day he met a woman who changed his wild ways . . . Mistress Lark had no need for passion. All her devotion went into a secret cause she embraced with her whole heart — until she met Oliver de Lacey. She looked into his soul and saw something worth saving. He looked into her heart and saw a hurt he could heal. Love was their most difficult challenge — and their greatest reward.

SUSAN WIGGS

VOWS MADE
IN WINE

Complete and Unabridged

NIAGARA

Ulverscroft Group Limited
England - USA - Canada
Australia - New Zealand

First published in the
United States of America

First Niagara Edition
published 1995
by arrangement with
HarperCollins Publishers
New York

ISBN 0–7089–5815–X

ULVERSCROFT
Large Print

Published by
F. A. Thorpe (Publishing) Ltd.
Anstey, Leicestershire
Set by Words & Graphics Ltd.
Anstey, Leicestershire
Printed and bound in Great Britain by
T. J. Press (Padstow) Ltd., Padstow, Cornwall

This book is printed on acid-free paper

To my fellow writer, Barbara Dawson Smith,
with love and gratitude
for all the years of friendship.

Acknowledgments

I wish to thank Joyce Bell, Betty Gyenes, and Barbara Dawson Smith for generously giving their time and support. Also, thanks to the many members of the GEnie® Romance Exchange, an electronic bulletin board, for so many interesting discussions.

Special thanks to Trish Jensen and Kathryn van der Pol for their proofreading skills.

I am falser than vows made in wine.
                    — William Shakespeare

Prologue

OLIVER DE LACEY had died badly. He had gone blubbering and pleading to the hangman's noose, and his last act as a mortal man had been to piss himself.

Aye, 'twas a bad death from the moment he had arisen in his dank cell in Newgate, begged one last time to sire a child on the warden's daughter, lied through his teeth to the priest who came to grant him absolution, and vomited up his last breakfast.

A singularly bad death for Oliver de Lacey. And now he was paying the ultimate price for his many sins.

The descent into hell was not what he expected. Indeed, it bordered on the peculiar. Darkness, aye, but what were those evil slits of gray light and that creaky, lumbering sound? And if he had left his mortal body behind, why did he feel this damnable pain in his neck? Why did he smell fresh-cut wood?

It was new and particularly awful for a man who had not expected to die by execution as a common criminal, of all things. He had always known he would die young. But he had worked hard to ensure himself a glorious demise. He had dreamed of perishing while fighting a duel, racing horses, perhaps even while bedding another man's wife.

Not — God forbid — swinging by the neck

while a bloodthirsty crowd jeered at him.

At least no one knew it was Lord Oliver de Lacey, Baron Wimberleigh, who had died at dawn. He had been arrested, tried, and sentenced in his guise of Oliver Lackey — a bearded, common rapscallion who had incited one riot too many.

Thank heaven for small favors. He had spared his family a great shame. They had all gone abroad until the spring; they would come back to find that Oliver had vanished without a trace.

Ah, what a waste, he thought in disgust as his strange conveyance transported him to eternal damnation. He had wanted to make his mark in his short time on earth. In pursuit of this, he had loved every woman he could find, fought every battle he could join, sampled every delicacy, read every book, embarked on every adventure available to an affable young lord. He had lived fast and hard and voraciously with the knowledge that his illness would one day conquer him.

And this morn, an hour before cock crow, he had died a coward's death.

"They say he died badly." The voice penetrated Oliver's hell-bound chariot. "Did you see?"

God's light, but it was a horrid, unholy voice.

"I saw." This voice, in contrast, was as sweet as the trill of a lark at dawn. "He showed no dignity whatsoever. I can't think why Spencer was so insistent about taking this one."

Spencer? The devil was called Spencer?

2

"Spencer," said the ugly voice, "like the Lord above, works in mysterious ways. Does he know you have come?"

"Of course not," said the woman. "He thinks I only help with the ciphering. He must never know."

"Well, pox and pestilence, I don't like it. Not one bit."

Amen, thought Oliver. Death was getting stranger by the moment. Descending into hell was an odd business indeed.

The creaking and jangling ceased abruptly.

Now what? Oliver wondered. He braced himself for an onslaught of fire and brimstone.

"Careful, now. Is anyone about?" the man asked.

"Just the chief gravedigger in his hut yonder. You did give him plenty of fortified wine?"

"Oh, aye. He won't stir his bones."

"But I see a light in the window," the woman said.

"Right. We'd best put on a good show, then. Move the cart just to the edge of the pit. Let's get this one out." The chariot lurched. "Easy now. Easy! Frigging slump-backed nag. Almost backed into the pit. Hand me that chisel. I'll just pry open this panel."

A screeching sound rent the air, followed by an equine whinny.

"Shrouds and shambles!" the man hissed. "Mind the box! You'll spill it."

A square of light opened at Oliver's lifeless feet. He began tilting, sliding, until his remains poured down a steep incline. He landed on

3

something dusty and infinitely more noxious than anything he had done inside his canions.

"Oh, no," whispered the female voice. "Dr. Snipes, what have we done?"

What indeed, Oliver wondered.

"He's fallen into the pit," she said as if she'd heard his question.

Ah, thought Oliver. At last it begins to make sense. Hell was a pit, exactly as Messer Dante had described. Except this place was cold. Bone-chillingly cold.

"We've got to get him out," said the man called Snipes.

Yes, yes, please. Oliver tried to speak, but no sound emerged from his brutalized throat.

"Dr. Snipes, look! He's come around. Sweet mercy, he is saved!"

Saved?

Oliver saw a pair of shadows looming above him, the sky a cloudy dark gray behind them.

"Mr. Lackey? Can you hear me?" the woman called out.

"Yes." The word came out as a thin wheeze.

"He speaks! God be praised!"

Why did this instrument of the Devil praise God? And why did she address him as Lackey? Surely the Devil knew his true identity.

"Mr. Lackey, we must get you out of there," Snipes said.

"Where am I?" There. He had spoken. A horrible rasp, to be sure, but his speech was intelligible.

"I, er, that is, you're near the City ditch across

4

from Greyfriars," Snipes said. "In a, er, in a pauper's grave."

"This isn't hell?" Oliver asked stupidly.

"Some would say aye," the woman murmured.

God, he loved her voice. It was particularly the sort of voice he adored in a woman — sweet but not shrill, crisp and precise as a well-tuned gittern.

"Surely it's not heaven," he said. "Purgatory, then?"

"Oh, Dr. Snipes," the woman whispered, "he thinks he is dead."

"I *am* dead," Oliver stated in his raspy voice. The dust and straw stirred as he lifted his fist. He sneezed. "I died badly. You said so yourself."

He could have sworn he heard stifled mirth. "Sir, you were hanged, but you did not die."

"Why not?" Oliver felt slightly miffed.

"Because we would not let you. We bribed the hangman to shorten the rope and saw to it you were cut down, pronounced dead, and nailed into your box before you died."

"Oh." Oliver thought about this for a moment. "Thank you." Then he groaned. "You mean I begged and humbled and pis — er, disgraced myself for naught?"

"It would seem so."

A distant cock crowed.

"Come, time is short. We must get you out of there. Can you move?"

Oliver tried to sit up. Jesu, but his limbs were weak! He managed to prop himself up. "This place is all lumpy," he complained. "What sort of hellhole is this?"

"Lark told you," Snipes said. "'Tis a pauper's grave."

Lark. Her name was as lovely as her voice.

"You might wish to make haste," she called. "You could catch a disease from them."

"From what?" Oliver asked.

"From the corpses. 'Tis a *pauper's* grave, sir. There's a heap of them down there, covered with straw and lime dust. When the grave is full, it will be covered over."

"All that lime makes for excellent grazing once the grass starts," Snipes remarked helpfully.

"You mean . . . ?" Bile rose from Oliver's stomach. He lurched to his feet. "You mean you dumped me into a heap of . . . of *corpses?*"

"A most regrettable accident," said Lark.

Oliver had spent weeks in Newgate, suffering from poor food and putrid air. He had been hanged nearly to death. There was no way he should have had the strength to sink his hands into the damp earth and scramble out of the grave.

But he did.

In mere seconds he was sprawled, gasping for breath, on the cold and dewy grass.

"God's shield, that's foul." Wheezing, he rolled over. His saviors bent to peer at him. Snipes wore the black cloak and tunic of an undertaker, and in the uncertain light Oliver could see a withered, twisted arm, a prominent nose and chin, wispy white hair beneath a flat cap.

6

"I'll just go and tell the gravedigger we've buried the poor sinner." Snipes lumbered off into the shadows toward a wattled hut in the distance.

"Have you the strength to rise?" asked Lark.

Oliver looked at her. "My God," he said, staring at the pale oval of her face, its delicate, dawn-limned features framed by a numbus of glossy raven hair escaping a plain coif. "My God, you are an angel."

Her full red lips quirked at the corners. "Hardly."

"'Tis true. I *am* dead. I have died and gone to heaven, and you are an angel, and I am going to spend eternity with you. Hallelujah!"

"Nonsense." Her manner became brisk as she stuck out her hand. "Here, I'll help you up. We must get you to the safe hold."

She tugged at his hand, and her touch infused him with miraculous strength. When he stood upright, he saw that he towered over her. Just for a moment he felt a sense of deep connection with her. He could not tell if she felt it, too, or if she always wore that wide-eyed, startled expression.

"A safe hold?" he whispered.

"Aye." She surreptitiously wiped her hand on her apron. "You'll stay there until your throat is healed."

"Very well. I have only one more question for you, mistress."

"Yes?"

He gave her his best smile. The one that

7

women of good breeding said could dim the stars.

She tilted her head to one side, clearly lacking the breeding to be properly dazzled.

"Yes?" she said again.

"Mistress Lark, will you have my baby?"

1

"SPENCER, you would *not* countenance what that yea-forsooth knave said to me." Lark paced the huge bedchamber of Blackrose Priory. "Of all the effrontery!"

"Said to you?" Spencer Merrifield, earl of Hardstaff, had the most endearing way of lifting one eyebrow so that it resembled a gray question mark. Sitting in his grand tester bed, his thin frame propped against a wall of pillows and bolsters, he eyed her in the early evening light that streamed through the oriel window. "You spoke to him?"

"Yes. I — at the safe hold." She cringed inwardly at the small lie and studied the pattern of lozenge shapes that tiled the floor. Spencer would object to her being present for the hanging. But the safe hold was run by godly folk whose goals matched Spencer's own.

"I see. Well, then. What did Oliver de Lacey say to you?"

She frowned and plopped down onto a stool by the bed, tucking her soft, kerseymere skirts between her knees. "I thought his name was Oliver Lackey."

"That is one of his names. In sooth he is Lord Oliver de Lacey, Baron Wimberleigh, son and heir to the earl of Lynley."

"He? A noble?" The man had been wearing a stained shirt and plain fustian jerkin over torn and ragged canions and hose. No shoes; those were always appropriated by prison wardens. He had looked as common as a mongrel dog — until he had smiled at her.

Spencer watched her closely as if seeking to peer into her mind. She was familiar with the look. When she was very small, she used to liken Spencer to the Almighty Himself, with all the powers of His station.

"Betimes he goes about incognito," Spencer explained, "I suppose to spare his family from embarrassment. Now. What did the young lord say to you?"

Will you have my baby?

Lark's face burned scarlet at the memory. Her response had been a drop-jawed look of astonishment. Then, humiliated to the depths of her prayer-fed soul, she had flounced away, instructing him to hide in the cart until Dr. Snipes joined them and they reached the safe hold.

"I shall lie low," Oliver had said, "but I should be more content if you were lying beneath me."

Thank heavens Dr. Snipes had returned and spared her from having to respond.

Now she looked at Spencer and felt such a wave of horror and guilt that her hands trembled. She buried them deep in the folds of her skirts.

"I do not recall his precise words," she said, lying again. "But he had a most insolent manner."

"Perhaps his brush with death put him in a foul mood."

10

It was an unusually tolerant observation from a man of little tolerance. Lark blinked in surprise. She tried to will her flushed cheeks to cool. "He could use a lesson in manners."

"Lark, be he rapscallion or man of honor, did he deserve to die?"

"No," she whispered, instantly contrite. She took Spencer's hand; his was cool and dry with age and infirmity. "Forgive me. I lack your generosity of spirit."

His fingers squeezed hers briefly. "A woman cannot be expected to comprehend the matters that move a man to courage."

She felt a sudden urge to snatch her hand away, then just as quickly buried the impulse. She owed all that she was to Spencer Merrifield. If from time to time his well-meaning comments grated, she should ignore them with good grace.

"And what lofty purpose do you have in mind for Oliver de Lacey?" she asked.

Spencer stared at her for a long time. She could see the flame of the dying sun reflected in his cloudy gray eyes. Ah, he saw her clearly — all the way through to her soul. Sometimes she feared his wisdom, for he seemed to know her better than she knew herself.

"Spencer?" She touched her stiff gray bodice, wondering if her partlet or coif had come askew.

"I've a purpose in mind for the lad. My dear," he said, "I am sick and getting sicker."

A lump of dread rose in her throat. "Then we shall seek a new physician, consult — "

He waved her silent. "Death is part of the circle of life, Lark. It's all around us. I have no fear of the hereafter. But I must make provisions for you. The manor of Evensong is already yours, of course. I intend to leave you all my worldly goods, all my monies. You'll want for nothing."

She did take her hand away then and tucked it between her knees, seeking warmth as an unbearable chill swept over her. He spoke so matter-of-factly, when in truth his death would change her life irrevocably.

"You are nineteen," he observed. "Most women are mothers by the time they reach your age."

"I have no regrets," she said stoutly. "Truly, I — "

"Hush. Listen, Lark. When I'm gone, you will be left alone. Worse than alone."

Worse? She caught her breath, then said, "Wynter."

"Aye. My son." The word was a curse on his lips. Wynter Merrifield was Spencer's son by his first wife, Doña Elena de Dura. Many years ago, before Lark's birth, the marriage had crumbled beneath the weight of Doña Elena's scorn for her English husband and her flagrant affairs with other, younger men. Like the Church of England and the Church of Rome, Spencer and Elena had been torn apart, the fissure created by infidelity and hatred.

And Wynter, now a strapping young lord of twenty-five, was the casualty.

When she had left Spencer, Doña Elena had

not told him she was expecting a child. While in sanctuary in Scotland, she had given birth and raised Wynter to be as bitter against his father as she was and as devoted to Queen Mary as Elena had been to Catherine of Aragon.

Two and a half years earlier Wynter had come back to Blackrose Priory to hover like a carrion bird over his father's wasting form. Each day Lark watched him furtively from her chamber window. As slim and darkly handsome as a young god, he rode the length and breadth of the estate, his black horse sweeping along the rich green water meadows by the river or racing up the terraced hills where sheep grazed.

The thought of Wynter made Lark fitful, and she stood and walked to the window. The sun was lowering over the wild Chiltern Hills in the distance, and shadows gathered in the river valley.

"By law," Spencer said wearily, "Wynter must inherit my estate. It is entailed to my sole male heir."

"Is he your heir?" she asked baldly, though she did not dare to turn and look at Spencer.

"A sticky matter," Spencer admitted. "I knew nothing of his existence when I put aside my first wife and had the marriage annulled. But as soon as I learned I had a son, I had him legitimized. How could I not? He did not ask to be born to a woman who would teach him to hate."

Lark heard the clink of glass as Spencer poured himself more of his medicine. "I should not have asked. Of course he is your son and heir." She shivered and continued to face the window, battered by a storm of bitter memories. "Your only one."

For her sake he had eschewed the chance to take another wife and father more sons. No matter, she thought, hugging herself against the chill air that slipped in through cracks around the window casement. More sons would not displace the first.

"Wynter is intelligent and educated," she said carefully, turning to face Spencer. "Surely he'll not misuse the estate."

"Do not be naive, my dear. Wynter wishes to exalt Queen Mary by reviving a religious house at Blackrose Priory. He'll turn this place into a hotbed of popish idolatry. I do not want him to have it. The monks who lived here before the Dissolution were voluptuous sinners," Spencer went on. "I sweated blood into this estate. I need to know that it will stay the same after I'm gone. And what will become of you?"

She rushed to the stool by the bed. "I try not to think about life without you. But when I do, I see myself continuing the work of the Samaritans. Dr. Snipes and his wife will look after me." It had occurred to her that she possessed some degree of cleverness, perhaps even enough to look after herself. She knew better than to point that out to Spencer.

He gestured at the chest at the foot of the bed. "Open that."

She did as he asked, using a key from the iron ring she wore tied to her waist. She found a stack of books and scrolled documents in the chest. "What is all this?"

"I'm going to disinherit Wynter," he said. She heard the pain in his voice, saw the flash of regret in his fading eyes.

"Oh, Spencer, how can you?" She closed the lid and rested her elbows on top of the chest. "You do love your son."

"I cannot trust him. When I see him, I notice a hardness, a cruelty, that sits ill with me."

Alarmed by Spencer's observation, she rose and fled to the hearth, staring down at the dull blue flames that wrapped around the great log. She thought of Wynter with his hair and eyes of jet, his lean swordsman's body, and his mouth that was harsh even when he smiled. He was a man of prodigious good looks and deep secrets. A dangerous combination, as she well knew.

"How will you do this?" she asked Spencer without turning around. "How will you deny Wynter his birthright?"

"I shall need your help, dear Lark."

She turned to him in surprise. "What can I do?"

"Find me a lawyer. I cannot trust anyone else."

"You would entrust this task to me?" she asked, shocked.

"There is no one else. I shall need you to find someone who is discreet, yet totally lacking in scruples."

"Spencer, this is so unlike you — "

"Just do it." A fit of coughing doubled him over, and she rushed to him, patting his back.

"I shall, Spencer," she said in a soothing voice.

15

"I shall find you the most unscrupulous knave in London."

★ ★ ★

Lark felt awkward, standing at the grand river entrance of the elegant half-timbered London residence. It was hard to believe Oliver de Lacey lived here, along the Strand, a stretch of riverbank where the great houses of the nobility stood shoulder to shoulder, their terraced gardens running down to the water's edge.

The door opened, and Lark found herself facing a plump, elderly woman with a hollowed horn thrust up against her ear. "Is Lord Oliver de Lacey at home?"

"Eh? He ain't lazy at home." The woman thumped her blackthorn cane on the floor. "Our dear Oliver can be a right hard worker when he's of a mind to be wanting something."

"Not lazy," Lark called, leaning toward the bell of the trumpet. "De Lacey. Oliver de Lacey."

The woman grimaced. "You needn't shout." She patted her well-worn apron. "Come near the fire, and tell old Nance your will."

Venturing inside a few more steps, Lark stood speechless. She felt as if she had entered a great clock-work. Everywhere — at the hearth, the foot of the stairs, along the walls, she saw huge toothed flywheels and gears, all connected with cables and chains.

Her heart skipped a beat. This was a chamber

16

of torture! Perhaps the de Laceys were secret Catholics who —

"You look as though you're scared of your own shadow." Nance waved her cane. "These be naught but harmless contraptions invented by Lord Oliver's sire. See here." She touched a crank at the foot of the wide staircase, and with a great grinding noise a platform slid upward.

In the next few minutes Lark saw wonders beyond imagining — a moving chair on runners to help the crippled old housekeeper up and down the stairs, an ingenious system to light the great wheeled fixture that hung from the hammer beam ceiling, a clock powered by heat from the embers in the hearth, a bellows worked by a remote system of pulleys.

Nance Harbutt, who proudly called herself the mistress of Wimberleigh House, assured Lark that such conveniences could be found throughout the residence. All were the brain-children of Stephen de Lacey, the earl of Lynley.

"Come sit." Nance gestured at a strange couch that looked as if it sat upon sled runners.

Lark sat, and a cry of surprise burst from her. The couch glided back and forth like a swing in a gentle breeze.

Nance sat beside her, fussily arranging several layers of skirts. "His Lordship made this after marrying his second wife, when the babies started coming. He liked to sit with her and rock them to sleep."

The vision evoked by Nance's words made Lark feel warm and strange inside. A man

17

holding a babe to his chest, a loving woman beside him . . . these things were alien to Lark, as alien as the huge dog that lazed upon the rushes in front of the hearth. The long-coated animal had the shape of a parchment-thin greyhound, but it had much longer legs.

A windhound from Russia, Nance explained, called borzoyas in their native land. Lord Oliver bred them, and the handsomest male of each litter was named Pavlo.

Lark forced herself to pay close attention to Nance Harbutt, the oldest retainer of the de Lacey family. The housekeeper had a tendency to ramble and a great dislike for being interrupted, so Lark sat quietly by.

She felt no immediate sense of urgency. Randall, the groom who had accompanied her from Blackrose Priory, was waiting in the kitchen. By now he would have found the ale or hard cider and would be useless to her. This did not bother her in the least. She and Randall had an agreement. She made no comment on his tippling, and he made no comment on her activities for the Samaritans.

According to Nance, the sun rose and set on Lord Oliver. There was no doubt in the old woman's mind that he had hung not only the moon, but also the sun and each and every little silver star in the heavens.

"I wish to see him," Lark said when Nance paused to draw a breath.

"To be him?" Nance frowned.

"To see him," Lark repeated, speaking directly into the horn.

18

"Of course you do, dearie." Nance patted her arm. Then she did a curious thing; she smoothed back the hood of Lark's black traveling cloak and peered at her.

"Dear God above," Nance said loudly. She picked up her apron and fanned her face.

"Is something amiss?"

"Nay. For a moment you — that look on your face put me in mind of Lord Stephen's second wife, the day he brought her home."

Lark recalled what Spencer had told her of Oliver's family. Lord Stephen de Lacey, a powerful and eccentric man, had married young. His first wife had perished giving birth to Oliver. The second was a woman of Russian descent, reputed to be a singular beauty. Though flattered by the comparison, Lark thought the elderly retainer's sight was as weak as her hearing.

"Now then," Nance said, her manner brisk, "when is the babe due?"

"The babe?" Lark regarded her stupidly.

"The babe, lass! The one Lord Oliver sowed in you. And God be praised that it's finally happened — "

"Ma'am." Lark's ears took fire.

"Weren't for lack of trying on the part of the dear lordling. 'Course, 'twould be preferable to marry first, but Oliver has ever been the — "

"Mistress Harbutt, please." Lark fairly shouted into the trumpet.

"Eh?" Nance flinched. "Heaven above, lass, I ain't so deaf as a stone."

"I'm sorry. You misunderstand. I have

19

no . . . " She lacked the words to describe how appalled she felt at the very suggestion that she might be a ruined woman carrying a rogue's bastard. "Lord Oliver and I are not that well acquainted. I merely wish to speak to him on a matter. Is he at home?"

"Sadly, nay." Nance blew out her breath. Then she brightened. "I know where he'd be. This time of day he's always going about important business."

Lark felt vastly relieved. Perhaps the young nobleman was engaged in lordly matters, serving his turn in Parliament or perhaps doing good works among the poor.

It might prove an unexpected pleasure to encounter him in his lofty pursuits.

★ ★ ★

Deep in the darkest tavern on the south bank, Oliver de Lacey looked up from the gaming table as the black-cloaked stranger entered. A woman, judging by her slight build and hesitant manner.

"Hells bells," said Clarice, shifting on Oliver's lap. "Don't tell me the Puritans are at us again."

Oliver sighed deliciously at the suggestive movement of her soft buttocks. Clarice was no more than a laced mutton in a leaping house, but she was a woman, and he adored women.

More than ever, now that he had been given a second chance at life.

"Ignore her," he said, nuzzling Clarice's neck,

20

inhaling the scent of lust. "No doubt she is a dried-up old crone who cannot bear to see people enjoy life. Eh, Kit?"

Christopher Youngblood, who sat across the table from Oliver, grinned. "In sooth you enjoy it too much, my friend. Such constant revelry does rob the savor from it."

Oliver rolled his eyes and looked to Clarice for sympathy. "Kit's smitten with my half sister, Belinda. He's saving his virtue for her."

Clarice shook her head, making her yellow curls bounce on her bared shoulders. "Such a waste, that."

The other harlot, Rosie, leaned toward Kit, caught his starched ruff in her fingers, and turned him to face her. "Let the lady have his virtue," she declared. "I'll take his vice." She gave him a smacking kiss on his mouth and pounded the table in high good humor as his face turned brick red.

Laughing uproariously, Oliver called for more ale and summoned Samuel Hollins and Egmont Carper, his favorite betting partners, to a game of mumchance. His spirits lubricated by ale and soft womanhood, he rolled the dice in the bowl.

And won. Lord, how he won. This was his first outing since that unfortunate incident — he refused to call it anything so grim as a hanging — and the luck that had delivered him from death now clung to him like a woman's sweet perfume.

Lucky as a cat with nine lives, he was, and it never occurred to him to wonder if he deserved it. Nor did it cross his mind that the whole incident had been very unusual indeed. Two strangers had risked their own safety to rescue him.

At a small, snug cottage near St. Giles they had provided him with a basin of hot water, a shaving blade, and a set of clean clothing. He had bathed, shorn off his blond beard, dressed, and returned home to sleep 'round the clock.

And he was none the worse for the wear, save for a bruised neck, now artfully concealed by a handsome ruff, and some redness in his eyes.

His saviors, Dr. Phineas Snipes and Mistress Lark, had wondered aloud why the mysterious Spencer had singled out Oliver for saving.

Oliver de Lacey did not wonder why. He knew. It was because he was blessed. Blessed with angelic good looks, for which he took no credit but which he used to utmost advantage. Blessed with a large, loving family whose only fault was that they were too hasty to forgive his every transgression. Blessed with a quick mind and a glib tongue. Blessed with a lust for life.

And cursed, God damn it to hell, to die young. There was no cure for his sickness. The attacks of asthmatic breathlessness were few and infrequent, sometimes giving him years of respite between episodes. But when they came, they struck like a storm. For years he had fought each battle, but he knew in the end the disease would conquer him.

"Ollie?" Clarice tickled his ear with her tongue. "Your turn to cast the dice."

Like a large dog shaking off water, Oliver rid

22

himself of the thoughts. He made a masterful throw. A perfect seven. Clarice squealed with delight, Carper grudgingly gave up his coin, and Oliver rewarded his woman by tucking a ducat deep into her doughy cleavage.

"M-my Lord?" A soft, uncertain voice broke in on his revelry.

With a grin of triumph still on his face, Oliver looked up. "Yes?"

The black-clad Puritan gazed down at him. A slim white hand pushed back the hood.

Oliver stood, dumping Clarice from his lap. "You!"

Mistress Lark bobbed her head at him. Her face was stark white, the eyes a luminous rain-colored gray, her lower lip trembling. "Sir, I would like to speak to you."

Without even looking at Clarice, he reached down and helped her to the bench. "Of course. Mistress Lark." He gestured at his companions and rattled off their names.

"Do sit down," he said. She made him feel the most uncanny discomfort. In the smoky lamp glow of the tavern, she did not look as ethereally beautiful as she had at dawn two days before. Indeed, she appeared quite plain in her coarse garb, her hair scraped back into a tight black braid.

"There isn't any room for me to sit," she said. "And besides — "

"I've a perfectly good knee just waiting for you." He grabbed her wrist and lowered her onto his lap.

She yelped as if he had set fire to her backside.

23

Her body went stiff as a pike, and she jumped up. "Nay, sir!"

Carper, Hollins, and Kit nudged one another and giggled. Clarice and Rosie laughed outright.

Mistress Lark, her mouth as prim as a dried prune, stood her ground. "I shall wait until it is convenient for you to speak to me. In private."

"Please yourself," he said, wondering why he felt this urge to bedevil her. "You might have a bit of a wait, then. Fortune is favoring me today." He held out his tankard. "Have some ale."

"No, thank you."

He had the most remarkable urge to kiss her prissy mouth until it became soft and full beneath his. To caress her slender body and melt her stiffness into compliance.

Aware now that he had set the rules of a waiting game, he winked at her and turned back to his companions.

Lark was certain that everything decent about her was being peeled away in layers. What a fool she had been to suppose Oliver de Lacey would be pursuing lordly goals. She was doubly a fool to have left Randall in drunken slumber and come here on her own. She had paid a ferryman to take her across the river. She had moved like a thief through noxious alleyways crammed with vagrants and cozeners, all for the sake of finding a man whom Spencer had, for once in his life, wrongly judged to be a man of honor.

All Lord Oliver seemed to be pursuing were the pleasures of the gaming table, the oblivion of

24

strong ale, and the fleshly secrets hidden beneath the laced corset of the woman called Clarice.

Bawdy talk rose like a fog from the gamesters, some of it so wickedly obscure that Lark did not understand. She felt like the flame of a candle buffeted by the winds of corruption. Stubbornly, she refused to be snuffed out.

If he meant to humiliate her by forcing her to wait her turn, then wait she would. Oliver de Lacey did not know her at all. She had learned duty and loyalty from the most honorable man in England. She would endure any torment for Spencer's sake.

Of course, Spencer would never know how she had suffered. She could not tell him she had stood amid ruffians and doxies and gamesters. And most of all, she could not tell him that she took a secret, shameful interest in her surroundings.

The blatant and lusty sensuality of the people around the gaming table shocked her. It was but mid-morning, and they were tippling ale and wine like wedding guests at a midnight feast.

And the center of all the attention, like the sun casting its fire on a host of lesser bodies, was Oliver de Lacey himself.

He bore no resemblance to the pitiful victim who had fallen into the dusty pit of corpses just two days before.

When she looked at him now, she discovered a new meaning in the word beauty. Aye, he was as comely as a prince, his hair a shimmering mass of white-gold waves, his face carved into a perfect balance of hard lines and angles harmonizing with a sensual mouth and eyes the color of a robin's egg. In some men such beauty might have created an air of softness, but not in Oliver de Lacey. His expression held a rare blend of humor and male potency that caused a flare of awareness in Lark.

He had little to show for his suffering in the bowels of Newgate prison. Most men who had been arrested and condemned for inciting a riot, then secretly saved from death, might be loath to flaunt their presence so soon after the event.

A splendidly cut doublet of midnight blue velvet displayed his broad shoulders to shameless advantage. Flamboyant gold braid laced his sleeves around powerful arms. And when he threw back his head to laugh, displaying healthy teeth and a musical tenor shuckle, she could hardly blame Clarice for clinging to him. He had that air of potency, of magnetism, that made even sensible folk feel safe and treasured when he was near.

Will you have my baby? The memory came unbidden; his words echoed in her mind, and she hated herself for clinging to them. He had meant it as a jest, no more.

It was chilly in the tavern, with its damp plaster and timber walls and the bleak light of oil lamps. There was no reason on earth Lark should feel warm. Yet she did, as if she possessed embers inside and some force from without fanned them.

"You're certain you don't wish to sit with us?" Oliver inquired, studying her so closely that she

26

was certain he noticed her hot throat and cheeks and ears.

"Quite certain," she said.

He heaved a great sigh. "I cannot bear to have you standing there in discomfort." He spread his arms as if to embrace all who sat around the table. "My friends, I must go with dear Mistress Lark."

She saw the disappointment on their faces, and in an odd, intuitive way she understood it. When Oliver withdrew from the table, it seemed the sun had drifted behind a cloud.

Then he did a singular thing. He sank to one knee before Clarice. Gazing up at her as if she were Queen Mary herself, he took her hand in his, placed a lingering kiss in her palm, and closed her fingers around the invisible token. "Fare you well, my lovely."

Watching the intimate and chivalrous farewell gave Lark the oddest sensation of yearning. Certainly there was nothing remarkable about a rogue parting from his doxy, yet Oliver managed to glorify the simple act with an air of wistful romance and tenderness. As if he cherished her.

Cherish. Lark wondered what it would be like to be cherished, even for a moment. Even by a rogue.

Then he spoiled it by reaching around and pinching Clarice's backside. She brayed with laughter. Oliver stood, and for the first time Lark was struck by his height. When he donned a blue velvet hat, the plume brushed the blackened ceiling timbers.

"Kit, I shall call for you later."

Kit Youngblood sent him a jaunty salute. Though somewhat older than Oliver, more blunt featured and quiet, he was nearly as handsome. Taken as a pair, the two were quite overwhelming. "Do. I missed our carousing while you were away. On a pilgrimage, was it?"

The look they shared was steeped in mirth and fellowship. Then, without warning, Oliver took Lark by the hand and drew her out into the alleyway.

As soon as she recovered her surprise, she snatched her hand away. "Kindly keep your hands to yourself, my lord."

"Is it your mission in life to wound me?" he asked, looking remarkably sober for all that he had quaffed three tankards of ale while she had watched.

"Of course not." She clasped her hands in front of her. "My lord, I came to see you to — "

"You held out your hand to me when I lay gasping on the ground at a pauper's grave. Why flinch when I do the same to you?"

"Because I don't need help. Not of that sort."

"What sort?" He tilted his head to one side. The plume in his hat curved downward, caressing a face so favored by Adonis that Lark could only stare.

"The touching sort," she snapped, irritated that her head could be turned by mere looks.

"Ah." All male insolence, he reached out and

28

dragged his finger slowly and lightly down the curve of her cheek. It was worse than she had suspected — his touch was as compelling as his lavish handsomeness. She had the most shameful urge to lean her cheek into the cradling warmth of his hand. To gaze into his eyes and tell him all the secret things she had never dared admit to anyone. To close her eyes and —

"I must remember that," he said, dropping his hand and grinning down at her. "The lady does not like to be touched."

"Nor do I like walking in a strange alley with a man I hardly know. However, it is necessary. You see, there is a matter — "

"Hail the lord and his lady!" A group of men in sailors' caps and tunics tumbled past, swearing and spitting and jostling one another as they shoved themselves into the tavern.

"Good fishing to ye," one of them called out to Oliver. "I hope the perch are biting fair." The door slammed behind the man, muffling his guffaws.

Lark frowned. "What did he mean?"

She was surprised to see the color rise in Oliver's cheeks. Why would so shameless a man blush at a sailor's remark?

"He must have mistaken me for the sporting type." Oliver started off down the alley.

"Where are we going?" Picking up her skirts, Lark hurried after him.

"You said you wished to talk."

"I do. Why not here? I have been trying to explain myself."

A creaking sound came from somewhere

above, where the timbered buildings leaned out over the roadway. Oliver turned, grabbed Lark in his arms, and pushed her up against a plastered wall.

"Unhand me!" she squeaked. "You rogue! You measureless knave! How dare you take liberties with my virtue!"

"It's a tempting thought," he said with laughter in his voice. "But that was not my purpose. Now be still."

Even before he finished speaking, a cascade of filthy wash water crashed down from a high window. The deluge filled the road where Lark had stood only seconds ago.

"There." Oliver eased away from the wall and continued down the street. "Both your gown and your virtue are safe."

Miffed, she thanked him tersely. "Where are we going?"

"It's a surprise." The sound of his tall, slashed knee boots echoed down the tunnellike lane.

"I don't want a surprise," she said. "I simply want to talk to you."

"And so you shall. In good time."

"I wish to talk now. Forsooth, sir, you frustrate me!"

He stopped and turned so abruptly that she nearly collided with him. "Ah, Mistress Lark," he said, his bluer-than-blue eyes crinkling at the corners, "not half so much as you frustrate me." She feared he would touch her again, but he merely smiled and continued walking.

She followed him along a pathway, passing kennels where dogs for the bull baitings were housed, trying not to gawk at a flock of masked prostitutes gathering to watch the sport.

The north end of the path opened out to the Thames. The broad brown river teemed with wherries, shallops, timber barges, and small barks. Far to the east rose the webbed masts of great warships and merchantmen, and to the west loomed London Bridge. From this distance Lark could not see the grisly severed heads of traitors that adorned the Southwark Gate of the bridge, but the whirling scavenger kites made her think of them and shiver.

Oliver lifted his hand, and in mere seconds a barge with three oarsmen at the bow and a helmsman at the stern bumped the bottom of the water steps.

Bowing low and gesturing toward the canopied seat of the barge, he said, "After you, mistress."

She hesitated. It had been a mistake to leave Randall behind. For all she knew, Lord Oliver was dragging her along the path to perdition.

Still, the open, elegant barge looked far more inviting than the dank alley, so she descended the stone steps to the waterline. The helmsman held out a hand to steady her as she boarded.

"The lady mislikes being touched, Bodkin," Oliver called out helpfully.

With a shrug, Bodkin withdrew his hand just as Lark had one foot in the barge and the other on the slimy stone landing. The barge lurched. She tumbled onto the leather cushioned seat with a thud.

Mustering courage from her bruised dignity,

she glared up at Oliver. His buoyant grin flashed as he grasped the pole of the canopy and swung himself onto the seat beside her.

Lark stared straight ahead. "I assume we are going someplace where we can speak privately."

Oliver nudged the oarsman in front of him. "Hear that, Leonardo? She wants to tryst with me."

"I do not."

"Hush. I was teasing. Of course I will take you to a place of privacy. Eventually."

"Eventually? Why not immediately?"

"Because of the surprise," he said with an excess of good-humored patience. "The tide's low, Bodkin. I think it's safe to shoot the bridge."

The helmsman tugged at his beard. "Upstream? We'll get soaked."

Oliver laughed. "That's half the fun. Out oars, gentlemen, to yonder bridge."

Lark hoped for a mutiny, but the crew obeyed him. In perfect synchrony, three sets of long oars dipped into the water. The barge glided out into the Thames.

In spite of her annoyance with Lord Oliver de Lacey, Lark felt a thrill of excitement. Turbulence churned the waters beneath the narrow arches of London Bridge. She knew people had drowned trying to pass beneath it. Yet the smooth, swift motion of the sleek craft gliding through the water gave her the most glorious feeling of freedom. She told herself it had nothing to do with the benevolent, lusty, and wholly pagan presence beside her.

Moments later, white-tipped wavelets lifted the bow of the boat. As the barge neared London Bridge, it bucked like a wild horse over the roaring waters around the pilings.

Lark lifted her face to the spray. She had come to London for a business transaction, and here she was in the throes of a forbidden adventure. She swirled like a leaf upon the water, buffeted, at the mercy of a whimsical man who, with sheer force of will, had turned her from her purpose and swept her up in an escapade she should not want to experience.

"I wish you would listen to what I have to say," she stated.

"I might. Especially if it involves wine, women, and money."

"I does not."

"Then tell me later, my dove. First we'll have some fun."

"Why do you insist on surprising me?" she demanded, gripping the gunwale of the boat.

"Because." He swept off his hat and pressed it over his heart. He looked boyishly earnest, eyes wide, a silver-gilt lock of hair tumbling down his brow. "Because just once, Lark, I want to see you smile."

2

SHE did not understand him at all. That much she knew for certain. She could not fathom why he insisted on entertaining her. Nor did she know why it pleased him so to wave to strangers boating on the Thames, to call out greetings to people he'd never met, to run alongside a herring-buss to inquire about a fisherman's catch.

Most of all, she could not comprehend Oliver's shouts of humor and ecstasy when they shot the bridge. The adventure was sheer terror for her.

At first. Her senses were overcome by the rush of the water with its damp, fishy smell. Her teeth jarred with the churning sensation as the bow lifted, then slapped down. The rush of speed loosened tendrils of hair from her braid and caused her skirts to billow up above her knees.

Terror, once faced, was actually rather exhilarating. Especially when it was over.

"Was that my surprise?" she asked weakly once the bridge was behind them.

"Nay. You haven't smiled yet. You're white as an Irish ghost."

She turned to him and forced up the corners of her mouth. "There," she said through her teeth. "Will that do?"

"It is precious. But nay, I reject that one."

"What is wrong with my smile?" she demanded. "We cannot all be as handsome as sun gods with beautiful mouths and perfect teeth."

He laughed, tossing his mist-damp hair. "You noticed."

"I also noticed your vast conceit." She poked her nose into the air. "It rather spoils the effect."

He sobered, though his eyes still shone with mirth. "I meant no insult, dear Lark. It is just that your smile was not real. A real smile starts in the heart." Forgetting — or ignoring — her interdict against touching, he brushed his fingers over her stiff bodice. "Love, I can make your whole body smile."

"Oh, honestly — "

"It is a warmth that travels upward and outward, like a flame. Like this."

She sat transfixed as his hands brushed over the tops of her breasts, covered by a thin lawn partlet. His fingers grazed her throat, then her chin and lips. She thought wildly of the oarsmen and Bodkin at the helm, yet even as a horrible embarrassment crept over her, she stayed very still, transfixed by Oliver.

"A true smile does not end here, at your mouth." He watched her closely. "But in your eyes, like a candle piercing the darkness."

"Oh, dear," she heard herself whisper. "I am not certain I can do that."

"Of course you can, sweet Lark. But it does take practice."

Somehow, his lips were mere inches from hers. And hers tingled with a hunger that took her by surprise. She wanted to feel his mouth on hers, to discover the shape and texture of his lips. She had been lectured into a stupor about the evils of fleshly desires, she thought she had done battle with temptation, but no one had ever warned her about the seductive power of a man like Oliver de Lacey.

Closing her eyes, she swayed toward him, toward his warmth, toward the scents of tavern and river that clung to him.

"I am touching you again," he said, and she heard the whispered laughter in his voice. "Please forgive me." He dropped his hands and drew away.

Her eyes flew open. He lay half sprawled on the tasseled cushions, one leg drawn up and one hand trailing in the water. "A rather cold day, is it not, Mistress Lark?"

She resisted the urge to make certain her partlet was in place. "Indeed it is, my lord." She was not used to being teased. And she was definitely not used to bold, handsome men who flung out jests and insincere compliments as if they were alms to the poor.

It mattered not, she told herself. Spencer claimed he needed Oliver de Lacey. For Spencer's sake she would endure the young lord's insolent charm. Certainly not for her own pleasure.

"Will you listen now?" she asked. "I have come a very long way to see you."

"Nell!" he roared, causing the barge to list as he leaned out from under the canopy. "Nell Buxley!" He waved at a shallop proceeding downstream, aimed toward Southwark. "I made

36

heaven in your lap last time we met!"

"Good morrow to you, my bed-swerving lord," brayed a wine-roughened female voice. A grinning woman in a yellow wig leaned out from the shallop. "Who's that with you? Have you ransacked her honor yet?"

With a moan of futility, Lark slumped back against the cushions and yanked her hood over her head.

★ ★ ★

"This is another place of iniquity!" Lark stood at the head of the street and dug in her heels. "Why have you brought me here?"

Oliver chuckled. "'Tis Newgate Market, my love. You've never been?"

She stared at the teeming swarm of humanity that pushed through the narrow byways, crowding around stalls or pausing to observe the antics of a monkey here, a dancing dog there. "Of course not. I generally try to avoid places frequented by vagrants, cutpurses, and no-account young lords."

Even as she spoke, she saw a lad dart up behind a portly gentleman. The child tickled the man's ear with a feather, and when the man reached up to scratch, the little rogue cut his purse and slipped away with the prize.

Lark clapped one hand to her chest and pointed with the other. "That child! He . . . he . . . "

"And a good job he made of it, too."

"He stole that man's purse."

Oliver began strolling down the lane. "Life is brutish and short for some people. Let the lad go."

She did not want to follow Oliver into the raucous crowd, nor did she wish to stand alone, vulnerable to the evils that could befall her. Despite his devil-may-care manner, Oliver, with his prodigious height and confident swagger, made her feel protected.

"Watch this," he said, sidling up to the dancing monkey. A few people in the crowd moved aside to let him pass. Lark fancied she could feel the heat of the sly, appreciative feminine glances that slid his way.

When the little monkey, garbed in doublet and hat, spied Oliver, it leaped excitedly over its chain. The keeper laughted. "My lord, we have missed you these weeks past."

Oliver bowed from the waist. "And I have missed you and young Luther."

Lark caught her breath. It seemed decidedly impious to name a monkey after the great reformer.

"Luther is a chap of strong convictions, are you not?" Oliver asked.

The creature bared its teeth.

"He is loyal to the Princess Elizabeth."

At the sound of the name, the ape leaped in a frenzy, back and forth over its chain.

"He has his doubts about King Philip."

As soon as Oliver named Queen Mary's hated Spanish husband, Luther lay sullenly on the dirt path and refused to move. Oliver guffawed, tossed a coin to the keeper, and strolled on while the crowd applauded.

"You are too bold," Lark said, hurrying to match his long strides.

He sent her a lopsided grin. "You think that was bold? You, who have been known to steal out in the night to save the lives of condemned criminals?"

"That's different."

"I see."

She knew he was laughing at her. Before she could scold him, he stopped at a stall surrounded by long canvas draperies.

"Come see the show of nature's oddities," a woman called. "We've a badger that plays the tambout." Reaching out, she grasped Oliver's shoulder.

Patting her hand, he pulled away. "No, thank you."

"A goose that counts?" the hawker offered.

Oliver smiled and shook his head.

"A two-headed lamb? A five-legged calf?"

Oliver prepared to move off. The woman leaned close and said in a loud whisper, "A bull with two pizzles."

Oliver de Lacey froze in his tracks. "This," he said, pressing a coin into her palm, "I have got to see."

He made Lark come with him, but she steadfastly refused to look. She stood in a corner of the stall, her eyes clamped shut and her nostrils filled with the ripe scent of manure. Several minutes passed, and she closed her ears to the whistles and catcalls mingling with the animal noises.

At last Oliver returned to her side and drew her out into the bright light. His eyes were wide with juvenile wonder.

"Well?" Lark asked.

"I feel quite strung with emotion," he said earnestly. "Also cheated by nature."

Lark shook her head in disgust. For once, Spencer was wrong. This crude, ribald man could not possibly be the paragon of honor Spencer thought him to be. "'An heart that deviseth wicked imaginations,'" she muttered, "'feet that be swift in running to mischief.'"

"I beg your pardon?" Oliver weighed his purse in his hand.

"Proverbs," she said.

"Why, thank you, my lady Righteous." With an insolent swagger, he plunged down yet another narrow lane, and Lark had no choice but to follow or be left alone in the crowd. They passed flower sellers and cloth traders, booths selling roast pork and gingermen. Oliver laughed at puppets beating each other over the head. He dispensed coins to beggars as easily as if he were passing out bits of chaff.

After what seemed like an eternity, they reached the boundary of the fair. In the distance they could see the horse fair at Smithfield.

"We'll venture no farther." Oliver's face paled a shade. "I mislike the burning grounds."

She followed him obligingly from the area. Though the blackened stakes and sand pits were not yet visible, she felt their proximity like the brush of a cobweb against her cheek.

"That is the first sensible thing I have

heard you say," She announced. "Think of the condemned Protestants who have been martyred here."

"I've been trying not to." As they walked past the fringes of the fair, Oliver heaved a great sigh. "I have failed."

"What do you mean?"

"I wanted to make you laugh and smile, and you have not. Where did I go wrong?"

"Well, you could start with our near drowning while shooting the bridge."

"I thought you'd find that exhilarating."

"I found it foolish and unnecessary. As was your greeting to the woman called Nell." Lark lifted a skeptical eyebrow. "'Heaven in her lap'?"

He had the grace to blush. "She's an old friend."

"What about your little treasonous exchange with a monkey?" Lark continued, enumerating the outrages. "And your prurient interest in a bull's, er, his two . . . "

"Pizzles," Oliver supplied helpfully.

"Hardly a cause for great mirth from me."

"I know." He had a rare gift for looking both sulky and charming at once. "I've failed you. I — " He broke off, glancing over her shoulder. The sulkiness disappeared, and his face glowed with sheer delight. "Come, Mistress Lark. Here is something you'll like."

Pulled along in the wake of his enthusiasm, she found herself at the stall of a bird seller. Wooden crates of burbling doves, huddled robins, and motheaten gulls were stacked about haphazardly.

"How much?" Oliver asked the man.

"For which one, sir?"

"For all of them."

The man's jaw dropped. Oliver grabbed his hand and dumped a small fortune of coins into it. "That should keep you in your cups a good while."

"My lord," Lark said, "there are hundreds of birds here. How will you — "

"Watch." He drew a silver eating knife from the leather sheath attached to his belt and pried open each cage. With a flourish he removed each little door.

"Oliver!" Lark barely noticed that she had used his Christian name. The bird seller uttered a blue oath.

Like a great, winged cloud, the once captive birds rose. The sound of beating and whirring feathers filled the sky above the fair. It was an awesome sight, darkening the sun for a moment, then turning light as the flock of liberated birds dispersed.

Oohs and ahhs issued from nearby fairgoers.

"'The stars compel the soul to look upward,'" Oliver de Lacey recited, "'and lead us from this world to another.'" He smiled at Lark beatifically. "Plato."

"I know." She squinted up into the brilliant sky at the birds, now mere specks in an endless field of marbled blue.

And against her will, a smile unfurled on her lips.

"Eureka!" Oliver spread out one arm like a seasoned showman. "She smiles. Oh, smile on, bright cherub. Eureka!" His grin turned wicked. "Archimedes. When he first said 'Eureka,' he went running naked through the streets."

"That," she said, her chest and throat warm with unaccustomed merriment, "I did not know."

"It is said he made his discovery about the displacement of water while in his bath. The insight so aroused him that he forgot to dress himself before running to tell his colleagues."

Lark pressed her fingers to her lips. "How did you know that?"

"I am a fountain of knowledge. Would you care to drink?"

"No."

"It was too much to hope for." Oliver lifted his face to the winter sun as the last of the birds disappeared. "There, you see, my angel. They can soar. I have set them all free."

"All of them," she agreed, feeling strangely content.

"Well, not quite."

She peered at the cages. Not a single bird remained. The bird seller was already stacking his crates in a two-wheeled cart.

Oliver slipped one arm around her waist, and his other hand rested on her bodice, the fingers drumming on the stiff corset of boiled leather.

"There is still one little lark in a cage, eh?"

His barb hit home with a sting of unexpected pain. She tried to look imperious. "Sir, I am insulted. Unhand me."

He bent low to whisper in her ear. "I could free you, Lark. I could teach you to soar."

Heat swept from her toes to her nose, and she could not suppress a shiver as his warm breath caressed her ear. Alarmed, she broke away and stepped back. "I do not want you to teach me anything of the sort. I simply want help with a certain matter. You have refused to listen. You have dragged me from pillar to post on a fool's errand. If you will not help me, I wish you would tell me now so I can be shed of you."

"You wear outrage like an angel wears a halo." He sighed dramatically, then lounged against a stone hitch post.

All her life she had been taught that men were strong and prudent, endowed with qualities a mere woman lacked. Oliver de Lacey was a reckless contradiction to that rule. Furious, she marched blindly down the road. She hoped the way led to the river.

With easy strides he caught up with her. "I'll help you, Mistress Lark. I was born to help you. Only say what it is you require. Your smallest desire is my command."

She stopped and looked up into his sunny, impossibly wonderful face. "Why do I think," she said, "that I shall live to regret our association?"

★ ★ ★

"I cannot understand why you agreed to this," Kit Youngblood muttered to Oliver. He glared at the prim, straight-backed figure who rode in the fore. They were on the Oxford road leading away from the city, on an errand Oliver had embraced

44

with good heart. The ride was enjoyable, for he loved his horse. She was a silver Neapolitan mare bred from his father's best stock. Big-boned and graceful as a dancer was Delilah, the envy of all his friends.

"Keep your voice down," he whispered, his gaze glued to Lark's gray-clad form. He had always found the sight of a woman riding sidesaddle particularly arousing. "I owe her my life."

"I owe her nothing," Kit grumbled. "Why drag me along?"

"She needs a lawyer. For what purpose, she has yet to disclose."

"You know as much about the law as I do."

"True, but it would be unseemly for me to practice a profession." Oliver feigned a look of horror. "People might think me dull and unimaginative, not to mention common."

"Forgive me for suggesting it, Your Highness. Far better for you to follow such lordly pursuits as drinking and gaming."

"And wenching," Oliver added. "Pray do not forget wenching."

Kit scowled, aiming another glare between the pricked ears of his mount. "How did she know where to find you?"

"She went to my residence. A footman told me she brought an escort called Randall, but he had no resistance to the seductions of Londontown. Nance Harbutt directed her to my favorite gaming house."

"Hunted you down, eh? And what have you done to the poor woman? She's barely spoken since we left the City."

"I took her to Newgate Market." Closing his eyes, Oliver recalled the rapt expression on her small, pale face when he had set the birds free. "She loved it."

"You've ever been the perfect host," Kit said. "I do not know why I put up with you."

"I wish I could say that it's because you find me charming. But alas, 'tis because you're in love with my half sister, Belinda."

"Hah! Faithless baggage. I've not heard from her in a year."

"The kingdom of Muscovy is not exactly the next shire. Fear not. She and the rest of my family will return before long."

"She's probably grown thin and sallow and peevish on her travels."

Oliver chuckled. "She is Juliana's daughter," he reminded Kit, picturing his matchless stepmother. "Do you really think such a lass could grow ugly?"

"I almost wish she would. Suitors will be on her like flies on honey. She'll take no notice of me, the landless son of a knight. A common solicitor."

"If you believe that, then the game is up before it's started. You — " Oliver broke off, scanning the road in the distance. "What's that, a coach?"

Lark twisted around in her saddle. "It looks as if it's gotten mired." She made a straight seam of her mouth. "You would have noticed minutes ago if you had not been so busy yammering with Mr. Youngblood."

46

"Mistress Gamehen," Oliver said with a smile, "one day you will peck some poor husband to the bone."

She tossed her head, the dark coif fluttering behind her. With a squeeze of his legs, Oliver guided his horse past her to investigate the distressed travelers.

The boxy coach had been traveling toward town. Rather than being pulled by big country nags or oxen, it was yoked to a pair of rather delicate-looking riding mounts. Curious.

Behind the coach was a bridge spanning a shallow, rocky creek. Apparently the conveyance had cleared the bridge and become stuck in the muddy berm at the roadside.

"Hello!" Oliver called out, craning his neck to see into the small square window. He waved his hand to show he had no weapon drawn, for travelers tended to be wary of highwaymen.

"Are you mired, then?" he shouted. No response. He drew up beside the coach, frowning at the horses. Indeed they were no draft horses. Smallish heads indicated a strain of Barbary blood.

"Hello?" Oliver twisted in the saddle to send Kit a quizzical look.

The coach door swung open. A blade sliced out and just barely caressed the nape of his neck.

"Jesu!" From boyhood Oliver had been blessed with quick reflexes. In the blink of an eye he had dismounted, drawing his rapier even before his feet hit the ground. Kit did likewise.

To Oliver's dismay, Lark did not stay

47

mounted and back away as any sensible damsel would do; instead she leaped out of her saddle, lifted her skirts, and rushed toward the coach.

Three men, wearing the tattered garb of discharged soldiers, swarmed out. From the grim expressions on their faces, they seemed bent on fair murder.

Oliver flourished his sword and feinted back from one of the soldiers, a bearded fellow.

"I say!" Oliver parried a blow and sidestepped a thrust. "We're not highwaymen."

His answer was a wind-slicing front cut that slit his doublet. A bit of wool stuffing bulged from the tear.

A feeling of unholy glee came over him. His blood thrummed through his veins. He loved this feeling — the anticipation of a battle joined, the lure of physical challenge.

"You're good," he said to the bearded one. "I was hoping you would be."

Danger always had this effect on him. It was a battle lust he had learned to crave. Some would call it courage, but Oliver knew himself well enough to admit that it was pure recklessness. Dying in a sword-fight was so much more picaresque than gasping his last in a sickroom.

"En garde, you stable-born dunghill groom," he said gleefully. "You'll not have the virtue of this lady fair but with a dead man's blessing."

The soldier seemed unimpressed. His blade came at Oliver with raging speed. Oliver felt the fire of exhilaration whip through him. "Kit!" he yelled. "Are you all right?"

He heard a grunt, followed by the sliding

48

sound of locking blades. "A fine predicament you've gotten us into," Kit said.

Oliver fought with all the polish he could muster under the circumstances. He would have liked to tarry, to toy with his opponent and test his skills to the limit, but he was worried about Lark. The foolish woman seemed intent on investigating the coach.

The soldier came on with a low blow. Like a morris dancer, Oliver leaped over the blade. Taking swift advantage of the other's imbalance, Oliver went in for the kill.

With his rapier, he knocked the weapon from the soldier's hand. The sword thumped into the muddy road. Then Oliver whipped out his stabbing dagger and prepared to —

"My lord, are you not a Christian?" piped a feminine voice beside him. "'Thou shalt not kill.'"

His hesitation cost him a victory. The soldier leaped away and in seconds had one arm hooked around Lark from behind.

"I'll break her neck," the burly man vowed. "Take one step closer, and I'll snap it like a chicken bone." Stooping, he snatched up his fallen sword.

"Don't harm the girl!" one of the other soldiers cried.

"Divinity of Satan," Oliver bellowed in a fury. "I should have sent you to hell when I had the chance."

Glaring at Oliver, Lark's captor drew back his sword arm.

"Thou shalt not kill, either," Lark stated. As

Oliver watched, astonished, she brought up her foot and slammed it down hard on the soldier's instep. At the same time her pointed little elbow jabbed backward. Hard. If the blow had met his ribs, it would have left him breathless. But he was much taller than Lark and her aim was low, and when it connected, Oliver winced just from watching.

The man doubled up, unable to speak. Then, clutching himself, he half limped and half ran into the woods beyond the road.

Kit's opponent, bleeding now, backed away. Swearing, he leapfrogged onto one of the horses, cut the traces, and galloped off.

Oliver raced toward the third soldier. This one fled toward the remaining horse, but Lark planted herself in his path.

"No!" Oliver screamed, picturing her mown down like a sheaf of wheat. But as Lark's hands grasped at the mercenary's untidy tunic, he merely shoved her aside, mounted, spurred, and was gone.

"Lark!" Oliver said, rushing forward. She lay like a broken bird in the path. "Dear God, Lark! Are you hurt — " He broke off.

It struck just then. The dark, silent enemy that had stalked Oliver all his life. The tightening of his chest muscles. The absolute impossibility of emptying his lungs. The utter certainty that this was the attack that would kill him.

The physicians called it asthma. Aye, they had a name for it, but no cure.

The world seemed to catch fire at the edges, a familiar warning sign. He saw Lark climb to her feet. Kit seemed to tilt as if he bent to pick something up. Lark moved her mouth, but Oliver could not hear her over the thunder of blood rushing in his ears.

God, not now. But he felt himself stagger. "Ahhhh." The thin sound escaped him. Shamed to the very toes of his Cordovan riding boots, Oliver de Lacey staggered back and fell, arms wheeling, fingers grasping at empty air.

3

"I'VE never stayed at an inn before," Lark confessed to Kit as she cut a strip of bandage.

Oliver leaned against the scrubbed pine table in the large kitchen and tried to appear nonchalant, when in fact he was doing his best to keep from sliding into a heap on the floor.

To focus himself, he stared at Lark. What was it about her, he wondered, that so arrested the eye and took hold of the heart?

Perhaps it was the childlike sense of wonder with which she regarded the world. Or perhaps her complete lack of vanity, as if she were not even aware of herself as a woman. Or maybe, just maybe, it was that sweetness. The quality that made him want to hold her in his arms and taste her lips, to be the object of her earnest devotion.

"Oliver and I know every inn and ivybush 'twixt London and Wiltshire," Kit was saying. Discreetly he sidled over to the table beside Oliver.

To catch me if I fall, Oliver thought, feeling both gratitude and resentment. Cursed with his baffling illness, he had lived a peculiar and isolated boyhood. When he had finally emerged from his shell of seclusion, Kit had been there with his brotherly advice, his ready sword arm, and a fierce protective instinct that surfaced even now, when Oliver had grown a handspan taller than his friend.

Kit held out his hand and clenched his teeth as Lark washed the grit from his wound.

"How did this happen?" she asked, wringing a cloth over a basin.

"I tried to pluck the dagger from my opponent's hand. He had a better grip than I thought."

She worked neatly, Oliver observed, her movements deft as she applied the bandage. He noticed that her nails were chewed, and he liked that about her, for it was evidence that she suffered unease like anyone else.

She wasted no missish sympathy on Kit but confronted his injury with matter-of-fact compassion and an unexpected hint of humor. "Try to avoid battles for a few days, Kit. You should give this gash a chance to heal."

"I wonder what the devil those bast — er, rude scoundrels were after," Kit said. "They didn't even attempt to rob us."

"Perhaps they were planning to kill us first." Oliver had become rather casual about his brushes with death. He could either fall victim to despair or enjoy the time he had.

Long ago he had decided to defy fortune. He refused to let the weakness of his lungs conquer him. He meant to die his own way. Thus far, the pursuit had been amusing.

"Thank you, mistress." Kit pressed his bandaged hand to his chest. "I feel much better now. But I would still dearly like to know what those arse — er, wayward marls

were about. Ah! I just remembered something."
With his good hand he reached into the cuff of
his boot and pulled out a coin. "I did find this
when we searched the coach."

Both Oliver and Lark leaned forward to study
the coin. Their foreheads touched, and as one
they drew back in chagrin.

"Curious," said Kit, angling the coin toward
the waning light through the kitchen window.
"'Tis silver. An antique shilling?"

"Nay, look. 'Tis marked with a cross."
Cocking his head, Oliver read the motto
inscribed around the edge of the piece. "'*Deo
favente.*'"

"'With God's favor,'" Lark translated.

Oliver discovered a useful fact about Mistress
Lark. She was incapable of keeping her counsel.
Like an accused criminal in a witness box, she
turned pale and ducked her head with guilt.

Damn the wench. She knew something.

"Who were they, Lark?" Oliver demanded.

"I know not." She flung up her chin and
glared at him. Oliver wondered if it was just
a trick of the sinking light or if he truly saw
the glint of fear in her eyes.

"I'll keep this and make some inquiries." Kit
left the kitchen through a passageway to the
taproom.

Oliver grinned and spread his arms wide.
"Alone at last."

She rolled her eyes. "Take off your doublet
and shirt."

He sighed giddily. "I love a wench who knows
her own mind and is forthright in her desires."

54

"My only desire is to find the source of all this blood." She pointed to the dark, sticky stain seeping through his clothing.

"Your barbed tongue?" he suggested.

"If I could inflict such damage, my lord, I'd have no need of a protector, would I?" She patted the tabletop. "Sit here so I don't have to stoop to examine you."

He hoisted himself up. Without hesitation she drew on first one lace point attaching his sleeve to his double and then the other. His bare, sun-bronzed arms seemed to stir her not at all. Did she not see how smooth and well muscled they were? How strong and shapely?

"Now the doublet," she said, "or shall I remove that as well?"

"It's so much better when you do it."

She nodded absently and began working the frogged onyx fastenings free.

Her hands were as light and delicate as the brush of a bird's wing. As she bent close to her task, he caught a whiff of the most delicious scent. It clung to her hair, her clothes, her skin. Not perfume or oil, but something far more evocative.

Woman. Pure woman. How he loved it.

"Why did you stop me from killing that sheep biter who tried to murder me?" he asked.

She parted the doublet like a pair of double doors. "You are no assassin, my lord."

"How do you know?"

"I don't know for sure. But instinct tells me that you have never killed a soul, and it would pain you if you did. You seem a compassionate man."

"Compassionate?" His doublet, finally freed, fell backward with a clunk to the table. "I am no compassionate man, but a bold and brash rogue. A brute of the first order."

"A brute." Her mouth thinned, and a sparkling echo of humor lightened her voice. "Who faints in the aftermath of battle."

He snapped his mouth shut. So, she thought the asthma attack was a swoon. Should he set her straight, or should he allow her to go on believing him a coward? Worse than a coward. A high-strung, tender, emotional, limp-wristed, sentimental man. A wretch beyond redemption.

She answered the dilemma for him, bless her. She turned those enormous rain-colored eyes up to him and said, "My lord, I do not impugn your manhood."

"Thank God for that," he muttered. Seeing that he had irritated her, he donned a look of earnestness. "Go on."

"Your behavior today marks you as a person of true courage. For a man who loves combat, to fight is no sign of bravery. But for one who abhors it, to do battle is a sign of valor."

"Quite so." The idea pleased him. If the truth be known, he loved a good swordfight or round of fisticuffs. But let her think he had been forced to drag courage from reluctance for her sake.

"This will hurt," she said. "The fabric of your shirt clings to the wound."

"I'll try not to scream when you remove it."

"Truly, you are never serious." Gingerly

56

she worked the caked lawn fabric from the gash in his side. He felt a burn, then a hot trickle as he began bleeding anew, but he'd be damned if he'd say anything. Compassionate man indeed!

She lifted the shirt over his head and removed it. Her exclamation was high-pitched, feminine, and wholly welcome to Oliver's ears.

"I do so love it when a woman cries out at the sight of my bare chest," he said.

"'Tis a terrible wound," she said, ignoring his conceit.

"Nay, just bloody. Clean it up and bandage it, and I'll be good as new."

He was hoping that as she worked she would notice that his chest was broad and deep, nicely furred with golden hair a shade darker than that on his head. But the silly witling had no appreciation whatever for his physique. His male beauty was lost on her. He wondered what the devil she was thinking.

Determined to keep her wits about her, Lark concentrated on her task. But her thoughts kept wandering. He was so dazzling that she could barely keep from staring. She caught her lip firmly in her teeth and tried to think only of cleansing the wound, not of the magnificent body of the man sitting on the table.

He was right about the gash just beneath his arm. It was shallow and should heal well. His thick doublet had protected him from the worst of his opponent's blade.

"'Tis clean now," she said, rinsing her hands in the water basin. She took a folded cloth and pressed it to the cut. "Hold this, please, and I'll bind it."

"This is such an honor."

He was the most obliging man she had ever met. Perhaps that was why Spencer had chosen him.

"I shall have to wrap you snugly to keep the pad in place," she said.

"Wrap away, mistress. I'm all yours."

This proved to be the most awkwardly intimate part of the whole business. She leaned close, practically pressing her cheek to his naked chest as she passed the strip of cloth around behind him.

She could feel the warmth and smoothness of his skin. Could hear his heart beat. Its rhythm quickened.

Nonsense. She was plain as a wood wren, and he was as beautiful as a god.

A god, aye, but he smelled like a man.

In truth the scent was as exotic to her as the perfumes of Araby. Yet some primal instinct inside her, some wayward feminine impulse Spencer had failed to suppress, recognized the scent of a man. Sweat and horse, perhaps a tinge of saddle leather and woodsmoke. Individually these smells provoked no reaction, but taken as a whole they made a heady bouquet.

She gritted her teeth and tried to keep from fumbling with the bandage. In one day she had seen and heard and felt more of the world than she had in all her nineteen years, and she did not like being thrust into such a feast of voluptuousness.

58

What she liked was life at Blackrose Priory. The quiet hours of study and prayer. The sober, steady rhythm of spinning and weaving. The safety. The solitude.

One day with Oliver de Lacey had snatched her out of that protective cocoon, and she wanted to go back in. To tamp down the wildness growing inside her, to deny that she had ever felt such a thing as excitement.

"Lark?" He whispered in her ear, and his breath was a tender caress.

"Yes?" She braced herself, wondering if he'd ask her again to have his child.

"My dear, you have bound me like a Maypole."

"What?" Lark asked stupidly.

"While I'm not averse to bondage in some situations, I think several yards of cloth is sufficient."

Startled, she stepped back. The makeshift bandage did indeed wrap him like ribbons round a Maypole. A strangled sound escaped her.

A giggle. Lark had never giggled in her life.

Oliver released a long-suffering sigh. "Had I known it was so easy to make you laugh, I would have gotten myself wounded much earlier in the day."

She sobered instantly. "You must not say such things." Seeking a distraction, she began to tidy the area, folding the unused bandages and removing the basin of water. "I never did thank you and Kit, my lord, for enduring such trouble on account of me."

"What man would not lay down his life for

a lady in peril?" he asked. "Happily, it did not come to that. In fact, I should thank you."

She emptied the basin out the door of the kitchen and turned to him, perplexed. "Thank me for what?"

"As you pointed out earlier, you stopped me from killing a man. For all that he did provoke me, I should not like to have his blood on my hands."

"My foolishness almost cost you your life. I let him grab me from behind."

Oliver slapped his palms on the tabletop. "Ah, you did fight like a spitfire, Lark. Your quick thinking and courage are rare."

"In a woman, you mean."

"In anyone." A lazy smile lifted a corner of his mouth. "When I remember that poor trot's face . . . He didn't expect to be stomped upon and jabbed by a mere slip of a girl."

Lark absorbed his words like a rain-parched rose. Never had she been praised before, not even for doing tasks of servile duty. Oliver seemed genuinely pleased with her.

He lifted his shirt to put it back on. "Why do you suppose the leader of the brigands was so adamant about not harming you?"

Lark ducked her head. After seeing the coin Kit had found, she had a very good idea indeed why the cutthroat had uttered the cryptic message. It was no coincidence that they had been waylaid en route to Blackrose Priory. The brigands were hirelings sent to stop them from reaching their objective.

They could have killed Oliver, she thought

with a nauseating wave of guilt. "I am so sorry," she said softly.

"Don't be." Oliver poked his head through the neck opening of his shirt, then winced as he tried to put his arm into the sleeve. Lark set aside the basin and hurried to help him.

"Here, don't twist around so," she said. "You'll pull at the wound." She held out one sleeve and took his hand to guide it.

Something strange happened. When their hands touched, there was an instant of deep connection, when she suddenly lost track of where she ended and he began, when she could feel her mind touching his, when such a profound sense of caring welled up in her that she could have wept.

She caught her breath and looked up into his face.

He had felt it, too; she could tell because she saw her own stunned expression reflected on his face.

They were strangers, and yet they were not. Some part of her understood that even though they had only just met, she knew him. Knew the way his eyes crinkled at the corners when he smiled, the way his throat rippled as he swallowed, the way his thumb felt pressing into her palm.

"Oliver?" Her voice sounded thin and bewildered.

"Hush." His fingers brushed a wisp of hair from her cheek. "Let not words get in the way."

"In the way of what?"

61

"Of this."

He moved his knees apart so that she leaned snug against him, and then he kissed her.

The very idea that he would actually do such a thing so stunned her that she stood there, as rigid and unresponsive as a hearth broom.

Until the heat started. It was a slow, searing burn that seeped through her body, warming the cold empty places inside her.

She gave herself up to sensation, not thinking, only wanting. The hand still clinging to his within the sleeve tightened, and she felt the answering pressure of his fingers. Her free hand crept up his bare chest. He was smooth and hard there, and the hair was slightly coarse. He was warm, so warm, she wanted to melt against him. She hooked her arm around the back of his neck. His fine, silvery hair felt as downy as it looked.

His lips were soft yet firm, and gentle, not grinding and demanding. They brushed slowly back and forth over her mouth, softening and moistening her lips until they parted. Then he did a most unsettling thing — he ran his tongue across her lower lip.

The shock first numbed her, then awakened her from the torpid, kiss-induced dream.

"Stop!" she shouted, and jumped back. And suddenly they were all entangled by shirtsleeves. The thin white fabric tore as she tried frantically to disentangle her arm.

On fire with mortification, she backed away, staring at him as if he held a mirror to her own wickedness. He could never know what a sin it was for her to covet him.

He looked as pleased as a fox in a dovecote. "Don't play the Puritan, sweetheart. I could have given you much more than a mere kiss."

A mere kiss. She clung to those words. People kissed when they said hello or good-bye. When they gathered for holidays or met each other after prayer services.

But not the way Oliver de Lacey had just kissed her.

Not as she had just kissed him back.

"That was an evil thing to do," she said, then braced herself, half fearing a bolt of lightning would strike her dead on the instant.

He chuckled. "Pity you favor Reformed principles, Lark. If not, you could wear a crown of thorns or a hair shirt."

"You're a wicked man," she said.

"And you are an excessively good woman. Don't you ever get bored with being so virtuous?"

If only he knew. She was not virtuous at all.

She could stay no longer, not with him still sitting half naked and tousled, eyeing her as if she were one of his lightskirt doxies. Without another word, she turned and fled.

★ ★ ★

It was the first time a woman had left him voluntarily. Oliver stared at the empty space. Lark had glared at him as if he had raped her.

"It was merely a kiss," he repeated to himself as he gingerly donned his doublet. "A kiss. 'Tis

63

not like I swived the saintly wench."

Wincing from the hot pain in his side, he slid down from the table and found a small cask of wine. He filled a clay mug and took a deep, cleansing swallow. "I've kissed half the women in England," he declared to the empty room, to the rows of pots hanging from the rafters, and to the iron tongs hanging over the hearth. "Or if I have not, it wasn't for lack of trying."

Yet he could not deny that holding Lark in his arms had caused a peculiar and unwelcome sentiment to rise within him. Sentiments that a man like him had no business feeling: tenderness and devotion and the utter certainty that he could be happy with this woman and this woman alone.

He was no stranger to wanting a woman, to having one. But the idea of being with anyone other than plain, shy little Lark was suddenly repugnant to him.

Holding her in his arms had given him a notion that had never before occurred to him. He wanted to live forever.

Forever.

And that, he knew as he took a glum sip of the cheap wine, was impossible.

In his finer moments, he was philosophical about his own mortality. His disability had always been a part of him. He accepted it. Sometimes he managed to convince himself that he was healed.

But then he'd get that horrible tightening in his chest, that insatiable hunger for air, that dark glimpse of eternity, and he remembered he was marked for an early death.

In some ways the knowledge had made him a better man — more daring, more bold.

Then he had kissed the prim, thin-lipped, disapproving Mistress Lark — the most unlikely of women — and suddenly he was desperate not to die.

He had entranced her with his kisses, had felt the desire emanating from her small, clutching hands. There was no surprise in that. He might be deficient in some skills, but kissing was not one of them. Aye, he could manipulate her body, could bring her to a state of near rapture if he chose to do so, but could he win her heart?

"Aye, that I could," he decided, draining his mug and slamming it down on the sideboard. Her aversion to his embrace at the last did not trouble him. He simply needed more time to convince her of his wonderfulness. "I could indeed. I could make her love me."

A painful dilemma, that. For if ever he won her heart, he was doomed to break it.

★ ★ ★

"You never finished explaining to me what you meant about the brigands," Oliver said the next day.

The three of them headed north, wary now in the winter sunshine, watchful for signs of more highwaymen. In the distance, pink-tinged clouds melted down onto the gentle Chiltern Hills, and forested mounds rolled out endlessly on either side of the road. Dry, frozen grass clung to the

65

sloping sides of the hills, and sleepy hamlets huddled in thatched clusters along the river.

Lark held her neck stiff and her chin high. Kit trotted up beside her. Saddle leather creaked as he leaned toward her. "Did you know them, Mistress Lark?"

She could talk to Kit. She did not look into his eyes and feel as though she were drowning.

"Not exactly. I think they were sent to stop us from reaching Blackrose Priory," she said.

"Really?"

"Aye." She had no choice but to admit her fears. "Spencer's sole enemy must have learned what he plans."

"What does the gentleman plan?"

She was keenly aware of Oliver's presence behind her. She felt the heat of his stare like a ray of the sun.

"I must let Spencer tell you that."

"You say he has an enemy. Who is that?"

"Wynter Merrifield." Lark paused as a cloud passed over the sun, then gave way to dazzling brightness. "His only son."

Kit gasped. "The man's son is his enemy?"

"Sadly, yes." She remembered the coin Kit had found. Of Spanish origin, it had been. "More I cannot say. Spencer will explain all you need to know when we arrive." She trotted on ahead, wishing the kiss had not happened, wishing she had not lain awake half the night thinking about his lips upon hers.

When Lark moved out of earshot, Kit glared at Oliver. "What in God's name are we doing?"

"Helping a damsel in distress?"

Kit studied her stiff figure riding in the fore. Mistress Lark rode as if she had a ramrod up her back. "She doesn't look distressed to me. Why is she being so secretive?"

"Because we're a pair of rogues. She doesn't trust us."

"And you trust her? Oliver, I need hardly remind you that she almost got us killed."

"It was exciting, was it not?" Oliver smiled, savoring the memory. "Swordfights have ever made my blood run hot."

"I worry about you, Oliver. I truly do."

He nodded at their silent leader. "She makes my blood run hot, too."

"Anything in skirts has that effect on you."

"Out of skirts is even better." Oliver studied her. To the undiscerning eye, she resembled her namesake — a small, drab bird. Yet he knew better. He knew there was softness beneath her rigid exterior, the heart of a woman beating in her breast, and a host of dreams inside her, just waiting to be set free. "That one's special."

Kit pushed back his hat and scratched his forehead. "Her? You're mad. Look at her."

"I've been looking, and I know what you're thinking. She's small and dark and plain. She's about the least worldly wench we've ever encountered. She has the disposition of a badger. And she bites her nails and quotes the scripture."

"And she fires your brand?" Kit demanded incredulously.

"The challenge of her stirs my blood, Kit. It is no great feat to desire a woman who is fair and charming. But this one." He nodded ahead, feeling a curious rapture. "If I could love her, I'd be capable of anything."

"She helped save you from hanging. It's disturbed your judgment," Kit said stolidly. Suspiciously.

"That's always been your problem, my friend. You lack imagination. You see only what is there on the surface. Mind, I don't blame you for loving my sister, but Belinda's easy to love. She's pretty, she has a charming temperament, and she loves you in return."

Kit thumped his fist against his chest. "She does?"

"Of course she does, you muttonhead, though I trow 'twas not your brains that won her."

"Why do I endure you?"

"To keep yourself from running quite mad with boredom. Tell me, Kit, how do you endure, toiling away at the law day in and day out?"

"Such toiling does earn me a living. Not all of us are born to wealth and idleness."

The laughter drained from Oliver. Most of the time he enjoyed the advantages of his rank. Every once in a while he wondered if he might be a better person were he forced to fend for himself. Fortunately his moments of doubt were few and far between, easily banished by thoughts of his own splendor.

Could he have been, even so slightly, wrong?

A short time later they reached the estate of Blackrose Priory. Oliver eyed it with appreciation. The long road, winding northward and westward, was kept free of deep ruts and holes and stones. The hedgerows were freshly clipped and alive with the music of thrushes.

Thick-coated sheep grazed on the gentle hills that rose behind the main building. The priory itself, once a haven for Bonshomme monks, had a good-size almshouse and a broad lawn with fountains and knot gardens. The path to the front had been paved with pebbles. The old Gothic hall, echoing with ancient, ghostly voices, had sprawling wings added on each end. It was built of native stone, which gave it a warm, brownish hue.

"The servants defer to her," Kit muttered, watching Lark.

It was true; the grooms who came to look after their mounts obeyed her murmured instructions. The pair of footmen who appeared at the main door bowed low to her.

"Who is she to this Spencer?" Oliver wondered as they followed her up the broad steps to the huge arched doors.

"Some relation," said Kit. "You ought to ask."

"I don't think she enjoys being questioned."

She stopped inside the door and turned to them. The weak light in the great hall leached her complexion of all color. The marble hardness of her face startled Oliver. He was hard-pressed to remember how she had looked last night when she had kissed him. She had been soft and warm and alive, a vivid contrast to the whey-faced stranger he saw before him now.

"Wait here," she said. "I'll see that you get

69

something to eat and drink. His Lordship will receive you shortly."

She turned like a soldier obeying an order and marched through a low door to the right of the hearth.

A door on the opposite side of the hearth opened, and in stepped a remarkable young man. "Charming, isn't she?" he said, a sardonic curl to his lip.

"Indeed," Oliver said. Without moving a muscle, he took the measure of the man. Of medium height and build, with glossy black hair and a pointed beard, he was dressed in black velvet, with a rapier at his hip and a wide smile of welcome on his face. His dark eyes flashed with the promise of a quick, observant wit. When he moved, it was with lithe, unconscious grace.

Oliver felt a shock of instant dislike as he fixed an equally charming smile on his face.

The newcomer held out a well-tended hand. "Welcome to Blackrose Priory. I am Wynter Merrifield, Viscount Grantham."

Ah, thought Oliver as he introduced himself and Kit. The heir. The enemy. The man who had sent hirelings to stop them from reaching Blackrose Priory. Was he the man who caused the hardness on Lark's face?

Oliver kept a bold grin in place. "My lord, we've already had a taste of your welcome."

4

WYNTER MERRIFIELD strolled to the hearth and propped an elbow on the massive mantelpiece. The hall must have once served as the refectory for the Bonshommes, for it was long, with a high, vaulted ceiling. Figures carved of stone and blackened with age-old soot leered down upon the tables and cupboards. Two low doors flanked the hearth, and above it hung a pair of crossed swords.

Wynter subjected the swords to a moment of contemplation. "I don't understand, my lord. Have we met?"

"The bridge at Tyler Cross," Oliver said. "Your welcoming party bared its talons."

Wynter turned, and his austere, handsome face went blank. "Welcoming party? I have no idea what you mean."

Kit regarded Wynter with unconcealed dislike. "We were attacked," he said. "Mistress Lark thought perhaps the brigands were in your hire."

"Mistress Lark is a strange bird." Wynter spread his arms to convey his bafflement. "She has ever been a victim of rampant imagination. Suspicious little mort. My father has done his best to reform her, but to no avail."

"Is she your sister, then?" Oliver braced himself. To think that Lark was kin to this

71

smooth, cold creature made his hackles rise. Or worse, was there a marriage in the works? He refused to dwell on the horror.

Wynter laughed, his amusement genuine and oddly seductive. He seemed a man who cloaked himself in shadows, hiding his true essence, showing only a chiseled and icy charm. "No."

"A cousin, then? Your father's ward?"

"I suppose you could term it that, after all these years."

Oliver went to a trestle table, pressed his palms on the surface, and leaned forward, forcing out the words. "Then is she betrothed to you?"

This time Wynter threw back his head and roared with laughter. "And I feared being bored today. My lord, you are too amusing. Lark is not betrothed to me. Far from it, thanks be to God."

Oliver's shoulders relaxed. He pretended it did not matter, that his question had been an idle one. "Just wondering," he commented.

Wynter pushed away from the hearth and strolled racefully toward Oliver and Kit. He held Oliver's gaze for perhaps a heartbeat longer than polite interest dictated, and in that moment they clashed.

They didn't touch, not were any words exchanged, but Oliver felt ill will emanate from Wynter like a breath of wind before a storm.

"Now then," Wynter said, a smile playing about his thin lips, "you must forgive my manners, but might I inquire as to your purpose here?"

"You might inquire," Kit said, beefy fists tightening, "but — "

"His Lordship will see you now."

Oliver turned to see a pale, soberly clad retainer at the main doorway, gesturing for them to follow him up a wide staircase.

Oliver bowed to Wynter. "Excuse us."

Wynter bowed back. Perhaps by accident, perhaps by design, his slim fingers brushed the hilt of his sword. "Of course."

★ ★ ★

Oliver paced back and forth in the master's chamber, a long, narrow room with a bank of shrouded windows at one end and a fireplace at the other. Spencer Merrifield, earl of Hardstaff, had banished everyone save Oliver from his bedside. But even the old lord's imperious command failed to evict the shadows that haunted the deep corners. Oliver guessed it had once been the abbot's lodgings. The draperies over the tall windows held the sunlight at bay and cloaked the chamber in mystery.

"You move like a caged wolf," Spencer observed in a calm voice from his bed.

Oliver forced himself to slow down. Spencer could not know it, but the darkness and the stale, lifeless smells of the sickroom were all too familiar to him. He had spent the first seven miserable years of his life in such a place, exiled there by the superstitions of his doctors and by the impotent grief of his father. It took the unexpected love of a most unusual woman to induce Stephen de Lacey to bring his ailing son into the light.

"Could I open the draperies?" Oliver asked.

"If you like." Spencer stirred, making a vague sweep of his arm. "My physician claims sunlight is noxious, but I feel equally ill in light or in dark."

Oliver parted the curtains. For a moment he savored the view, a beautiful valley cleaved by the silvery river, a patchwork of fields and meadows, all embraced by the forested hills.

Then he turned to get his first good look at the man who had saved him from hanging and then summoned him from a perfectly good day of gaming and wenching. Afternoon light showered through the lozenge-shaped panes of glass, making shifting patterns of black and gold on the flagged floor. Long, dappled shafts fell on a frail man whose skin hung loose upon his skeletal frame. He had wispy hair that might have been black at one time, proud aquiline features, and keen eyes.

He hardly looked the hero or the crusader, yet there was something about him. The aura of a powerful mind that had outlived its useless body.

"Why did you tell Kit to leave the room, my lord?" asked Oliver.

"We'll need him, but not yet. Do sit down."

Spencer had a pleasant way of giving orders. He was, taken as a whole, a rather pleasant man. The fact that Oliver owed his life to the earl made it easy to like him.

"I should thank you," he said. "I thought

I was done for, that it would all end at the gallows. I don't mind telling you I did not make a graceful exit. My lord, I am in your debt."

Spencer nodded. "The life of an innocent man is payment enough. Still, I do need your help."

"What is it, my lord? What can I do to repay you?"

Spencer stared at the foot of the bed, where a great chest with a mounded lid stood. "The deed is possibly illegal. At best, it's a manipulation of the law."

Oliver grinned. "I've been known to break a statute or two in my time. In sooth, Oliver Lackey was not wholly innocent. I did indeed incite riots and mayhem when the mood took me."

"There are those who would thank you for your mischief. The spirit of honest Englishmen must not be ground out beneath the heels of the queen's corrupt ministers."

"Such were my thoughts," Oliver said, delighted to find a kindred soul in Spencer. "Tell me more of this task."

"It's dangerous."

"My forte."

"It involves a great deal of record searching."

Oliver's spirits fell, for such work bored him. "Not my forte."

"That is why we'll need your friend, Kit."

Oliver was suddenly impatient with the whole affair. He resisted the urge to start pacing again. Even in sunlight the room held the dank promise of death. Blackrose Priory was a strange place indeed, peopled with strange inhabitants, not the least of whom was Mistress Lark. He much preferred the rollicking atmosphere of London.

"Why don't you simply tell me what you require?"

"Ah, youth." Wistfulness crept into Spencer's tone. "I was hoping you'd be eager to serve. You have not disappointed me."

"My lord," Oliver said, "I cannot help but wonder. Mistress Lark went to a great deal of trouble to find me and bring me here."

Spencer clutched the tapestried counterpane as if he wished to leave his bed. "You gave her trouble?"

The ferocity of the question took Oliver aback. "No, my lord. But I do confess I wasn't sitting at home waiting for her to come calling. She found me" — he dropped his voice to a mumble — "at a Bankside tavern."

"God's shield," Spencer snapped. "I expected better from you."

He sounded like someone's father, Oliver thought. "She is incredibly loyal to you, my lord," he observed, hoping to turn the subject.

"Of course she is," Spencer grumbled. "I have raised her from infancy. Given her every advantage, taught her a woman's duties — "

"A woman's duties? And what might they be, my lord?" Oliver had a few ideas of his own, but he wanted to hear Spencer's answer.

"Obedience. That above all things."

"Ah." Oliver had to remind himself that Spencer was his host and responsible for saving his life. He had to content himself with the

76

mildest comment he could muster. "My lord, I have never subscribed to the view that women are inherently sinful and need to be brought to heel like mongrel puppies."

Spencer wheezed out a long-suffering sigh. "You still do not understand, do you, my lord? You believe I summoned you here to help me. It's Lark, you jolt-head. I brought you here to help Lark."

★ ★ ★

"He wants us to what?" Kit demanded.

They strolled in the parkland north of the old priory. The forest in the distance covered the rising hills with skeletal gray trees. Archery butts and a quintain, long idle, rose from the yellowed lawn amid a tangle of wild ivy. An abandoned well, surrounded by rubble, stood amidst the disarray. A broken stone pedestal lay near the well, where doubtless some saint or other had once reigned in serenity.

"Break the entail on this estate," Oliver explained. "He doesn't want Wynter to inherit."

"Wynter must inherit, since you say he's the eldest — and only — son." Kit picked up a rock and tossed it at the ragged target. It hit dead center, tearing a gaping hole in the weather-worn leather. "Unless he's been declared illegitimate. There's always that. Wasn't Spencer's marriage to Wynter's mother annulled?"

"Yes, but Spencer refuses to declare Wynter a bastard." He grinned. "Legally, that is. According to the old man, Wynter is not trustworthy. I gather the lordling's a bit too Catholic for his very reformed father."

"Then the old man should have raised him in the Reformed faith."

Oliver watched a flock of rooks take flight from the trees that fringed the park, black wings beating the pure white of the winter clouds.

Ah, but he did like Kit. Simple, solid as the earth beneath his feet. In Kit's mind there was no question as to what was right and what was wrong. Kit knew.

"I expect Spencer would have done just that," Oliver said. "But Wynter's mother had other ideas, and did her utmost to instill them in her son. She was Spanish."

The one word explained all, and Kit nodded. "A servant of the queen, was she?"

"Aye, one of Catherine of Aragon's ladies. Passed away a year ago, but she's having her revenge on Spencer now. She lives on in Wynter. Apparently her devotion to Queen Catherine is reflected in Wynter's allegiance to Queen Mary. If he inherits this place" — Oliver swept his arm to encompass the rambling priory — "Spencer fears it will once again become a Catholic stronghold, perhaps placed at the disposal of Bishop Bonner." He winked. "Perhaps given back to the Bonshommes, the religious order that once inhabited Blackrose. I understand they were a naughty lot."

Kit shuddered. "Bonner. Just the thought of him clouds a sunny day." He picked up another stone and hurled it, hitting the archery butt again. "Lord Spencer does not wish his property to fall to his son. Where shall it go, then? To Lark?"

"Yes. To Lark. He claims it is a fairly simple legal procedure."

"When legal procedures become simple, people will no longer need my services," Kit said. "But why you? Why us? There are a thousand London lawyers he could have chosen."

"I pointed that out. He claims to know my father. Claims I inherited his deep sense of honor." Oliver bowed with a mocking flourish.

Kit laughed. "Little does our host know."

Just for the smallest fraction of a second, the comment bothered Oliver. He recovered instantly. "It matters not. He arranged for me to be saved from the gallows. He needs our help. So we'll help him."

"We?"

"You and I, dear Kit."

"I haven't agreed to anything."

Oliver crossed his arms over his chest. "You will."

"I won't."

A bell sounded.

"Let's go in to supper," Oliver said, striding toward the priory.

He ignored Kit's protests all the way to the dining hall. Sparsely furnished, it was a cavernous room with a hammer beam ceiling and painted hangings on the walls. Not exactly a warm, relaxing place in which to take supper.

More chilly than the room were the two people who waited to dine with them.

79

Oliver had not thought it possible that there could exist a gown plainer than the one Lark had been wearing earlier. Yet she had managed to find one. It was dyed unevenly in shades of black and ash gray. The bodice was flat and unadorned, the sleeves so narrow and tight he wondered how she managed to move her arms.

Yet it was her face that disturbed him most. Framed by the ugliest of coifs, it was stone cold, the light gray eyes empty, the mouth stiff.

Oliver strode across the room and snatched her hand. As he sank to one knee and bent to brush his lips over her chilly fingers, he whispered, "Where did she go, the woman of fire and spirit who all but dragged me from London?"

He was beginning to fear she was not Lark, but a cold, look-alike stranger. Then he felt it: the profound connection he had experienced the first time she had touched him. It was like the throb of a heart or a spark rising from a fire. Instantaneous, unmistakable, deeply felt.

Her face showed only brief recognition; then she blinked and the icy mask fell back in place. He wanted to ask her what was wrong, why she acted so strangely, but not in the present company.

He straightened, released her hand, and turned to greet Wynter. "My lord." He offered a nonchalant bow. "I see you bring out the best in Mistress Lark."

Wynter sent him a conspiratorial wink. "Then I shouldn't like to see her at her worst, should you? Welcome to my table." He nodded at Kit to include him.

"Your father's table," Oliver corrected with his most pleasant smile. "Lord Spencer is an admirable man."

"Lord Spencer is dying," Wynter said without concern. "I assume he sent for you in order to cheat me out of my rightful inheritance. I won't let you. Let's eat."

He planted himself on the canopied chair at the head of the table. Oliver shot a 'what an arsehole' look at Kit and held Lark's chair out for her.

She stared at him blankly.

"Do sit down, Mistress Lark," Oliver murmured.

A smooth, melodic chuckle flowed from Wynter. "Do forgive our Lark. The social graces seem to be beyond her grasp."

She didn't even flinch. It was as if she were accustomed to his biting comments. She seated herself with the unthinking obedience of a beaten spaniel.

Oliver sat across from her, and Kit took the seat at the foot of the table. Wishing he could kiss some life back into Lark, Oliver grabbed the pewter wine goblet at his place.

Lark cleared her throat and clasped her hands in prayer.

Feeling sheepish, Oliver released the goblet, and when she finished asking the Lord's grace, he and Kit dutifully replied, "Amen." Wynter made an elaborate sign of the cross.

Eager to have done with the tense and silent

meal, Oliver was pleased to see a small army of well-trained retainers break into action, flowing in through a small side door from the kitchen. He savored the fresh bread and butter, a salad of greens and nuts, a delicious roasted trout.

"Thank you, Edgar," Lark murmured to a boy passing the bread basket.

"Took me months to get the servants in hand," Wynter explained, reaching up without looking around, confident that the bread basket would appear. It did. "I suppose dear Lark did her best — didn't you, Lark? — but of course that couldn't possibly be good enough. Not for these rough, country types."

He could not see the blaze of anger that lit the serving boy's eyes as the lad withdrew. Oliver stifled a laugh. "You just won them over with your charm, my lord."

Wynter had a rare gift for focusing his gaze as sharp as a blade. "My lot has not been easy. Spencer disgraced my mother and sent her into exile. Whatever charm I possess, I did not learn at my loving father's knee."

Kit, ever the guardian of right and wrong, lifted his cup and released a huff of breath into it.

Oliver wished he, too, could remain the skeptic, but he could not. Wynter bore the scars of wounds for which he was not responsible. Just as Oliver hadn't asked to be born with asthma, Wynter hadn't asked to be born to a woman whose morals were too loose and a man whose morals were too rigid.

"No one's lot is easy," Lark stated. She turned

to Oliver. "Except perhaps yours, my lord."

"Indeed," he said wryly, angling his wine cup toward her in a halfhearted salute. He contemplated telling her what it was like to turn blue for want of air but decided it was inappropriate conversation at table.

The main dish arrived, the platter borne high on the shoulders of two footmen. They planted it with a flourish in the center of the table.

Wynter closed his eyes and inhaled. "Ah, capon. A favorite of mine."

"Lord Oliver," said Lark, "Why don't you do the honors and serve yourself first?"

Between his sympathy for the nasty Wynter and his distate for the main dish, Oliver felt queasy. "No, thank you. I never eat capon."

Kit smothered a laugh.

Lark tipped her head to one side. "Whyever not?"

"It's a castrated cock, that's why. Gives me a bad feeling."

He expected her to be shocked by his bluntness. Instead he saw a faint spark of amusement in her eyes.

"I take it you'd never ride a gelded horse, either," she said.

"I ride only mares." God, he liked her. She stood for everything he hated, everything he found tiresome, and he liked her immensely.

"I have no qualms about eating capon." Kit wrenched a leg from the roasted bird and bit into it. Wynter took the other leg. Oliver held out his goblet for more wine.

"How is the weaving coming along, Lark?"

Wynter asked quite cordially.

"Well enough," she said without looking at him.

He lifted an eyebrow. "Is it, then? It appeared to me that you've been neglectful of late. I've seen no progress on the tapestry you've been weaving."

"I didn't realize I was under your scrutiny."

"One can't help but notice when a woman neglects her duties to go traipsing off to London."

Oliver looked from one to the other as if they were engaged in a tennis match. What an extraordinary pair they made, despising each other with such civility.

"And what have you done with yourself, Wynter?" Lark's voice was low, yet dripping with venom. In contrast with the servile spaniel who had first entered the room, she seemed to be coming out of herself, brandishing words like a sharp blade. "Turned in any heretics lately?"

Wynter smiled as if at a jest. "Dear Lark. You are always so full of pointed humor."

Oliver watched Wynter's hand clench around the ivory handle of his knife.

When Spencer did finally die, Oliver knew that Lark would have to beware Wynter Merrifield.

★ ★ ★

"'Wardens' Temporal Act . . . Treasonable Offences by Rank Villains' . . . None of these will do." Kit frowned at the thick, heavy tome on the long library table.

84

Lark knelt on the bench beside him and dragged a fat, smoking candle closer. "What about this one?" She pointed to an entry on another page of the huge tome. "'An Acte for the Disbursement and Recovery of Real Property.'"

Oliver rubbed his weary eyes. Midnight was but a vague memory, and they had been in Spencer's amazingly huge library since sunset, poring over law books and legal tracts.

"We'll have to go to London," Kit said, blowing out a sigh that caused the candle flame to waver. "We'll never find what we're looking for here." He closed the huge book with a thud.

"Ouch!" Lark said. "You've closed my finger in it!" She yanked the book open.

Oliver's mind kept toying with what she had said earlier. "Disbursement," he said to himself. "Recovery . . . " As a youth fleeing the boredom of polite nobility, he had gone to St. John's at Cambridge to hear shockingly reformed ideas on the law. Unfortunately his memories of that time were obscured by a pleasant mist of women, gambling, drinking, and general mischief.

Kit took a sip from the wine jug. "You carry on the search. I'm but a common lawyer. A very weary common lawyer." Yawning, he left the library.

"Is he really a commoner?" Lark asked.

Common. Oliver's mind clung to the word for a moment. "His father was a knight who had eleven sons. Kit fostered with my father." The recollection plunged Oliver into the past. There had been a time, long ago, when his father had barely acknowledged Oliver's existence. Kit had been the substitute son, the golden lad who learned to ride and hunt and fence at Stephen de Lacey's side.

If there were wounds from that time, they had healed nicely, Oliver decided. He adored both Kit and his father.

He brought his thoughts to the present and looked at Lark. The pale stranger at supper had given way to the lively maid who had braved a Bankside tavern to find him.

What a charming scholar she made, so sweetly unaware of her provocative pose. She had her elbows planted on the heavy tome, her knees on the bench, and her startlingly shapely backside thrust out and upward in a way that brought the devil to life in Oliver.

Wisps of dark hair escaped the detestable coif, and the locks curled softly around her pale face. The hunt for a loophole in the law seemed to animate her, causing her eyes to dance and her lips to curve into an artless smile. Even better, the angle of her pose allowed Oliver to peer unobstructed into the bodice of her dress. It was a beautiful bosom indeed — what he could see of it. High, rounded breasts, the skin like satin or pearls, and if he craned his neck, he fancied he could just barely make out a shadow where her skin darkened —

"Are you ill?" she asked.

Oliver blinked. He shifted on the bench. He glanced down at his codpiece. Other than being

86

too tightly trussed, he felt fine. "No. Why do you ask?"

"You were looking at me rather strangely."

He laughed. "That, my darling, was lust."

"Oh." Her gaze dropped to the page. Something told Oliver that she had little experience with lust.

"Don't worry," he said. "I assure you, I can control my base impulses."

"Perhaps." She drummed her fingers on the page. "'Tis true, I sense no danger when I'm with you. Yet at the same time, I feel as defenseless as a fledgling fallen from the nest." A single crease of bafflement appeared between her brows.

He touched the tip of her nose. "That's because I threaten the most vulnerable part of you, my pet. Your heart." He gave her no chance to ponder that, but forged on. "Now. What is it you keep reading on that page?"

"It's about the disbursement and recovery of — "

"That's it!" Oliver jumped to his feet. He strode to her side of the table, leaned down, and skimmed the page. Even as his eyes absorbed the printed words, he noticed her scent of fresh laundry and femininity.

"What's it?" Lark blinked at him.

He lifted her bodily from the bench. He wanted to share his exuberance, to show her the clean, effervescent joy of a puzzle solved. While she gaped at him as if he'd gone mad, he planted a brief, noisy kiss on her mouth, then spun her around, throwing his head back and laughing.

"Lark, you have the wit of a scholar!" he cried.

"I can't." The spinning seemed to render her breathless, so he stopped and held her by both hands.

"Why not?" he demanded.

"Well." She looked up at him with heart-breaking earnestness. "Because I'm a woman."

"So was Eleanor of Aquitaine. Christine de Pisan. Perkin Warbeck."

"Perkin Warbeck was a pretender to the throne," she stated. "And he was a boy."

"Don't be so certain." He couldn't help himself. Such sweetness as he saw in her face should be outlawed as a strong intoxicant. He tipped up her chin and brushed his knuckles along her jawline. "Why in God's name do you believe such humble ideas?"

She tried to look away. He held her chin again, his touch gentle yet compelling. "The most learned men of the age have made a great study of the minds of women. They have proven that women are weaker."

"Learned men also once claimed the world was flat. Lark, you just gave me the key to breaking Spencer's entail."

"I did?" For a moment sheer joy transformed her face into a vision of loveliness. He had no idea how she could seem so plain and lifeless one moment, so glowingly beautiful the next. She presented a far greater puzzle than English law, a far more interesting one, too.

"The Common Recovery," he said with satisfaction. "I never thought of it until you

88

suggested it. You've a fine mind, Lark, and the man who says otherwise is a fool." He smiled down at her, his hands cradling her cheeks. "I could kiss you."

"You've already done that, thank you very much," she said. "How does it work?"

He found himself staring at her face. Candlelight had such a happy effect at moments like this. The warm gold glow healed her pallor, brought out the elegant shape of her nose and cheekbones, and flickered in the velvety depths of her eyes.

"How does it work?" he repeated, mindless now with desire. "Well." He pulled her toward him, passing one hand around to the back of her waist. She gasped, and he smiled.

"It would help if you were not so stiff in your upper body."

"My lord — "

"And you should hold on with both hands — just so." He took her hands and brought them to his shoulders, then around behind his neck.

"But — "

"And for Christ's sake, don't talk. That spoils everything."

"What I meant was — "

"You talked. Disobedient wench." He cut her short with a kiss. When he had kissed her in the tavern, he had been woozy from his attack. He was recovered now, and he meant to prove to himself that he could control his desire for her. That she was no different from the dozens of other women he had wooed and won. He wanted to obliterate that one frightening moment when

89

she had made him feel deeply. Care deeply. Want something that could never be.

He opened his mouth over hers, brandishing his tongue like a weapon, smoothing his hands over her shape. She was a woman like any other. A nicely put together bundle of hip and tit and silky hair. An object to be enjoyed, not enslaved by.

Even as he told himself these things, he felt the truth crashing down around his ears. Lark was special. Lark was the one woman who could make him feel these things. Lark was —

Oliver's breath left him in a whoosh. He staggered back and glared at her.

"Why did you do that?"

She glanced at her fist, then relaxed her fingers. "Punch you in the stomach? You'll notice I was careful not to hit your wounded side."

"I was kissing you, and you punched me." The blow to his pride cut deeper than any flesh wound.

A wry smile curved her lips. Her mouth was soft and moist, and he wanted it again, but he was too angry to try.

He began pacing the room. "Don't you like me, Lark?"

"Truthfully, I think not. No matter. Spencer needs your help. I am loyal to Spencer. Ergo, I shall endure you. I must be careful with you, Oliver. I wanted to know how the Common Recovery worked, and you showed me how a kiss worked."

"Given a choice of the two," he said dryly,

"I'd choose the kiss every time. The Common Recovery is a heaving bore."

"But we can use it to bar Wynter from inheriting the priory."

"Aye, we can." A delightful notion occurred to him. "It is very complex, Lark. It will take much hard work and many hours of preparation from Kit and me. And you."

"Me?" Her eyes went wide. Adorably wide.

"Aye. We shall have to work very, very closely, Lark. Can you do that?"

She seemed entranced by his look. "Aye. That is, if I must."

He caught her hands in his and drew her close. "You must."

★ ★ ★

"What an amazing coincidence," Kit said the next day. "A whole tract on the Common Recovery right here in the Blackrose library."

"Convenient, is it not?" asked Oliver.

Lark studied him in the pure morning light. Such strong early sunshine would surely expose his flaws. Yet she realized, with a sinking feeling in the pit of her stomach, that in looks, at least, Oliver de Lacey had no flaws.

The sunlight only enhanced the spun gold of his hair, brightened the sky blue of his eyes, and brought out the bold structure of his face and physique.

Just the sight of him tugged at something deep and elemental inside Lark. And, heaven help her, Oliver knew. Even as she chastised

91

herself, he caught her staring and gave her a smoldering look followed by a wink that she felt all the way to the bottoms of her feet.

Shaking sense into herself, she pointed at the legal tract Kit was studying. "Is that rare?"

"Aye. Why would Lord Spencer possess it? Has he a particular interest in the law?"

Only his own rigid rules, she thought, then flayed herself for disloyalty.

"Not that I know of. But His Lordship is a learned man who has many interests." She deliberately kept her gaze from wandering to Oliver. "Lord Oliver wasn't able to explain exactly how the Common Recovery works."

"I could've explained," Oliver said with a sulk that was every bit as appealing as his smile. "I just didn't see the point of going into it at so late an hour. The heart of the night was not meant for legal debates."

She continued to ignore him. "I want to know, Kit."

The mild surprise in Kit's regard was gratifying. Most men would be shocked and dismayed by a woman's interest in the law.

"'Tis a lawsuit," he said. "By using Oliver as a party in the suit, I can prove Lord Spencer came by his estate through irregular means."

"But he didn't."

Kit grinned. "You must think like a lawyer. Of course he did. And Oliver is entitled to both compensation and the right to dispose of the estate as he chooses."

"Oliver? He doesn't own the estate."

"For our purposes, and only on paper, he does."

"Oh." She disliked the sticky dishonesty of it, yet she saw the merit in the plan. "And naturally Lord Oliver would not choose to confer the estate on Wynter Merrifield."

"Naturally," Oliver said. "I would give it to you, my fair Lark."

"What must we do?" Lark asked, tossing away his glib compliment with a wave of her hand.

"We must take a long walk and discuss this," Oliver suggested. "Intimately, at great length."

"Why should we walk outside?"

Oliver cast suspicious glances to and fro. Lark suppressed a smile at his overblown gestures. "No one must hear our plans."

Kit nodded. "He's right. Wynter knows we're up to something. I'd not like to encounter his friends again."

Oliver touched his side where Lark had bandaged him. "Nor I. Fighting is so distressful to me."

Kit shot him a look of amazement. Oliver put on an appealing, earnest look and led the way out of the library.

Blackrose Priory and its vast grounds seemed to be awaiting the spring, the trees with buds still tucked within themselves, the sere, colorless lawns barren. At the far reaches of the estate, the gardens ran wild and tumbled into the majestic disarray of the forested hills. Lark took her companions to a high walk along the ridge of a rise above the river. The air smelled of cold river water and dry reeds.

93

"When Spencer was well we used to come here often," she said, speaking over the soughing wind and the rustling of tall grasses. She remembered the feel of his hand firm around hers, the certainty of his voice as he taught her her place and her role. Bridle the body and press down feeling, he used to say in all earnestness. Quench the heat of youth. He was very convincing. A single errant thought sent her to the chapel to kneel for hours in prayer.

Yet even Spencer's best efforts had been for naught.

Before the shame could engulf her, she lifted her skirts and picked her way over to the edge of the walk. There was a sheer drop to the river, and along the face of the cliff, rock doves nested. "Sometimes," she said, "boys from the village used to climb down and rob eggs from the nests. It looked like such an adventure."

"You never tried it?" Oliver asked.

"I know better than that." She glanced around. "Where is Kit? I thought he was coming with us."

"He dropped back a few moments ago," said Oliver. "He has work to do. We're devising a lawsuit, remember?"

She turned her face out to the view of the valley. It had always seemed so deep and distant, illuminated by long rays that touched places she could never go. "You will pretend Blackrose is really yours, given to you in a prior grant the year you were born." She squinted at the sun-struck river far below. "Won't that make Spencer look rather stupid?"

"Not at all. He wouldn't defend his right. He'll swear that a third person — "

"Who?" Lark demanded. She was unhappy enough being party to deception without bringing in more cheaters.

"He need not exist; let's name him Mortimer."

"I hate that name."

"He's not real, Lark. Now, Mortimer has always been an obliging sort." Oliver touched her arm, and she forgot to tell him not to. "He's the defaulter."

"Oh." She glanced at his hand. It was quite an ordinary hand. Large and squarish, sprinkled with golden hair. She wondered why the touch of so unremarkable a hand could make her go warm inside, all trembly with yearning. Did Oliver de Lacey possess some special magic, or was the magic inside her?

Suddenly afraid to find out, she took her arm away. "Go on. Spencer will swear that Mortimer did what?"

"Sold him the estate. Illegally."

"Ah. Then Spencer would be entitled to compensation from Mortimer."

Oliver nodded. He leaned back against a broad, rounded boulder, crossing his booted feet at the ankles and eyeing Lark as if he had not eaten in days. "Lands of equal value would be nice."

"But where would this mythical Mortimer get — "

His fingers touched her lips. She wanted to moan with the pleasure she felt, to melt in a puddle at his feet. She should have punched

95

him harder last night.

"Just listen, darling," he said, his fingers tracing her jawline, moving lower, toying with the locks of hair that had escaped her coif. "Our dear Mortimer will disappear at that point."

She steeled herself against the impulse to lean toward him, to let his hand travel lower. "Then he'd be in contempt of court."

Oliver's gentle, knowing smile confirmed it — both her statement and his acknowledgement of her need.

Lark forced herself to step back, to escape the tender bond of his caresses. "I've got it all worked out now. Since Mortimer's in contempt, judgment must be given against him."

He shoved off from the rock and took a step toward her. "Aye. The court will say Mortimer had no right to make the sale to Spencer."

She edged backward, away from him. "And the estate must therefore be awarded to you."

He advanced, his pace unhurried yet unrelenting. "And I can do what I like with it."

Lark pretended not to notice what he was doing. "What about Spencer? He's still entitled to compensation from Mortimer."

"Spencer and I will work that out." Each time he spoke, Oliver came closer. "I can keep the estate and pay him a fair price for it. Or I can sell it to anyone Spencer designates. It doesn't matter. The entail will be broken."

Lark felt the wind tease more tendrils of hair from confinement. "'Tis cold-blooded and dishonest," she said, still edging backward. "But there is a certain beauty to it."

"Why is it," Oliver asked, "that we cherish beauty more when we find it in unexpected places?" He reached for her. "Lark, sweetheart, the cliff — "

She took another step back and started to fall. Even before a scream could gather in her throat, he had her by the waist. He brought her toward him, slamming her so forcefully against him that the breath left them both.

She pressed her cheek against his shoulder. He was shaking, and for some reason that made her like him better.

He took her by the hand and started down the rubbled path back to the estate. He stopped and turned, smiling as the breeze tossed his hair into splendid disarray. "I promise you," he whispered into her ear, "I am not so deadly as a fall from a cliff."

5

"**A**N excellent plan," Spencer declared in his quavering voice. "Quite ingenious."

"Lord Oliver and Kit think so. You'd think the two of them had discovered Atlantis."

Almost under his breath, Spencer said, "I made a wise choice indeed."

Unsure of his meaning, Lark spooned up more oxtail broth seasoned with leeks and carrots and fed it to him. "Choice?"

"They are clever and good-hearted young men," Spencer said, turning his head away from the next spoonful of broth. "Honorable men."

"Kit Youngblood is." Lark waited, trying not to seem impatient. Spencer had been endlessly patient with her all her life; she should show him tolerance now. Of late, this was a nightly occurrence. If she didn't feed him, he wouldn't eat.

"And Lord Oliver?" he asked.

"A knave," Lark pronounced. "A typical idle nobleman."

"You voice a strong opinion." Spencer spoke mildly. He never had to raise his voice to her. He asserted his command in subtler ways — a meaningful pause, a lifting of the chin, a narrowing of the eyes.

Lark flushed. "No doubt he's only helping because you ordered him to be saved from hanging. Once he considers that debt repaid, we'll see no more of him."

She told herself she should cease dwelling on thoughts of Oliver de Lacey. With a pang of restless worry, she thought of the communiqué in cipher that lay concealed inside the stomacher she wore around her waist. She had not yet decided whether she would tell Spencer of it.

That thought alone flayed her with guilt. She had never, ever deceived him. Until lately.

"He's more than a knave," Spencer said.

"A rakehell?" she suggested. It felt rather nicely wicked to defy good manners every so often. "Coxcomb? Rascal? Foe to decency?"

Spencer lifted a trembling hand to silence her. "It's unbecoming to speak so carelessly. Not like you at all, Lark, and the worst of it is, you are wrong."

"Am I?"

"Beneath his roguish surface beats the heart of a man of honor. It might take time for you to realize this."

Her guilt sat like a knot in her throat. Spencer was going to die. Surviving grief was the one lesson he could not teach her. "What does it matter what I think of him?" she asked, offering another sip of broth. "He will serve his purpose and then be gone."

Spencer took a few more swallows, then turned his head away again. "Enough. I am helpless as a babe."

"So was I when you took me in," she said with a rush of sentiment. "I was a babe." They shared a history of nearly twenty years. The

99

thought of losing him made the future careen off kilter. What had once seemed certain was now uncertain, without depth or color.

To keep from wringing her hands, she took up her ever-present sewing and stabbed idly at the chemise she had been stitching for the past several months.

"Taking you in was no great sacrifice for me, dear Lark. The rewards I have reaped far exceed the commitment I made. You've become a woman of great virtue, obedient and humble, a joy to me."

Hating herself for deceiving him, she put down her sewing and withdrew the ciphered letter from her stomacher. "Spencer?"

He let out a wispy sigh. "Another rescue?"

"Aye."

"Be careful, Lark. I have never liked your role in this."

He would like it even less if he knew of all her adventures. "I'm good at ciphering," she said. "This one's based on the birthday of the pope. Interesting. I think it could be traced to someone very close to the queen."

"A woman who thinketh alone thinketh evil," Spencer reminded her.

As always, Lark sank her teeth into her tongue until it hurt. Arguing with Spencer was never worth the cost to her pride, for he never failed to win.

"Don't let anyone know you have this knowledge," he continued. "Thank God you're a woman and can't endanger yourself with these rescues."

Little did he know she was much more deeply involved than that. She told herself her deception in this and in the other, darker matter was a kindness. Spencer was sick. If he knew what she planned, he would worry and fret and further weaken himself.

Worse, he would try to stop her. And not even for Spencer would she agree to that.

★ ★ ★

Oliver lay wakeful long into the night. Every day he spent with Lark made him want her more, and in a way he was not used to wanting a woman.

He glared up at the pleated canopy over the bed-stead and scowled at the play of shadow and candle-light in the velvet folds. There was a time when any woman would do — so long as she was warm, pliant, and of a decent age.

Lark had destroyed his breezy disregard for virtue and chastity. She had made him want her and her alone. Now only one woman would do. She was warm, aye, and of the right age, but she was definitely not pliant.

Muttering under his breath, Oliver rose from the bed. He took a drink of water straight from a large ewer, then pulled a loose shirt over his naked form and stepped out into the darkened passageway.

The countryside was insufferably silent. He missed London and the sounds of revelry, the stomping feet and jangling harness, the call of the sleepless bellmen on watch. This

101

place, buried in river-fed hills, was as quiet as a crypt.

As he had done each night, Oliver moved soundlessly along the upper passageway, stopping at the door to Lark's chamber.

Each night he simply stood there, weighing the merits of either entering her room or slinking back to his own quarters.

Thus far, he always chose the slinking.

Did she lie alone and dream of him, he wondered, or were her dreams locked away in a cage like the rest of her?

Was she by nature pure of heart and mind, or did she work at her virtue as a swordsman practiced his stance?

And why, by all that was holy, did he find her so appealing? She was so damned good. All the time. Even on the two fondly remembered occasions when he had kissed her, she had managed to hold part of herself back. To resist, as if she feared committing some terrible sin.

He clenched his fists at his sides. He wanted to sweep her into his arms and make her cry out in ecstasy. Didn't she know what she was missing?

He took a step toward her door. He pressed slowly and steadily and silently at the latch.

As he did, with his face screwed up in anticipation of the noise the latch would make, he heard voices from within.

Lark's angel voice, murmuring in hushed tones. Followed by a low, deadly, masculine rasp.

Devil take the wench on her back! She had a lover!

On fire with curiosity and gut-tearing jealousy, Oliver leaned his ear against the door. He ceased pushing on the latch, for he did not want to miss a word.

" . . . sooner than we thought," Lark was saying.

Oliver pictured her bent over her lover's supine form, that long hair she took such pains to conceal dragging over the scurvy jack-dog's chest.

"Careful now," said the gravelly, half-familiar voice. "It won't do for us to get caught before we're even out of the gate. Are you sure that bit of blond London fluff is none the wiser?"

The rude scall. Blond London fluff indeed! Surely Lark would set him straight.

"Lord Oliver remains as blissfully ignorant as a shrieve's fool," Lark said. "He takes a bottle to his room each night and drinks himself into a stupor."

Oliver seethed, then froze as he heard a strange creaking like the sound of leather straps.

"Mind, it's a tight squeeze," said Lark with a gasp.

Oliver broke out in a cold sweat. The deceiving little lightskirt! What sort of perversion was she practicing?

"I'm almost there," said the lover.

Lark whispered something swift and unintelligible. The heavy breathing exploded in a burst of relief, then ceased.

Oliver pressed his ear even harder to the

door. In one lightning movement, the door whipped open.

Oliver fell into the room. Blinking, he tried to take in his surroundings: blowing curtains, guttering candle, the watery scent of the river, a man stradling the window casement, half in and half out.

They were on him like a pair of St. Bartle's footpads. Lark landed with her knees on his chest. Her lover heaved himself back into the room to clamp a hand around his neck.

Sweet Jesu. It was what he dreaded above all other tortures. The slow strangulation. The chest-ripping starvation for air. Oliver's eyes flew open wide, and he tried to protest, but no sound came out.

"Let up," Lark whispered, parting her knees to ease the pressure on his chest.

The hands stayed in place.

"For the love of God, look at his eyes! He's having some kind of fit. Let up!"

The hand loosened. Oliver dragged in a great gasp of air, then slowly, painfully, released it. He gazed up at Lark. The single candle, burning on the mantel, tinged her pale skin and dark hair in precious gold.

He smiled, acting as if such things happened to him often. "I'm naked beneath this shirt."

She jumped off him so quickly that she landed with a thud on her backside, her skirts riding up over her knees. "How dare you listen at a lady's chamber door!"

Thank God she was still fully dressed, that he had arrived before she had disgraced herself.

Imagining her hulking lover waiting behind him with knife drawn, Oliver tamped down his fear. "Are you a lady? Do ladies in this part of the country entertain men in their private chambers at night?"

"No!" she snapped. "I mean, yes! That is, it's none of your affair!"

Oliver sat up. Her lover loomed like a shadow against the blackness outside the opened window.

"Have you no shame, sir?" Oliver asked with dramatic outrage. "Will you leave Mistress Lark to defend her honor all on her own?"

"My honor is none of your concern," Lark retorted. "Good night, my lord." She looked pointedly toward the door.

Oliver jumped up, glaring at the intruder. A breeze through the window caused the candle to flare, and at last he recognized the man. The heavy jowls. The soft eyes. The withered arm hanging at his side.

In the private darkness of her room, Lark had been entertaining Dr. Phineas Snipes.

"A married man at that," Oliver said in disgust. "And his wife is a friend of yours, or so it seemed at the safe hold."

Lark and Snipes exchanged a glance — not one of lust or guilt, but of collusion.

Comprehension hit Oliver like a slap in the face, leaving him relieved and oddly excited. "It's your secret work, isn't it? The work of the Samaritans."

Lark clasped both her hands around his. "Pray do not betray us, my lord. I beg you."

Lark. Begging. How he loved it.

He was tempted to take advantage of her, to put a price on his silence, yet he found himself saying, "Of course I won't betray you. I'll help you."

She dropped his hand. Head down, eyes looking up through her lashes, she regarded him dubiously. "This is no romp to amuse an idle cove."

Her stab cut his pride. "Do you think I'm made of no more substance than that?"

"You've given me no reason to suppose otherwise."

"He owes us a blood debt, Lark," Snipes said quietly. "And Piers is nowhere to be found. That's why I risked coming here."

"Who is Piers?" Oliver asked.

"A river pilot. He is also a loyal man who specializes in a certain type of escape. We need him now, and we cannot find him. It's sometimes necessary for our confederates to disappear from time to time."

"Then let me play his role." Oliver was caught by the secrecy and urgency of the plan. "I won't disappoint you."

"'Tis risky," Snipes warned.

"I thrive on risk. What was Piers's specialty?"

"Helping prisoners escape."

"From Newgate? By now I know every foul passage and oubliette of the place."

"Not Newgate," Lark whispered.

"Smithfield," said Snipes.

A swift image of sand pits and blackened stakes swept like a shadow through Oliver's mind. "Ah, gross spectacle."

"Go back to bed, my lord," Lark said, not unkindly.

"I'm coming with you."

"What about your promise to Spencer?"

"Kit will work on it while we're away."

Lark and Snipes exchanged another long, considering look.

He wanted to shake them both. "Why do you doubt me?" he demanded. "A 'bit of blond London fluff' indeed! Why do you think me a shallow, frivolous nobleman seeking the thrill of a daring escape?"

"Isn't that what you are?" Lark asked.

"Do not believe everything you hear."

"I'll remember that next time you lie to me," she shot back.

"You need me," he said in his most imperative tone. "At the very least, you need my hands at the oars, since your pilot is missing." He hiked his chin to a lofty angle. "If I fail at Smithfield, you can let me burn there."

"I like it not," Lark said slowly.

"You have no choice," Oliver pointed out. "For if you leave me behind, who's to stop me from divulging your plan?" He hoped they didn't realize he would never betray them. He might be a bit of fluff, but he was a loyal bit of fluff.

Their silence seethed with desperate indecision. He had them.

* * *

To Lark's annoyance, he did look rather dashing. True to his word, he had readied himself in haste and joined them at the river landing. He wore tall boots, fashionably slashed, the tops turned down just above the knees. His cloak was long and dark, and it gave off a rich rustle of silk when he moved. His sword rode discreetly at his hip — a quiet, elegant threat that a thief would not want to test.

"You're staring, sweetheart," he whispered. "Is my codpiece unlaced?"

Chagrined, she backed against a mooring post. In the swift wherry, Dr. Snipes was busy preparing to cast off. Lark cleared her throat. "You look too perfect for the dirty work ahead of us."

He gave a supple bow. "Is this a problem?"

The problem, she decided, was not with the clothes, but with the man himself. He was simply conspicuous. Even in black garb, with nary a bauble or plume in his hat, Oliver de Lacey stood out. It was his height and breadth, his pale silver-blond hair, which caught the moonlight and shimmered like a halo.

He had a presence. A high vigor, an almost frenzied lack of restraint, an ineffable yet undeniable quality that commanded attention. Not just from women, though on their journey from London not one female they passed had failed to eye him longer than she would eye an ordinary man. Many of those women had misinterpreted Lark's relationship to him. They had gazed upon her with envy. It had been a strange feeling — and

108

so gratifying that she was sure it must be a sin.

"Lark?" he prompted.

It was in his voice, too. A certain tone that summoned and held the attention.

She scowled at him. "I cannot think how to make you less noticeable, my lord. Let us go. We should hurry."

The grin he flashed her shone like a beacon through the darkness. She shot him a quelling look. "Do not smile. It makes you even more conspicuous."

"Ah." He sobered instantly. "No smiling. I can't think why I would smile around you anyway."

"Our work is deadly serious," she snapped, giving vent to her temper. "The life of an innocent man is in danger. We do not break into prisons, risk our lives, stop executions, and defy the law to amuse ourselves, but because it is right."

"And if you should happen to have a good time doing it?" Mockingly he fanned his face with his cap. "Jesu forfend!"

She brought her fist down on the mooring post. "You'll probably be caught and named a fugitive."

His laughter caressed the night air. "A vain hope, sweetheart. It was Oliver Lackey they condemned and hanged. If you did your job well . . . "

"We did," Snipes assured him.

"Then no one even remembers the poor sod." He spread his arms, the magnificent black cloak fanning out around him. "I ask you, what resemblance bear I to that rude, unshaven, unwashed, ill-mannered commoner?"

"He talked just as much," Snipes observed. His withered arm stirred uselessly at his side. "I wish you would have more respect for the risks you're taking."

Oliver swallowed. He seemed discomfited. "You were caught, weren't you, Phineas? That's how your arm was injured."

Snipes turned to face the river. The cold breeze blew his loose breeches. "It was a long time ago. I broke."

"Dr. Snipes," Lark said softly.

"I broke," he said, his voice harsh. "I think about it every day." He shook his crippled arm. "This is my reminder. Snipes was a coward. Snipes betrayed his friends."

"As you said, it was a long time ago. We should go," Oliver said.

Lark allowed him to help her into the wherry. As always, there was more to his touch than simply a handhold. It was a lambent heat that grazed her, subtle as a secret kiss. He made her breath catch and her stomach lift.

That was the problem, she decided, settling on the low-backed bench. She tried not to watch him as he swept off his cloak and pulled on a pair of shiny leather gloves, slashed at the cuffs. He picked up the oars and began rowing with a graceful, concentrated rhythm. She felt too much pleasure being around him. It couldn't be right.

And Lark had spent all her nineteen years

110

being taught what was right. She had faltered only once, and that memory was as much a part of her as Phineas's bad arm was to him. But like him, she had to go on.

Turning astern, she glanced at Dr. Snipes, who worked the tiller. A staid and silent man, he rarely revealed his thoughts as he had a few moments earlier. Yet he, too, seemed caught by Oliver de Lacey, watching the younger man as a bettor might eye a champion prior to a wrestling match.

Once they were out in the middle of the river, Oliver's powerful oar strokes enhancing the strong current, he began to talk.

"Tell me about this man we're going to rescue, this Richard Speed."

Lark looked to Dr. Snipes again. How much should they reveal? Snipes lifted his shoulders in bewilderment.

Oliver seemed to sense the unspoken question. "Surely you can tell me those things which are a matter of public record. If the poor cove's to burn at Smithfield, then he's gained some fame."

"He preaches the Reformed faith," Lark said. "He's a young man, but very learned, a powerful orator. He has been known to persuade whole towns to renounce the pernicious evils of the Church of Rome."

Never breaking the rhythm of his oar strokes, Oliver fixed her with a probing stare. She wondered if he could see her in the moonlight, or if her hooded cloak kept her in shadow.

"Are the pernicious evils of the Catholic

Church any more odious than those of Reformed nobles who stole church treasures during the Dissolution?"

She clutched the sides of the wherry as it whispered through a burble of rapids. "Richard Speed gained no personal wealth by espousing his beliefs. He preaches that faith — and faith alone — saves. Not paying church indulgences. Not chanting spells or counting beads. Faith. A simple enough concept, don't you think, my lord?"

"So if I believe in God, I go to heaven? Even a sinner like me?" he asked, reaching forward, drawing back, somehow teasing her with the motion.

"I find it beautifully complex," Lark said. "Mysterious. To the queen's advisers, it must be horrifying."

His grin flashed like quicksilver. "True. The idea that a soul can be saved without paying the church for the privilege must be unthinkable to Bishop Bonner."

She was pleased and surprised by his insights. "Precisely."

"Why did you wait until now to rescue this paragon?"

"We didn't know he'd been taken. When we discovered he had, we could not determine where he was being held. That's usual, you know. The most dangerous prisoners are held in secret places so the populace won't rise to free them."

He continued to question her about Speed. Long after ordinary oarsmen would complain of

112

burning shoulders and blistered hands, Oliver continued to row, covering the distance with a velocity even Piers could not have matched.

The slightest hint of the new day tinged the horizon. The creak of fishing gear joined the sound of lapping oars, and the watery smells of the river grew dank with the hint of sewage, for they were nearing the City. The spires of London rose, ghostly shadows in the distance: St. Paul's like a hatless gent, its dome destroyed by lighting two years before. The rambling turrets and lance-sharp weather vanes of the famous Strand residences, including St. James's Palace, the queen's favorite London lodging.

From deep within a pink fog of smoke and morning mist thrust the four turrets of the White Tower in the middle of the Tower of London.

"I had a brother named Richard," Oliver said abruptly.

Lark felt a pang of curiosity. In truth she knew little of his background save that Spencer admired and trusted the de Lacey family.

"He was called Dickon," Oliver went on.

There it was again, Lark realized. That low, vibrant quality of his voice. The tone that made her want to sit forward, enraptured, and listen to him for hours.

"Dickon," Oliver repeated. His voice grew soft and heartbreakingly wistful. "I never knew him. He died before I was born."

"My lord, I am so sorry," Lark whispered, and without planning to, she reached out and touched his knee. She wondered what it was like to have brothers and sisters — a true family, for that matter. She would never know, for she had grown up isolated and shut away from other children. "I'm certain the two of you would have been very close."

"Aye." A mysterious, pained expression crossed his face. "I wish to God I had known him."

For a moment his sorrow was so devastating and real that she yearned to take him in her arms, to press his head against her breast and weep for him.

Then, of a sudden, the sun broke through the clouds behind him. It had an almost eerily propitious timing, like the midsummer sunrise over the giant stones of Salisbury Plain.

Just for the blink of an eye, the red fire of the rising sun gave him a glowing halo. More than ever he looked like an angel, pious and pure, too perfect to be mortal, his pain raw yet somehow otherworldly. Yearning and wonder rushed through Lark, and a thickness came to her throat.

"Oliver," she whispered helplessly.

He glanced down at her hand upon his knee. A devilish gleam sparked in his eyes, and the moment was gone. It had passed so quickly that Lark decided she had imagined it.

"I say, Dr. Snipes," Oliver declared, "I think the lady's beginning to like me."

She snatched her hand away. "Your insolence is boundless, sir."

"So is my patience, where you are concerned."

She hugged her knees to her chest and studied the looming shadows of the city. "Almost there."

She twisted around to look at Dr. Snipes. "We have never risked Smithfield before."

"No." He ran a finger round his high collar. "It won't be the same as a hanging. Even bigger crowd. The queen has mandated that a member of her council be present. Besides that, there will be churchmen, wardens, aldermen, hangers-on."

"Relic collectors," Oliver added. "Abraham men, cutpurses — "

"There's usually one executioner and his assistant," Snipes said.

"Does he take bribes?"

"Of course. They all do. But he can only do so much. Wet the kindling. Start the blaze downwind. Those techniques are hardly merciful. They merely prolong the agony."

"Or prolong a man's life until we intervene." Oliver seemed none the worse for having rowed all night. "What is your plan, then?"

Lark twisted to look at Dr. Snipes once again. He huffed out his cheeks, adjusted his hat, and seemed to concentrate intently on the tiller.

She turned back to Oliver. "I'm afraid we don't exactly have one."

Rather than voicing disgust, Oliver winked at her. "Leave it to me, then. You'll not regret it."

As he explained his intentions, Lark found herself both caught by his enthusiasm and distrustful of it. He seemed driven to seek out excitement. He spoke and acted like the most committed of Samaritans. Yet she had no doubt that once the work became tedious, he would abandon it. He was capricious and easily bored.

Rescuing a famous man from Smithfield was a challenge he could not resist. To him, it was a whim. A means to feed his masculine pride.

"Ever seen a burning?" Dr. Snipes asked Oliver.

Oliver never broke his rhythm. "'Tis not a favored entertainment of mine. But I understand they draw quite a crowd."

"Aye. Everyone from piemen to aldermen to Gypsies."

"Gypsies?" Oliver looked up, hot energy dancing in his eyes.

"Of course," said Snipes. "A crowd is a Gypsy's livelihood."

"All those purses to cut," Oliver said.

Lark heard a curious sharpness in his tone. She had never met anyone even remotely like him. He gave her a crooked smile filled with humor and joy, yet at the same time the murky shadows still haunted his eyes.

Neither his mind, nor his tongue, nor his rowing arms rested during the voyage down the Thames. When the travelers disembarked, he insisted on stopping at Bridewell Bridge over the river Fleet. There he made an odd sign with grass and sticks, refusing to explain his actions except to say they would aid his scheme.

Half running in their haste, the three wended their way northward, to Smithfield. The crowd thickened around St. Bartholomew's. People's faces were hard, their eyes bright with morbid anticipation. An air of barely suppressed violence

116

hung like a fog over the masses as they moved and shifted across the broad field.

Lark stared with her mouth open and her heart thudding almost painfully. Oliver removed his hat, furrowed his hand through his hair, and said, "God's teeth."

"I've never seen so many people in one place before," Lark whispered.

"My father used to come here to trade horses," Oliver said with a shudder.

"This is impossible," Dr. Snipes conceded wearily. "They have defeated us this time. We shall never get him free with this crowd all around us."

"No!" A sense of dread and loss pounded inside Lark. She knew Richard Speed only through his writings, but those had convinced her that the man was touched by grace. His ideas were so simple. So pure. Faith brought a soul to God. Faith alone.

For that, the Catholics would put a man to death.

"We cannot let them murder him." By standing on tiptoe, she could see the tops of the stakes, black with soot from the many fires before this day. She shuddered. "And in such a fashion."

Oliver's hand closed around hers. She would never get used to that jolt of sensation she felt when he touched her. In fact, it was getting worse. Sometimes she felt it when he merely looked at her.

"I said I would help you do this." The certainty in his tone was that of a man who did not know the meaning of the word failure.

Snipes wiped his brow. "We can't even get near the pits. He'll be gone by the time we fight our way through this crowd."

In her stomach, Lark felt the echo of an ominous drumbeat. A cluster of chanting clerics surrounded a mule dragging a hurdle. The prisoner was being brought to the execution pits.

Oliver tossed his cloak back over one shoulder, cupped his hands around his mouth, and called, "Reprieve!"

"Oh, that's wise," Lark snapped. "We're supposed to be inconspic — "

"Reprieve! Reprieve!" Others took up the call. "Save him! Reprieve!"

Oliver made a bow, flourishing his cloak. "You see, the crowd is our ally, not the enemy."

"You heard only a few voices out of thousands," Lark said. "The rest would riot if they were deprived of the spectacle."

"Oh, they shall riot." As they passed through the thick of the mob, Oliver seemed more and more agitated. Almost pleasurably excited. "You must move in close to the pits so you can help the good reverend to safety when I give the signal."

"Safety?" Snipes peered about skeptically.

"What signal?" Lark asked. She heard the droning monotone of a chanted prayer.

"I suppose the signal isn't necessary. Simply wait for the hue and cry to begin, and then run."

"What makes you so certain there will be a hue and cry?"

"I assure you, there will. Ah. I knew they would come." Oliver pointed at a brightly painted wagon lumbering toward the field. It creaked to a halt, blocking the narrow way at Pie Corner and St. Sepulchre's Alley. A canvas flap gaped open, and a group of rag-clad Gypsies swarmed out, sinking into the crowd. "There," said Oliver. "Take him there and keep low."

"To a Gypsy wagon?"

"Trust me." Oliver gave her that look. The one that was filled with lust and tenderness. The one that caused her to feel as if her feet had left the ground.

"Trust you," she repeated, her tone heavy with irony.

"I knew you would." He gave her a swift kiss that made her head swim and Dr. Snipes's jaw slacken, and then he was gone, shouting and waving at the Gypsies as if they were old friends.

"We'd best do as he says." Lark took Dr. Snipes by the sleeve. "It's better than no chance at all."

"He'll land us all in prison." Snipes shuddered, and the color dropped from his cheeks.

"Perhaps." She refused to dwell on the possibility.

"They'll torture us." His arm trembled beneath her hand. "I could not stand torture. I consider myself a man of deep, abiding, and unshakable faith, but I am also a coward."

She tightened her grip on his arm. "You're no

119

more a coward than the next man." Her gaze caught Oliver's receding form. He was taller by a handspan than anyone else in the crowd, his blond hair spilling from beneath his dark velvet cap. "Less so than some others," she added, speaking too low for Dr. Snipes to hear.

It seemed to take an eternity to wend their way through the noisy throng. Lark recoiled from the avid stares trained on the stake. Normally they executed people in groups, but Speed was special. Richard Speed was to die alone. The queen's ministers meant to make an example of him.

She and Snipes passed St. Bartholomew's, an Augustinian priory church that fronted the square. Beside the church stood a reviewing platform with plank seating for the dignitaries. She glanced up, saw an impression of dark velvet robes, gleaming chains of office, and loathsome self-righteousness. The lord mayor and aldermen would be there, along with the bishop of London's chancellor, a member of the queen's council, and attendant clerics. The officials were as ugly as the stone deities carved into the walls of the church.

The hunger in the eyes of the spectators sickened Lark. It was the same hunger she'd seen in bettors at a bearbaiting or a cockfight. True, she did notice tears streaming from the eyes of some. But not many. Not enough.

The arrogant officials inadvertently aided Lark and Snipes. They prolonged the spectacle with prayers and repeated readings of the charges. A gray-robed cleric was shouting threats of fire and brimstone when Lark reached the front of the crowd.

Here, men-at-arms leaned indolently on a stout wooden rail surrounding the pit. The chanting monks, mindlessly and brutally pious, lifted their faces to the February sky.

The railing groaned as the busy, babbling mob pressed against it. Lark felt panicky as she imagined herself squeezed to death against the rail.

Then her gaze found Richard Speed, and she forgot her own discomfort. Barefoot, dressed in a tattered shirt, he stood in the circular pit, anchored to the stake by a thick chain around his chest.

A chancery official read a list of Speed's heresies and proclaimed the sentence — death by burning.

Speed held his head proudly aloft and listened. He was a young man, but his gaunt cheeks and sunken eyes made him look ancient. His legs had been stretched, the joints grossly swollen. His ripped shirt flapped against his skeletal frame, and his chin jutted forth in a final gesture of defiance.

Lark placed one foot on the lower bar of the fence and boosted herself up. Twisting around, she spied Oliver, his head bent as he laughed and flirted with a Gypsy girl.

Her heart sank. She had been right about Oliver de Lacey. He was true only as long as the work was amusing. Once the challenge became too great, he fell back into his old ways.

The Gypsy girl spoke to others nearby, who

121

in turn whispered to their neighbors. And so it went, no doubt bawdy talk and gossip. Lark turned away in disgust and stepped up another rung.

Richard Speed raised his bound hands. "Good people of London, today I preach my last."

Lark's mouth dropped open. Near her, the jostling ceased and people shushed each other. Never had Lark heard such a voice. This broken man, half dead already, snared the attention of thousands. It was like hearing a lion's roar come from the mouth of a kitten.

"I have been told that I am a heretic," Speed shouted.

"No!" people called. "Never that!"

"I have been told that I have no reverence for the sacraments. And that is true."

Horrified gasps seemed to suck the air from the field.

With fire in his eye, Speed leaned forward. "I have no reverence for the sacraments because the scriptures do not command me to."

"Thief!" The shout came from somewhere behind Lark.

Bracing a hand on Dr. Snipes's shoulder, she turned. Two portly men glared at each other. From her high perch, Lark saw a Gypsy youth slinking away, head low.

"I believe no more and no less than I read in the scripture, which is the word of God," Speed roared.

"My purse!" a lady shrieked. She shook a fist at the startled boy next to her. "You stole my purse, you thieving little herring."

122

But he hadn't. From her elevated perch, Lark could see a Gypsy girl sidling away, dropping a fat purse into her laced bodice.

"He *pinched* me," wailed a plump matron. Her husband grabbed the man beside her and proceeded to shake him. Meanwhile, a dark-bearded Gypsy looked skyward, his face the picture of innocence while his victim blamed her neighbor. People nearby swore and jostled one another.

"I *am* guilty!" Richard Speed shouted. "Guilty of believing in God as He is revealed to us in the scripture."

"*Fiat justitia!*" The shout came from the reviewing stand. In response, the hooded executioner lowered a hissing torch to the straw and kindling, which lay in heaps at the foot of the stake. His assistant set out bladders of gunpowder as well. They would use the explosives to speed the burning, for roasting a person alive was an inexact science that sometimes required an extra charge.

"Stop, thief!" Yet another robbery occurred in a different part of the crowd. "Stop that bilking cull!"

The executioner and his assistant hesitated, torches hovering over the firewood and gunpowder. They looked to each other for guidance. The assistant reached under his hood and scratched his head.

"If this be heresy, then I am a heretic!" Speed's sermon, moving as it was, began to drown in a sea of angry shouts.

The Gypsies were gifted thieves. They made

their cut and slipped away — and managed to implicate a bystander in the process.

A movement caught Lark's eye. Oliver had climbed up on the Gypsy wagon wedged in the mews and was gesturing to her. He wore an insolent grin, looking more fit than he should after rowing down the Thames all night.

The burgeoning riot, incited by the light-fingered Gypsies, was clearly his doing. Before she could stop herself, Lark smiled at him. She should have trusted him. Riots and mayhem were his specialty; that was what had landed him in Newgate in the first place.

"Dr. Snipes," she said, climbing down from the rail, "I do believe — "

A cursing man plowed into her. He was pressed from behind by the angry crowd. They panicked at having lost money; it was the only thing more important than watching a man being burned alive.

Lark reached for Dr. Snipes, but in the blink of an eye a half dozen people filled in the breach between them.

Lark tasted the panic that was infecting the crowd. She heard an ominous creaking sound. The wooden rail bowed out, groaning with the strain of the throng. Seconds later the rail snapped.

A mere step from being crushed, Lark lurched forward. To her astonishment and dread, she found herself at the very edge of the sandpit, staring in horror at the condemned man.

6

MEN-AT-ARMS fanned out to enclose the burgeoning mob. Spectators tumbled, crushing and cursing one another. Barriers around the pit collapsed beneath the rush of the crowd.

The executioner, bellowing oaths beneath his half mask, stumbled back. A sun-browned Gypsy hand plucked the flaming torch from his grasp. A cart piled with straw took fire, spooking the mule. The squealing animal reared and plunged into the throng.

Someone shoved Lark from behind, pushing her to her knees in the sand. The bundles of kindling scratched her. A rotten egg odor of sulfur wafted from the bladders of gunpowder piled nearby.

Gasping in fear, Lark dragged herself to her feet.

She came face-to-face with the rebel minister, Richard Speed.

"Reverend sir!" she cried.

"God be with you," he replied, looking as calm and holy as an angel in marble.

"I — we've come to save you." She whipped a glance around and saw the seething, screaming mob closing in on them. With a sick feeling in her stomach, she teetered on the brink of failure. Oliver and Dr. Snipes had vanished. She was but a woman who had spent her life locked

125

in a grim battle against sinful impulses. How could she ever have thought she possessed the fortitude to rescue Richard Speed?

A woman who thinketh alone thinketh evil. Spencer had recited the proverb to her often. She should have heeded him.

Reverend Speed glanced up at the groaning plank stands. From that lofty vantage point, the captain of the guard gesticulated furiously and shouted orders. The soldiers had been all but trampled in the stampede of angry people. A few attempted to use their pikestaffs to clear a path, but the staffs were broken or snatched away by the rushing crowd. A pall of smoke from the burning cart shrouded the field.

"I am much obliged," Speed said. "And I mean no lack of gratitude, but perhaps you could hurry."

Lark looked helplessly at the thick chain that circled his chest, mooring him to the stake. "I know not what to do," she said, almost sobbing. "The soldiers will be upon us soon, and — "

A great screeching, splintering sound stopped her. She looked back at the reviewing platform.

And spied Oliver de Lacey. Beneath the straining planks, he was using a pikestaff to dislodge the supports from under the platform.

For the first time, Lark let herself hope for success.

The chain was not locked but looped around a wickedly long nail in the back of the stake. Sometimes, to show mercy, the executioner drove the nail into the victim's neck to hasten his death.

126

With frantic fingers, she worked at the chain. Soot blackened the iron, reminding her that other martyrs had not escaped the flames.

She firmed her trembling lip, scraped the link off the nail, and the chain fell free. Richard Speed started to collapse onto the piled kindling. She hauled him up by the wrist and shouted, "Make haste!"

Ducking her head, she plunged into the raging crowd, following a vague path cleared by the fright maddened mule. Squinting through the pall of smoke, mothers separated from their children screamed in panic. People injured in the stampede moaned and cried for help. Officials shrieked out orders that went unheeded.

Oliver flung away his pikestaff and darted out from beneath the reviewing stand. The platform holding all the stuffy dignitaries of London collapsed in a heap of broken boards and bellowing men.

And in the midst of it all, Lark and Richard Speed found a way out.

★ ★ ★

"What *is* this place?" the reverend asked, blinking in the dimness. His pale skin pulled taut over the bones of his face, and his eyes peered out from purpled sockets. Still, he retained a misty air of majesty that made Lark proud to be in his presence.

She felt a suspicious crawling in the blanket beneath her. Bedbugs or lice . . . or worse. She shuddered. Outside the painted canvas covering of the vehicle, the crowd still rioted.

"It is a Gypsy caravan," she explained. "I was told to come here. Perhaps we had best conceal you in some way." After rummaging in a heap of soiled clothing, she found a length of cloth, which she draped over his head. As she tucked it around his shoulders and arranged the ends to hide the manacles on his wrists, she felt him tremble.

Her heart went out to him. "You'll be all right now," she whispered. "Truly, you have many friends who will protect you."

He let out a shaky breath. "It is a blessed miracle."

"No. It is our Christian duty." She found a moth-eaten shawl and layered it over the dull cloth.

"Who are you, mistress?"

"My name is Lark."

"You have risked much for me this day."

She looked up at him, her hands upon his knees and her throat suddenly tight. Despite the odd, womanish disguise, she noted a certain masculine beauty in his face — it was nicely sculpted, and his eyes were deep and kind. He lacked the loud, lavish, golden handsomeness of Oliver de Lacey. Speed's was a quiet appeal, one that did not shout but beckoned.

"God will reward you for your courage," he promised.

It was a far more appropriate remark than asking her to have his child, she decided.

She squeezed the reverend's hands. The noise of the crowd seemed to fade for a moment.

128

Richard Speed's face was close — close enough for her to see the thick fringe of lashes around his rich brown eyes and to see the weariness and pain in the creases of his pallid cheeks.

"I fear I possess little courage," she admitted. "But I have been taught to do my duty."

The caravan lurched. Lark tumbled against Richard Speed, and he grasped her shoulders, cradling her cheek to his chest.

At that very instant, Oliver de Lacey climbed into the caravan.

For a moment he simply stared at them. Then a self-deprecating and humorless grin slashed his mouth. "I know just how you feel, old man," he said to Speed. "And in truth, I wish you better luck with her than I have had."

★ ★ ★

It was dusk by the time the train of caravans stopped. Tired of the uncomfortable closeness of the covered van, Oliver leaped out through the back. They were north of London, and the high ridge of the Chilterns rose in the distance. Long purple shadows painted the flanks of the hills, and a mist, fine as a fairy's whispers, softened edges and deepened hues, turning Oliver's mood reflective and melancholy.

It had been an eventful day indeed. No doubt the authorities were going mad searching for the escaped prisoner. Even as the caravan had pulled away from Smithfield, Oliver had heard people muttering that a miracle had occurred, that the hand of God had swept Reverend Speed up to heaven.

He glanced around him, watching the other caravans lurching up to the broad green clearing near a russet beechwood grove. The clearing, beside a rushing stream, would be their camp for the night.

He started to stalk away from the vehicle, then turned and walked back. The ugly truth jabbed at him. He was humiliatingly jealous of the tender regard in which Lark held Richard Speed. But he would die before he would let her know that.

Parting the curtain of leather strips that formed the doorway, he scowled into the shadowed van. "We'll stay the night here. Reverend, let me help you out. We'll get Rodion to strike your manacles."

"I would be much obliged." The reverend rose slowly, laboriously. Oliver envisioned the torture the man must have endured, and suddenly he did not feel so angry.

"It's all right to whine or curse if you like," he suggested, studying the tormented look on Speed's face.

"Why would I whine or curse?" Speed asked in genuine confusion. "Being among Gypsies is better than being burned alive."

"Such high praise! You cannot help but love him," said Rodion, grinning and putting down a step stool. The Gypsy held out his hands to help Speed down. The preacher half fell into Rodion's arms, and Rodion carried him away to a pallet on the ground, where some of the women were building a fire.

"Ah, mind the poor man's wounds," called a brusque, familiar voice.

A comfortable warmth seeped through Oliver, and he turned to smile at her — a woman he had loved since he had learned the meaning of the word.

"Jillie, my dove! Come give us a kiss!" He barely had time to call her name before her embrace engulfed him.

The speed with which Lark appeared was gratifying. Like a hedgehog emerging from its hole, she popped out the back of the van. No doubt she wished to see just whom Oliver would address with such affection.

Jillie of the yellow hair, cornflower blue eyes, and arms the size of a blacksmith's. Jillie, the West Country maid who had been swept into adventure by her Romany husband — Rodion, chief of the Gypsies.

Pity she had been married a score of years and had borne a half dozen children, for Oliver adored all eighteen stone of her.

She had an embrace like that of a mother bear and a grin as big as her generous heart.

Smiling back just as broadly, Oliver stepped away. "That hug, dearest Jillie, was worth waiting for."

She cuffed him on the side of the head. "Two years it's been, you cozening rogue."

"And your beauty has grown in bounty with each passing season."

She cuffed him harder. "Listen to the unlicked little whelp, thinking to flatter me. I'm big as a

131

barge, and proud of it." Beaming, she turned to Lark. "And who might this be?" Oliver had forgotten how loudly Jillie's voice boomed. "Is she your current tup?"

Lark had the most extraordinary way of blushing. She seemed to color like a glass jar filled with wine — from chin to scalp, quite visibly. Yet even as she flushed a deep, attractive pink, she managed to find the poise to step down from the caravan and curtsy to Jillie.

"Mistress, I am not his tup, nor ever shall be."

Jillie looked Lark up and down, her pale eyebrows lifting at Lark's plain black mockado gown. "Pity. I trow he'd make you happy as a milkmaid tumbled off her stool."

Lark's flush deepened a shade. "He has indeed made me happy." She grasped his hand and pressed it to her bosom.

He could feel the beating of her heart, and the sensation made his head spin. He disliked the response intensely. She made him feel like a green and callow youth, enslaved by the first stirrings of manly desire.

Her expression glowed with ill-aimed worship. "My lord, you saved a godly man today. I can think of no way to express the depths of my gratitude."

He could have suggested a few ways, but none of them involved hero worship.

Damn it to hell and back, he wanted her to *want* him.

"Aye, well." He extracted his hand from hers. "It seemed a fair thing to do at the time."

132

Jillie lumbered off, bellowing orders. The Gypsies drew their wagons into a half circle in the wood-fringed clearing. Men went off to survey the road-stead to make certain no one had followed them. Others hobbled the horses and set them to graze in the sere grass.

Women built a great cookfire and set a big pot to boil. Children hauled water up from the stream, and a few musicians tuned their guitars and harps and shawms for music.

Old Maida, the healer, had laid Richard Speed upon a pallet and busied herself doctoring his wounds. She fed him a draft of anise and rosewater, thickened with honeyed wine, and soon the good reverend had sunk into deep, healing sleep.

"I love the Gypsies," Oliver said, loosening the laces of his doublet and happily surveying the activity.

Beside him, Lark raised her eyebrows. "Why?"

"Why not?" He shrugged out of the doublet and dropped it carelessly to the ground. Within seconds a lad happened by, snatched up the garment, and walked away, rolling his eyes and whistling to make certain Oliver noticed him.

With a growl of mock outrage, Oliver bent low and chased the boy, tumbling with him to the ground and tickling him until he surrendered the doublet. The lad's peals of laughter were the sweetest music Oliver had heard in weeks.

He sent the boy on his way with a pat on the backside. Shaking out his doublet, he returned to Lark.

"They seem pagan, homeless wanderers," she observed.

He suspected she was mouthing nonsense drummed into her by the redoubtable Spencer.

"Spencer once said their race comes from the tinkers who made the nails used to crucify Jesus Christ," she added.

Now Oliver was certain he'd guessed the source of the nonsense, but he was in no mood for arguing. With his lawn shirt flapping loose, he took her hand and led her toward a group sitting round the fire.

The flames bathed the Gypsies' faces in warm hues of amber and gold. Their smiles were broad, their gestures easy — a man smoothing his hand down his wife's curling hair, a mother gathering a babe to her breast, a young boy bringing an old woman a slice of bread slathered with lard.

"Pagan?" Oliver asked with a hint of exasperation. "Homeless? Look at them, Lark. They love their children. They inflict pain on no one. And just because they don't own a sad little patch of tillage means naught. In truth they are free, unfettered by greed and ambition. Can you say as much for Christian Englishmen?"

"No." She shivered, hunching her shoulders, and Oliver wondered if she was thinking of Wynter. "No, I cannot."

He sat cross-legged on the ground amid the group of people and drew her down beside him. Lark accepted a clay bowl of soup and a bit of bread, sipping daintily from the rim of the bowl.

Oliver liked watching her. She was as bright as new-minted copper, absorbing all that she saw with a hunger that made him angry for all the years she had been sheltered at Blackrose Priory.

He spied a new face in the crowd — a woman. She came and sat near him, arranging her layered skirts around her like the petals of a flower. The fireglow bathed her in friendly hues, shadowing her age-weathered face and burnishing her white hair gold. Though he had known the members of this tribe for years, he did not recognize her.

Summoning up his knowledge of Romany, he said, "I have not met you before, have I?"

Lark glanced at him sharply. "You speak their tongue?"

"Aye."

"How singular."

"No more singular than knowing Latin, a language no one speaks yet everyone must learn."

"I am Zara," said the woman, her voice deep and husky, her eyes sleek and sanguine. "A wanderer from afar."

She was most intriguing, her white hair oiled to a sheen and pulled tautly into two glossy braids. She had a ready smile, revealing a missing tooth on the lower front. When she turned her head toward the fire, Oliver saw that upon her cheek blazed a remarkable star-shaped strawberry stain.

No wonder she bore herself with such confidence and sat in a place of honor next to Rodion. Those born with such marks were considered blessed.

"Where did you come from?" Oliver asked.

"Far beyond the Narrow Sea. From the kingdom of Muscovy."

Oliver felt a twinge of familiarity. "My honored stepmother comes from a place called Novgorod."

Mystery and magic glowed in Zara's gleaming eyes and shaped her smile into a learned arc. "I know."

Zara. Juliana had spoken of such a woman. A seeress, she was, the one who had prophesied Juliana's journey to England.

Although Oliver put little stock in stargazing and soothsaying, Juliana had always maintained that the woman called Zara had once tapped into her soul and foretold events that shaped her life.

"'Tis you!" he said in an astonished whisper, abandoning Romany for English. "But how — "

"One of your own father's ships brought me after . . . " Zara, too, switched to English, spoken with a broad, guttural accent. She looked into the heart of the fire, and reflected flames danced with misty memories in her eyes. "After Czar Ivan's men killed my husband and made slaves of my children."

"Ah, you poor woman!" With a catch in her voice, Lark put down her bowl and reached across Oliver, grasping Zara's hands.

The Gypsy woman took in her breath on a hiss, as if Lark's touch had burned her.

"I'm sorry," said Lark. "I didn't mean to hurt you — "

136

"Hush. Do not move."

"What have I done?" Lark asked. She caught her lower lip in her teeth and dropped one shoulder as if bracing herself for a blow.

Zara leaned forward, her eyes keen with fascination, the strange star on her cheek shining in the fire-light. She turned Lark's hand over in her own, spreading it out, tracing her slender finger along the palm. "It is you."

"I don't know what you mean."

"You are one of the three." With a jerk of her head, she motioned Oliver away.

He edged back so that the women sat facing each other. A powerful tension seemed to pulse in the air and flow across the bond between them.

"I still don't understand," said Lark. "What three?"

"I saw your fate before you were made," Zara said. "It was on a night of fire in Novgorod. Three women. Three fates flung like seeds upon the wind." She smiled into Lark's shocked face and clutched her hand tightly. "The circle was begun before you were born, and will endure long after you are gone. You are but a part, a ripple in the water."

"Circle?" Lark tugged at her hand, clearly discomfited by Zara's strange musings.

Zara held fast to her. "The circle of fate."

"Why me?"

"Because of vows that flow from a young man's lips." Without ever taking her gaze from Lark, Zara took Oliver's hand and linked it with Lark's. The Gypsy woman stood, looking wholly refreshed, and wandered off to the musicians.

Feeling intrigued yet unsettled, Oliver extracted his hand from Lark's. "Wine," he muttered, and brightened. "This calls for wine! Let us vow, Lark, to drink and make merry."

Lark pushed the stew around in the clay bowl. Apparently she had lost her appetite. "What do you suppose she meant by all that?"

Oliver shrugged. He did not enjoy the vague, prickly feeling at the back of his neck. "Perhaps it is the way an old woman enlarges her own importance. The poor soul has no more family. 'Tis a sad thing to feel useless, and so perhaps she makes prophecies to prove her worth."

"As a Christian, I can but agree," Lark said. "Still, she gave me such an odd feeling when we touched."

Oliver laughed. "To you, all touching is odd, sweetheart." He ran a teasing finger down her cheek and tickled her ear. She gave a little cry and drew away, and he laughed again. "See? You squeak and squawk like a hen for the stewpot."

She sniffed and turned her attention to the Gypsies sharing London gossip. They possessed a wealth of it, for in their travels they had learned to become both open-eared and unobtrusive.

"The she-king is said to be desperate for an heir." Rodion uncorked a flask of plum wine, took a drink, and passed it on.

Jillie cupped her hands around her mouth and said loudly, "One of Queen Mary's advisers even consulted Zara to divine Her Majesty's chances of having a child."

Oliver gave the flask to Lark. "You need this, my dear, for you've gone quite pale."

"I don't often find myself privy to treasonous talk," she whispered. Then she took an impressively long drink of the plum wine.

"'Tis said," Rodion continued, "that Queen Mary is conspiring to steal someone's newborn babe. Fact is, they arrested a tailor's wife for saying another lady's child would be named the queen's own."

Lark nearly choked on a mouthful of wine. Oliver patted her back until the spell passed.

"I don't believe that for an instant," Oliver felt obliged to say.

"Nor do I," said a Gypsy man. "For all that she is a sickly, bitter, and ill-advised woman, the queen adheres to strict principles."

"Pity the same is not true of her chief minister, Bishop Bonner," Rodion said. At the mention of Bonner's name, his listeners tucked their thumbs and crossed their fingers. Old Maida clutched at the rope of white garlic hanging from her belt.

A tambour rattled suggestively. The mood of the gathering lightened as if a pall had been lifted from their midst. Laughter erupted, and people stood up, clapping raised hands.

"I don't suppose you dance," Oliver said.

"Of course not," Lark retorted.

"Would it disturb you if I did?" he asked, jumping to his feet.

"Would it stop you if I said aye?" she fired back.

Disagreeable stick, he thought, walking away from her. Why did he let her bother him?

Laughing he joined hands with the Gypsies forming a circle.

As he took up the whirling motion of the round dance, he let the rhythm sweep him back to the summer-gilt days of his boyhood. Thanks to his step-mother, he had learned to love the ways of the Romany people. They cared only for the moment, never fretting about what the morrow would bring. Certainly they never wrung their hands about the fate of their immortal souls.

Bare Gipsy feet thumped upon the trampled ground. The inner circle was comprised of women, and facing them were the men, forming a circle of their own. They never touched their partners yet moved with such harmony that the men and women seemed to be joined in some primal way. The shadowy rhythm suggested the music of love played between two bodies.

Oliver tried to focus his attention on the Gypsy girl vying for his attention. She was as dark and sweet as a ripe cherry. She did not cage herself in busked corsets or stays but decked her body in a loose, low-cut blouse and colourful skirts.

Even so, Oliver was shocked to discover that he could not summon the easy, earthy desire he usually felt for women. A cold horror seized him. Perhaps this was the beginning of the end. Perhaps this lack of passion was the first herald of his inevitable march toward an early death.

No. Sidestepping his dance partner, he glanced over his shoulder at Lark. She sat clutching her skin wine flask. Her face held a most gratifying look of shock and yearning.

His blood began to heat. Lark was the key. Somehow, his passion and desire all centered her. And of all the women Oliver de Lacey had held in his arms, only Lark felt exactly right.

Deep in a secret, unacknowledged part of him, he remembered Zara's prophecy. She had joined his hand with Lark's as if it were an act ordained by a higher force.

★ ★ ★

The fire had spent itself to embers. The frenzied, exotic music had faded to echoes of plucked strings and drum rattles, and the dancers had drifted into snoring heaps of tangled limbs and blankets.

Oliver was nowhere to be seen.

Joints creaking with stiffness, Lark rose to her feet. The wine she had drunk rushed to her head, and she listed like a wherry on a wave.

"Steady," she muttered to herself, stepping gingerly over a sleeping man. She passed a group of children lying intertwined like a litter of puppies. What strange and wondrous folk these Gypsies were.

A few weeks earlier she never could have imagined that she would be among Gypsies. Spencer had assured her that they were lawless beggars and thieves. In truth they were a joyful lot who loved good food, fruity wine, and wild dancing. They harmed no one.

She crept close to the pallet where Richard Speed lay. Thick, coarse blankets covered him to the chin. In the uncertain moonlight he appeared pale and peaceful, his wounds salved and bound by the woman called Maida.

Lark walked on, her skirts rustling over the night-dewed grass. She felt oddly alert, her imagination still aflame, hours later, with the words Zara had spoken.

Vows that flow from a young man's lips. Surely Oliver was right. They were an old woman's musings or perhaps a trickster's ploy. Yet Zara had asked for nothing. Or had she? Lark remembered the look in the Gypsy's eyes when Zara had linked her hand with Oliver's.

Lark inhaled deeply of the cold night air and eased the frown from her brow. There was no use fretting. She should enjoy the pleasant numbness of the plum wine, and she should not neglect her prayers.

Leaving the circle of caravans and the horses sleeping with heads hung low, she went down beside the river. There she found a mat of soft grass and fell to her knees.

She had always found a certain spiritual rapture in prayer, but tonight the feeling eluded her. Instead her mind clung to images of the Gypsy dance and Oliver de Lacey. Closing her eyes, she saw him again. The flickering firelight. The pure gold of his hair. The loose eddy of his unbound sleeves. The flash of his smile.

He danced as he seemed to do all other things — with his whole heart, with every fiber of vitality he possessed. Though Lark rubbed her eyes with her fists, she saw him still, his powerful arm wrapped around the

142

waist of a smiling Gypsy maid, his crooked smile heartbreaking and enigmatic, hinting that his temperament could change in a blink from joy to melancholy.

Dry leaves rustled beneath her as she shifted and forced her eyes open. She stared at the gleaming black ribbon of the river flowing past, the secret gurgles whispering to her. Still she thought of him, of Oliver de Lacey, so fair and rowdy, so comely, amusing, bright, and aggravating that he seemed almost a character of myth rather than a real man. He was possessed by a vigor and lack of temperance that both fascinated and frightened her.

She had grown exhausted simply watching him.

And yet she couldn't *not* watch him.

It was time to confess the truth to the Almighty.

She pressed her hands together — palms damp, nails chewed — and squeezed her eyes shut again.

"Lord," she whispered. Her tongue felt thick, stumbling over the words. She drew a deep breath. "I have been possessed by an evil temptation."

There. She'd said it. Lightning did not strike her dead, so she rushed on. "It is Oliver de Lacey, Lord. I cannot stop thinking about him. Forgive me, but more than once I have wondered what he looks like without his . . . his clothes. When he was dancing tonight I kept staring at his legs. His *legs*."

She paused, listening to the night wind

143

sifting through the long grasses nodding at the riverbank. She still seemed to have the ear of the Almighty, so she continued baldly. "I feel a ripple of *something* — heat or cold, I know not which — up my spine when I hear the sound of his laughter. And dear Lord, he laughs far too much. Though it is no affair of mine, I cannot help but feel pleased that his face is not marked by pox scars. And when I see the sky reflected in his eyes I almost forget I am a godly woman and — "

"Sweetheart, your prayers are about to be answered."

Lark shot to her feet as if something had exploded under her skirts. "How dare you disturb my privacy!"

Oliver de Lacey grinned. It was the same lazy, insolent smile she had just complained to the Almighty about. Oliver strolled down the riverbank on the silk-clad legs she had just described to her heavenly host. And then, self-assured as any actor on a stage, he laughed. And aye, it was the same spine-shivering sound she both craved and dreaded. Heat, she decided insanely. The shiver was heat, not cold.

Oliver bowed deeply before her. "Aye, it makes me happy indeed to learn that I have led the saintly Mistress Lark into temptation."

7

S HE was glad for the shadowy darkness, for her cheeks were on fire with humiliation. "You are the first man I've met who considers causing me discomfort a worthy deed."

"You are wrong, my lady Righteous." He stopped just in front of her, so close she could feel the heat of his body and recognize his unique scent. A heady, shockingly familiar essence.

She knew he meant to intimidate, to make her quail in awe like . . . like . . .

Like the helpless, smitten sinner she was.

"I meant no insult," he said in a rich, intimate whisper. "'Tis only that I had feared you were made of stone."

"I?" Incensed, she spun away and stalked back and forth along the bank of the river. "I — made of stone? Just because I don't drool over a conceited Lord — Lord *Worm* like you? I care about the poor and infirm," she declared. "I love God with tenderness and reverence. I — "

"Indeed." Clearly unmoved by her tirade, he handed her a dipper of water from the stream. "Cool your tongue, Mistress Firebrand, lest you sear someone with it."

She stopped and took a drink of the fresh, chill water. On her second swallow she realized she was obeying him, spat out the water, and simply glared at him. She always did as she was told. Lately that had not been much of a virtue.

"It is admirable to care about the poor and to love God." Oliver lounged against the trunk of a tree, his face in shadow, his voice betraying sardonic amusement. "But where in the scripture is it written that a woman should not be human, should not feel the desires and yearnings of a healthy young body?"

"A good Christian is chaste in thought and deed." Even as she spoke the words, she knew they were not her own. Spencer had taught them to her. Spencer had taught her everything.

Oliver de Lacey made her doubt long-held beliefs when it was so much easier accepting them as fact.

"A good Christian," he countered, "is one who can tell good from ill. One who can confront and conquer temptation."

"I can tell good from evil."

"Then what am I, Lark? Am I good? Or evil?"

His bald question startled her. "I was never meant to judge you, my lord."

"Oh no?" He pushed away from the tree, detaching himself from the concealing shadows. For the first time Lark realized he was angry. Truly angry, and he was barely in control. With his shoulders taut, his prowling gait restrained, he reminded her of a predator about to strike.

"Never meant to judge me, were you?" His mocking tone cut like a blade. "My dear

146

Countess of Contempt. My dear, pious, holier-than-a-nun's-arsehole Lady Lark." He grasped her by the upper arms and forced her to look up into his face. "Since the moment you pulled me out of a pauper's grave, you have done nothing but judge me."

She flinched, though his hold did not hurt. "You were insolent to me that night! You asked me to have your baby!" She had not meant to remind him. She wished she could take it back. Mortified, she twisted herself out of his grip.

"Which some women would take as a compliment," he shot back.

"Well, *I* did not."

"And from that moment on, you considered me a flesh-loving beast."

"When have you shown me otherwise?" She was shouting now, but she was past caring. "I sought your help, only to find you in a gambling den draped with a — with a — "

"With a ha'penny whore," he filled in for her. "And a jolly good day it was, until *you* came along with your big black cloak and your little pinched face and your 'burn in hell' attitude."

"Which you promptly proceeded to scorn." She poked her finger at his chest for emphasis. "You all but drowned me in the Thames. You dragged me to a fair I did not wish to attend. You — "

"Enough!" He caught her finger in his fist. "You win. I am the blackest of sinners." The raw, pained note in his voice made her want to cover her ears, to run and hide. "The fact that I braved an attack by brigands for your sake, that

I roused a crowd to riot so you could rescue Richard Speed, were only temporary lapses into virtue."

She did not want to think of him as a man who could be hurt. "It's not that I'm ungrateful." Her voice was soft and low-pitched.

He put one finger beneath her chin and stared into her eyes. "Am I truly that repulsive to you, Lark? So odious, so tainted by evil, that you would pray on your knees to escape me?"

"I was praying for my own sake, not yours." How had he done it? How had he managed to turn things around and make her feel guilty for something she said in private prayer?

"Begging for release from temptation, were you?"

She didn't answer. She avoided his gaze.

"Temptation!" he roared, grabbing her again. "You do not even know the meaning of the word."

She winced, and he took a deep breath. "I have never met a woman who could so easily arouse me. To anger," he added quickly. His hands began to ride slowly up and down her arms. "Lark, I don't claim to be an expert in theology like the most holy Mr. Speed, but I have learned something about temptation. Something I can teach you."

His gentle caresses soothed her. "Yes?"

"I know you think you should banish me from your presence, from your thoughts, from your life if need be, in order to triumph over temptation."

It was exactly what she had been thinking. "Go on."

"That would be no victory at all. True triumph and true grace come from confronting temptation."

"Confronting it?"

"Aye, and exploring it at its deepest level within yourself. And ultimately, sweet Lark, finding the strength to resist."

"I don't know what you mean." She felt light-headed now, lulled by fatigue and by the tender stroking of his hands on her arms, up and down, shoulder to elbow.

"Let me show you," he whispered. "When I lean down and touch your ear — like so — *that* is temptation."

The moist flick of his tongue on her earlobe nearly set her aflame. She knew she should run — far away, to a place where he could not find her — but instead she stayed riveted and spellbound by the sorcery of his touch.

"When I slide my hands down your back" — he demonstrated — "and then cup you against me" — he pulled her so close, she could feel the entire length of his body — "*that* is temptation."

He brought his hand up, smoothly removing the fabric partlet that covered her décolletage. "When I caress you here, where your breasts rise against your bodice, *that* is temptation."

She was truly on fire now, and the worst of it was, she did not care. All the reliable old proverbs and cautions flew out of her mind.

He bent to skim his lips over her bared flesh,

then lifted his head, pressing his brow against hers and staring into her eyes. His mouth hovered close, tantalizing, its shape imprinted on her senses, its texture and taste evoking forbidden memories of other moments.

"And when you kiss me?" she heard herself ask boldly. "Is that temptation?"

"Oh, yes, my love. Of the sweetest sort." He bent his head, his lips coming closer and closer. "Yes indeed." He paused when his mouth came nearer still, a mere breath away. She could almost feel his kiss. The hunger to experience it flared out of control. Passion was contrary to all of her training, all of her hard-won self-control. Lessons and lectures burned away like so much kindling on a bonfire.

"What are you feeling, Lark?" he asked in the softest of whispers. "Tell me. Describe it."

"I feel . . . " She wanted to grasp him and press his mouth down over hers, to punish herself with sinful yearning. "Overly warm."

"Where?"

"I . . . everywhere," she replied, taken aback.

She felt the soft hum of his mirth as he chuckled. "Can you be more specific?"

"I could. But there are certain things I do not . . . I cannot name."

True warmth flowed through his laughter then, and genuine affection radiated from him as he slid his arms around her and pressed her cheek to his chest. "Dear Lark. You do have much to learn."

She realized that he referred to the act of physical love. The old guilty horror crept over her, and she shuddered. "Suppose I don't wish to learn?"

"There is no shame in naming body parts and knowing how they work. Trust me." Before she could stop him, he let his hand stray. "Now, this is a — "

"No!" She clapped her hands over her ears. "That is vulgar."

He lifted her hand and spoke into her ear. "Then what about — "

"Stop that!" Yet even as she spoke, she was intrigued by his game and by the stragely liberating feeling it gave her to speak frankly of things she had been taught to keep secret. She felt both shame and curiosity, wanting to know what a real wife knew. Curiosity won out, grinding the last flicker of guilt beneath its heel. "I shall listen if you promise to whisper."

"Of course," he said, all seriousness.

"And if you swear you won't use those horrid low German terms."

"Very well."

They settled — he with vast amusement, she with uncomfortable fascination — on terms more suited to animal husbandry than lovemaking. Although her cheeks burned, she was an avid listener, forgetting her shame as he described a world of sensation, of temptation, of ravishing sensuality. It was nothing like the world she knew. It was brighter, bolder, and infinitely seductive.

"Now then," she said with false briskness when he finished, "I have confessed to what I feel. I am ready to be tempted." She raised

151

herself on tiptoe, so eager now for his kiss that she almost wept when he held her off once again.

"Patience, Lark. I'm not convinced that you've truly confronted temptation."

"But I told you about the heat. I even told you where I felt it."

"What else, Lark?" His hands continued to tease and torment her, massaging her shoulder blades, meandering around — just barely, to touch the fullness of her breasts.

As though I shall die if you don't kiss me, she thought.

"I feel strange, in a pleasant way," she confessed. "As if I could know something, see a new world, if I let myself. Have you ever stood at the edge of a cliff in the dark and wondered what lay below?"

"It's a hard decision, is it not?" He did something new and shocking with his tongue, and shivers passed through her body, starting in the place she had just learned the name of and radiating out to the tips of her toes, her fingers, her breasts.

"Aye," she whispered helplessly. "A hard decision."

"So what shall it be, Lark?" His warm lips touched the pulse in her neck. "Stay where you are, in tedious safety, or fling yourself off the cliff to see what awaits you?"

"A great danger might await me."

"Or something wonderful."

She clutched at the front of his shirt. "It is easy for you, Oliver. You are a born cliff jumper.

You have no obligations. No commitments. No responsibilities. No one expects anything from you. You can afford to take risks."

"In other words, the world cares not whether Oliver de Lacey lives or dies, is that it?"

He spoke quietly, but she heard the venom in his voice.

"It would not be so if you would become a responsible man." She wanted to lash out at him for making her experience this yearning, this vulnerability, this passion she had no right to feel. And for not kissing her when she needed it more than air.

"Like your precious Richard Speed. He can move the masses to tears, Lark. But can he make you feel like this?"

Oliver turned her, pressing her back against the tree, and finally, just before she screamed in frustration, he kissed her.

Truly kissed her. Deeply. Wickedly.

She responded with an ardor she knew she would be ashamed of later. But she could not help herself. That was the worst of it. The loss of control. The stripping away of her will until there was nothing left but the wanting, the ache.

His tongue slid in and out of her mouth. Slowly. Rhythmically. To her shock, she felt the echo in her newly named body part.

Her fists tightened on his shirt, then went slack and slid downward. The shape of his chest was fascinating. His midsection was still bandaged, but lower she discovered interesting ripples on his stomach. Good Lord, he was wonderfully put together!

When her fingers brushed the tops of his blousy canions, she froze. The dark time reared in her mind, but she shied from thinking about that now.

"Ah, sweetheart," he murmured against her mouth, "we've barely begun."

"We must stop." Tears burned her eyes. She did not know if the tears sprang from grief or frustration.

"Nay." He cupped his hand around the back of her head. "Lark, we can't stop."

"I thought your purpose was to teach me the true meaning of temptation so I could resist it."

"I lied."

"You did?"

"My true purpose was to seduce you."

She ducked beneath his arm and stepped away so she was no longer pressed between him and the ancient tree.

"You're wicked, Oliver de Lacey!"

"But I'd never bore you, dear. And in truth . . . " He raked a hand through his hair and gazed at her, looking genuinely perplexed. "I've never known anyone like you, Lark. Here's the truth. I've never, ever felt so aroused as I do at this moment."

She felt a thrill in spite of herself. "That is your problem. You won't solve it by harassing me."

"If I did not revere each and every member of your fair sex, I would fling you onto the riverbank and touch you in all the places I described a few moments ago."

Though she would have died rather than admit the truth to him, his words summoned an image that excited her. At the same time, she knew that she was perfectly safe. For all of his faults, Oliver did truly respect women. She could not imagine him doing harm to her or any other.

He began to pace, restless as a stallion. His tall knee boots crunched over the loose sand and gravel of the bank. "I'm confused, Lark. I know not why, but kissing you is more fun than bedding a legion of willing wenches." He swung around and challenged her. "Why don't you want me?"

"Why should I?" she shot back.

"All women want me," he said with a surprising lack of conceit. "I've never encountered rejection before."

"Then you have led a charmed life," she answered primly.

"And why *you*? I've known women more lavishly beautiful and, God knows, more worldly. I've known women of lofty accomplishments who have the confidence of queens." He seemed almost to be speaking to himself. "Why *you*?"

"Ah." She was able to hold the hurt at bay, but her temper had reached the boiling point. "That is what galls you. Veritable princesses have fallen into your lap. And then there is me. Lark. Mousy and brown and timid." She glared at his codpiece, the contents of which he had modestly referred to as "His Highness."

She tossed her head and said, "I am surely

too much an oaf to appreciate the near sacred gift you offer me."

"Lark, that is not what I meant."

"It is what you meant, and you know it," she shouted. Lord, it felt good, sinfully good, to vent her temper. She had always been instructed to keep hers in check. Now she knew the disgraceful pleasure of pouring it all out. She stalked back and forth on the bank. "I could give you a hundred reasons why I do not want you to seduce me. You are spoiled, conceited, irresponsible." She counted them off with her fingers. "Faithless, truthless, lawless — "

"But enough about me." He caught her raised hand in his. "You are quick to enumerate *my* faults. Have you none of your own? No reason of your own to deny yourself a perfectly good night of love?"

"I have a reason." The old shame seized her in its grip. She tore her hand away and resumed pacing. So did he, following her. At the bank of the river, she stopped and turned. They both assumed the time-honored stance of a bickering couple: hands on hips, noses thrust toward each other, brows almost touching.

"Well?" he prompted furiously.

She took a deep breath. It was about time he learned the truth. He was bound to find out eventually anyway.

"Because," she said in a nervous rush, "I am married."

8

"**M**ARRIED!**" Oliver squawked. He cleared his throat. "Married! How on earth can you be *married*?"

Reeling in shock, he peered at her through the darkness. Lark. She looked the same as she ever had. Not beautiful. Beyond beautiful.

The moonlight fell like a veil over her, glinting in her dark hair like filaments of silver. She was no raving beauty, he assured himself for the hundredth time. But there was that air about her. That rare combination of delicacy and strength. That intriguing allure of self-denial and barely repressed passion.

"This is a joke," he said. "You cannot possibly be married."

"People get married," she stated. "It happens every day."

"Not to you." The denial leaped from him. He had suffered many surprises in his time, but never one that *hurt*. Lark could not be married. She was sweet. She was innocent. She was *his*.

Apparently not.

"Not to me?" she asked, thrusting up her chin. "And pray you, why not? Ah, I see. I am too timid and mousy and plain to be the wife of anyone, is that it?"

You are too naive, he thought. Too pristine. Too . . . *mine*.

He loosened the laces of his collar, for despite

157

the cold night he had begun to sweat. "What sort of wife goes traipsing around the countryside risking her life to rescue condemned men? What sort of husband would *allow* it?"

She shrugged, her defiance dimming a little. "He does not precisely allow it."

He. Oliver's stomach churned. *He.* The husband. A man who had an identity, who commanded Lark's heart.

"Who?" Oliver forced himself to ask. "Who is this husband whose wife defies death and sleeps amongst Gypsies?"

She squared her shoulders. He braced himself, certain she would name the handsome yet oily Wynter Merrifield.

The thought that Wynter — or any man — might know her and touch her in the way Oliver wanted to know her and touch her was unbearable.

"Who?" he demanded again, preparing himself for the news that she had wed Wynter, who was bolder, stronger . . . and longer lived than he.

"Spencer Merrifield," she replied.

Oliver broke into relieved laughter. "Your jest is strange indeed, Lark."

"'Tis no jest. Spencer is my husband. I am Lark Merrifield, countess of Hardstaff."

Oliver mouthed the name and the title, but no sound came out. *Please be lying.*

But Lark never lied. Lark never jested. He suspected she did not even know how. In this, as in all matters, she was deadly serious.

"But he's old!" Oliver burst out at last.

"Forty-five years my senior."

"Then why . . . how . . . wherefore . . . "
Oliver raked all ten splayed fingers through his hair, wishing he could comb away his sense of horror and betrayal. "I need a drink," he mumbled.

She unbent enough to offer him a slight smile. "So do I."

They crept back to the encampment. Lark checked on Richard Speed; he still slept a sound, healing sleep. Oliver nicked a jar of wine clad in wicker from where it hung on one of the wagons. He took a woolen blanket and two battered pewter goblets as well, and they stole away together — like two lovers in the night, he thought with an ironic smile.

He led her up a slight incline to the top of a grassy knoll overlooking the river. The scent of the water freshened the breeze that drifted up from the valley. Oliver welcomed the coolness on his face. Lark had some explaining to do, and he would not let her rest until she confessed all.

Scowling, he spread out a blanket, sat down, and patted the spot next to him. She lowered herself somewhat warily.

He uncorked the bottle, filled both goblets, and handed one to her. "Drink. Something tells me this is going to be a long night."

She took an admirably lusty pull from the cup. He pretended not to notice the arc of her throat as she drank or the way her long eyelashes fanned her cheeks. He knew nothing quite so flattering as the silver light of a winter moon.

She finished, setting down the cup. "Why do you stare at me so?"

159

"With such tippling skills, you'd not be out of place in one of my London haunts."

She stared down at her lap. "Yes, I would."

He touched her shoulder. When she looked up at him, he saw the moon reflected in her great, sad eyes.

"Lark, why did you not tell me you were married? And to Spencer Merrifield, of all people?"

"It seemed imprudent, especially at first."

"And you are, above all, a prudent woman."

She tightened her fist around the base of her goblet. "Of necessity. At the start, I knew virtually nothing of you. Like the court that condemned you to the gallows, I thought you a common rabble-rouser. I felt no need to share my life history with you."

"Then why not later? Why not after you learned my true identity and came looking for me?"

"Ever since I joined Dr. Snipes and the Samaritans, I have always tried to keep my part in this work private."

"Because Spencer has no idea about the risks you take."

"He believes I do no more than help Mrs. Snipes at the safe hold at Ludgate and decode messages in cipher. If he should happen to hear that a woman was seen rescuing prisoners, he'll be less likely to associate that woman with me."

"Ah." Oliver savored the burn of a long swallow of wine. "Is that why you act the downtrodden female when you are at Blackrose?"

160

She sniffed. "I shall ignore that."

"You still haven't said why you kept this a secret from me. *I* would not have told Spencer," Oliver grumbled.

"I feared what you would think if I introduced myself as Spencer's wife and then told you the plan to disentail Wynter."

"You thought I'd assume you were acting out of greed, wanting the inheritance all for yourself."

"I do not," she said vehemently. "But neither do I want Wynter to have it. In the days before the Reform, Blackrose Priory was a place of corruption and superstition. Wynter would restore it to that state."

Oliver held up a hand. "You need not exert yourself to make me believe *that*, Lark. What I was wondering about was a bit more . . . personal."

She drank again, pulled her knees up to her chest, and set her chin upon them. Clearly she was unaware that the pose made her look younger and more untried than ever. Good Christ. *Was* she untried? Had she and that wasted old man shared a bed?

"Just start at the beginning," he said, wishing the thought had never occurred to him. "I want — I *need* — to understand."

"Shortly after my birth, both my parents died of the sweat."

He nodded and took a drink. The dread horror of the sweat had been known to empty whole manors and towns, so the situation was not unusual.

"They were Lord and Lady Montmorency," she said.

"I have heard the name. Estate in Hertfordshire?"

"Yes. It's called Montfichet. And I, just three months alive, was the sole heir." She held up her hand as if she knew what his comment would be. "Spencer had little interest in the land. He already possessed a manor called Eventide — that will fall to me upon his death — and Blackrose Priory, which King Henry granted to him in the first phase of the Dissolution."

With random, nervous movements, she plucked strands of dry grass and arranged them on the blanket in front of her, forming the roman numeral *VIII* with the blades. "Blackrose was granted on condition of entail, for at the time, the realm needed stability. The king could not know that Spencer's son would embrace the corrupt Church of Rome when he was man-grown."

She helped herself to more wine. Oliver stifled his own impatience to learn the answer to the only question that truly concerned him.

Did you bed him, Lark? Are you that old man's lover?

"After my parents died, a number of men vied to make me their ward. I'm told the petitioning became quite competitive, for the wardship was lucrative."

"And Spencer was among those offering to be your guardian?"

"Being a friend of the Montmorencys, he heard of my plight, learned of unsavory schemes

162

to bribe the Court of Wards and take possession of my estate." With a restless hand she whisked away the bits of dried grass. "My father summoned Spencer to his bedside. He begged Spencer to look after me, to protect me."

"Ah," Oliver commented. "The fated deathbed promise."

She looked at him sharply. "*Some* people take such solemn oaths quite seriously. Spencer did. He wed me out of a sense of duty to his old friend. He's told me this many times."

A sense of duty. No wonder the woman had no notion at all of her own worth.

She gazed off at the moon-silvered distance, the roll of hills delving toward the river valley. A light mist stole through the dale, its moody presence giving the land an aura of mystery. "At that time, I suspect Spencer's life was quite empty. He had just put aside his Spanish wife — Wynter's mother. He forced her to annul the marriage on grounds of her imprudence."

"You mean she cuckolded him?"

Her cheeks darkened. "Aye. She left in high dudgeon and went north to a Catholic sanctuary in the Borders."

"Leaving Spencer without wife or child." Oliver was beginning to see a horrible sort of logic in the tale.

"In practice, yes, though once he learned he had a son, Spencer made certain Wynter would always be recognized as his legitimate heir. It is a decision he came to regret." She tilted her head slightly as an owl called from the woods. "When Spencer's petition to the Court of Wards was denied, he went to King Henry and asked permission to marry me."

"And the king allowed it?" Oliver thought for a moment. Aye, old Harry would have found it quite amusing. Oliver remembered the king — corpulent, belligerent, dangerously intelligent, yet woefully ignorant in matters of the heart right up until the end.

"Of course he allowed it." Oliver answered his own question. "It would leave a loyal noble — an adherent to the Reformed faith — in charge of three important estates — Montfichet, Eventide, and Blackrose."

"Aye. Spencer was extremely loyal to the king." Lark spoke slowly, thickly.

Good Lord, was the woman getting drunk? "You became the infant countess of Hardstaff. How very singular." His nerves were stretched to their limit. "Lark, I must ask you . . . "

She flung out one arm, then flopped back on the blanket, propping herself on her elbows. "Ask away," she sang out. "Dissect me like a cadaver of the Royal College. I have no more secrets. Though I can't think why my life would interest you."

Nothing could have made him feel more guilty. But he well knew how to ignore guilt. "You see" — he cleared his throat — "I have come to care about you."

She regarded him with a twinkle of suspicion in her half-lidded eyes. "No doubt."

He hated it that she did not believe him. But then, why should she? Spencer had been telling her for years that he had wed her out of duty, not love.

Oliver's frustration escalated to anger. He pressed her back against the blanket, their position — if not their attitude — that of two lovers. He could feel the firmness of her flesh beneath his fingers, could smell her scent of perfume and wine. An overpowering desire flared through him, and he wanted to punish her for making him want her so badly, for being the woman he could not have.

"What was it like?" he demanded.

"Let go of me." She wrenched herself away and sat up on her knees. "You have no right — "

"Did he raise you to his particular tastes?" Oliver couldn't help himself. He chose each word as a dart, dipping its point in poison. "Did he wait until you had your first monthly, or did he simply bed you from the time you could walk — "

Her slap, when it struck, was powered by a surprising force. One of passion and rage.

Oliver felt a curious sort of relief. She was not always totally in control. And she knew how to stop him when he got carried away.

He poked his tongue at the lining of his lip and tasted blood. "On my troth, you've a good arm."

She held out her hand, staring at it as if it belonged to someone else. "What right have you to ask such questions?"

"Because I feel betrayed."

"You're the only person I've ever hit." She

165

glared in fierce accusation. "But then, you're the only person who has ever been so impertinent."

Oliver grabbed the wine and refilled the two goblets. "It was stupid of me to ask." He drained his glass, flinching as the wine stung his lip. "Stupid, for I do know the answer."

She gulped back her wine and sent him a lopsided grin. "Do you?" She rolled over on her stomach on the blanket and cupped her chin in her palm. Slapping him had evidently drained all the anger from her, and now she was an amiable drunk.

The night had begun to yield its dense shadows to the coming dawn, and the soft early light bathed her, gilded her, transformed her from woman to sprite. He saw her then for what she truly was, a girl raised by a stern yet good-hearted man, taught to loathe passion and physical need, untouched by any man — save Oliver de Lacey.

He knew this as well as he knew how to load a pair of dice. He should not have made such ugly accusations. "Ah, Lark." He caught a silky lock of her hair in his fingers. "Spencer has been father to you, not husband."

She tilted her head to one side, nuzzling her cheek into her palm. "I shall always be grateful to him."

He knew she meant the words. He knew Spencer deserved her gratitude and loyalty. He had risked his reputation to take in an orphan, had forfeited any chance of taking a true wife.

"I'm grateful to him also," Oliver said. "If he had not made such an unconventional marriage

166

to you, then by now you would have been snatched up by some randy young buck."

Just for a moment, the light died in her eyes. She turned her head away. "And that would disturb you?"

"Aye."

She caught her breath, and it sounded like a sob. Oliver had a horror of weeping women, so he braced himself for a storm.

Then she surprised him by laughing softly. "You are a wicked and thoroughly likable man, my lord. I need more wine."

He loved the effect it was having on her. The glow it lent her cheeks, the gentle languor of her limbs, the soft curve of her mouth, no longer pruned in disapproval but moist and relaxed. He gladly refilled both their goblets.

She sat up, stopping him just as he raised his to his lips. "Wait. What shall we drink to? Long life and happiness?"

A shadow passed over his heart. He covered the chill he felt with a jaunty grin. "Long life, my lady? Why not simply happiness?"

"To happiness, then." She touched the rim of her glass to his.

"May we grab life by the throat and wring it dry."

"Gruesomely put."

They sipped their wine, and she frowned. "In sooth we cannot be happy, not so long as the people of England are chained by intolerance and superstition."

"Then let us drink to breaking those bonds."

The sun rose higher, its pink radiance speeding

up over the gentle swells of the Chiltern Hills. Her laughter chimed like a song, and without warning Oliver thought of the words Zara had spoken earlier. *The circle was begun before you were born, and will endure long after you are gone.* Somehow his fate had become linked with the one woman he could not have.

They toasted the dawn and each other, and just for a time, neither worried about what the future held.

★ ★ ★

Leaving the Gypsies in the river-fed hills to await the springtime, the three travelers rode southeastward toward sanctuary. Richard Speed was thin and bruised, yet in high good humor. His companions were withdrawn and bleary eyed as a pair of Sauce Lane tipplers.

"You never said it would be like this." Lark held the reins in one hand, her head in the other, and moaned.

Oliver sat his Gypsy-trained horse, a spirited mare, as if he had never ridden before. "My lady, all pleasure has its price."

She pressed her lips into a grim line. "Is he not profound, Reverend Speed?"

"All men are profound if you pour enough wine into them." Speed, blond and lovely as a painted icon, smiled at them both. "How much farther to our destination?"

"We'll be there by dusk. I hope to make Gravesend the day after that," Oliver said, mussing his hair with a restless hand. "At

Gravesend, you'll board a ship bound for the Netherlands and eventually make your way to Switzerland."

Richard's smile melted into sadness. "I never thought I should see a day when I would leave my beloved England."

Lark's throat burned to hear him speak so. "Your exile is only temporary. Queen Mary cannot reign forever." She hated herself for wishing her sovereign ill. But Mary allowed Bishop Bonner to abuse and murder innocent men. She let King Philip's advisers dictate her policies.

"True," Speed admitted, "but suppose she gives birth. One is always hearing that she is expecting. Then, even if she dies, Philip of Spain will rule as regent. What hope have we then?"

Lark had no answer. She was silent for a time, remembering the night before, the way Oliver had shown her the meaning of temptation, their stormy quarrel, their truce, the vows with which they had greeted the dawn.

Oliver de Lacey was a strange, wonderful, and reckless man. Suddenly afraid for him, she spoke her thoughts aloud. "I think you should go into exile with Reverend Speed."

He snorted. "I?"

"Yes, you. What if someone discovers you cheated the hangman?"

Dry humor rustled in his throat. "Not likely, madam. Surely you remember my disguise. They hanged a bearded commoner called Oliver Lackey. A stranger. No one knows that the poor sod was pulled from the pit of death and revived

169

by an angel of mercy."

No one save me knows what you said that night, Lark thought, then chided herself for dwelling on his reckless, romantic words.

"Let Oliver Lackey rest in peace," he said. "I see no reason for me to leave England."

She couldn't help herself. She said, "*I* do."

"Ah." Understanding hardened his features. To her mortification, he spoke his mind despite the presence of Richard Speed. "You want me as far from you as possible so I don't remind you that you're a woman. A healthy young woman with healthy desires — "

"Enough!" she shouted, kicking her horse so that it trotted ahead.

As she rode away from her tormentor, she heard him say, "You're a learned man, Reverend Speed. What would *you* do in my situation?"

Lark pretended to ignore the holy man's reply, but she could not mask her shock at what he said.

"My lord, were I in your predicament, I would first pray for guidance. And then I'd probably tup the wench."

★ ★ ★

The manor house was surrounded by a broad lawn, stone walls, and iron gates. A gruff guard challenged the travelers, and Lark began to fear that her trust in Oliver's plan had been mislaid.

She held fast to her horse's reins, expecting any moment to be arrested. "Where are we?"

she whispered to Oliver.

"You'll find out soon enough," he whispered back. Then he fixed a look of lordly disdain on his face, glared at the gatekeeper, and announced his name and title.

"You may pass within," the guard said, stepping back from the gate. "The grooms will see to your horses."

A light, icy rain had started, and they hastened to a torchlit hall. Lark was finally recovering from the effects of her binge the previous night, but she knew she looked a sorry mess. Her gown was wrinkled, the skirts and shoes spattered with mud from the road churned up by her plodding horse. Her hair was damp, and when she removed her coif, curls sprang awry like unbaled wool.

Aside from feeling gritty and tired, she was in a foul temper with both of her traveling companions. With Oliver for making her quite weak with desire and with Richard Speed for sympathizing rather than sermonizing.

Perhaps that was the way with all men. Fleshly desires had the power to blur the line between right and wrong.

Even now the two of them were happily clinking their ale mugs and tearing into a crusty loaf of fresh bread.

Incensed, Lark cleared her throat. Both men stopped, uneaten bread in their unwashed paws.

Pointedly she clasped her hands and took a deliberately long time asking the blessing. At the end she added, "Thank you, Lord, for our safe deliverance. Give us the strength to revere you

171

with our faith, our devotion, our *sobriety*, our *chastity* — "

"We ask this in the name of Jesus Christ, *amen*," Richard Speed interrupted.

"Amen," echoed Oliver, his mouth already full of bread.

Lark scowled at them both. A servitor brought forth a platter and lifted the lid to reveal a succulent roast capon. At the same moment, a small, slim woman entered the hall, speaking in a ringing voice.

"As I recall, you never eat capon, do you, Wimberleigh?"

The remarkable flame-haired creature stopped and fixed Oliver with a dazzling smile. He leaped from his bench. She held out her arms. "I, on the other hand, find capon the daintiest of delights. Come now, dear Oliver. Greet me."

With a gut-deep twist of some emotion she did not recognize, Lark watched them. She had never seen Oliver look so awestruck and worshipful as he took the woman in his arms and said, "Bess. It's been a long time."

A long time since what? Lark wanted to demand.

"Too long," the striking woman said, dealing him a playful slap to the cheek. "If you weren't so pretty to look at, I'd have you punished."

"And I'd endure it with pride."

Lark rolled her eyes.

"My companions," Oliver said, bringing Bess to the table. Both Richard Speed and Lark stood. "And this is — "

"My friends call me Bess," the woman said.

Up close, she lost none of her stunning presence. She was neither tall nor beautiful, yet she bore herself like one who was both. She held out a slender hand to Reverend Speed, who bowed and kissed it while Lark curtsied.

Throughout the meal, Bess held all of Oliver's attention. He hung on her every word, cut her food into dainty bits, tasted it himself with old-fashioned gallantry, and fed her morsels from his own fingers.

He loved women, Lark told herself, wishing the knot in her stomach would loosen. He had said so from the start. And Bess was obviously a special woman.

His lover?

Finally Lark recognized the emotion that had been gnawing at her since Bess had entered the room. For the first time in her life, she felt the sharp stab of jealousy. It was a small, evil death inside her, unbidden, unwanted, yet out of her control. She felt actual pain in the area around her heart.

"And from where do you hail, my lady?" Bess asked, favoring her with a controlled smile. It was impossible to tell whether she was genuinely interested or merely being polite.

"Hertfordshire," Lark replied. "At Blackrose Pri — "

"I do so love the hills there, do you not, my lord?" Bess turned to Oliver. "Such fine hunting to be had."

There goes civility, Lark realized. She began to appreciate the wisdom in Spencer's approach to rearing her. It was less painful by far to keep one's feelings in check. To hold others at a distance. What sane person would want to feel the wild thump of desire, the sharp bite of envy?

" . . . the usual court gossip," Bess was saying.

Lark forced herself to listen. There was no point in tormenting herself.

"The queen fancies herself with child — again," Bess stated, dipping into her finger bowl. She seemed to have no need of another voice in the conversation. "A false hope, alas."

Lark held her breath and looked, goggle-eyed, from Bess to Richard Speed. She had heard such talk from the Gypsies, but they were not likely to attract the attention of the court. Bess, on the other hand, was a gentlewoman. She should know better.

The reverend sat pale and still, doubtless as shocked as Lark. No one, *no one*, said such things about the queen and lived.

"Do you think so?" Seeming to lack Lark's concern, Oliver filled a wine goblet and handed it to Bess.

"Of course. She is past her fortieth year, her husband has gone abroad, and she is ill." Bess put aside the finger bowl and held out her hand, studying the back of it. She nodded as if satisfied with its perfection. "I assure you, Reverend Speed, I am quite the innocent maiden, but even I am aware that, under those circumstances, the likelihood of a child is slim."

Lark darted a glance at Oliver. Did the

woman's treasonous talk not affect him in the least? Nay, he continued to worship Bess with his big, soft, blue eyes.

No wonder Bess possessed such confidence. A man's affection and regard were potent indeed. Powerful enough, Lark knew now, to lure her from her life of unquestioning obedience. Powerful enough to reawaken the dreams she held in her heart.

Without warning, Lark recalled the day Oliver had freed the caged birds at the market. *I could teach you to soar.*

A wave of realization washed over her. It was true. Oliver de Lacey possessed some sort of gift that made people want to push at the edges of life, to pound on the doors at its boundaries, to demand more than they should, to expect more than they deserved. She had seen Oliver affect people that way — Kit and perfect strangers and Gypsies and Bess — and now her.

She toyed with her food. When is my turn? She wondered. When do I get to soar?

"Don't you think so, mistress?" Bess's voice startled Lark.

"I do indeed," Lark said firmly, having no idea what she was agreeing to.

Richard Speed caught his breath, and his cheeks reddened. "Perhaps Lady Lark did not understand the comment."

Bess sent him a brazen wink. "I said, no expectant mother in England is safe so long as Queen Mary desires a child." She belted out a hearty laugh, clapped her hands, and called for a chessboard to be brought.

175

"Do you play?" she asked Lark.

"A little," Lark murmured, still reeling with shock at Bess's latest comment.

"Excellent." With a wave of her hand, Bess dismissed Oliver and Richard, and five minutes later she had captured three of Lark's pawns.

"Did you ever wonder why the queen is the most powerful piece on the chessboard?" Bess asked.

"To protect the king," said Lark. "And in sooth I've heard it said that long ago, the queen was actually a minister of sorts." As she spoke, she took one of Bess's knights.

"Oh, meager wit," muttered Bess. "I didn't see that coming." She shook her head in self-disgust, the torchlight catching the sparkling beads in her elaborate coif. "I am far too bold and impulsive."

"And I lack both of those virtues," Lark admitted. Bess eagerly seized yet another pawn, inadvertently clearing a path for Lark's rook.

"Not everyone sees boldness and impulsiveness as virtues. Besides, you're wrong, my lady. Are you not the one who has saved the lives of no fewer than eleven condemned prisoners? And isn't it true that you devise the cipher used by the Samaritans? I've been stumped by that cipher for months. Is it built on someone's birthdate or — "

"My lady," said Lark, terrified by Bess's uncanny knowledge. The activities of the Samaritans were supposed to be kept strictly secret. "You are misled, I'm not the one — "

Bess laughed, throwing back her head so

that the torchlight caught the gold filaments and jewels in her coif. "Self-effacing to the last. Never mind, I'll not force you to admit you played a role in stanching the flow of Englishmen's blood."

As if you ever could, thought Lark. She captured Bess's bishop with her rook.

"Still, it is an admirable thing, the way you hide your cleverness behind the guise of a simple woman without a thought in her head. I must remember that for the future."

"Remember what?" asked Lark.

"To fool them. To claim I am no more than a lowly woman — "

"Your Grace?" A servant stepped hesitantly to the table.

Lark frowned. Was Bess a duchess? But she claimed she was not married.

"Aye, a lowly, ignorant woman," Bess continued, disregarding the servant. "When in sooth I know I shall always be smarter than them all." She lifted her chin and favored the servant with a dazzling smile. "I do beg your pardon, Cuthbert. Idle female chatter. We are so hopelessly shallow, we can't seem to help ourselves." She winked at Lark.

Cuthbert held out a purse of leather. "Ma'am, the letters have come from your sister the queen."

"Thank you, Cuthbert. Set them on the table. My poor, unfortunately female brain will have to cope with them later. It is so hard to reason when one is but an addle-witted woman."

Cuthbert bowed and left, frowning and scratching his head.

Bess scanned the letter. Just for a moment, stonecold fury hardened her face and flared in her night-dark eyes. The moment passed in a heartbeat, and Bess beamed at Lark. "This is useful indeed. Oh, I am an imp. Poor Cuthbert doesn't know what to think."

Nor did Lark. She simply sat there as if someone had planted her on the bench and she had grown roots. Her head throbbed with the echo of Cuthbert's words. *Your sister the queen. Your sister the queen.*

Good God in heaven. Bess was the Princess Elizabeth, heir apparent to the throne of England.

9

"**Y**OU might have told me," she snapped at Oliver as they left the residence the next day.

"Told you what?" He massaged his temples and blinked at the early morning light. Unlike Lark, he had stayed up until dawn, drinking and playing at cards.

"That this is Hatfield House," said Lark, pleased to see him flinch when she raised her voice. "That Bess is the Princess Elizabeth."

They left behind the handsome palace and gardens, taking a well-traveled road through a great oak forest. The clack of dried reeds along the verge mingled with the muffled, steady thud of the horses' hooves.

Oliver rubbed his palm over his chin, where a light, golden stubble grew. "As I recall, you did not have much to say to me after I pointed out your fear of letting yourself feel a woman's passions."

Lark scowled at the memory. In sooth she *had* been silent. Determinedly so. "Still, you might have — "

"Hush!" Oliver stood up in his stirrups and twisted around, looking back over his shoulder.

Lark reined in her horse. Then she, too, heard it — hoofbeats.

In one fluid motion, Oliver dismounted and helped Lark down. They led both horses to the bracken at the side of the road. A concealing growth of reeds and genet plant hid them from view. His hand rested on the hilt of his sword.

The sight of that hand — the same hand that had taught her temptation so tenderly — poised to do violence sent chills through Lark. She studied his face and noted the tautness of his jaw, the expectant heat in his eyes.

"You *like* this," she whispered. "Why is it that you *like* this?"

He lifted one eyebrow, one side of his mouth, in the most endearing expression she had ever seen. With gentle lover's fingers, he touched her beneath the chin. "Because it reminds me that I'm alive," he said.

The rider came into view. Unbarbered yellow hair flying out behind him, he sat the horse awkwardly, yet with great command. Tension flowed out of Lark on a surge of relief. "'Tis Richard Speed," she said, leading her horse back onto the road. Oliver remounted his mare and joined them.

"Something's amiss," he said.

Speed nodded miserably. With his soiled tunic and uncombed hair, he looked for all the world like an angel recently banished from paradise.

"Well?" prompted Oliver.

"We've been found out. All Bishop Bonner's henchmen are afoot, looking for me."

Oliver swore. "Are you certain?"

"The Princess Elizabeth received a communiqué only last night."

Lark stiffened in surprise as she remembered the letter delivered by Cuthbert and the icy rage she had seen, just for a moment, in Elizabeth's eyes. Could Queen Mary herself have warned her not to be caught harboring a fugitive?

The idea revolved round and round in Lark's mind. She had always regarded Queen Mary as a remote, immovable obstacle to the cause of Reform, certainly not as a woman who cared deeply about her sister.

"Bonner's spies always lurk like a plague near Bess," Oliver said. "The creeping, unmannered dogs seek any excuse to find her guilty of treason or heresy. They know she'll crush them if she takes the throne."

"That's why I left Hatfield so quickly. She offered to shelter me until I could plan another escape, but I did not want to risk tarnishing her reputation."

"God's heels, you *are* a martyr, aren't you?" Oliver said in disgust. "You should have stayed."

"And if they found him with the princess?" Lark asked.

He glared at her for precisely a heartbeat; then his eyes danced with pleasure. "For someone so well convinced of the inferiority of women, you do make a valid point."

His easy acceptance of her opinion startled her. Spencer would have sent her off to memorize pages of proverbs.

"So what was the warning?" Oliver asked.

With a shaking hand, Speed raked the loose, long hair back from his face. "Bonner's men have sealed the ports, and they inspect every ship be it incoming or outgoing."

"So Gravesend's out." Lark thought quickly

as she studied her companions. They were alike enough to be brothers, both blond and fair and excessively handsome. Yet where Richard's face held earnestness and fortitude, Oliver's was blasé and cynical.

Even so, she saw something in Oliver, a raw, restless pain that engaged her sympathy. He lived in a state of debauchery and even took pride in his venial lusts. Equal measures of agony and exuberance and cleverness formed his character. There was no reason she should like him, yet he fascinated her. Much more, she was ashamed to admit, than did the holy Richard Speed.

"We must go to Blackrose Priory," she said. As soon as she spoke the words, she felt a deep tug of certainly and knew she had chosen wisely.

Oliver pulled idly at the pheasant feather in his hat and scowled at her from beneath its shallow brim. "The Reverend Speed will be a fine gift for Wynter. A lamb to the slaughter."

"Wynter won't know."

"He's not stupid, Lark. A brain-infected villain, perhaps, but not quite a fool."

"Nor am I." She caught her breath, aware that she had never before truly believed that. She squared her shoulders and, all on her own, mounted the horse. "I have a plan."

★ ★ ★

"Incredible." In an innyard northwest of London, Oliver walked in a wide circle

182

around the Reverend Richard Speed, looking the preacher up and down with wide, laughing eyes. "If I did not know your true identity, even I would believe the disguise."

"I feel ridiculous. A misbegotten mongrel." Speed glowered at his two grinning companions. "Is this absolutely necessary?"

"I fear so," said Lark. "You'll get used to it. You look splendid."

"Quite splendid," Oliver agreed. "Gorgeous, in fact." It took all his restraint to keep from breaking into great peals of laughter. "You make a most convincing woman, my dear Speed. Or shall I say, Mistress Speed?"

Because he was a godly man, Speed did not curse, but his glare held pure poison.

"Of course," Oliver continued as Lark bent to sift through the garments they had — by hook *and* by crook — acquired, "we cannot call you by the name Speed at all, for by now it's notorious. What shall it be, then? Lady Lackbeard? Dame Deviant?"

"Enough. I won't stand for this another moment." Red faced and exasperated, Speed reached up to tear off his demure coif.

"Wait!" Lark straightened, putting a hand on his arm, raising a pleading face to his. "You are too quick to give in. Think what is at stake, Richard."

Oliver snapped his fingers. "Quick. Mistress Quickly! You'll go down in history as the martyr in petticoats," he couldn't resist adding.

Speed conceded the point with a disgusted nod. "I suffer in the name of the Lord," he grumbled, kicking sullenly at the hem of his overskirt. The gown, pilfered by Oliver himself from a bawdy house in Shoreditch, fit snugly across the shoulders but too loosely in the front.

"You need a bit more up top." Oliver plucked a handful of straw from a pile beneath the eaves of the stable. "Hold still." He pulled at the neckline of Speed's coarse lockeram chemise and inserted the straw, fluffing out the busked bodice of the dress.

"It itches," Speed protested.

"Not so much as a hair shirt," Oliver said. When he finished with the straw, he added a somewhat crushed ruff collar to conceal Speed's Adam's apple.

Lark continued exploring the contents of the sack Oliver had gotten from the leaping house. After a moment she straightened, holding an odd, furry object dangling from a string. "What on earth is this?"

Oliver nearly choked on suppressed mirth. These two green Protestants were going to be the death of him. "That," he said, his face determinedly solemn, "is a merkin."

Lark cocked her head and frowned. "I still don't — "

"It's just the touch we need to perfect the disguise." Oliver snatched it from her. He stooped in front of Speed and hiked the reverend's skirts. "It's a privy wig."

Lark gave a squeak of horror and turned away, covering her face with her hands. Speed froze with revulsion. When he found his voice, he said. "There's no need to carry the disguise this far."

"You never know where spies might be lurking, my dear Speed," Oliver said. He would burn in hell for this jest, but he couldn't resist. "Put it on."

Just as Speed finished tying on the odd hairpiece, a groom brought their horses around. He gaped at Speed for a moment, then clapped his hand over his mouth and fled. When he ducked out of sight, they could hear his guffaws.

"There goes dignity," Speed grumbled.

The three of them mounted and left the innyard just as the sun was chasing off the damp chill of dawn. Speed rode sidesaddle, one leg hooked awkwardly over the bow, his feet pushed into tight fustian slippers. He complained loudly and steadily, his straw-stuffed bosom jouncing with each step of his trotting horse. At noon they passed the bridge at Tyler Cross.

Though he laughed and joked about Speed's costume, Oliver never forgot that the reverend was a fugitive running for his life. Neither did he forget what had happened the last time they had crossed the bridge here.

But today they encountered no winter travelers, no coach conveniently embedded in the roadside mud.

By the time the rising, round hills came into view, Speed had grown quiet and resigned. If he managed to keep his face free of whiskers and his big hands and thick wrists hidden, if he managed to temper his voice, no one would suspect he was a man.

"Lark, my felicitations," Oliver said. "The disguise is clever."

"We shall see how clever," she said in her typical cautious way.

It was happening again, a shutting-down that came over her when she approached Blackrose. She was like a flower caught in a sudden frost. She lost the color and life that made her vibrant and special. She became withdrawn and somehow damaged.

Oliver thought he knew why now. Spencer was her husband. That gaunt, dying old man in the master's chamber was her *husband.*

And — irony of ironies — Wynter was her stepson. He was several years older than she, but he was her stepson. It boggled the mind.

Quite unexpectedly, Oliver felt a small, hot pang of sympathy for her. He imagined what her life must have been like here — wife to a man who was father instead of husband, mother to a stranger who clearly despised her. How bizarre and sad it all was.

As they passed through the gatehouse of the priory, he caught up with her, reached across, and touched her shoulder.

She turned to him, and he saw that the transformation was complete. Lark was gone; the marble-faced stranger had taken over.

"Yes?" she asked. "What is it?"

"I just want you to know, I'll stay here for as long as you need me."

Bitterness tightened her smile. "Nay, my lord. You'll stay for as long as it pleases you."

"And how would you know that?"

"I am coming to know you, my lord. You are quick to take up a cause and just as quick to abandon it. Truly, you have the loyalty of Simon and Peter."

A blaze of fury lit Oliver's chest. She was right, damn her. It had ever been the way with him. He pursued those things that interested him; when interest waned or he felt the least bit threatened, he moved on to the next adventure. The difference was, this time he did not want the adventure to end.

"You're wrong." He reined in, and they waited as two stable lads ran forth to take their horses. "This time I shall stay and see this through. Did I not so vow that night on the hill?"

"Vows made in wine seldom hold." She dismounted without assistance and tossed her reins to one of the lads. Oliver leaped off his mare and made a great show of helping Richard Speed dismount.

The reverend's beskirted form dropped clumsily to the stone-paved drive. He tugged at his tight bodice and ran a finger around the rim of his ruff.

"Thank you, my lord," he muttered under his breath.

Oliver grinned and whispered, "Try that an octave higher, and I'll believe you."

Lark led the way into the great hall. With long, manly strides, Speed stalked toward the door. Oliver grasped his elbow. "You walk like a ploughman, not a lady. Slow down.

187

Tiny mincing steps. A slight sway to the hips. Like this." He demonstrated, then turned to see Speed gawking at him.

"My lord, pardon me for asking, but where the devil did you learn to walk like that?"

Oliver laughed. "Years of careful and diligent observation, my dear Speed."

They entered the hall to find Lark being greeted by a worried-looking servant.

"What is it, Crispus?" she asked.

The man clutched at the edges of his ill-fitting jerkin. "'Tis the master, ma'am. He's taken a turn for the worse. The physick were with him all the night through, and now Goody Rowse has come from the village to sit."

Lark spared not a glance at Oliver and Richard. She picked up her skirts and raced for the stairs.

Over her shoulder she said, "Where is Lord Wynter?"

"Gone," Crispus called. "Took the wherry toward Londontown, he did. The queen summoned him to court, or so says his manservant."

Lark grabbed the banister at the first landing and fairly swung around it. Oliver caught a glimpse of her face. It was white with terror and with something he had to force himself to acknowledge.

By God's eyes. She really did love the old man.

* * *

188

Lark dropped to her knees beside the bed. The air *whoosh*ed from beneath her travel-stained skirts. The branched velvet pooled around her in a gray lake.

"Spencer!" she whispered.

"He ain't been awake save for a few minutes now and then." Goody Rowse got up from the armed chair where she had been seated, knitting. "Took some broth, but no more than a sip or two."

"I see." With a nod, Lark dismissed the woman. An awful sense of guilt assailed her. He ate best when *she* spooned the broth, but she had been off on an adventure with a man she found fascinating, a man who kissed her at will, a man who was not her husband. "Spencer?"

He lay in repose like a corpse, his head centered perfectly on the pillow, his spotted hands crossed upon his chest.

She could not remember the last time she had touched him. It was not that they were averse to one another; quite the opposite. Spencer was simply not one for touching. He had always relied on the powers of the mind.

But what happened, Lark wondered helplessly, when touch was all that was left?

Spencer was so unlike Oliver.

She formed the comparison before she could stop herself. Oliver didn't simply *like* touching; he seemed to crave it. To need the contact as most men needed food.

And when she was near him, she needed it, too.

Ashamed of her straying thoughts, she said

189

more loudly, "Spencer!" She needed to banish her mind of Oliver de Lacey. Emboldened, she laid her hands upon Spencer's. "'Tis Lark," she said. "Can you hear me?"

His hands were cold. The flesh felt thin and dry, excruciatingly tender. But slowly, almost magically, it grew warm where her hand covered his.

The warmth brought on memories of long ago. For the most part, he had been stern and demanding. But always, his deep, abiding regard for her underlay the rigid exterior. Every so often she would catch a glimpse of affection and warmth.

Suddenly she had a clear picture of him lying beneath an apple tree in springtime. She must have been four or five at the time and had managed to climb the blossoming tree. She remembered laughing with delight as she shook the branches, causing a rain of petals to fall on him. He, too, had laughed, his face covered with snowy petals. He was so handsome when he smiled.

A tear slipped down her cheek.

"None of that." Spencer had awakened. He was hopelessly weak, but a fire of discontent still burned deep in his eyes.

Lark smiled and swallowed the lump in her throat. "I was just remembering how good you've always been to me."

"Good. Hmph. Whatever good there is in you, Lark, you were born with. Had I been able to lecture it out of you, I'm sure I should have done so."

"You don't know what you're saying," Lark protested. The Spencer she knew would never question himself. He knew right from wrong as if the Lord had handed it to him on a stone tablet.

"Nay," he said. "Dying is a marvelous thing, Lark. It forces a man to be honest with himself, and with those he loves. Where is Oliver?"

"Why would you wish to see him?"

"I need him, Lark. Please. There's not much ti — "

"My lord, I am here." Unbidden, large and golden as an archangel, Oliver strode into the chamber. Skirts swishing, Richard Speed bustled in after him.

Lark jumped to her feet. "Were you listening at the door?"

"Aye, Lark." He touched her cheek briefly. "I'm so sorry you came back to this. I — "

She ducked her head and stepped away. "Spencer, this is Richard Speed."

"Ah. The one who just escaped Smithfield, praise be to God." Spencer turned his head toward the door, looking past Speed. "Move aside, mistress. I cannot see the reverend."

Speed bowed, the movement awkward and stiff. "My lord, *I* am Richard Speed."

"Odd vestments," Spencer muttered.

Speed's cheeks colored. "It's a disguise. I must remain in costume until it's safe to leave England."

Spencer closed his eyes. "God save us from an England that puts godly men to death." He opened his eyes again. "Sir, your presence is a great comfort to me."

A transformation came over Richard Speed. Despite the ridiculous costume, he became a man in his element. He alone knew what to do in the presence of a dying man. His beautiful young face was suffused with a comforting glow of reverence.

"The Lord is with thee," he whispered, and despite his soft voice, certainty echoed through the chamber.

"In that, I do have faith." Spencer was quiet a moment. "I stand between two worlds. One foot here, and the other elsewhere. I want to go."

A whimper jumped in Lark's throat. She felt Oliver's hand at her back, steadying her.

"And yet I linger here," Spencer said.

"Don't be afraid, my lord." Speed cupped his hand over Spencer's brow.

"I'm not. But I have unfinished business."

"Perhaps that is why you suffer still."

"Is our legal matter concluded?" Spencer asked Oliver.

"Kit has taken the suit to court. You need worry yourself no further on that. Wynter will never take over Blackrose."

Spencer sighed. His lips were blue, and Lark knew she was losing him. He took a labored breath and said her name.

"I'm here." She went to the side of the bed, sank back to her knees, and took his hand in hers. The warmth she had imparted earlier was gone.

"You are a remarkable young woman, Lark."

192

Never had he paid her a compliment. She was too stunned to reply.

"There was a time when I might have claimed the credit for your noble heart, your honor, your learning. I know better now. I have done you a terrible injustice."

"Pray do not say that," she whispered. "You have been my savior, my guiding star, for all the days of my life."

Speed moved to stand at the foot of the bed. Oliver was on the opposite side from her, and his eyes met hers.

It shouldn't have happened, but when she gazed at him, she felt an overwhelming sense of connection, an intimacy she had never shared with another person.

How could it be that the man who had raised her from infancy seemed so distant and remote, while a man she had known but a few weeks seemed to hold her heart in his hands?

Spencer cleared his throat with an alarming rattle. "I brought you up as I thought best, hammering away at your spirit, trying to grind out the qualities that glowed brightest within you — your lively mind, your fervent craving for learning, your inborn tenderness, your . . . " He seemed reluctant but plunged on. "Your womanliness. I was wrong. You were just too *alive* for me, Lark. Your vigor frightened me. I tried to kill the spark that lights your soul."

She suffered a brief memory then, of being made to kneel and pray, to study and spin and sew, to suppress her laughter with sober thoughts, and to stifle her opinions in favor of parroting proverbs.

"You did your best," she protested. "You — "

"Hush. I did try to douse that ember in you, but the fire never died despite my efforts. Do you know how I know that?"

Tears blurred her eyes. "No, Spencer. You have ever been a mystery to me."

"I know it because I now realize that one man kindles that spark. I see it in your eyes when you look at him."

"No!" Guilt prickled like a rash over her. Oliver made a strangled sound in his throat.

"Do not deny it, Lark," Spencer said. His chest convulsed, but he conquered the gasping through sheer force of will. "Rejoice. Here I am, at the end of my life, and I see so clearly now. I was bitter. I thought all marriages were bound to bring naught but pain. Now I know better. Marriage between two who hold each other in such tender regard is a gift from God. I need to know someone will care for you and protect you."

His voice grew stronger and wavered less. "That man is Oliver de Lacey."

She dared to peek at Oliver then. He wore a stunned expression, as though he had just eaten a poisonous mushroom.

Spencer managed a weak squeeze of her hand. "I want you to marry him as soon as I'm gone."

"Never!" She lifted her hands to her ears. "Please God, I am not hearing this."

His bony, wavering hand lifted, reaching like

a claw, uncovering her ears. "Do not tarry and grieve for me. Don't even wait until I'm cold. Swear it, Lark! Swear you'll take him as your husband."

"Please, I can't — "

"Swear it," he pleaded. "I'll have no peace until you do."

Her mind whirled in an agony of confusion. Of all the deathbed requests Spencer could have made, this was the most unexpected, venial, and unthinkable of entreaties.

"No," she whispered. "I can't."

"Lark, I beg you." Spencer had never suffered pain from his illness; torment twisted his features now. His face was contorted, and though his eyes were dry and rimmed with red, he seemed to be weeping.

She had never seen Spencer weep.

"Please," he said. "Please, Lark. Please."

She so wanted his passing to be peaceful. But how could she marry Oliver? She barely knew him, and what she did know of him, she did not like. He was reckless, capricious, and unpredicatable. He made her feel like a woman. Made her tremble inside with wanting him. Made her remember why she could never, ever succumb to fleshly desires.

"Please," Spencer whispered, his voice a dry rustle in his throat.

"For God's sake, *swear it*!" Oliver burst out. "He's begging you, Lark!"

Her head snapped up. Frustration darkened his face as he grasped Spencer's other hand. Before she could speak, Oliver said in a rush,

"If it will give you peace, my lord, then I will vow to make Lark my wife. I'll cherish and protect her, and God strike me dead if I fail."

At Oliver's startling words, Spencer seemed to relax. His chest rose and fell more easily, and a tiny smile curved his blue-tinged lips.

"Then we are halfway there." The reedy whisper thrummed with hope. "Lark, say you'll have him. And none of this in-name-only blather. You've been trapped in a marriage of convenience for twenty years. Time to take a real husband."

She looked in desperation at Richard Speed. He simply stood amazed, his hands clasped in prayer. Then she studied Spencer, who seemed to be drifting farther and farther away even as she watched.

"Please, Lark."

She could barely hear his whisper, but even now she felt his strong will pressing at her heart. How could she deny him at such a time?

"Very well," she said in a stranger's voice. "If marrying Oliver is what you wish for me, then that is what I'll do."

"Do you swear it before God?"

She hesitated. If she made such a vow, it would be irrevocable. Her chin lifted; her gaze clashed with that of Oliver de Lacey. She saw a flawed yet exuberant man, one who coaxed passion from her, who listened to her opinions, who respected her will, who made her feel protected, cherished, important.

Her heart said *yes*.

"Very well," she said in a rush. "I swear to

God I'll do as you ask."

Silence hung in the room for a moment. Then Spencer took each of their hands and joined them with his own.

A pale, distant light glowed in his eyes. "It is done, then."

His blue lips smiled. Neither Lark nor Oliver dared to move their hands, though it felt odd to have them entwined with Spencer's.

Richard Speed prayed softly.

Lark had no idea how long they stayed there. After a time, Spencer's breathing seemed to change. It was shallow, irregular, punctuating Speed's ceaseless prayers. Then Lark heard an odd clicking sound, followed by the softest of sighs.

He was gone.

She leaned forward and pressed her lips to his. In life he had never let her kiss him, and the piercing injustice, the sense of chances lost, tore at her heart. His lips were cool and dry until her warm tears wet his face.

She and Spencer had shared an unusual yet deep love, one that she would carry like a precious relic for all of her days. By her own words she had tied herself to Oliver de Lacey, but she could not think of him now, could not take time to wonder if he was capable of that sort of abiding love.

"How will I live without you?" she whispered. "In God's name, Spencer, how will I go on?"

★ ★ ★

"How can I possibly shackle myself to the one woman who cares nothing about me?" whispered Oliver. The cool breath of the wind stole in through the cracks around the chapel windows.

Three days after Spencer's death, he and Kit stood on the threshold of the chapel at Blackrose Priory. At the altar Lark and Richard Speed waited, both wearing dark mourning gowns relieved only by the pleated white barbes that covered the bodice from neck to waist. Lark's peaked mourning veil covered her hair and contrasted starkly with her pale cheeks.

"It's a bit late to cry off now," Kit said. He had returned from London, the lawsuit neatly concluded, the day before.

"It was too late the moment I made that idiotic vow." Oliver fingered his dress sword nervously. What a dilemma she had put him in. Her heartbreaking farewell to Spencer had made it clear that she would never love another.

"Kit, I am the blackest of black sheep. A rake and a rogue. A blackguard, a skirt-lifting womanizer. Surely a poor candidate for a h — h — " He couldn't bring himself to say it.

"Haven't you always claimed you wish to experience all of life? To try everything? Marriage is the one adventure you have not braved."

"I only wanted to experience the fun parts. The great challenges."

Kit sent a significant look at Lark. Expressionless and dull eyed, she clutched Spencer's illegal Book of Common Prayer like

198

a shield to her buckram-stiffened chest.

"I ask you, Oliver," Kit said, "what greater challenge than *that*?"

"You are such a comfort to me, Kit." Anger uncurled like a flame inside him. He felt used, coerced, driven to this spot by forces beyond his control. Aye, control. Even from beyond the grave, Spencer remained in command of him.

Richard Speed beckoned them with an impatient wave of his hand.

Feeling no less dread than he had the day he had gone to hang, Oliver de Lacey went to claim his bride.

10

WHILE promising her future to Oliver de Lacey, Lark peered at him through the screen of a black mourning veil. He stood with his weight shifted negligently on one hip, his hair mussed as if by a lover's hand, and a look of boredom on his too handsome face.

Richard Speed read through the betrothal agreement and marriage settlement, hastily arranged by Kit. Oliver caught her staring and gave her a broad, insolent wink.

She sniffed and glanced away, pushing aside a sudden thought of Wynter. He would be livid when he discovered what she had done. Nagged by unease, she forced herself to concentrate on Reverend Speed. His health was improving at a rapid rate; soon he would outgrow the hated gowns he wore as a disguise. He appeared almost as uncomfortable as Lark felt, his feet shifting beneath the hem of his skirt, his arms bulging inside the tightly laced sleeves. He had begged to don a cleric's robes, but Oliver had declared it too risky.

Knowing Oliver's sense of humor, Lark suspected he found it amusing to be wed by a minister in skirts. Kit Youngblood, standing as witness at Oliver's side, pressed his lips together hard, as if holding in an explosion of mirth.

Kind, helpful Kit. Thanks to him this marriage

would be legal, a solemn contract entered into for life. Over cups of wine the night before, Kit had recorded the betrothal. He had overseen the financial arrangements, negotiated a dowry, and drawn up the marriage settlement.

Now Richard Speed hammered the last nail into her fate. He gave them one final opportunity to disclose any impediment to their union.

Lark took a deep breath. She wanted to turn and run, to declare her unwillingness. Then she heard Spencer's last words again. *I want you to marry him as soon as I'm gone. Do not tarry and grieve for me. Don't even wait until I'm cold. Swear it, Lark! Swear you'll take him as your husband.*

She had given her word to a dying man.

Oliver nodded to Richard and said, "Proceed."

And so they vowed, in the dark, windy chapel of Blackrose, to be husband and wife. Lark heard herself promise to be chaste, submissive, and fruitful and was glad the veil hid her blush as she remembered that marriage had been ordained for procreation.

Then it was Oliver's turn to speak his vows. She expected him to enumerate them as casually as if he were counting tithes.

Instead he snatched off her peaked veil and grabbed her by the wrist. Her hair, like a maiden's now, spilled down her back.

"My lord!" She felt naked and frightened. His eyes were the burning blue of the sky on a hot day. "What — "

"I want to see your face when I make my pledge," he said. "I want to make sure you hear me, Lark." Without looking back, he held out his free hand, and Kit gave him a golden ring.

"I vow to provide for thee," he said, "and to guard thee from danger and want, to be faithful and vigilant over thy welfare." He stared down at the ring. Lark wondered if she imagined it or if Oliver's hand actually trembled as he placed the ring on each successive finger of her hand. "With this ring I thee wed, with this gold I thee honor, and with my body I thee worship."

Lark could not say why, but his words made her seem to float far above the ground.

"Until death us do part," Oliver concluded. As he spoke the final pledge, the intense merriment left his eyes; they clouded and darkened, and his mouth went taut as if a sudden pain had gripped him. Then the moment passed, and Lark decided she had imagined his torment, for he was smiling down at her once again.

She barely heard Speed's awesome proclamation: "Those whom God hath joined together, let no man put asunder."

Oliver touched her chin, gaining her attention. "Lark? It's over."

"Over?" she asked stupidly.

"Aye, sweet. Well, the boring part, anyway."

"Would His Lordship like to kiss the bride?" Speed asked.

Oliver's grin was wry, possibly bitter. "Now the interesting part begins."

★ ★ ★

202

Alone, Oliver entered the bride's chamber and found it empty. Their wedding supper was a simple affair of bread and wine and apples set out on an oval table. Sullenly Oliver poured himself a goblet of wine and went to the window to await his bride.

The house servants and retainers had taken the news of the marriage with surprising aplomb, as if Spencer, even in death, had the power to make them obey.

A bird alit on the ledge outside the open window. Oliver noticed that someone had left crumbs there. Lark. He imagined her alone in this room, year after year, setting out crumbs to draw the birds, perhaps craving their company while she worked at her tedious spinning and sewing.

The sky was a deep, twilight blue pierced by the first winking stars of evening. The bird chirruped. Oliver drank his wine in one gulp and belched loudly. The bird flew off.

"I'll have another little lark to manage tonight," he muttered. "Pity she doesn't scare as easily." A twist of apprehension knotted his gut. He had no fear of making love to her, of course, but what if she became pregnant? He had often daydreamed about having a child, but it was always in the abstract, and the child in his imaginings did not have a real child's need. In truth, Oliver knew it would be best never to father a child. His illness was unpredictable. He had every reason to suppose it could be passed to one's children, much like one's looks. His own brother had suffered from the same ailment, and

Dickon had not lived to see six summers.

Even if Oliver sired a perfectly healthy child, he himself was far from perfect. What good was he, a profligate likely to die young, to a son or daughter?

Damn her. She had trapped him into this marriage.

Lark came into the room a few minutes later. At first she didn't spy him by the window, and she leaned against the door, closed her eyes, and wiped the back of her hand against her brow.

"Don't be so quick to breathe a sigh of relief." Oliver pushed away from the window ledge and sauntered toward her. He spread his arms wide. "Madam, felicitations. You and Spencer have managed to land the Wimberleigh heir."

A fire blazed in her gray eyes, like globed flames on a rainy day. "What on earth are you implying?"

He stopped at the table, set down his goblet, and pressed his palms to the smooth surface. Leaning forward, he said, "I am implying that you and Spencer — God rest his soul — went to a great deal of trouble in order to bring me to heel. First saving me from the gallows, then using me to break the entail, and finally closing the trap just as Spencer turns up his toes. Very well executed, if you'll pardon the expression."

"That is the most outrageous, conceited, wormwitted nonsense I have ever heard."

"You deny it?" He lifted one insolent eyebrow.

"Of course I deny it. You practically forced me to make that deathbed promise to Spencer."

"I wish I had come to realize your ruse sooner.

204

You're a fine little actress, Lark. You made me pity you."

She, too, put her hands on the table and bent toward him. They were nose to nose, each trying to outglare the other. "That was no act. I had no idea Spencer meant to pair us off. It was the last thing I wanted. In fact, *you* arranged it to trap *me*!"

"Ha!" Disbelief exploded from Oliver, but she didn't even flinch. "Now that, sweetheart, is the most ridiculous bit of fiction yet. Why in God's name would I want to trap *you*?"

The ugly words hurled out before he could stop them.

She caught her breath as if he had struck her.

He froze, wishing he could reel them back in. He was tempted to tell her the truth, but the truth was, he was scared. He had wanted her for weeks. Now that she was finally his, he realized that it was not enough simply to have her. He was now responsible for her safety, her happiness.

Happiness? What in God's name did he know about making a woman happy outside the bedchamber?

"Why?" she echoed. "Because I'm a wealthy widow."

The way her voice faltered over the word *widow* gave him pause. He cleared his mind of the wine he had drunk and remembered. He recalled Lark bending over Spencer at the moment of his death, giving him a kiss of depthless grief and tenderness. She had loved the old man, and by dying, he had broken her heart. *How will I live without you?* Her agonized whisper haunted him still.

Oliver cursed under his breath and shoved away from the table. "Why should we argue about it? 'Tis done. I vowed I would take you as my wife. And so I have." He walked to her side of the table, took her hand, and raised it to his lips. "Almost."

Touching her had its usual unsettling effect on him. He noted the softness of her skin, the clean womanly scent of her, the warmth that seemed to emanate from her.

When he lifted his lips from her palm and looked up, he saw the wounds in her eyes. Her expression made him forget his concerns about fathering a child, even as it made him remember the rest of his vow.

"I promised Spencer I would protect and cherish you."

She snatched her hand away. "I've fared perfectly well without you for the past nineteen years. As for the cherishing, I don't need it."

He took a step toward her. "Aye, Lark. You do."

She inched backward. "Not from a man who sees all of life as a series of sport and jest. Who makes a game of toying with a woman's feelings. Who keeps the vows that amuse him and discards the ones that lose his interest."

What bothered him most about her tirade was that she was right. Prim mouthed, excruciatingly virtuous, and as unbending as a battle lance,

she enumerated his faults and flung them in his face.

He backed her up until she had nowhere else to go. Her rigid spine pressed against a paneled wall. He flattened his palms to the wall and lowered his head to look her in the eye.

"That may be true, Lark." He smiled and played his trump card. "But I'm all you've got." Without even meaning to, he brushed his lips over hers, drawing a gasp of surprise from her. "You would not dance with me earlier, during supper."

"It would be unseemly for me to dance so soon after the death of my — of Spencer."

"There is no one to see now, Lark. No one but me. Dance with me, Lark. Dance with your husband."

"No," she whispered, her face going pale. "We cannot. There are no musicians — "

"I can hum a tune."

"That is not the point, Oliver! I will *not* dance with you."

"Very well," he said, growing aroused by her nearness and, surprisingly, by hearing his name on her lips. He wondered if she could feel the heat that fired his blood. "It's our wedding night. Let's not talk. Every time we talk, we end up quarreling."

She stared at him for a long, long time. Her face never changed. Her eyes never left him. He started to feel uncomfortable. He wondered what she could be thinking — if she was taking his measure and finding him wanting, if she thought Richard Speed was more handsome, or

Kit more reliable or — heaven forfend — better endowed.

"I don't know what you want me to do," she said at last.

He nearly collapsed with relief. So *that* was what had her so bothered. Dear Lark. Ever competent in all things, she was ashamed of this one shortcoming, if it could be termed that.

"Ah, Lark." He cupped her cheeks in his palms, marveling at the pearly texture of her skin. "I beg you, do not worry about matters of protocol tonight. Besides, what of our talk we had beside the river? Do you never think of that?"

"You never told me how to feel, what to say."

"I beg you, just this once, not to worry about the proper thing to say and do."

"But I must explain something — "

"Hush." He dropped his hands to her shoulders and started massaging them gently. He could feel the tension in her coiled muscles and stiff posture. "Do you remember the birds at Newgate Market?"

She nodded. "How could I forget?"

"Do you think, when I set them all free, they worried about how they were going to fly, where they were going to go?"

"Certainly not. They're *birds*, my lord. They but did what instinct told them to do."

"And so must you, my Lark." He bent and blew softly into her ear. "Enough of fretting and worrying about right and wrong. You are God's creature as much as any bird or beast. You have

to stop thinking so much and simply *feel*."

"I don't think" — she shuddered as he blew into her ear again — "I can do that."

"Sweetheart, you just did."

"I did?"

"You did."

It was the most unusual seduction Oliver had ever performed. It was not simply that Lark was so naive, that she was wrapped in layer after layer of puritanical beliefs and rhetoric. Such virtues might have been good for the soul but had no place in a seduction.

More than that, his heart was caught. That was the true source of his anger, his fear. That had never happened to him before, and he did not quite know how to cope.

He had wanted a challenge. How many times had he declared as much? Kit was right. She was the challenge of his life. Marriage was the one adventure he had not yet sampled.

"Come here by the fire." He took both her hands and walked backward, holding her gaze with his, not even daring to blink for fear of losing that rapt, spell-bound look in her eyes.

They stood upon the hearth facing one another while the soft red glow of embers lit them. He pressed his lips to her brow — lightly, reverently. He didn't want to scare her.

If it took all night, if it took a fortnight, a year, a lifetime — he would teach her to love passion.

He could not say why it was so important to him. Only that something critical hung in the balance. Lark. Her happiness. He had not

thought himself capable of caring so much, caring until it hurt.

She reached up to touch her coif, which she had modestly donned immediately following the wedding. He lifted her hand and held it to his heart.

"Nay," he said. "Do nothing. Think of nothing. Tonight the labor is mine."

Obediently she dropped her hand. He found the two wooden combs that held the peaked coif in place and slid off the starched linen, dropping it to the rush mat.

Her hair seemed to move with a life of its own, inky waves bouncing and shimmering from her shoulders to her hips.

Oliver caught great handfuls of her hair in his hands, burying his face in it, inhaling deeply. "If I went to sleep now and never woke up," he declared, "I should die a happy man." For this moment, it was true. He thought often of death, so often he no longer feared it. "How soft your hair is, how silky." He cupped his palms and drew great piles of locks like a shawl around her shoulders. With the onyx curls framing her face, she looked beautiful. There was no other word for it. *Beautiful.*

He told her so, several times, kissing her face and her neck and her hair as his fingers found the laces binding her mourning barbe and sleeves. He drew on the strings, loosening them until her stiff bodice fell with a faint clunk to the floor and the sleeves slithered down to join it.

Oliver sank to one knee to remove her shoes and stockings; then he stood. Clad in her

holland chemise and that soul-stirring cascade of hair, she looked pale and vulnerable. Yet his undressing seemed to hold her fascinated, so he kissed her mouth — savoring the taste of her — and untied her overskirt.

The heavy black garment collapsed like an unstaked tent, revealing a more sheer underskirt, which met the same fate. And then he saw her farthingale.

He had always known the infernal thing was there, but seeing it stirred his outrage. The brittle cane hoops imprisoned her slender form. "When I called you a lark in a cage," he said, working at the back fastening of the apparatus, "I was not far wrong." Offended, he removed the skeletal frame and watched it drop, a tangle of concentric hoops, to the floor.

Then, as if beginning a dance step, he took her hand and led her away from the oppressive costume. With less effort and greater pleasure, he removed her long-sleeved, high-necked chemise.

When he finished, she stood before him clad in her shift — bare armed, her slender shins peeking from beneath the hem.

She had gone a shade paler. Oliver stepped back and drank in the sight of her. "How different you look," he said.

"I am no different than I was five minutes ago," she insisted. "They are only clothes."

"Only indeed. I shall remind you of that the next time you try to truss yourself up like a goose for the roasting pan." He pulled her against his chest and cradled her head there. "You're not comfortable like this, are you, Lark?"

She shook her head. "I wish you would let me explain — "

"There's no need. The birds in those cages were safe. But miserable. Once freed, their future is less certain — "

"Safety is not everything," she said.

Oliver's heart lifted. It was the first bit of encouragement she had given him. He led her to the bed, a simple affair with no ornate carvings or hangings but a wealth of comfortable bolsters and embroidered coverlets. He pressed her shoulders to make her sit and then began to disrobe. He had deliberately moved away from the light of the fire, for he did not want to frighten her. He was a large man, and he wanted her badly. The sight of him, the evidence of his desire, might jolt her out of her compliance.

With quick, easy movements, he shed his doublet and hat and boots, then paused to refill his wine goblet.

"Here." He handed it to her. "Drink. 'Twill keep you warm while I am otherwise occupied."

She took a deep drink, though her wide gray eyes watched him over the rim of the cup.

He took his time shedding canions and hose and let his long shirt cloak him. A bitterly amusing irony struck him. She had been married for almost twenty years, and she was a virgin.

That was why, he decided, she seemed such an enigma to him. In some ways, she was wise beyond her years. In others, she had not grown past girlhood.

The thought roused such a feeling of

tenderness in him that he delayed even longer, unlacing his chemise at the neckline at an agonizing pace. Finally he dropped the garment.

Her breath caught, a small, harsh gust of surprise. He lowered himself to the bed and reclined beside her, taking the wine from her and setting it aside. "Are you afraid, Lark?"

"No, of course not." She looked away. "Yes."

Sadness tugged at his smile. "I would never, ever hurt you."

She shivered. "I wish you would just have done with this. Please. Be swift."

"That, my sweet, I will not do. I shall take my time, and when we're through, you'll be glad I did."

"I doubt it."

He slid his arm under her and pressed her close. She felt tense, yet curiously fragile. Leaning down, he took her lips and kissed her lightly, patiently. For good or for ill, she was his wife. He would treat her with all the gentleness and passion he had promised.

After a time, her mouth softened. She wound her arms around his neck, clinging to him. Oliver felt a surge of triumph. His hands skimmed up and down, up and down, discovering the slim shape of her, learning that she possessed an unexpected, wiry strength. His lips left her mouth and traced her jawline, dipped to sample the softness of her skin in the little hollow above her collarbone. He drew on the laces of her shift, the last vestige of her modesty. Down and down the garment moved, baring her inch by inch, and as he disrobed her, he tried to remember how in God's name he could have ever thought her plain.

In the dim glow from the hearth fire, she seemed made of alabaster, though her silken skin was warm and alive, flushed by anticipation. Her breasts filled his cupped hands, and he kissed them over and over again until her faint, shocked protests stopped. He continued downward, drawing open the shift, revealing her tense, flat belly, her thighs, and the beautiful feminine part of her.

She made sweet, wordless sounds of bewilderment and denial mingling with rising passion. His hands slid down, cradling her, his mouth kissing her, until the shift was gone.

Then he returned to her mouth, his tongue tasting the warmth within while his hands never ceased their exploration.

"That was not so terrible, was it?" he asked.

"You're finished?"

He laughed quietly. "My love, I've barely begun."

Lark studied his smiling face. She didn't want to mislead him. She didn't want to need him like this. She didn't want to look into his eyes and forget to breathe. She didn't want to crave his kisses and caresses as if she were starving, but she did. God help her, she did.

And Oliver de Lacey, for all his swaggering conceit and self-seeking attitude, seemed determined to give her pleasure. He kissed her again, deeply and thoroughly.

While his tongue plunged in and out with

214

an insistent rhythm, she felt herself relax. This was different. The past was behind her. He was her husband. Her reason for marrying him no longer mattered. This felt good, felt right, and her conscience began to ease, ever so slowly, toward total surrender.

Why had she wanted him to be brief? A foolish notion, that. It sprang from that other moment of darkness that had left her shaking with shame. This was different, she thought once again. *Different.*

She wanted this feeling to go on forever. His searing kisses and his restless hands had an extraordinary effect on her. She had not drunk much wine, but a delicious sense of intoxication flowed through her and brought every inch of her skin to a state of burning sensitivity.

She knew it was not love she felt, for love was a quiet warmth, not this raging hunger. With a cry of abandon, she slipped her arms around his neck and crushed their lips together, wanting a closeness, a completion she could not name. She knew it made no sense, but she felt that if she found joy with Oliver, perhaps she could forget her haunted past.

Even as he kissed her, she heard his sound of muffled mirth. She had not known it was possible or even permitted to laugh in bed. His laughter was not mockery, but sheer, exuberant delight, so typical of Oliver.

Oliver. How deliciously odd to think of him by his given name.

All the bleak, empty years made desire keen as a blade. She arched her back so that her bare breasts brushed his chest. The light contact made her crave more. She wanted his kisses there, but she had no idea how to make her needs known.

And yet he knew. He groaned deep in his throat and lowered his mouth, suckling, while his hand eased down and down, parting her thighs.

No. Her mouth shaped the protest, but the sound that came out said yes, and his fingers slid over her, finding a small, secret place that turned desire into a burning conflagration, out of control, until she did not feel like herself at all. Lost, she was lost, and Oliver was her only anchor as she drifted higher and higher, lifted to the places he touched her — breasts and thighs, making something inside her coil tightly, ready to explode.

"Please please please," she heard herself whisper.

"Soon, my love," he mumbled, moving his lips over the tips of her breasts and then returning to her mouth while his other touch changed, his fingers brushing her and then moving inside, imitating the motion of his tongue. The tandem rhythms took her higher yet until she teetered, helpless and lost, while little sobs tore from her throat.

He moved then, looming over her, between her parted thighs. The hot velvet of him touched her. She raised her hips, and then she felt a pressure, strong but not painful, increasing her yearning. For a moment he stopped kissing her and gazed down.

"Are you all right?"

"No. Yes. I don't know." She was in a fog, her mind as dull as a witling's.

"If it hurts, I shall stop." His beautiful, sad smile appeared and then fled. "It will probably kill me, but yes, I'll stop. Shall I?"

"Yes. No. Don't you dare, Oliver."

He kissed her, lowered himself another fraction of an inch. "I love the way you say my name."

They kissed again, sharing breath, hearts beating as one, and he continued his tender, relentless journey. The pressure built and built, not pleasure, not pain, but some irresistible mélange of torment and rapture that spiraled into a deep, velvety sting.

She gasped. "Oliver!"

He cursed. "You're hurt." He started to draw away.

Her hands, quicker than her mind, grasped him by the hips and held on. "Don't . . . you . . . dare," she repeated.

He covered her again, filled her, and paused, just for a heartbeat. She could not be sure, but she thought surprise flickered in his face, and she braced herself for the storm of his hatred and disgust. But instead he started to move. The rhythm was slow and subtle at first; then he quickened it. Abandoning the last vestiges of her apprehension, she rose to meet each thrust.

She flew higher and higher, grasping at the unnamed joy that seemed to hover just out of her reach.

"Almost there, love," he whispered in her ear. "Almost there."

When the moment came, she cried out in anguish and ecstasy, for to feel so intense a pleasure must be sinful, forbidden. Oliver sank down upon her and stopped, yet the rhythm had taken on a life of its own — warm, long ripples from muscles she didn't know she had.

A hoarse cry broke from Oliver. She felt a renewed burst of heat and then a gentle pulsing that prolonged the moment until time had no meaning.

They lay together, his weight a sweet burden upon her, their bodies intimately joined. The bond was deep and mysterious, reaching her heart and causing a beautiful ache within her.

Lark's thoughts swirled in a pink mist of delight and confusion. All her life she had been taught to guard her heart and her body. Tonight she had let down her guard, bringing him into her life, into her body, part of him buried in her, touching her deep inside and fitting perfectly, a bond forged by nature. She had trusted him, had taken the ultimate risk, and she was fiercely glad.

"You're crying." His gentle lips caught the tear that slipped down her cheek.

"Am I?"

Very gently he moved off her and lay on his side next to her. "Aye. I'm sorry if I hurt you."

"'Tis not that. I feel different. Unlike myself. Is this what you meant by soaring?"

"I believe, my love, that it is."

"Oh."

"Did you like it?"

"How can I answer that?" She felt raw and vulnerable, and suddenly she wanted to hide from him.

But he wouldn't let her. He pulled her close, cradled her head in the crook of his shoulder. "Then don't answer, Lark. Sleep. It's been a long day for you."

"I could not possibly sleep." Even as she spoke, a pleasant lassitude slipped like a silken scarf over her, and she snuggled closer still. The smell of him wrapped her in thoughts of warmth and comfort, and her breathing slowed, long savoring inhalations.

"Lark?"

She smiled at his gentle, endearingly uncertain tone. "Mm?"

"I meant to tell you something earlier. Don't fall in love with me, Lark."

"Mm?" she said again. "Why not?"

"I saw your heart break when Spencer died. I'd not want you to suffer like that again."

Her eyes fluttered shut. "Fall in love with you, Oliver? Now, why would I commit such a folly as that?"

★ ★ ★

In the days that followed, the air was piercing and clear, and springtime swept down from the Chiltern Hills, blanketing the landscape in green. Drovers herded flocks of sheep up for their summer grazing. Copyholders plowed the

219

outlying fields, and their children broadcast the rye seed.

Lark fell into the routine that had ruled every season at Blackrose Priory. She supervised the rents, saw to the making of candles and sausage, ordered the scrubbing of floors and walls and halls.

Aye, she thought, making her way to the sewing room to help Florabel with stuffing a mattress, the days passed as they always had.

But not the nights.

The mere thought quickened her blood, and she felt a warm spasm low in her belly. She paused outside the small room off the kitchen and tried to conquer her unbidden blush.

The maid must have stepped out. The mattress, just half filled with straw and sweet herbs, hung in the middle of the room. Lark stepped to the other side and began gathering up armfuls to stuff in the mattress. After several minutes had passed, she heard a footstep outside the room.

"Florabel," she said without looking up, "I expected all the retainers at Blackrose to abhor me for marrying Lord Oliver so soon after Spencer's death." She poked more straw into the mattress. "In truth, everyone seems so accepting. What do the servants say when I am not around to hear?"

Florabel worked in silence; Lark could hear the soft rustle of straw as she cut it.

"Ah. You needn't answer, then," Lark said, "and I shouldn't pry. But tell me, Florabel, what *do* you think of my lord husband?"

Lark was obsessed with him. She wanted to talk about him to anyone who would listen.

More silence. Lark imagined the girl's cheeks ablaze with embarrassment and smiled. "You needn't answer that, either, Florabel. It's plain to see everyone finds him charming. He is boisterous and funny and bright and exasperating." She closed her eyes, collapsed onto the full mattress behind her, and savored the spice of dried lavender and bay. "Also, he is quite insufferably handsome, don't you think? Of course you do. All women do." Since Florabel was of an age with Lark and newly wed herself, Lark added boldly, "I get very little sleep these days, for Lord Oliver is very . . . active at night."

"To say nothing of the days," said a low, decidedly masculine voice. A warm weight fell upon her. Her eyes flew open. Before she could cry out, Oliver kissed her, long and hungrily, pressing her into the mattress while the clean ticking billowed up around them.

For a moment the intense pleasure that rushed over her obscured all else. She felt an almost painful joy, as if her thoughts and words alone had summoned him.

She tore her mouth from his long enough to rouse indignation. "Where is Florabel?"

He laughed and touched his tongue to her ear. "I gave her tuppence and sent her to market."

"But we have work to do."

He pressed his hardness into the cradle of her hips. "So we have."

Suspicion chilled the inevitable heat he

221

kindled. "How long have you been here?" she demanded.

He tugged at her bodice and sleeve lacings. "Long enough."

"Long enough? What does that mean?"

He laughed again and tugged at her chemise until her breasts were bared to his mouth, his tongue, his lightly nipping teeth.

"Long enough to hear myself called charming, funny, bright, handsome . . . I blush to continue."

"And so you should." In spite of herself she weakened, lifting herself toward the wicked delights offered by his mouth. "I didn't mean a word of it."

"Of course you didn't." He hiked her skirts and lowered his canions.

"I won't love you," she said, opening to him helplessly, raising her hips and sighing as he sank into her.

"Of course you won't."

She let out a soft sob as he began to move. "Then why . . . do I let you . . . want you . . . " Her voice trailed off.

"Because you can't help yourself, my sweet. Nor can I."

★ ★ ★

Oliver did not know how much time had passed. He did not care. He looked through the single, unglazed window of the sewing room and saw that the sky had darkened to the color of Lark's blushing cheeks.

222

Lark.

He glanced down at his sleeping wife. The mattress cradled them like a cloud, keeping the chill air at bay. When he was a lad, dry straw used to irritate his lungs, but it had not bothered him in years, God be thanked. Now only the occasional London summer or sometimes a sense of anxiety brought on the illness that would ultimately conquer him. Here, the air was soft and safe, and he had not suffered a seriously anxious moment yet.

Lark sighed and curled herself closer against him. She had fallen asleep in his arms, as sweetly exhausted and trusting as a babe.

For weeks Oliver had lived in a state of confusion. He was a rake. A prodigal. A daredevil. This bucolic, monogamous life was not for him. His mission was to go adventuring, to sample all of life's pleasures, to consume delight in great gulps, not caring what wounded rubble he left in his wake.

But something terrible — something unthinkable — had happened.

Oliver de Lacey had fallen in love with his wife.

He spent a few minutes wondering when it had happened. He decided it had not come upon him all at once, like a direct hit from Cupid's arrow. Instead his feelings had spread gradually, sprouting from the germ planted the moment Lark had pulled him from a pauper's grave. Nurtured with humor and sympathy when she had bravely faced him in a Southwark tavern and endured his antics at Newgate Market. Leavened with admiration when he had realized the risks she took to save the wrongfully condemned. Grown with tenderness when he had watched her weep at Spencer's deathbed.

And finally and irrevocably sealed when she had surrendered to him on their wedding night.

He frowned slightly at the memory. He had gone about it all wrong, letting his fear turn to anger and accusing her of conspiring to trap him into marriage. They had argued their way out of that, thank God, but she had surprised him yet again . . . the moment he had joined with her.

Oliver was a man of vast experience. He knew a maiden when he bedded one. Lark was as virginal as any he had known; she was innocent in all ways . . . but one.

He told himself he was wrong, that perhaps she was made differently, that her maidenhead had yielded without the usual resistance. Yet every so often doubts nagged at him. He had never placed a high value on the insubstantial shield between innocence and knowledge, but at odd moments he did wonder if Lark hid something from him.

It mattered not. Oliver leaned down and kissed a stray curl that adorned her temple. That was the beauty of love — it made such things cease to matter. Love was a curious affliction. He felt as if all his life he had been running a race and now, at last, he had found the finish line.

Gone was the restlessness that once drove him to live his life at a frantic pace. Lark made it seem all right to slow down, to watch the color of the sky deepen at twilight, to listen to the laughter of children at play, or to lie motionless, for hours, with his sleeping wife in his arms.

His finger traced the delicate line of her brow and temple. He wondered if anyone else suspected the passion that burned beneath the plain, scripture-quoting Lady Lark. What a wonder she was in bed, hungry and inquisitive, shamelessly adventurous, playful, and so generous that it stole his breath away.

The love came over him in great heaving waves. Sometimes it would happen when Lark was far away, yet near in his thoughts. The emotion was so staggering that he had to stop what he was doing and sit down.

How could one small, prim woman wreak such havoc on a man's heart and soul?

Oliver sighed and gazed down at her. Soft skin, dusky eyelashes shadowing her cheeks, a bowed mouth that was beautiful when she wasn't pursing it in disapproval.

The wave struck with unusual force. Oliver felt a tightness in his chest, braced himself. An attack. Not now. Not here.

The familiar darkness never came. He let out a breath of relief when he realized it wasn't an attack. It was something quite different.

He realized that there was one flaw in loving. It hurt when it wasn't returned.

I won't love you. Her breathless, almost desperate declaration echoed in his mind.

He curved his mouth in a bittersweet smile. "Then I hope you don't mind," he whispered, "if I love you."

It was the first time he had spoken the words aloud, and he waited for lightning to strike.

Instead, a hammering sounded at the door of the sewing room.

Lark blinked herself awake. "What is it?" she mumbled.

"My lord! My lady!" Florabel's voice shrilled with anxiety. "Come quickly! Lord Wynter has returned!"

11

WHEN Oliver and Lark found Wynter, he was pacing in the great hall and questioning the steward like a Spanish Inquisitor.

"Why weren't the rye fields left fallow? And what about the western uplands? I thought I ordered the grazing there."

The steward, a thin-necked man called Cakepen, wrung his hands. "Quite so, my lord. But there were a few cases of the bloat, and then — "

"Wynter!" Hiding his annoyance behind a broad grin, Oliver strode forward, both hands outstretched. Wynter was a handsome bag of male pride, Oliver acknowledged. And perhaps, like Oliver himself, no stranger to using his looks to advantage.

Shamelessly, Oliver gave him a back-pounding hug. "Welcome to Blackrose."

Wynter hauled himself free, flinging out his arms to rid himself of the hug. "What do you here?" Without waiting for an answer, he glared at Lark. "I should have known your wit was too small to dispose of a mere houseguest. Why *is* he still here?"

Oliver gave Lark no chance to reply. "I can see you're consumed by grief over your father's passing." He pressed a cup of ale into Wynter's hand. "Apparently you were so sick with mourning that you failed to come and pay your respects at his burial." He patted Wynter on the shoulder. "Time will heal your heart, son."

Wynter gulped the ale and rolled his eyes. "Son? Have you taken vows while I wasn't looking?"

Oliver laughed. He heard Lark catch her breath and hold it in agonized, waiting silence.

"Aye," he said, "I have. Marriage vows."

Wynter's eyes narrowed.

"'Tis true." Oliver refilled Wynter's glass. "And since Lark was your father's wife, and therefore your stepmother, I might well be your stepfather." He winked at Lark. "Have I got that right? Does marrying the stepmother make me this young landraker's — "

The ale cup slipped from Wynter's hand and spilled into the rushes on the floor.

Lark was no help at all. She stood there pale and goggle-eyed, looking as if she had swallowed a live toad.

In a single stride Wynter had her backed against the wall, his hands gripping her upper arms and his furious face mere inches from hers.

"*Is this true?*" he demanded.

Just for a moment, Oliver stood perfectly still. He had never, ever felt this way before, so at first he didn't recognize the feeling.

Then he identified it: rage. Clean and sharp and brutal. It was as if someone had put a glowing brand to his brain. The heat was so tremendous, he thought his head would explode.

With his blood boiling, Oliver leaped forward, grabbing Wynter and spinning him around. Wynter's arms exploded outward, shoving Oliver away and unbalancing him. He staggered back while Wynter's hand found the hilt of his sword.

No one, but no one, was quicker with a blade than Oliver de Lacey. Even before he found his footing, he had his weapon drawn, the tip of it pushed into the tender hollow between Wynter's collarbones.

Wynter's eyes widened in astonishment. Then he nearly crossed them as he looked down at the sword. His own weapon dropped with a defeated clatter to the floor.

Oliver usually grinned good-naturedly at his victims before he bested them. This time he did not smile. His own fury worried him. His control hung by a slender thread — a thread controlled by the small, frightened woman who watched them both.

"Please don't kill him," she whispered.

The faint, pleading words reined in his rage. He could not trust himself to move, but he did manage to force himself to put on an expression of paternal disapproval. "Here now, my boy." He spoke calmly enough. "If you persist in being naughty, I shall have to send you to your room."

"You meddlesome knave," Wynter said. "They gossip about you in the lowest dives in Southwark."

Oliver hooked a thumb into his balderic. "There is much of me to gossip about," he couldn't help commenting. "And how would you know the dives of Southwark, hmm?"

Wynter tossed away the question with a blink and countered with one of his own. "How can you think to keep a wife? And Lark, of all women! I've known her far longer than you. I know how to handle her. She is — "

"My wife," Oliver snapped. "I have never had a wife before, and I rather like this one, so I mean to keep her. Much to my surprise, I am possessive of her."

To reinforce his meaning, Oliver increased the pressure of the sword point. "So you see, Wynter, I cannot allow you to touch her. Nor to make any remark I could construe as insulting. Is that clear?"

"Yes." Wynter spoke very softly, as if in fear of deepening the pressure of the steel on his vulnerable neck.

"Excellent." Oliver winked and sheathed his sword. "If you had any idea, Don Weasel, how close I just came to killing you — "

"Oliver, never mind." Lark put a hand on his arm and kept her eyes downcast. "You've made your point."

He had just rescued her from a twisted, hateful man. Wasn't she grateful?

"Indeed you have." Wynter swallowed hard and touched his throat. "Though my mother raised me to be a hospitable host, I'm afraid I'll have to ask you to leave Blackrose. Now that my esteemed father — of well-beloved memory — is gone, I have work to do." He sent a thin smile to Lark. "You have done an adequate job of managing the estate. But, as I expected, you've not been nearly as thorough as a man."

If Oliver had made such a taunt, she would have flown in his face and proven him wrong. With Wynter, however, she simply clasped her hands in front of her and said, "You know I am a hard worker, Wynter."

"Ah, indeed you are. I wonder if our dear Lord Oliver wed you for that virtue alone." Wynter kept the open door at his back, no doubt well aware that Oliver would attack again if provoked. "I think not. Anyone with half the wits of a hen knows he wed you for your property — that which is legitimately yours."

"You pretend to know much of what happened while you were off to London," she said, but her voice was uncommonly soft.

"You believe everything Oliver de Lacey tells you," Wynter said, disgust curling his lip. "Maybe you're a gull rather than a lark. No matter. When you discover his game, you'll come running back to me."

With that, he turned on his heel and left the hall.

Lark stood rigid, pale, watching him depart. It worried Oliver to see her like this — his Lark, his hardheaded outspoken Lark, quelled into weak silence.

Back to me. Oliver frowned at Wynter's words. Not *to me*, but *back to me*, as if he had possessed her before.

The thought was so outrageous that he tossed it away like so much offal. Trying to lighten the moment, he said, "I suppose I'll have to wait until supper to tell him the suit is concluded and he's been disentailed."

"Aye," she said.

Her meekness infuriated him. "Look at me, Lark! Now!"

She lifted her gaze to his. Her great mist-colored eyes, bruised by the shadows of her thick lashes, reflected ancient wounds that made him want to shake her — or take her into his arms.

He did neither. "What poison does he feed you, Lark? A half hour ago I looked into your eyes and saw naught but passion and wonder and joy. Five minutes with Wynter and you're like a candle that's burnt itself out. It hurts me, Lark. It hurts me to see you like this."

"Ah, and there we have it," she said, crushing her fists to her sides. "*You* feel hurt. You always see things in terms of yourself. You never try to understand *me*."

"Then make me understand," he snapped. "Why do you cower before him? Has he hurt you, abused you? By God, if he had, I won't even need my sword to kill him."

"No! Oliver, if you truly care about my feelings, you'll stop interfering. And *I* shall deliver the news about the entail."

"That should be interesting to watch. You can barely get three words out when he's around."

She clenched her fists at her sides. "Excuse me, for I must see about supper."

In a whirl of stiff skirts and indignation, she was gone.

★ ★ ★

That evening at supper, Lark served capon. She made no apology to Oliver when the hapless roasted bird arrived at the high table. She merely stared straight ahead, out at the lower tables where the stewards and overseers, footboys and maids, and occasional wayfarer took their meal.

Ironically, her quarrel with Oliver had given her the strength to endure this evening. She had vented her temper, that unseemly, angry passion Spencer had so disliked, and she had survived the ordeal. She would survive tonight. She would not let either Oliver or Wynter make her cringe.

Wynter sat at her right, Oliver at her left. On the other side of Wynter sat Mr. Belcumber, the portly and empty-headed mayor of Hempstead.

Oliver chattered blithely with Mr. Nettlethorpe, a successful breeder of horses who had promised to locate a stud for Oliver's prized Neapolitan mare.

As she had been for the past score of years, Lark was left alone with her thoughts.

How ironic, she thought bitterly. Spencer had been convinced that Oliver would be her salvation. That with his youth and beauty and charm, he would fling open the cage and she would soar.

She took another sip of wine and thought back to Wynter's arrival. She had felt that familiar thud of trepidation she always experienced in his presence.

It was a rare gift, indeed, to be able to rip a person to shreds without even touching her. Wynter had a way of using words like a tarred lash, stripping away at her until she shrank like a defeated dog. She had given him that power over her.

From time to time she tried to make excuses for herself — she had met him at the tender age of seventeen; her judgment had been blurred by his sleek beauty and magnetic air. But when she was honest, she admitted her own shameful weakness. The ugly past was her secret, her carefully hidden sorrow.

Every once in a while she had tried to fight back, but always on behalf of innocent folk accused of heresy, never herself. Even Oliver had failed to repair her pride. Aye, he had put Wynter in his place, had threatened him, and she had been filled with hope. But Oliver had acted for his own benefit. Because *he* hurt. *His* pride was at stake.

She sighed and set down her wine, having no taste for it. Of late, she had a sour stomach. Her gaze strayed to the coat of arms above the door. Spencer's device, a hart passant, still adorned shields and hangings throughout the house.

'Tis not your fault, Spencer, she thought. The fault lay with her. She could not find happiness. She never would. And two years earlier, she had flung away her own peace of mind.

"Who is that woman there?" Interrupting her reverie, Wynter pointed at a lower table. "The one in the gown of dark blue."

Lark's heart leaped as she followed Wynter's

234

pointing finger. Richard Speed's outlandish disguise had proved to be unusually successful. With his yellow curls and broad face, Reverend Speed resembled a handsome, upcountry maid in simple garb.

"Well?" Wynter prodded.

Lark gave him the explanation they had settled upon. "Mistress Quickly is a poor widow fallen on hard times."

"She looks lonely. Where are your manners, Lark?"

Before she could contrive an excuse, Wynter sent a servant to fetch the buxom Mistress Quickly.

Lark gripped Oliver's knee under the table.

He smiled and whispered, "So you're over your pique? Can't keep your lovely hands off me?"

Scowling with impatience, she whispered, "I fear Wynter has taken a fancy to our guest."

She expected Oliver to think and act quickly to avert the disaster. Instead he threw back his head and hooted with laughter. Moments later he stood to help Mistress Quickly up to the raised head table.

Lark saw Oliver lean down and say something into Speed's ear. Speed went pale, but that only enhanced the illusion of maidenly trepidation. His curtsy, when he was presented to Wynter, seemed endearingly clumsy. His blush, as he took a seat on the bench between Wynter and Lark, was genuine.

When Wynter's hungry eyes fixed on the

tightly filled bosom, Lark wished she had not been so liberal with the straw.

"Try the capon," Wynter said, pushing the salver toward Speed. "'Tis unusually succulent."

Speed sniffed and waved a dainty handkerchief in front of his face. "Capon makes me bloated. You'd not want me breaking wind at the high table, would you?" Batting his huge, guileless eyes, Speed gazed at Wynter.

Oliver made a gurgling sound, almost choking on his wine.

Yet wonder of wonders, Wynter seemed enchanted. He regaled Mistress Quickly with tales of his travels, boasting that the queen had received him with a special kiss only a week earlier and that Bishop Bonner was considering him for an official post as undersecretary to the undersecretary of heretics' widows and orphans. The office made certain that those who had lost their providers to heresy suffered no lapses of their own.

"How exciting for you," Speed piped. "Imagine, rooting out all those dangerous old women and small children. I've always considered them a threat to the security of England."

Wynter squinted at Speed.

Speed bowed his mouth into a sweet smile.

"Of course," Wynter continued, "that would only be a start. Once I carry out my plans for Blackrose, I'll surely earn a more influential post." He leaned over to whisper in Speed's ear, then left the table to ask the musicians to play a love song.

Speed nudged Lark in the ribs and spoke out

of the corner of his mouth. "He wants to meet with me later!"

"Oh, didn't you know?" she said. "'Tis the lot of women to deal with noxious suitors."

Wynter returned as the lute player began a new tune. He settled himself next to Speed, but Mr. Belcumber distracted him with a question.

"He's got his hand on my knee!" Speed hissed at Lark.

"So remove it," she murmured.

"I did! He put it back!" Horror and panic rasped in Speed's voice. Wynter did not seem to notice, for he was still speaking to the mayor.

For a moment, for one wicked, delicious moment, Lark let him suffer. Women were constantly embattled by unwanted male attention. They endured gropings and worse. Yet even virtuous men made light of women's troubles.

Finally, when it seemed Speed would burst his false bodice, she relented and cleared her throat. "My dear, did you ever discover the cause of those running sores on your — " She leaned over and pretended to whisper in Speed's ear.

Wynter sat forward to glare at Lark.

With newfound strength, she ignored him.

"Sores?" Speed asked stupidly.

"Aye." She paused and gritted her teeth. She had hoped Speed would not be so dense. "Did you find Grizzell Forrest, the healer? And did she tell you if it was leprosy, or the French pox?"

Speed squeaked as if someone had pinched him. Wynter shot to his feet, the bench scraping the floor as it pushed back.

237

"What a pity for you to leave so suddenly," he cried. "Mortlock! Pyle!" Two maids scurried forward. "Help Mistress Quickly to the parish house. I'm certain she'll wish to — to recuperate in private."

A gleam flashed in Speed's eyes. "But what about our meeting?"

"I — I just remembered," Wynter said. "I have a previous engagement."

"I had hoped for my sake you would break it."

"Impossible. Quite impossible."

Muffled chuckles came from Oliver. Speed seemed to sense that he was pushing his luck. "A disappointment, my lord." His parting curtsy was even clumsier than his first, and Lark wondered if Wynter heard Speed mutter, "Kiss my breech, you oily swasher," under his breath as he left the hall.

"I can see I'll have much work to do around here," Wynter said, fanning the air with his napkin. "Lark, what on earth were you thinking, letting a hideously diseased woman into my house?"

Lark glanced at Oliver. She could see the laughter hiding in the blue depths of his eyes, and for a moment she took pride in his pleasure.

The moment passed quickly, though. It merely acknowledged what she already knew in the pit of her stomach. She should delay no longer.

She resisted the urge to grasp Oliver's hand under the table. She told herself she did not need his help in taking this step. She gathered

238

her courage on a deep breath of air, braced herself, and turned to Wynter.

"I take it you have not read Spencer's will."

He narrowed his eyes. "Don't tell me the old worm fodder left you without a penny. Not that it should matter now that you've landed yourself the Wimberleigh heir." He jerked his head resentfully at Oliver.

Ill will thickened the air. Lark tightened every muscle to keep from trembling.

Oliver's knuckles turned white around the handle of his eating knife. Still, he kept quiet, and with dawning gratitude she realized he would allow her to tell Wynter in her own way.

"Spencer was generous with me," she said. "We knew he would be, of course. I brought him Montfichet as my dowry, and that will revert to me." She dragged in a deep, steadying breath. "He was generous with you as well, Wynter." She was not sure what prompted her to add, "He loved you, in his way."

Just for a moment, sentiment softened Wynter's handsome face. His chin trembled, and a strange, sad hunger flared in his dark eyes. Lark wondered, in that blink of time, what sort of man he might have been had he been taught to love rather than to hate.

"How fortunate," he muttered, holding out his goblet for more wine. He was himself again, harsh and suspicious and filled with loathing.

"He left you half interest in the clothworks at Wycherly. Also the house in Fleet Street and the sum of a hundred pounds in silver. As for

239

Blackrose Priory . . . " She forced herself to be steady of voice and demeanor. "He left it to me."

Wynter snorted into his cup. "Don't be stupid, Lark. The property is entailed. Like it or not, it falls to me."

"The entail has been broken."

"Quite legally," Oliver chimed in. "You see, a lawsuit has proven that it never belonged to Spencer in the first place."

"Of course it belonged to Spencer," Wynter said. "King Henry granted it to him."

"Not quite." In his cheerful, breezy style, Oliver explained the law of the Common Recovery.

Lark barely heard. She found herself spellbound by the look in Wynter's eyes. It was a fury so distinct and icy that she was transfixed like a mouse by the jeweled eye of a cat.

It would have been easier to bear if he had flown into a rage. But of course, Wynter held his emotions in check. With sinking dread, she realized she was more like him than she thought. She might never be free of him.

He listened to Oliver's rambling recitation. Then he bathed his hands carefully in the finger bowl and dried them with a napkin. He stood, holding his fists clenched.

"I do not accept this, I shall contest it."

Oliver grinned, but by now Lark knew him well enough to see the steel behind his smile. "Kit Youngblood is a most excellent lawyer. You'll get nowhere, I assure you."

"So." Wynter's manner became brisk. "The

240

battle lines are drawn." Almost as an afterthought, he turned to Lark. "You plotted against me. I shall never forget your treachery."

In military fashion, he snapped a turn and stalked out of the hall, calling for his retainers.

"'Tis done, then," Oliver said.

"Nay," Lark whispered, the queasiness bolting through her once again. "'Tis not even begun."

★ ★ ★

"I'm afraid," said Lark.

Puzzled by the quaver in her voice, Oliver drew rein and held up his hand to signal Speed to stop. "Afraid? Wynter can't hurt you. Whatever hold he had over you is broken."

Her face was pale and drawn, the shadows under her eyes making them appear larger than ever. A sting of tenderness jabbed at Oliver. He could never look at her without wanting to put his arms around her and hold her close.

"I mean I'm afraid to meet your family," she confessed.

He swept his arm toward the magnificent panorama rolling out before them. His parents' Wiltshire estate was matchless in its symmetry and beauty, from the pocked limestone gatehouse to the rambling, gabled manse, to the long gardens and mazes that led to the wild woods to the south and west.

"I thought it only proper to introduce my wife to my family now that they've returned from Muscovy. Besides, poor Speed needs to

241

escape England. If anyone can help him, my father can. At last count, I believe his fleet numbered a dozen ships."

"You're right." She sent the gowned and coifed minister a wan smile. "Reverend Speed, you have been most patient with us."

"Indeed." He dug his finger beneath his starched headdress and scratched his head. "You've both been more than generous, and you've taken enormous risks for my sake." He grinned at Lark. "I've even forgiven you for telling Lord Wynter I have the pox."

"No one will ever accuse my wife of being dull witted," Oliver said, his chest filling up with pride.

Lark ducked her head, and he wanted to shake her. Why did she persist in thinking herself unworthy? How could he convince her that she truly was as he saw her? Radiant with an inner beauty, fiercely clever, worthy of love.

Aye, love.

He threw back his shoulders. "We are at Lynacre. Do we turn back or will you meet my family? Come, Lark. Be adventuresome."

Her gloved hands gripped the reins tighter. "Of course I shall meet them. It's just that I've never before had a real family. It will seem strange to me."

Oliver laughed, thinking of the menagerie within the walls of Lynacre. "Oh, they are strange, I promise you that."

★ ★ ★

242

They did not disappoint. Once the travelers had surrendered their horses to the grooms and waited in the shadowy main hall, the exuberant de Lacey clan descended like an ill-matched flock of exotic birds.

Oliver accepted hugs from his father, his stepmother, the two girls, and the twins. Hollering above the babble of greetings, he said, "I've gotten married, and I've brought my wife to meet you."

Instantly the babble started up again and crescendoed to a roar. To Oliver's horror, they surrounded Richard Speed, hugging the poor man, kissing him, welcoming him to the family. Lark stood by silently, doubtless mistaken for a lady's maid, her hands clasped and her eyes downcast.

Simon and Sebastian, the twins who were identical in all ways but one, began nudging each other and whispering.

Stephen de Lacey, Oliver's father, bellowed a hearty welcome to Speed. Like Oliver, he was a big man. Aside from his wife and family, the thing he loved most was the joy of invention. Around his neck hung no fewer than three pairs of spectacles, one of which seemed to have a tiny set of backward-facing mirrors attached. Along with the spectacles were two different watches on leather thongs, and one of them suddenly let loose with a tinny gong. Speed yelped in surprise and jumped back, shaking his skirts as if a mouse had run under them.

Stephen chuckled and turned to Oliver. "If I

get this mob quieted down, would you introduce her to us properly?"

Speed moaned with the frustration of it all.

Oliver's chest felt as if it might burst from inappropriate mirth. "Of course. Father, Lady Juliana."

His stepmother, plump as a ripe peach, turned with a sparkling smile. "Please do. Oliver, this is a most rare honor." The special flavor of her native Novgorod still lilted in her voice.

"There's been a mistake," Oliver said when he could finally control his laughter. "That is the right Reverend Richard Speed."

"Richard Speed!" shouted Natalya, clapping her hands. "I have studied your sermons for years." Dark, dainty, and as graceful as a cat, she was an avid reader of philosophy who had, thus far, frightened off all suitors with her intellect.

"Ha!" Simon burst out, jabbing his twin brother in the ribs. "I *told* you something was amiss!"

Sebastian, who understood such attractions, shoved Simon away and sent a boggle-eyed stare at Oliver. "You wed a *man?*"

"God save me from unnatural brothers!" Simon shouted. "First Sebastian, and now *you*, Oliver?"

Belinda swore, no doubt echoing invective learned during her frequent visits to the gunpowder merchant in Bath. Wearing a man's riding clothes and armed with a leather whip, she stumbled back against a sideboard.

Sebastian slapped his thighs. "Of course not, merkin-breath," he said to his twin. He pointed to Lark, who still stood frozen and silent off to one side. "*That's* his wife."

"Sweet Jesu, thank you!" Simon bellowed, thumping his fist three times upon his chest. With the swagger of a ship's captain, he swept across the room, picked Lark up in his arms, and whirled her around.

Oliver started forward to rescue her, but his family thwarted him. They smothered poor Lark with love. She, who had known only the stern regard of a strange man many years her senior, was suddenly swallowed by the unabashed adoration of the de Lacey clan.

Juliana lapsed into a string of Russian endearments. Belinda insisted that Lark be entertained with a fireworks display; Natalya wanted to show her the library. Simon and Sebastian began to argue, loudly and passionately, about whom Lark more closely resembled — Artemis or Perpetua.

Stephen de Lacey stepped back and simply wept for joy. It was like seeing a mountain weep; he was so huge and his happiness was so heartfelt.

Oliver didn't have the heart to tell him they had married to honor a deathbed promise. His family always worried about him, always seemed certain he avoided marriage because of his condition, which was true.

Then his thoughts fled as a faint cry broke from Lark. Her eyes rolled up and she pitched forward, collapsing into Simon's brawny arms.

"My God!" Natalya shouted accusingly. "We've smothered the poor woman!"

12

"HOW long have you known?" asked a gentle, darkly accented voice.

Lark blinked at the fuzzy shape looming over her. She swallowed past the dryness in her throat. She felt the billowing softness of a downy mattress beneath her, the comforting weight of a counterpane covering her. Inhaling, she smelled the pungence of dried flowers. She blinked again and the shape resolved itself into a beaming, round-faced woman with vivid green eyes.

Lady Juliana, Oliver's stepmother.

"Known . . . what?" Lark asked.

With deft hands, Juliana held Lark's head and pressed a cup to her lips. As she took a sip of the broth, Juliana said, "About the babe. How long have you known?"

Lark nearly choked on the drink, and Juliana took the cup away.

"Babe?" Lark managed to gasp.

"Ah, you poor child. I thought you knew. I suspected it the moment I saw you."

Lark's hand slipped down to her midsection. It was as flat as unleavened bread. "How?"

Juliana smiled. "I daresay I have a gift for such things. There is a pallor, and a sort of dreamy wistfulness in the face. Then when you fainted, I became quite certain. Do you not know the signs?"

Lark shook her head. How would she, raised in a solemn household by a man forty-five years her senior, a man who all but denied that she even possessed a female anatomy?

"Are your monthly courses late?" Juliana inquired.

"Aye. I think so." Indeed, when that female event had first happened, Lark had been sure she was dying. Spencer then subjected her to a lecture on Eve's sin that left her more confused than ever.

"Waves of nausea? Sickness in the mornings?" Juliana asked.

With growing fright, Lark nodded.

"Tenderness in the breasts?"

A flush scalded Lark's cheeks and she nodded again, mute and guilty as a felon.

"No one told you of these signs? No one prepared you?"

"No. I had no idea."

Juliana whispered something in a foreign tongue. Lark did not understand the words, but she comprehended the heartfelt catch in the lady's voice and the diamond bright sparkle in her green eyes.

"I am so happy for you and Oliver," Juliana said in English. "I never thought . . . that is, I worried that Oliver would not settle with a wife and start a family. He has ever been one to shy from devotions of the heart. I am so glad he has changed."

Lark lay speechless as the revelation tumbled through her mind. A babe. She had never even seen one up close. The idea that she would

247

give birth to a naked, helpless creature was overwhelming. Awesome. Unimaginable.

"I'm afraid," she said.

"Of course you are." Juliana's tenderness and sympathy were so natural and so comforting that Lark wanted to weep. She had never known true friendship, never known the simple solace of quiet talk between women. At the same time, Lark felt deceitful, for she knew Juliana did not understand the truth.

Oliver had undergone no epiphany. He had not suddenly changed from reckless rogue to family man. He had married out of a sense of obligation. His vows sprang from duty, not love. From a promise wrung from him by a dying man.

She still saw the hunger in his eyes, the need for adventure. She knew he would always put his own feelings and pleasures before those of anyone else. He would probably hate the idea of a child.

"Do not tell Oliver," Lark pleaded.

"You will tell Oliver in your own time." Juliana hesitated; then her smile grew pensive. "I made that mistake myself once, long ago," she said. "Had I told Stephen, I could have spared us both a great deal of hurt."

"How so, my lady?"

"I let myself believe the bitter words he flung at me, rather than listening to the silent words of his heart. He loved me. He wanted our child. I just did not trust that love." She seemed to catch herself and said, "Listen to me, passing out advice like old Zara."

248

The name sparked a memory in Lark. "The soothsayer? Oliver and I met her just after leaving London. She said that she knew you."

A puzzling array of emotions lit Juliana's face — shock, fear, amazement, and finally, an odd look of satisfaction. "I have known her since I was a girl in Novgorod. She came to England a few years ago." Juliana smoothed Lark's hair on the pillow.

Lark lowered her eyelashes. "I was prepared to dislike the gypsies, but I found I couldn't. I was drawn to them, especially to Zara."

Juliana smiled. "She has a kind heart. And a very powerful presence."

Lark held up both hands. "Before I quite knew what was happening, Zara was studying the lines of my palm and speaking in a strange, dark voice."

Juliana did not move; her expression did not change, yet Lark had the impression Oliver's stepmother was riveted, her attention completely caught. "What did she say?"

Lark frowned, trying to remember.

Juliana spoke another foreign word. "Ah, you are tired. I shall leave you — "

"No, please." Lark caught her hand. She felt a bashful, awkward affection for Oliver's stepmother, and she did not want to lose that. "I was trying to recall what she said."

"And do you remember?"

Lark pinched the bridge of her nose. She still had not quite absorbed the news about the child, and her thoughts were scattered. "She said I was . . . one of the three."

Juliana drew a quick breath.

"She claimed that she saw my fate before I was made. There was something about a circle."

"Yes?" Juliana's question was taut with anticipation.

"The circle of fate." Lark shrugged. "I confess I paid her little heed. She . . . disturbed me. Not by intent," she added quickly. "I felt a strange tingling when our hands touched, and she seemed so certain of all she said."

"She is very wise." Juliana patted Lark's hand. "I, too, feared her sometimes. Other times, I felt that her words guided me. I feel them guiding me now." She hesitated for a moment, closing her eyes and murmuring something in Russian or Rom, Lark did not know which. Then determination firmed Juliana's mouth.

She unfastened a large jeweled brooch from her shoulder: "This ornament is very special to me, and I want you to have it. Let it be a symbol of your welcome to this family. There is much sadness attached to this, but much triumph as well."

Lark stared, gape-mouthed, at the gift. The setting was gold, a cruciform shape thrust through a circle of gold encrusted with pearls. At the apex of the cross gleamed a large, glorious, blood-red ruby.

The ornament had a curious effect on her. The jewel glowed as if the light were shining from behind it. Lark had never seen the piece before, but it looked hauntingly familiar to her.

"It is too dear," she said. "I can't accept — "

"Then you will insult me," Juliana said

briskly, as if she had made up her mind. "I am certain you do not want to do that. This brooch is a relic of my family, the Romanovs of Novgorod." Solemn remembrances hovered in the faraway look in her eyes. "They are all gone now, my parents and brothers. They perished in an uprising many years ago. I escaped with this."

Hot tears filled Lark's eyes. "Oh, my lady, you should keep it."

Juliana shook her head, her gray-misted curls framing her face. "I have a new family and a new life. As will you. Someday, you will give it to my grandchild, and so the circle will be complete. This was meant to be; I feel certain."

The circle was begun before you were born, and will endure long after you are gone. Lark heard the gypsy woman's words as if someone had whispered them in her ear. She shivered, drawing the covers up over her shoulders. Thinking of the babe as someone's grandchild made the pregnancy painfully, frighteningly real.

"I can but thank you, then," she said after a long silence.

Juliana showed her strange etchings on the back of the brooch. "This is the Romanov family motto in Russian."

Lark squinted at the pretty, Cyrillic characters. "What does it say?"

"'Blood, vows, and honor.'"

There was something both fierce and touching about the motto. A steely certainty that made Lark feel stronger simply repeating the words.

"And look." Juliana touched a tiny catch.

251

The brooch separated, and a pointed dagger of polished steel emerged. "There was a time when this was quite useful to me." She put the weapon back and placed the brooch in Lark's hand, closing her fingers around it.

"You'll not need a weapon," Juliana said with a broad, bright smile. "After all, you have Oliver to look after you now."

★ ★ ★

"I have no idea what to do with a wife," Oliver admitted glumly to his father. A week had passed since their arrival. Lark had recovered from her unfortunate spell in the great hall. Never had Oliver felt such a sick, overwhelming, helpless fear. Seeing her carried off, pale and limp, had chilled him to his bones. When Juliana had emerged from the bedchamber to announce that Lark was fine, Oliver had nearly staggered with relief.

It was a strange and sad notion that family love proved toxic to Lark.

Cantering along beside him on a tall Neapolitan mare, Stephen de Lacey chuckled. "I never thought you'd be at a loss in regard to a woman."

They were riding the high chalk hills of Wiltshire, where the sheep were gray-white clumps against the deep, eye-smarting green of the high pastures. The air smelled richly of earth and dung and new spring growth.

Oliver reined his horse toward a treeless, grassy down that led toward the royal hunting

252

park. Years earlier, Stephen had been named perpetual warden of the holding, a high royal honor.

"I did not mean in *that* regard," Oliver corrected him, "but the other — the worrying, the *caring*."

Stephen's face hardened. "It hurts sometimes, doesn't it? To care for another more than for your own life."

Oliver heard layers of meaning beneath his father's words. Then he scowled, his riding boot brushing a scrubby hawthorn bush beside the path. "I never asked for this. Never asked for someone to love. I tell you, Father, it makes a man daft, even just the day-to-day living. Waking up to the same woman every day is a new notion for me."

"Ah. I wonder that you did not consider that before marrying Lark."

"I considered very little before marrying her." Restless with frustration, Oliver spurred his horse. The mare took off at a gallop, her long, fluid strides sailing over furzy heath and rubbled, ancient rises.

With a shout, Stephen followed, and they raced without aim across hills and ridges, finally plunging along the rich verge of the royal forest. Blue succory and dawn-hued lady's-glove whizzed past in streamers of vivid color. The breeze was keen and piercingly fragrant, and for these few moments Oliver was supremely happy.

He glanced over his shoulder at his father. Stephen had the better mare — he *always* had the better mare — but it was only slightly better, and he held back so that Oliver could take the lead. Age had silvered Stephen's tawny mane and etched lines of contentment about his eyes and mouth. In his early boyhood Oliver had seen helpless torment in that regal face. Juliana had changed Stephen's grief to hope and joy, and ever since, he and his father had been as boon companions.

Oliver slowed his horse to a walk along the fringe of the forest. No matter how fast or how far he rode, he could not outrun the events of the past weeks.

"The marriage took place against my will," he confessed. "And Lark's." He watched Stephen's eyebrows lift and then told him of Spencer, with whom Stephen had been acquainted during the reign of King Henry.

"He was a curious old man," Oliver said. "A keener mind I've yet to encounter. But for some reason, he took it into his head that Lark and I should marry." He spoke only briefly of Wynter and Blackrose Priory. He did not want to worry his father.

Stephen was thoughtful, absorbing the extraordinary tale.

"So you married her because of a deathbed promise?"

"Aye."

To Oliver's surprise, Stephen laughed, his massive shoulders shaking with mirth. "The reason was no worse than my own basis for marrying your step-mother. And I have no regrets. So shall it be with you."

"How can that be? Lark's so . . . so *proper*. And virtuous. And self-righteous. She hates the things I like. Sometimes — outside the bedchamber, of course — I think there's no pleasing her."

"But she loves you," Stephen said. "When I saw her watching you at breakfast today, the look in her eyes was filled with that bewildered wonder of a woman newly smitten." With a lopsided grin, he added, "De Lacey men are simply irresistible to a certain type of female."

"The difficult type," Oliver said.

"You would not want an easy one. You have ever thrived on a challenge."

"Quite so. Which brings me to my other problem — Richard Speed."

Stephen's brow blackened with a scowl. "Your sister Natalya is unhinged over him."

"I noticed." Oliver shuddered. "All those sighs and bovine gazes. Disgusting."

"So he's a scoundrel?" Stephen asked. "A jackanapes? Should he be sleeping in the stables?"

"Certainly not. He's a good man. I've met none better. But who, I ask you, is good enough for *my* sister?"

Stephen grinned. "Precisely. I've given the matter some thought, and I have a plan for Speed."

"If it involves donning skirts again, he'll revolt," Oliver said.

★ ★ ★

"Are you sure you're strong enough?" Oliver asked, holding open a garden gate on rusty hinges.

The look of tenderness and concern on his face flustered Lark. She clutched at the jeweled brooch that fastened her cloak at the shoulder and wondered if . . . no, he could not know about the baby. Lady Juliana had sworn she would say nothing.

"Lark?" With his shoulder propped against the ivy-covered wall, he looked boyish and appealing. As usual, his uncommon allure scattered her thoughts. Some men had beautiful eyes, others a strong and pleasing form, still others a wonderful, sculpted face and a smile that dimmed the sunlight. Oliver had it all.

"Of course." She cleared her throat and spoke loudly. "I am completely recovered." And so she was, since Juliana had taken her into her care. Before she was allowed out of bed in the morning, she drank a draft of mare's milk. Tisanes of mint kept the nausea down through the rest of the day, and Juliana insisted on a nap every afternoon.

"You're sure?" he asked.

"Quite sure. I must have been overtired from traveling. That's all."

"Completely recovered." He stroked his chin and eyed her with a frank lust that brought a jolt of heat to her loins. Without even touching her, he had the power to rouse her ardor. To make her want him with an intensity that frightened her. All her life she had been taught that base yearnings of the flesh detracted from her devotion to God. She had learned the truth of that first hand. She wanted to explain her feelings to Oliver, but she could only stare at him, helpless and spellbound, a victim of his smoldering, suggestive stare.

"You have no shame, my lord." Her cheeks burned with color.

"I should hope not." He used one hand only, reaching around behind her and sliding his hand down, teasing, his eyes laughing at her. He did this often and with startling inventiveness, whether he was chastely pressing her arm during morning devotions or snatching her into the shadows of the hall and kissing her deeply and seductively while musicians played.

"Oliver, please." She tried to keep the smile from her voice.

"Then let's go," he said at last. "I want to show you something." He put his fingers to his lips and whistled. A pack of graceful borzoya hounds came streaking across the freshly scythed yard. As the tall animals streamed through the gate, Oliver stroked their silky coats.

"My first real friend was a windhound," he said, half to himself.

Lark stepped through the gate, pausing to look up at him in surprise. "A dog? Didn't you play with other children?"

The merest tinge of bitterness hardened his smile. "Sweetheart, I did not even know other children existed."

Finding that difficult to believe, she moved along the path, flanked by a low, well-tended hedge.

"This used to be a maze," Oliver said, tucking her hand into the crook of his elbow. The dogs leaped the hedges at will, eventually disappearing into a profusion of woods. "For years, no one save my father even knew this garden existed." He gestured upward. "The hedges were tall, touching like archways at the top. Very few who blundered in were able to find their way out."

"It sounds rather dangerous. Why would your father cultivate a maze like that?"

"To keep this part of the estate separate. Secret."

He came from a family of eccentrics, she reminded herself. A father whose odd inventions made Lynacre a place of wonder, a stepmother who had lived with gypsies, brothers and sisters who pursued unusual vocations. Inadvertently she touched her stomach and wondered, for the first time, what her child would be like.

"You're certain you feel up to a walk?" Oliver said.

Though flustered, she managed to nod — thinking of the babe as a *person* had a profound effect on her. Soon she would tell Oliver. Part of her dreaded that. Although he had spoken of children from the very start, it had been teasing, abstract. He had no real desire to take responsibility for a child.

She feared, too, that he would make her stay here with his family through her confinement. She did adore his parents, but she did not want to spend so many idle months in the countryside when there was important work to be done.

She told herself not to worry. Wynter had

disappeared to London. She and Oliver had brought Richard Speed to Wiltshire without incident. When they lay in each other's arms at night, nothing in the world seemed amiss.

And so she kept her secret locked in her heart, just for a little while longer, she told herself. Just until she was certain Oliver would not run from the responsibility or leave her to bear it alone.

They wended their way along the path, and at the end, stepped beneath an arbor.

Lark gasped and squeezed Oliver's arm. "What an extraordinary garden."

"Isn't it?" They passed a line of wych elms and arrived at a fountain. Winged fish and carved dragons spouted water into a basin of blooming yellow brandyball lilies. All around them grew a menagerie of topiary, giant ivy lions, gryphons and mythical beasts with wings and horns.

"Your father's doing?" she asked.

"Yes."

"And who lives in that cottage?" She pointed to the snug, half-timbered building all draped in morning glory.

"I used to live here." He spoke without his usual jaunty, devil-may-care attitude.

There it was again, that shadowy anguish, hinting at a darkness he kept hidden from her and from the world. "Oliver — "

"Come." He took her hand and led her to the house. "When the gypsies pass through on their wanderings, they often stay here."

He pushed at the door and let her into a small, sun-flooded hall. The cottage smelled of dried herbs, which hung in ribbon-tied bunches from the rafters above the hearth. The furniture consisted of a trestle table and benches, a box chair, and a wooden settee.

"I don't understand," said Lark. "Why did you live here and not at the manor house?"

Oliver spun a geared iron device attached to a quern, and the round stones grated against each other. "I was ill and not expected to live."

"*What*?" She wanted to run to him, but he was withdrawn now, half turned from her.

"Sickly children die." He shrugged and stopped working the quern. "It happens. My father thought it best to keep me away from the perils of everyday life."

He spoke matter-of-factly, yet the revelation chilled her. At last, she began to understand why he seemed to live his life so recklessly, so voraciously. "What illness was this?"

"Asthmatic fever. An inflammation of the lungs." He walked to the hearth and fingered a bundle of greenish twigs hanging from the rafter. "The attacks of breathlessness came and went. Nothing seemed to help until Juliana arrived. The Gypsies brought this herb with them from the distant east. It's called ephedra. Boiled in tea, it eases the breathing."

"Then you recovered," she said.

He looked away. Just for a moment, just for a heartbeat, his face went dark and unreadable. Then he grinned and spread his arms. "Tell me, do I look like a man about to keel over of a mortal illness?"

She could not help but laugh. "Marry, my

lord, you are the picture of health." Yet she could not forget that, for a moment, he had not met her eyes.

Discomfited, she strolled through the hall, pausing to examine a few books stacked in a cupboard. Books on gardening and husbandry, a child's hornbook on a paddle, religious tracts.

"We both had rather strange, sheltered childhoods," she said.

"Aye. Yours turned you into a sober, solemn woman dedicated to doing the Lord's work, and denying herself anything that might smack of pleasure."

She flushed. His summation was correct. She felt compelled to reply, "And you turned out to be a rogue who would not dream of denying himself any amusement."

"Touché, sweetheart," he said in a low voice. "I am a vain and shallow man. No doubt I'll suffer the torments of the damned one day." He crossed the room and pulled her against him. "All the more reason to take pleasure where I find it, eh?"

Despite what he had said about her piety, Lark felt anything *but* pious when she was in his arms. To distract him, she indicated a narrow, winding set of open wooden stairs. "What is up there?"

"I thought you would never ask," he said with a wink. He brought her up the stairs to a narrow gallery with a ceiling so low that he had to stoop. He ducked into one of the two rooms, and she found herself in a tiny bedchamber with a low bedstead and a basin on the windowsill. Once again, she saw a shadow pass over Oliver's face as if he were the sun with a cloud briefly obscuring his radiance.

Then he grinned in that way of his that made her melt inside. "The sight of a bed always has such a profound effect on me."

She shivered.

"You too?" He lifted her coif and removed the pins from her hair. "Did anyone ever tell you that you have the most lovely hair?"

"No. Of course not." She knotted her hands in front of her and stared at the warped wood of the floor. "It would be immodest for me to listen to such talk. 'Woe unto them that draw iniquity with cords of vanity.'"

He walked in a slow circle around her like a warden unsure of what to do with a recalcitrant prisoner. "'If a woman have long hair,'" he countered, "'it is a glory to her.'" He brought the heavy masses of her hair down around her shoulders. "Isn't that how the proverb reads? 'For her hair is given her for a covering.' That said, my darling," he whispered, freeing her of oversleeves and bodice at the tug of a lace, "what need have you of clothes?"

"I had no idea you could quote scripture."

"Your virtue is rubbing off on me." There was magic in his touch, she thought, and she had no power to break the spell. God help her, she wanted to resist him. Somewhere deep in her mind, a voice cried out that she should not allow desire to rule her will.

But the voice was very faint, quickly drowned by the roar of passion in her ears.

And so she stood unresisting as he removed

262

her clothes, item by item, setting the garments on the box chair. His leisurely pace nearly maddened her. She wanted to tear at her stockings, her chemise, her shift, urging him to hurry before she burned to ashes.

But she bore it all, endured his tender ministrations because he had taught her that anticipation only honed the pleasure later.

After seemingly endless moments, she stood naked and so did he, and she stared at him. They had never made love in so private a place before. The little cottage was an intimate bower deep in a forest where no one could reach them.

He took both her hands in his and pulled her toward him. She came willingly, expecting him to crush her in an embrace. Instead he bent slightly and pressed a chaste kiss to her brow. There was a strange, golden purity in the moment, and she had a fearful thought. To Oliver, this seemed a certain form of worship.

"I cannot help but feel afraid sometimes," she said.

He lifted her hands and pressed her palm against his chest. "Afraid? Of me?"

"Of everything *but* you."

"Ah."

The pounding of his heart beneath her hand raised an answering pulse deep within her. "I worry that we won't be allowed to stay like this. Content. Free of worries."

He threaded his hands through her hair and took her mouth in a kiss that was decidedly unchaste. "My dear, the only people I know

263

who are free of worries are dead."

He laughed at her expression and kissed her again, deeply but not as hard as she wanted him to. With a faint whimper in the back of her throat, she tiptoed high and crushed herself closer.

He seemed surprised and wholly delighted by her eagerness. Somehow, she knew that few men were so obliging; that Oliver's patience, his tenderness and compassion were extraordinary. And so she dared. Dared to look upon him with a bold, exploring eye. Dared to mold her hands to the shape of him — arms and shoulders, hips and buttocks. Dared to touch her mouth to his and slip her tongue inside.

A groan of pleasure rumbled from him, and he fell back on the bedstead, bringing her with him. The bedclothes were soft with age, faintly perfumed with lavender. Her senses were fully engaged; tastes and scents and textures filled her to brimming.

Their kiss was the sharing of one breath, one heartbeat, one moment in time. She felt herself opening to him like a door flung wide, and she covered him with her body. When she kissed him, she heard only silence, and yet she spoke and he seemed to understand. It was a wordless, intimate communion, and although she never consciously formed the thought, her heart told her the truth.

She loved him.

The shattering certainty urged her to boldness; she wanted to devour him, to inhale him, to show him that her robust hunger matched his perfectly. Their warm breath mingled and fused, and her heart rose, for she felt a magic in the moment. Their souls were merging, becoming one; she was losing a part of herself yet at the same time gaining something precious and new.

"Come to me, Lark," Oliver whispered in her ear. "Be with me."

She lifted herself above him and for a moment, let the exquisite torment of anticipation linger. Radiance bathed the room, the bed, the moment, and at last she joined their bodies with a slow, settling movement of her hips.

She cried out, feeling his touch in places he wasn't even touching. She was in control, and yet she was not. With his hands and mouth he took her will from her, and she surrendered it willingly, voluptuously, wantonly.

Though it was too soon for Oliver to notice, her breasts were heavier. More sensitive. When he fondled them, she moved restlessly until a rhythm began.

And there, bathed in glowing afternoon light, on an old bed that smelled of autumns past, Lark discovered a new side of herself. She broke free of the bonds of her upbringing, the tenets and strictures that condemned her to feeble obedience. Oliver coaxed the aggressor from her, and she was soaring at last, exactly as he had once promised she would.

Afterward, she felt sweetly drowsy and lethargic, lying in his arms, her chin propped upon his chest as she studied his face. "Was that legal?" she whispered with false solemnity.

"Probably not. Shall I ask Kit?"

She slapped him playfully on the arm. "Don't you dare."

He sent her a smile, one of the soft ones that touched her heart. "You seem different."

She forced herself not to look away. "In what way?"

He toyed idly with her long hair, spreading it out across his chest and stroking it with his open hand. "You seem less worried. Less trussed up by ideas of what's proper. Less *old*."

"Less *me*," she said, trying to hide her relief.

He misinterpreted her wandering gaze, and with his fingers under her chin he brought her back to him. "That's not true," he said, his voice uncharacteristically fierce. "You are becoming more like yourself each day, and less like the gloomy and bitter little creature you used to be."

"I think I'm insulted."

"You know better than to take offense. I love you, Lark. I would never hurt you."

The lancelike rays of sunlight through the window touched her bare back and shoulders. She spoke her most heartfelt fear. "You love easily, Oliver."

"And why should I not? The members of my family, the friends I have made, inspire affection. It feeds my soul to love."

"And to be loved," she said.

"That is true."

Tell him, urged her inner voice. Tell him that you love him.

"Oliver."

"Yes, sweetheart?"

She changed her mind, decided to wait until her feelings did not bleed like raw wounds.

She wanted to be more than food for his greedy soul. She wanted him to look upon her and feel the same silent exultation she felt when she gazed at him. She wanted him to feel the same helpless wonder that nothing, no one, would ever mean as much to him as she did.

"We had best start back," she said, improvising. "Now that I am feeling well, your parents have invited guests to dine with us at Lynacre."

He blew out a reluctant sigh. "I'd nearly forgotten. All the tenants and townspeople. Also Algernon Basset, earl of Havelock. And Kit's father, Sir Jonathan Youngblood."

"You know them well?"

"Very well indeed. Havelock is the most prolific gossip in all England. No doubt he'll have plenty to say about our hasty marriage. He has probably set the date for the birth of our first child. A pity he'll be disappointed."

Maybe not, thought Lark. Before she could stop herself, she asked, "Do you look forward to that? To our first child?"

He chuckled, sitting up to don his blousy chemise. "In sooth, I had not thought that far ahead." He kissed her briefly, letting her taste their spent passion. "I rarely think past tomorrow."

"So I've noticed." She had made the right choice in not telling him.

"I want you all to myself, sweetheart." With

lascivious glee, he fondled her breasts. "I can't imagine sharing you."

She blushed and gathered up her clothes.

He laughed and continued dressing. "You will be proud to learn that my father and I have determined a way to smuggle Richard Speed out of England."

She poked her head through the neck opening of her shift. "Is it safe?"

"It shall be an adventure. We'll travel to London. The *Mermaid*, one of my father's Russian fleet, will be arriving to dock at the Galley Key in London late in the summer. After its cargo is offloaded, the ship will be careened and repaired. Then it will return to St. Petersburg by way of the White Sea. Calling, of course, at Amsterdam."

She clasped her hands together. "Where Richard can be put into the hands of Dutch Protestants." The southern Low Countries suffered under Spanish domination, but in the north, amid the icy seas and tidal islands, the Dutch fought for their freedom.

"Aye, that is the plan."

Half clad, she rushed across the room and threw her arms around him, covering his face with kisses.

He staggered back in surprise. "If I'd known it would mean that much to you, I would have told you sooner."

She laughed and picked up her petticoat, shaking it out. "The safety of the Reverend Speed means everything to me."

"Does it? Why?"

"Because of what he stands for. The work he does." She frowned, trying to twist around to tie on her skirts. Oliver stepped behind to help. Lark went on, speaking over her shoulder. "Richard has the power to affect many, and the grace to use his power to do good. To save souls. To question authority and preserve freedom."

"It is that power that the men of the Church fear," Oliver pointed out. Accomplished as any lady's maid, he helped her don her bodice and lace up her oversleeves.

She reached for her coif. Before she put it on, he turned her to face him and plunged his hands into her hair. "Such a pity to hide it."

His flattery warmed her face, and she kissed him. "You give me sinful vanities."

"A little vanity is healthy." He kissed her back. "I *do* love you."

She raked back her hair and slid the coif in place. "That's because it's easy for you to love. If it were difficult, you would not bother."

"Wench," he said, clutching his chest as if wounded. "Your tongue is a rapier. One day you'll find a better use for it."

She shook her head. He was charming and incorrigible. Hardly the qualities for a good father. If only she could be certain he would not grow restless, eager for the next adventure, she would confess all to him, about the baby, and even about the secrets in her past.

"Oliver?"

"My love, I have an idea." He seemed not to have heard the question in her voice. "Let us go abroad with Richard Speed."

269

Her heart sank. Their problems loomed before her, insurmountable as an icy mountain. "Oliver, I am committed to helping the Samaritans with their work here."

"You've served them well, Lark, but think of yourself for once. Think of it! We'd have the most splendid time, sailing the churning seas, eluding the Spanish navy, perhaps engaging in a battle or two." Laughing, he drew an invisible sword and assumed a fighting stance.

Lark turned away to hide the wistfulness in her eyes. She looked at the gardens, where the late afternoon sunlight lay softly upon the hedges and lawns, and stifled a sigh. Just when she was preparing to settle down, he wished to go off on yet another adventure — as if the past few months had not been adventure enough.

And that, she realized, was the wall between them. He lived from one reckless exploit to the next, little caring for the grinding labor and distant rewards of less dazzling pursuits. The excitement of playing husband and father would likely pall for a man like Oliver.

13

"SHE thinks I love her because it's easy," Oliver complained to Richard Speed at supper that night. In honor of Oliver's marriage, a great banquet had been set up on one of the broad greens of Lynacre. The elaborate food and entertainments had drawn a boisterous crowd of merrymakers from town and country alike.

Speed offered no sympathy, merely gazed with longing at Natalya, who watched the dancing on the torchlit tennis court. "*She* thinks I love her not at all," said Speed.

Kit, who had arrived that afternoon, made calf eyes at Belinda. Peculiar as ever, Oliver's sister ignored her suitor. The celebration had given her a chance to indulge her dearest passion — setting off explosives. "*She* thinks I love her too much."

Oliver filled their goblets with dark claret. "What a miserable lot we are." He glared across the lawn at Lark, who sat in earnest conversation with his stepmother. "Why do we let them do this to us?"

"Because our brains are in our — " Kit caught himself. "Sorry, Reverend."

"Do not apologize. I am beginning to despair of ever wearing a codpiece again." His gaze held a world of torment. Peculiar in her own right, Natalya was pacing up and down, practicing a

271

sermon under her breath.

"'Tis good to see you're human, at least," Oliver said. "I was beginning to think you were above matters of the heart."

"I was," Richard said with a desultory tug at his starched ruff. He had no choice but to stay in disguise; news had come from Essex that four men had been burned just a week earlier. Bishop Bonner's attacks on Protestants were escalating in frequency and viciousness. Kit's report from London was that the authorities had been thoroughly humiliated by Speed's escape.

"Until I met Natalya," he concluded, watching her gesticulate to make a point in her sermon. He lifted his eyes heavenward. "By all that's holy, what right has she to be so lovely? So dainty and sweet? She gives me no encouragement at all, yet I yearn for her."

Oliver thought of his sister's bovine glances and wondered how Speed could be so blind.

"Does it help to pray?" Kit asked. His attention was fixed on Belinda. She had climbed to the top of a rise in the middle of a formal knot garden. There, she and her assistant, Brock the Alchemist from Bath, set their charges. The display of flying fire would culminate the evening's entertainment.

"It helps some." Richard scowled. "But not when I see her sitting there, nattering away while I malinger here imprisoned by this ridiculous costume." Glumly he kicked at the hem of his gown. "I can't even ask her to dance."

"Patience, Richard," Oliver cautioned him. "Havelock would have a scold's day at the

272

gossip mill if he knew we harbored a fugitive Protestant."

Speed glared at the earl, a pretty man of middle years. An hour earlier, Havelock had entered talking and had yet to pause. Like a stream in a spring melt, he brimmed and overflowed with gossip.

In December of the previous year the English garrison at Calais had failed to defend itself; England's last foothold in France was lost. Those who dared, Havelock said with bitterness, blamed the queen's husband, Philip of Spain.

In March the queen went to Greenwich to await the birth of her child. Despite her stubborn delusions about the false pregnancy and the state of her own health, she made out a new will. Frightening business, that, for the document made Philip regent of England.

Recently, seditious pamphlets had flurried like a storm over London, declaring the queen a raging madwoman and cruelly jeering at her sad, fruitless marriage.

Havelock had related all this with an uncustomary lack of relish. He did love gossip but preferred the sort that titillated one's sense of the ridiculous. The current tidings simply filled men of reason with bleak despair.

Oliver had absorbed the news silently, thoughtfully. Not with his usual firebrand flare of temper. Of late he had learned to smolder slowly, to conserve his righteous anger.

Sebastian, the younger twin by moments, clapped his hands at the musicians. "If you

273

please, my masters," he called. "A new dancing measure."

A tambour rattled. The head musician whistled a salute on his pipes, and then the slow, measured beat of a pavane commenced. Simon drew a partner from the visiting ladies. Sebastian paired up with a journeyman weaver of Malmesbury. Though their friendship always caused a few eyebrows to lift and ears to redden, the sight of the two no longer created a stir. Oliver did not pretend to understand his brother's preference, but considering his own past way of life, he was hardly in a position to condemn anyone.

Speed looked mildly curious.

Oliver chuckled. "The fact that Sebastian has an identical twin makes for no end of fun. Usually at poor Simon's expense."

Stephen de Lacey bowed low before his wife; they stepped down from their table to lead the set.

Oliver caught Kit's eye. "Shall we?"

Kit blanched. "Shall we what?"

"Ask the ladies to dance, minnow-brain."

"What if she says no?"

"Then you can hurl yourself off a parapet."

"Really, Oliver, I — "

"Hsst!" Richard clutched Kit's arm. "I see trouble coming."

As splendid as one of the peacocks that roamed the grounds, Havelock was making his way toward them. He favored Speed with a broad smile, his intention clear. Oliver leaned over and murmured an order into Kit's ear.

274

Kit went from pale to red in an instant. "No," he whispered.

"You must," Oliver hissed.

"You'll owe me a blood debt." Kit rose and ungraciously dragged Richard up with him, leading the mortified, beskirted reverend to the tennis court to join the other dancing couples.

Oliver lifted his cup to greet Havelock. "You're too late, my lord. That lady is spoken for."

Havelock looked wistfully at Speed. "So I see."

"She is not your sort anyway. Too robust." Sending Havelock on his way with a brimming goblet of claret, Oliver crossed the grassy sward.

Lark had been watching the revelry from the bride's seat of honor, a canopied, thronelike chair at the high table. The massive seat, carved with leering gargoyles and oak leaves, dwarfed her. To Oliver, she looked like a little girl playing at being a princess. Her face reflected a childlike wonder; her rain-soft eyes seemed to drink in the entire merry scene. He didn't have to ask if she'd ever seen a fête before; he knew she had not. Filled with bittersweet affection, he sank to one knee before her.

His easy gallantry never failed to startle her. Oliver liked that, liked the way her cheeks flushed and her breath caught when she looked at him and put her hand in his.

"You think that's interesting?" he asked, indicating the dance on the tennis green. "Watch my sister."

Belinda and Brock were in rare form with their

incendiary display. With the basin of a fountain reflecting their artistry, they set off sizzling stars and great wheels of burning color, a *miroire chinoise* that launched a spectacular glowing bird. Each child received a pharaoh's serpent egg, a black pellet that hissed and grew into a snakelike shape.

"It's wonderful," Lark cried, and the exploding stars were reflected in her eyes. "Your sister makes magic."

"She's actually quite practical. Her formulas for gunpowder are much in demand. She put her foot down, though, when my father attempted to launch a rat into the air with a rocket tied to its back."

"He should use Bishop Bonner instead."

For a moment her solemn look deceived him. Then he realized she had made a jest, and he burst out laughing. "If anyone can draw you out of your shell, my lady Lark, my family can."

For the pièce de résistance, Belinda had fashioned several great aerial shells. But something went wrong; within seconds of the fuse being lit, the entire garden was shrouded in smoke.

Oliver waved away a thick, sulfurous cloud and felt an ominous tickle in his lungs. Panic jolted through him. Not now, he thought, forcing his chest to relax in the way that sometimes warded off an attack. Not with Lark watching.

"She must've mismeasured the charge," he said, trying not to wheeze, "or failed to mix the powder correctly."

"I can see nothing!" Lark said, squinting

through the jaundiced fog. "Is everyone all right?"

For a moment the breeze parted the smoke. He saw Kit running up the hill toward Belinda and then noticed, with a twinge of brotherly concern, Richard Speed stealing a kiss from Natalya.

"Everyone is fine," he said, willfully denying the twitching in his lungs. "Lark, I want you to stay here with my family while I take Speed up to London to await a ship to carry him abroad."

"No." Her instantaneous denial both gratified and frustrated him.

"You'll be safe at Lynacre."

"My own safety concerns me little."

"Oh. I feared you would say that. Don't you like my family? I know they're a bit odd, but they're people of good heart."

A timely wind slowly lifted the shroud of smoke to reveal the merrymakers back at their dancing and laughter. Oliver expelled a relieved breath; his lungs were clear again.

Lark looked at his family with her heart in her eyes. "They are an amazing, marvelous, magnficent clan," she said softly.

"Then why won't you stay with them?" Oliver asked.

"They are not *mine*."

He felt a curious squeezing sensation in his chest, and the feeling had nothing to do with the smoky air. "To God, Lark," he muttered, "you do tug at my heartstrings."

She laid her hand over his. "No one has ever said anything like that to me before."

"Perhaps no one's ever cared for you as I do."

A cautious joy lit her gaze. "Perhaps. But you are so capricious, Oliver. Only this afternoon you were begging me to go sailing off to Amsterdam with you. Now you want to leave me here with your parents. Tomorrow you might want to ship me away to Smyrna."

"I have given it much thought, Lark. We've been lucky, running with Richard, keeping him hidden. But if our luck runs out, the game is up."

"Game," she said, her voice harsh. "That's all it is to you."

"Lark, I — "

"I do not fight for justice to amuse myself, Oliver."

His temper sparked. "*That*, madam, is painfully apparent. However, I have decided that it's safer for you to stay at Lynacre."

"And *I* have decided to go with you and Speed to London."

"No." Lord, but the woman kindled his ire like no one else. "You can't go. And that's final."

★ ★ ★

In London, Lark and Oliver and Speed stayed at the large, elegant Wimberleigh House situated between the Strand and the Thames. To the vast dismay of Richard Speed, the Russia Company ship had been delayed. He moped like a lovelorn boy, penning letters to Natalya in Wiltshire and

278

seemingly oblivious of the tension between his host and hostess.

Lark had won the battle over whether or not she would stay at Lynacre, but Oliver extracted his price. He did nothing blatantly cruel; in fact, in her company he was his usual attentive and tender self.

But he was not always with her. He made a point of leaving for long periods of time each day.

One evening she sat in the withdrawing room on the main floor of the house, and when she heard his step outside the door, she did not look up from her reading.

"There you are, my love," he said, striding into the room with loose-limbed grace. He stopped in front of her, bent, and framed her face with his hands. "Good Lord, but you look luminous. I should have stayed abed with you all day long."

She could not help but smile. "Where were you?"

"Out and about." He went to a side table and poured himself a cup of wine. "Down to the keys to watch the shipping."

"No sign of the *Mermaid*?"

"None. And what have you been doing?"

The question never failed to startle her. He was inordinately interested in her opinions, her thoughts, the things she knew and read and dreamed about. She had never known any truth save what Spencer had told her. With Oliver, she was learning that beliefs could — and sometimes should — be challenged.

279

"Reading Erasmus." She indicated the book in her lap with a nod. "*The Apothegms*. No wonder the church has banned his writings. I think tomorrow I should read some poems to lighten my mind."

He laughed. "Read the Latin ones my brother Simon brought from Venice. The illustrated ones."

"Those are bound to be banned for an entirely different reason," she said, blushing. She felt that Oliver tried to expunge the ideas Spencer had drummed into her: that women were inherently unwise, venial creatures. That they had no thoughts of their own and that their time was best spent in menial, somber pursuits such as sewing and reading scripture.

He taught her chess and backgammon and mumchance. He gave her books by Heywood and Calvin. He watched with delight as she read John Knox's latest diatribe against women and grew furious enough to pen a challenging letter to the radical Scotsman. Some evenings Oliver read her the old, aching sonnets of Petrarch in a voice that made her melt with emotion.

Feeling her usual confusion of affection and exasperation for her husband, Lark took her sewing from the basket by her chair. She acted out of long ingrained habit rather than conscious thought, deftly stabbing the needle into the fine white lawn of the tiny chemise.

A baby's garment. Too late, she realized her error.

"Oh, drudgery!" Oliver snapped. He snatched the chemise from her and balled it in his big fist.

"How many times must I tell you, Lark, I don't want you laboring over menial chores."

It was a labor of love, but she could not tell him that. She stared in horror at his fist, wondering when he would realize what he held in his hand. He had eased the way for her to avoid telling him about the baby. Her initial reluctance was fast turning to deception.

Just as she gathered breath to blurt out the truth, he tossed the wadded chemise into the basket without another glance. Then he knelt in front of her and took her hands. "Talk to me, Lark. You're hiding something."

She hesitated, frozen with surprise and fear. She had no idea he was so sensitive to her moods and nuances. "I never meant to hide it. H-how long have you known?"

He held her gaze with his. "Since our wedding night."

She pleated her brow in a frown. "But that can't be. I — "

"Lark. The fact that you were not a maiden is nothing to me. You're mine now. That's all that matters."

Her head began to throb, her heart to pound. It wasn't the baby at all, then. This, though, was infinitely worse.

He caressed her hands lightly. "It would hardly be fair for me to condemn you, given my own adventures. Yet you seem troubled."

The color dropped from her face. Memories roared out of the past, and her heart seemed to shrivel in her chest. Like a fool, she thought she had escaped the shadows.

She could not find words to form a lie, so she merely drew her cold, shaking hands away from his and clenched them into fists on the book in her lap.

"Lark?" The very gentleness in his voice broke her heart. "I did mean what I said. Some men put great stock in virginity. In you, there is so much more to treasure."

"No," she managed to whisper at last. Her eyes drowned in tears of shame. "There, you are wrong." Her vision blurred from the tears, and she was back in that place again, that shadowy room where the dark, masculine voice called to her, taunted her, never ceasing until she yielded. "I should have stood firm, but I — he — "

Oliver's hands captured hers again. "Stood firm? But Lark, Spencer was your husband."

"Not Spencer!" She snatched her hands away and stood. The book fell with a thud to the floor. She hurried to the tall, narrow window and pressed her burning face to the glass as sickness rose in her.

"*Wynter.*" Behind her, Oliver spat the name like an oath. Then, with calm, deadly intent, he added, "I'll kill him."

"You will not!" She spun around, her hands clasped as if in prayer. "I beg you, Oliver, don't harm him."

For the first time he looked at her with suspicion. Eyes narrowed, lips taut. "Why not?"

"Because he is dangerous. Because I don't want to lose you."

He stood unmoving, his eyes bluer than the

summer sky and bright with fury. "Tell me the truth, Lark. Is your concern truly for me — or for *him*?"

"That's vile. You know I hate him."

"Then let me avenge you. He took your honor. He treated you like dirt beneath his heel. He deserves to be punished."

She sank to her knees before him. How could she explain what had happened that one night, what she had said, what she had felt? She could not, for she barely understood herself. "Oliver, I beg you. Leave this be. It is over. We never even see Wynter anymore."

He grasped her shoulders and yanked her up to face him. "You would beg me on your knees to spare him?"

"You're not a violent man. Why sully yourself with the blood of someone like Wynter?"

"Because he hurt you. Because you cringe whenever he walks into a room."

"It would hurt me more if you attacked Wynter. Don't you see, Oliver? *No one knows.* If you seek revenge, all the world will know."

"I see. And the world is not as forgiving as I am." He let go of her and stepped away, backing toward the door. "I should have been prepared for difficulty," he muttered, and she could see the barely contained rage in the color of his cheeks. "You accused me of loving you too easily, so I suppose I should not be surprised that you are making it difficult. If not impossible."

★ ★ ★

283

In the weeks following their quarrel, they never spoke of Wynter again. Lark passed many hours in the sloping, shady gardens. She remembered the first time she had come here to seek help for Spencer. Not in her most mad fantasies had she imagined that within a year she would be married to the de Lacey heir and expecting his child.

She certainly hadn't imagined falling in love with Oliver.

Or had she?

One of the first things he had ever said to her was to ask if she would have his child. His query had been impertinent, improper, and wholly inappropriate. Yet she had not been able to deny the thrill that had eddied through her like the first breath of spring after an endless winter. Had it started even then?

On a warm afternoon, she stood in the ornate river garden and watched the constantly flowing river. Barges and lighters, tilt boats and ferries, slipped past, their hulls gilded by the sun, tillers scoring the surface of the water with their wakes. It was an idyllic, peaceful scene, viewed from the rose-decked garden.

How odd to know that just a small distance down-river, the severed heads of traitors and heretics leered from the gates of London Bridge. Or to imagine the queen, fighting constant illness, still trying desperately to govern her squabbling councillors. Or to picture the hidden mews and alleyways, rife with squalor.

London festered with secret sores. Lark did not blame Queen Mary. The problems were too many and too deeply rooted to be solved by one woman — a woman who probably had no idea how much her subjects despised her Spanish advisers and chief ministers, Bishop Edmund Bonner in particular.

It was odd to think of Queen Mary pining for her absent husband, pining for a child.

Odd indeed. Mary yearned for a child she could not have. Lark had never dared to dream of having a child, and yet in five short months she would give birth.

And she still had not told Oliver. She had come so close, that night he had made her confess about Wynter. If Oliver had only stayed silent, had only listened, she would have told him.

"Froth and bother," she muttered under her breath. She plucked a daylily and ripped the delicate blossom to shreds. Oliver had taught her a few choice oaths. From time to time she would let one loose, revel a moment in the delicious wickedness of it, then repent.

It was a strange, waiting time. She had expected her growing body to give away her secret much sooner, but she retained her slim shape, save for a gentle roundness easily concealed by her gown.

The weeks had flown by at a furious rate, like leaves blown before a stiff wind. At first the excitement of being in London, the private thrill of harbouring Richard Speed, had been amusement enough. She drank it all in like a parched tree in a soft rain, and time passed, and she did not notice the days drifting by.

Until lately.

Oliver still smoldered about their quarrel, still watched her with hooded suspicion and hurt. Although he was affectionate and caring, he held part of himself at a distance. He left her much to herself, even at night, and she missed him. Ached for him.

A gloomy restlessness blanketed the entire household. Richard Speed was about to go mad from the isolation. He was not allowed to leave the house. No one was allowed in to see him. He was a man accustomed to walking out among people, to talking and preaching of great matters. Hiding for so many weeks was beginning to wear on him.

Lark marked the changes in herself as well. As each day passed, she glowed brighter with high health. At the same time, Oliver drifted farther away.

The changes were subtle, yet she could no longer deny that he stayed out later at night, drank more, laughed louder, and brooded longer when he thought she wasn't looking.

At first she attributed his mood to his anger about Wynter. After several weeks she began to think it was only an excuse. He longed to go back to his bousing and carousing, to the dark dens of Bankside and Southwark, where no one judged him, no one expected anything of him, no one cared.

Grumbling another borrowed oath, she told herself to cease her moping. The garden was fragrant with late roses and borage, and the lowering sun turned the river to a ribbon of amber.

The day held a peculiar magic for Lark. For whatever else was happening to her life, she knew unequivocally that a miracle was taking place inside her.

This morning, while lying in bed and wishing Oliver were beside her, she had felt *something*.

Low in her belly. A flutter. A lifting sensation. A quickening.

It was her baby.

Even now, hours later, the memory had the power to touch her soul with wonder. She had not grown fat; the rounding of her belly had been imperceptible. It was easy to let the weeks slip by, to put off thoughts of the future.

Today, the child had sent her a message. *I am here. Love me. Acknowledge me.*

Lark tipped back her head and let the breeze cool her face. "I promise you," she whispered as a barge nosed up against the water steps at the end of the garden. "I swear to you I'll tell him."

★ ★ ★

Oliver kept a false, teeth-gritting smile on his face as the barge pilot guided the craft up to the water steps. In sooth he felt nigh to dropping like a felled tree. The sickness was on him, worse than it had been in years.

All summer long he had passed terrible, restless nights, barely able to expel the shallow breaths he dared to draw. Each day he struggled

287

to deny the tightness in his chest.

He tried to pretend he was as hale as any Hog Lane meat cutter. Though he yearned to spend every spare moment with Lark, he distanced himself a-purpose, using their quarrel over that jack-dog Wynter as an excuse.

The truth was, he couldn't bear for her to guess he was ill. He did not want her to know he was afflicted with the murderous lung ailment.

He hoped none of the occupants of the barge would see him clutching at an iron loop behind him to steady himself. "Fare you well," he told his friends. "We shall lift a toast again tomorrow."

Egmont Carper laughed. "I'd welcome it. Your skill at primero has weighted my purse."

Oliver gave him a self-deprecating grin. "And lightened mine."

Samuel Hollins doffed his cap. "Until the morrow, then."

Oliver sent them a hearty salute and stood on the water steps, cocky as any dockside dandy, until the barge departed. Only then did he allow himself to sink back against the stone bulkhead, drop his head into his hands, and force out a long, labored breath.

"Are you quite well?"

He nearly jumped out of his skin. Scrambling to his feet, he looked up and saw her. Lark. His wife, who had grown so confident, so wise, and so radiantly lovely that she scared the hell out of him. These days he wondered if he knew her at all.

"I didn't see you standing there." He bounded

288

up the steps and vaulted the garden terrace. "Of course I'm well." He grasped her shoulders and kissed her, those soft pink lips, and when she kissed him back, he thought for the thousandth time. *She cannot truly be mine.*

And yet she was. Or at least she had been, until their quarrel. She'd been warm and willing in his bed, night after night. Taking his love, yet holding hers back. If she learned of his illness, she might never again offer the splendid comfort of her body.

She pulled away and smoothed a tumbled lock of hair back from his face. "Where have you been?"

As if she didn't know. The ale and tobacco and tavern smells clung to him like a dark aura.

"Out working for the cause, of course." That, at least, was not wholly a lie. The authorities still sought Richard Speed, and Oliver was anxious to get him out of England. He took Lark's hand and strolled up through the garden. He needed a draught of Nance's special tea, the one the Gypsies had taught her to make with the twigs of the ephedra shrub.

"Were you?"

"I was. Reverend Speed is going to pine away to nothing if we don't get him out of England soon."

"I know. Is there news of the *Mermaid*?"

"Aye, she made port a week ago."

"Oliver! Why did you not tell me?"

"She's being careened and readied to sail. I've told the ship's master to expect a femme sole bound for the Continent."

"Oh, Oliver — "

"Not to worry." To cover his breathlessness, he drew her down next to him on a wrought-iron seat. It was another of his father's inventions, a swing worked by a rope pull. It hung from a branch of the tallest tree in the garden. Nearby, a brass sundial thrust up from a clump of flowers. "I was painfully discreet."

"So you told no one."

"None save Dr. Snipes." He tugged at the rope, and the swing began to move. What he did not say was that something was not right with the plan. He could not put his finger on it, but an ominous premonition prickled at the edge of his awareness. He kept thinking of Snipes with his useless, twisted arm and his fearful eyes.

"We can trust him," Lark said, clearly relieved.

"And what of me?" Oliver asked, squeezing her hand. "Can you trust me?"

Her eyes widened. "When have I ever failed to trust you?"

When you spurned my love, he wanted to shout at her. *When you diminished it by saying it was easy.*

No sound came out. Oliver felt himself teetering on the brink of a full-blown attack. He looked at the ground; it seem to tilt madly.

His hand waved away her question. After a long moment he managed to exhale. "'Twas a foolish thing for me to ask."

Why is it so difficult for you to love me?

She fell silent. The boats slipped by. Gulls

and kites screamed over the river. The barge returned from delivering Oliver's gaming mates, and the oarsmen loitered on the quay, sharing a flask. The shadow of the sundial lengthened. Her hand was small and warm in his. He could feel her pulse beating softly against his own. He could feel his whole chest turning to stone, slowly, inch by inch, until he barely had the power to breathe.

He must tell her before it was too late. He must promise to become the man she could love. A man of honor and commitment. A man who adored her with his whole, aching, unworthy being.

"Lark?"

"Oliver?"

They both spoke at once, and she laughed. "What were you going to say?"

He kissed her brow. His numb lips could barely feel the texture of her skin. "You first."

"Oliver, I — " She drew a deep breath.

Say it, his heart urged her. *Say you love me.*

"Yes?" he asked.

"I'm going to have a baby."

The world fell still. It seemed that the leaves ceased to tremble in the breeze; the river halted its flow. Then a roaring started in his ears. A baby? A baby? Emotions tumbled through him like water over a cataract. Elation, dread, horror, and a terrible, heart-deep joy.

"A *baby*?" he heard himself say.

She sent him a radiant smile. "Aye."

"But how — "

"Oliver, really." She gave a nervous, awkward laugh.

"I mean, when?"

"It will be born come November."

"But that's less than five months from now. A baby takes what? Ten months? A year?"

"Nine months." She seemed amused by his ignorance.

He hated her having this secret knowledge. Being part of a mystery he could never share. "How long have you known?"

She looked down at their linked hands. "I've known . . . for a while. Since we first visited Lynacre."

The darkness raced at him. The attack was coming, barreling like cannon shot. Fear mingled with his rage. He clutched her shoulders and jerked her around to face him. The sweat poured down his temples.

"You are four months quick with my child and you did not tell me?"

"I did not know how, what words to say — "

"Jesu! Am I the last to know I'm going to be a father?"

"No, only Juliana — "

"Jesu," he said again, and then he could speak no more. The black nothingness engulfed him, squeezing his chest, imprisoning stale air in his lungs. Never, not since boyhood, had he felt such an intense episode coming on.

Run, he commanded himself. *Run. Don't let her see! Don't make her watch you die!*

He ripped his hands away from her and lurched to his feet.

292

"Oliver, please!" It sounded as if she were shouting down a tunnel.

He jerked away. Half blind, he stumbled along the terraced garden to the water steps, nearly collapsing into the barge. A wave of his hand commanded the pilot and oarsmen to cast off.

Even as his vision dimmed, he caught a last, shining glimpse of Lark. Her eyes wide and shattered. Her shoulders trembling. Her mouth moved, but he could not hear her words. Then she lifted her skirts with one hand, put her other hand to her mouth, and ran up to the house.

★ ★ ★

Lark could not sleep that night. She had taken supper quietly with Richard, listened to his reading of the scripture, and excused herself early.

Nance Harbutt, yammering at the two footmen who worked the windlasses of her special lift for mounting the steps, had hobbled in to see the mistress off to bed.

The plump old harridan had thumped her cane on the floor and glared at Lark. "Where is he?"

Lark had winced at Nance's accusing tone. Leaning toward Nance's ear trumpet, she'd said, "Out. I know not where." Then she had plucked courage from her own ire and said, "Your fair-haired lad can do no wrong, Nance, so you need not worry."

"Humph!" The huffy sound held a world of accusation. Nance set aside her cane and

293

began unfastening the hooks and laces of Lark's buckram bodice and velvet skirts. As she helped Lark don a clean shift, she spoke once more. "I take it you've told him, then?"

Lark tipped back her head so Nance could comb out her hair. "Told him?"

"About the babe."

Lark had whirled on Nance, heedless that the comb yanked at her hair. "How did you know about that?"

Nance guided Lark to the great curtained bed. "Lass, I've acted the lady's maid since you arrived. I've bathed and dressed you, lacing and hooking day in and day out, laundering your smallclothes. You don't show much, but I noticed."

"You said nothing."

"'Tweren't my place. But the greenskeep saw the master go roaring off in the barge, and you standing there watching with your poor heart pinned to your sleeve, and I guessed that you told him."

"Why are you angry at me?" Lark had demanded.

Nance had cradled her cheeks in palms molded by years of toil. "You should have made him stay, lass. You should have made him stay."

Now, as she remembered Nance's words, Lark pounded her fist into the bolster. "She knows better than that," Lark said aloud. "No one can make Oliver de Lacey do anything against his will."

She swung her legs over the side of the bed

and jumped down. Nance would have scolded her for going barefoot on the cold floor, but Lark didn't care. She paced back and forth, muttering to herself that life had been much simpler before Oliver.

Before she had known what it was to love a man.

Before she had known the terror and wonder of carrying a baby.

She could not deny it; her life held a richness now, a texture of deeply felt moments of pain and elation that had been missing in her former existence.

Being the object of Oliver's affection was like being given a precious gift, only to find that the true cost of the gift was to be borne by her.

She tried to summon resentment, to feel horrified at his reaction to the news. For the moment, all she could think of were the things she loved about Oliver. She saw him in all his many moods and guises — laughing at one of his own jests; peering lustily at her above the rim of his wine goblet at supper; bowing solicitously over her hand as he invited her to dance; slamming Wynter up against the wall in defense of her; proudly introducing her to his friends and family. Perhaps, in his easy, affectionate way, he did love her. But was that love strong enough to embrace their child?

The truth was, he frightened her with his wild nature, his leaps from light to darkness, from torment to joy. He seemed to feel everything more intensely than ordinary men.

Everything but a sense of responsibility for his

unborn babe, she thought, flopping back on the bed and scowling into the darkness.

She punched the pillow again and tried to decide how and when she could forgive him.

★ ★ ★

He sank into darkness, into gaping black vast emptiness where he found nothing but pain. The agony was intense: chest full to bursting, unable to expel and expand with new breath; heart pounding like a cudgel against the wall of his ribs, head so feverish that his eyes seemed to boil in tears.

He was aware of nothing else, no sound save the hiss of blood in his ears, no sensation save the blinding pain that seized and squeezed and shook him as if he were in the grip of some great, taloned beast of prey.

Time had no meaning. The moments were measured by the devastating peaks of agony and by the crazed hammering of his heart.

So this is dying, he thought, and then all thought was swept away on a great wash of torment, and naught formed in his head save a ceaseless, silent inner screaming.

The pain became a transcendent thing, and he rode high on its crest, sailing above it, weightless and numb.

Coolness spread like a balm through him, and suddenly the black void took fire, with blood-bright scarlet at the edges and the center burning white and pure. A splendid silence descended, blanketing him in a sense of fearlessness.

As from a great distance of time and space, he saw himself clearly, rakish as any common swindler, caring for naught, for no one save himself and his own pleasure. What a stupid, wasted life he had squandered on wine and women and wagering. What a desolate tragedy that the moment he had discovered true purpose with Lark and their child — when he'd learned that love was no easy sport, but a battle for the highest stakes of all — he should have it ripped from his grasp.

Of all his regrets, the most profound was that Lark would never know the sort of man he might have been.

Angry black broke through the white nothingness. The pain returned with a vengeance. He felt as if he had been dropped from a great height, landing flat on his back. The air emptied from him in a huge *whoosh*, and the world returned, amber sky and sailing pink clouds, the gurgle of the river past the hull and finally, startlingly, a voice.

"My lord?"

Oliver blinked. He saw a coarse red face, a broad brow pleated with creases of worry.

"Bodkin?"

"Thanks be to God, my lord," the pilot said. "We thought you'd . . . gone."

Oliver became aware of the velvet cushions of the barge beneath him, the river-cooled air rushing over him. He forced a smile. His lips, his fingers and toes, were numb and cold, bluish and stiff.

"Nonsense, my good man." He paused,

gasped, and hiccuped. "I was taken ill. Perhaps the oysters I ate today were bad." With shaking, chilled hands, he pushed himself up and looked around. They were in the middle of the Thames, downstream from his house, drifting toward the south bank. The oarsmen gawked at him as if he were a ghost.

"Would you like us to take you home, my lord?"

"Not yet." Oliver's mind whirled, snatching at the strange incandescence that had engulfed him only moments before. Clearly he was about to die. He knew not what sort of time was left to him, but that time was short. "We shall return after dark. And my wife is not to know of this little spell. Do you swear?"

"Of course, my lord." The oarsmen nodded.

Oliver knew he looked as ashen and exhausted as he felt. Lark would worry, unless . . .

The plan came to him, dark and deceptive as the whisper of a courtesan. Lark would hate him, but he couldn't help that.

★ ★ ★

By the time the City bells clanged and a bellman called out the midnight hour, Lark had decided to forgive Oliver. She, too, had been shocked to learn of the babe. Perhaps he simply needed time to —

"I need more *wine!*" His rough bellow accompanied the opening of the chamber door. The fanning motion caused the fire in the grate

298

to flare, and for a moment Oliver was bathed in gold.

The light outlined his unkempt hair and unfastened clothing. Forgetting her resolve to be patient and forgiving, Lark marched across the room and planted herself in front of him.

"You do *not* need more wine." She stared into his hazy and reddened eyes. "You have already had plenty by the smell of you, and nasty, vinegary stuff it was."

"Then give me good wine to cleanse my palate." He sidled over to a table. His doublet was undone, flapping like a set of broken wings. Mud from the London streets and wharves clung to his boots, and his shirt had come untucked. He had lost his cap, and his hair was a tangle of golden waves.

No one, thought Lark resentfully, should look so comely when he was in this condition. Yet Oliver did. He resembled not so much a fallen angel as one who had willingly left his state of grace.

He scowled into the jar on the table. "Not much left."

She advanced on him. "You don't need another drop. You need to go to bed."

He grabbed her and pulled her against him. "Aye. Bed. We — "

"Oliver!" She reared back, aghast. He reeked of cheap scent. The coarse, heavy odor of a woman like Clarice or Rosie. Women who sat on his lap and rubbed themselves against him.

He spread his arms, looking the soul of innocence. "Is something amiss?"

"You smell like a woman's perfume!"

"Then I'm improving. A moment ago it was cheap wine."

She stared in horror at his ashen, exhausted, handsome face. The pain of betrayal drove like a lance into her. A burning wad of sobs constricted her throat. Calling on all her years of training for self-control, she swallowed hard, conquering her tears.

"You disgust me," she said fiercely. "How dare you go out carousing on the very night you learn you are to be a father?" She stalked back and forth in front of him. "You spoke of wanting a child, but they were just words. Idle wishes. The actual fact frightens you, doesn't it, Oliver?"

He tossed his head like a lion shaking out its mane. "Hardly."

She had been schooled in reserve. The chaos of emotion he stirred in her was unnerving. She realized that she did not *want* to love him, for he drove her mad. She had to abandon him quickly, letting anger replace love, letting it insulate her from the pain.

Even as the insane thought crossed her mind, she felt a great, tearing grief. "Why can't you behave like — like a *husband*?" she demanded, ashamed of her strident voice. "Why can't you be — be — "

"The sort of man you can love?" he asked acidly.

"I didn't mean that." Although, to her horror, Lark realized that she did. "I just want you to tell me you'll love this child. Not with that

300

easy, laughing love that comes and goes like the tide, but with depth and constancy. Can you do that?"

"If there's a question in your mind, Lark, then I doubt it."

Frustration seared her like a flame. "You will never grow up! Never take responsibility for a wife, a family." She picked up the clay jug. "*This* is your wife, your refuge. You made many promises, Oliver, but I understand you now. Your promises mean nothing."

She thrust the jug at him. It slipped from her fingers and shattered on the floor. The dark liquid bled into the rushes and the cracks between the flagstones. Shards of pottery littered the floor around her bare feet.

Oliver swore. In one swift motion that belied his drunken state he swept her up in his arms. With pottery crunching beneath his boots, he stalked to the bed and deposited her there.

"So you don't trust me to honor vows made in wine?" he asked with a cocky grin. "Marry, I should hope not. I suppose you will only believe in me when I ink a vow in blood."

"Get out of here. I never want to see you again!"

Lark hurled herself facedown in the pillows. She held back her sobs until she heard him stumble out and shut the door.

★ ★ ★

Hours later Oliver crept back into the bedchamber. He stood by the bed, holding a candle and gazing down at his wife. She had cried herself to sleep. Misty tracks of dried tears marked her cheeks.

She had believed his wastrel lie, as he had planned. He just hadn't planned on hurting her.

A magnificent sense of irony gripped him. Tonight, while concealing his weakness under raw wine and cheap perfume, he had stumbled across an opportunity to transform himself from knave to hero. For some weeks he had been aware that he was being watched, followed, spied upon, though he had said nothing to Lark.

The trouble with informants, he thought sarcastically, is that they trusted one another too easily. It had not taken him long to find one whose tongue could be oiled by fine claret and whose purse welcomed a sovereign or two.

The news was bad. Bishop Bonner's informants were certain Speed would soon attempt to escape aboard a ship. All that remained was to locate the rebel and condemn him and his collaborators.

"I've thought of a way to work this," he whispered to his sleeping wife. "For you, Lark. And for Richard and even for poor Dickon." Tiptoeing from the room, he made his way to his office, found parchment, quill, and ink.

He set the candle in a holder, pushed back his sleeves, and, because he expected that his role in the escape would be the death of him, began to write a love letter to his unborn child.

Onto the page he poured his thoughts, trying to record all those things a father needed to say to a child, in case he was not here to say them.

After a time he put a sheaf of papers into a drawer and penned several letters.

By dawn Oliver had managed to throw Bonner's hounds off the scent for a few more days, perhaps. He must use his time well. He must, he thought with a self-mocking smile, be a hero even if it killed him.

14

"WHAT does the message say?" Richard Speed asked, impatiently pushing a lock of hair back under his coif. In the past weeks his hair had, to his great shame, grown quite long and curly.

Lark scowled at the smudged page. "Give me a moment. This cipher is a new one."

Feeling groggy from too much wine, too little sleep, a brush with death, and a risky conspiracy, Oliver crossed his arms on the gallery table and lowered his head. He had nearly died the previous day. He had slain Lark's regard for him the previous night. But the arrival of the letter from an agent of the Samaritans made his own concerns seem small.

Unbeknownst to Lark and Richard, Oliver had spurred the Samaritans to action, for he alone knew that time was running out. A hatter from London Bridge had sent pearled kid gloves and a swan feather cap to Lark. Though she possessed less vanity than one of the borzoya dogs, she professed delight in the gift. Then, when the messenger had departed, she had unfolded a tiny, pleated bit of parchment from one of the fingers of the gloves.

Now she frowned in concentration at the communiqué. Oliver rested his chin on his forearm and stared at her.

A baby. She was going to have a baby. *His* baby.

She looked no different from the day before, when he had wallowed in blissful ignorance of her condition. She was still his pale, dark-haired wife whose beauty was obvious only to those who loved her.

And, by God's holy light, how he loved her.

A moan of despair slipped out before he could stop it.

Lark and Speed looked at him. Both their gazes held a detached, impersonal concern that made Oliver want to scream.

"Are you ill?" Lark inquired.

"Ill with wanting you," he said, just to make her mad.

But this time she did not get angry. She simply cleared her throat, said, "Indeed," and picked up her quill to continue working on the cipher.

He watched them, the man of God and his pale disciple, and he thought how well suited they were to one another. Spencer should have chosen someone like Speed for Lark's husband.

Not a shallow, self-serving profligate who was doomed to die young.

There was a pendulum clock in the gallery. Oliver's father had designed the timepiece, a handsome affair with polished brass weights and a moon face. It ticked off the seconds like heartbeats, accentuating the tense, concentrated silence.

At last Lark set down her quill. "I've got it."

305

"Well done!" Speed exclaimed, covering her hand with his.

Oliver forced himself to pretend that it did not matter. "So?" he said in a bored voice, pretending he had no idea what the message said.

"Tonight," said Lark. "We're to meet Dr. Snipes at the Galley Key. Reverend Speed is to board the *Mermaid*. He'll sail with the midnight tide."

More silence. More mechanical pulse beats from the clock. Speed left the table and went to the broad oriel windows that overlooked the garden and river.

He bowed his head, and Oliver could see him speaking silently to the Lord. Lark sat with her hands clasped, her eyes closed. Oliver wondered what it was like to have a faith so pure and unshakable. He was beginning to think he might need a faith like that.

The only time he felt that purity of purpose was when he was making love to Lark. Which in itself was probably blasphemous enough to damn him to hell.

"You'll soon be a free man," Oliver said heartily, crossing the room to clasp hands with Richard.

Speed's beatific face, pretty as any bridegroom's, softened into a smile. "Some men yearn for freedom. Others have no idea what to do with it. I fear I am of the latter sort. I'm so used to running and hiding, to secret sermons in shadowy places, I won't be used to liberty."

Oliver grinned. "Were you a man of lesser

306

virtue, I would have plenty of suggestions."

Behind him, he heard a self-righteous sniff from Lark.

"You could write sermons and memoirs," Oliver suggested innocently. "I know that is what *I* would do."

Speed chuckled. "Indeed, my lord. So now I must go collect my belongings." But he didn't leave right away. His face grew solemn. "I don't think I've ever thanked you properly. And Lady Lark as well. Few would be so selfless and daring as to snatch a man from the flames at Smithfield and then to flee with him, to hide and shelter him for months. Thank you."

Oliver did not have the heart to tell Speed he had embarked on the adventure because he had been bored with life and lusting after Lark. At first that had been his sole driving force. Later he had found a deeper satisfaction in working against injustice. He smiled and said, "You're welcome."

Speed hugged him hard and fast, and Oliver couldn't bring himself to speak, even to tease the reverend about his skirts. Just for a moment Oliver thought of Dickon, the brother he had never known.

Dickon, who had died because he could not breathe.

* * *

Oliver obviously thought she had not noticed his affection for Richard Speed. Lark watched them as they hurried down to the water steps. The

307

two had grown as close as brothers. Different as they were they shared a rare, luminous friendship that sometimes made her yearn for a friendship of her own.

It was deep night, the sky a black velvet canopy over the Thames. London lay sleeping, with only the gurgle of the river and the occasional call of a bellman to disturb the silence.

Lark could not stop thinking about Oliver. When he and Richard had embraced that afternoon, she'd had the strange sensation of looking into her husband's mind. He claimed he did not take life seriously, that his own pleasure was more important than great matters of church and state. Yet he had, for a moment, looked utterly stricken. For once, he'd revealed a pain and depth that made her ache for him.

She shivered, not so much from the night air as from a feeling that she was drawing closer and closer to a man she was not certain she should love.

They reached the water steps, and Speed placed his small bundle of belongings in the wherry. They would use no river pilots for this voyage.

From the corner of her eye, Lark saw a shadow move. She froze and grabbed Oliver's arm. The touch must have conveyed her urgency, for he fell still.

"There," she whispered, nodding in the direction of an arbor of espaliered yew trees flanking a garden path.

His rapier hissed from its sheath as he stole

toward the shadows. Though Lark could not see him clearly, she watched his broad shoulders square off in determination, and a cold fear squeezed her stomach.

Oliver rushed toward the arbor. "Who's there?" he demanded.

A branch moved, black and jagged against the blacker sky.

Oliver disappeared behind the arbor.

Lark pressed her palms together and tried to pray, but no words would come. Instead she could only whisper, "I can't lose him. I can't lose him." A terrible rustling sound from the arbor spurred her into action. She yanked her small dagger from its sheath. She wore Juliana's gift at all times, but she had never expected to use it.

"Out of there, you lurking knave!" Oliver shouted. Even in danger he retained his sense of drama; she could hear the excitement in his voice.

A thud and a moan issued from the darkness. Oliver burst onto the path, dragging a small, struggling figure with him.

"Christ on a crutch!" he spat. "What are *you* doing here?" Even as he spoke, he sheathed his blade.

Lark expelled the long breath she had been holding. She and Richard Speed drew together on the river landing and waited.

Shoving the intruder in front of him, Oliver returned, sputtering all the while. "Oh, mistress of calamity! God's truth, you are the most vexing, vile, villainous little ronyon — "

"My love!" Richard Speed sprang up the water steps and grabbed the captive in his arms. "Somehow, I knew you'd come. I had faith."

Lark stumbled back against the stone wall. "*Natalya?*"

" — bird-witted, infinite and endless wretch — "

"Do hush up, Oliver," Natalya said, nestling her cheek against Richard's chest. She was dressed all in black, wearing a man's tunic and hose under a plain fustian jack. "I could not let you leave without me."

"What are you doing here?" Speed asked.

"I grew tired of waiting for news, so I came to London."

"None but the three of us and Dr. Snipes are supposed to know of the plan."

She kissed him on the nose. "I saw your name on the ship's manifest."

"My name!"

"Madame Vitesse." Natalya brushed past Oliver and settled herself in the wherry. "Is that not French for Speed?"

Oliver's oath was as blue and as cold as ice. "Lord preserve me from scholarly women."

"I'm going with him," Natalya announced.

"Over my rotting corpse, you saucy little giglet. You can't go." He turned to Lark. "Tell her she can't go."

Lark studied Natalya's implacable face. "She's going."

Oliver swore again and wheeled on Richard. "Tell her she can't go."

Speed boarded the wherry and helped Natalya in. "She's going."

Oliver lifted his face as if to howl at the moon. "Have the wits left all but me?" He paced up and down the narrow landing. "Richard, she is my sister, damn your benighted eyes! De Lacey women do not run off with fugitives! I'll not see Natalya shamed, her reputation ruined."

It was strange and rather endearing to see him condemn her for the very behavior he himself reveled in, Lark reflected.

"For godly shame! Nails and shackles! Disgrace, thy name is Natalya! God's lid, that she should gad about like — "

"Oliver, there is something you should know," Natalya said calmly.

" — like some hefty wharfside mutton — "

"We're married." said Richard Speed.

"My sister is a woman of honor! She deserves better than — " Oliver broke off and went as stiff as a pike. "*What*?" he roared.

"Married," Natalya said simply. "We wed in secret at Lynacre. I knew Papa would fret, so we told no one."

Oliver deflated against the stone wall. "Married."

"We are," Richard assured him.

"You unbolted rogue!" With jerky motions, Oliver rolled up his sleeves. "How dare you — "

"I insisted," Natalya said. "He wanted me to wait for him, but I refused."

"You'll wait, by God, until your *teeth* fall out!"

Natalya regarded him with a steely conviction that reminded Lark of Juliana. "My brother, you do me honor with your concern. But this is

311

my life. It is what I want. I'm going with my husband."

Oliver dropped his arms to his sides. Slowly, sadly, his sleeves unfurled. "You want to flee in the night with an outlaw."

"Yes."

"Journey to a foreign land and live in exile."

"Yes."

"For God's sake, *why?*"

"Because I love him." Natalya's voice grew husky with emotion. "Can you understand that, Oliver? Do you know what it is like to love so truly that you would hazard all? Your reputation, your wealth, your family?"

Oliver stood silent for a long time. Lark held her breath. Here was a love that would not be easy; it demanded risk and promised nothing in return. She yearned to hear Oliver concede, to say that he, too, had learnt to love in that all-giving way.

Instead he treated them to several more minutes of fine invective, helped Lark into the wherry, and cast off down the Thames.

★ ★ ★

Hours later, dawn tinged the spires of London and traced a long gold filament on the calm waters of the Thames. The wherry bumped against the water steps of Wimberleigh House.

"So they're off, then." Oliver ruffled his hair with a weary hand.

"It was decent of you to wish them godspeed," said Lark.

"My father will nail my ears to the stocks," he muttered, mooring the boat.

"Why do you suppose Dr. Snipes was not there?"

Oliver still bent over the mooring cleat, yet his hands stopped moving. She saw him take a deep breath; then he said, "I do not know."

Lark stood, and the craft listed. Oliver caught her against him. With effortless grace he set her on the landing and stepped out. His touch lingered. He held her close for a moment, inhaling deeply, his face buried in her hair. His hand cupped her cheek. "You're tired, love. Are you all right?"

They were the first tender words he had spoken to her since she had told him about the baby. Foolish tears burned her eyes, and she looked away, burying her face against his shoulder.

A lump had been lodged in her throat from the moment they had bade farewell to Richard and Natalya. Seeing them face their perilous future with such fortitude had touched her heart.

She had tried to give Juliana's brooch to Natalya as a talisman. Natalya had refused. "Mother gave it to you for a reason. Keep it well," Natalya had said.

"I shall be all right," she told Oliver.

"I thought that in your . . . delicate state . . . " His voice trailed off.

"You cannot even say it, can you?" she whispered. "You cannot even admit that I am going to have your baby."

313

"Because it scares me," he said fiercely. "There. I've spoken the truth. The idea that you will be in agony and danger scares me!" He pressed her cheek to his chest. "My mother died giving me life."

His stark honesty stunned her for a moment. "I didn't know," she said.

"Now you do."

She stepped back, catching his hands in hers. "I cannot change what is. I cannot stop being with child. I'm afraid, too, Oliver. I had no mother, no woman to instruct me in the ways of a wife or a mother."

"Lark." Her name sounded hollow as it echoed off the water. "Lark, I *will* change. You'll see. I'll prove to you — "

"Don't you understand?" She touched her fingers to his lips. "You should not have to prove anything. If you feel you must, then you should blame me. What happened with Wynter — "

"You made it clear you wish to forget that. I'll honor that, Lark. I swear I will. I'll be different, I — "

"Hush. You talk too much." A vast tenderness, mingling with relief, washed over her. "I want to go to bed."

"Of course. You're tired. You've been out all night."

"I don't want to sleep," she announced baldly. It was true. Seeing Richard and Natalya embark on their dangerous voyage had reminded her of the fleeting quality of joy and the necessity of capturing happiness when one could.

"Then what do you want to do?"

314

"Oh, Oliver. Are you going to force me to say it?"

"My sweet, sweet, Lark!" Laughing, he swept her up into his arms with a motion that made her heart soar.

She knew she would always remember this moment. It was a small, sparkling treasure she would keep in a secret place in her heart like a perfect rose pressed between old parchment pages. Many years later the memory would still stir her, like the subtle perfume and soft magic of the preserved rose.

She drank in every detail, the way the dawn light mingled with river mist to give the quiet gardens a dreamlike splendor. The lilting notes of a bird's morning song trilling in the dew-clad trees. The aroma of river and wind that clung to Oliver's hair. The mellow sadness of his smile. The thud of his heart. The promises he whispered in her ear.

It was a moment when the world seemed to hold its breath. She gathered it into herself and held fast, watching the garden drift by as he strode with her to the house.

A charwoman and a potboy in the kitchen looked up from their chores, blinking sleepily at the lord and lady as they passed.

He climbed the stairs with fluid ease and went straight to his own chambers, not even pausing at her adjoining rooms.

"I should get my shift and robe," she suggested.

He lowered her to the bed. "Love, that won't be necessary."

The deep timbre of his voice raised gooseflesh on her arms, and she found it oddly thrilling to surrender to him in this way, to put aside her usual impulse to control and direct things. He made her see the value in simply *being*, in flowing along like a leaf on a current.

As Oliver began, with deft solicitousness, to disrobe her, she sank deeper and deeper into the stream of feelings, and she floated farther and farther from reason and logic. It mattered not at all that he had taken her will from her. This time she wanted to surrender. Completely.

She felt the morning breeze through the open window swish over her body, over breasts and belly and legs Oliver had bared without effort. This, she thought, watching him shed his own clothes, the golden light limning him from behind, this is true trust — to give herself fully, holding nothing back.

And there was nothing in the least frightening about it.

Before, when he made love to her, Oliver had done so with alternating dark intensity and lighthearted humor. This time he was intent in a different way. It was as if a new facet of him had turned toward the light and she were seeing him for the first time.

He bent down and kissed her, and his lips were warm and firm, moist as the fronds of the lilies blooming in the garden. His hands glided like the wings of a bird, touching her breasts, circling them, slipping round and round as pleasure coiled inside her. He lifted his head to catch his breath, and then he bent to kiss her breasts. He went lower, fingers and mouth lightly caressing the subtle mound of her belly.

"'Tis unthinkable that I did not notice," he whispered. "Now 'tis all I see. A miracle, Lark. Nothing less. And I, like a blind beggar, failed to see it."

"I hid it," she confessed, brushing her fingers through his silky hair. "Because I was afraid."

He turned his head to press his lips to her palm. His kisses continued, swirling in ever-tightening circles, drawing closer as if he understood the need coiled inside her, waiting to be sprung. His hands eased her thighs apart and opened the petals of her womanhood, first to his fingers, then, shockingly, to his mouth. Surprise and blade-bright pleasure held her spellbound, suspended, and the coil drew tighter, unbearably tighter, until, all at once, she was flung free, launched like the birds over the Thames, airborne.

Soaring.

He joined with her, and she could hear his voice but not his words, and it did not matter. He gave himself up with a deep shudder, and he kissed her, startling her with the flavor of herself. She knew not how long the moment lasted. Eternity might be reached in the blink of an eye. A heartbeat had the feel of forever.

Lark drifted back slowly, a feather on a capricious breeze that rocked her slowly back and forth, down and down into a satiated stupor.

"Are you — " Oliver broke off, cleared his throat. She heard a curious note of wonder in his voice. "I didn't disturb you in any way? The baby, I mean."

She smiled at his awkwardness and twined her fingers through the golden-brown hair on his chest. "No, but for some reason I cannot name, I am filled with the most exquisite melancholy."

He caught her chin with his fingers and turned her face to his. "You felt it, too, then. The French say it is *la petite mort.*"

She swallowed, her heart still pounding. "No, it was not at all like dying! You have given me pleasure many times, Oliver. But this morning you gave me joy."

He smiled his dear, crooked, half-sad smile. "Then my duty will be to give you many such moments."

Fatigue rolled over her in a great warm wave, and her eyelids drooped. "Your babe is as willful as his sire," she explained. "Having his way with me. Demanding sleep when I wish to stay awake with you."

"Sleep, wife," he said, pretending brusque command. "There is plenty of time for talk later."

"Later," she whispered. "Later I might show you that I can make love just as wickedly as you can."

"Madam, I shall take you at your word," he said.

★ ★ ★

Oliver awoke from a splendid dream to a hideous nightmare. At first he could not place the muffled pounding, the odd clanging.

He blinked himself awake to see that they had slept the day away. Twilight, that shadowy dawn of night, bruised the patch of sky he could see through the window.

He wondered if a shutter flapped loose; perhaps that was the source of the pounding. He started to ease himself free of Lark. Her hair dragged like raw silk across his bare chest.

She looked so sweet as she lay there, a bare shoulder angled toward him, her lips bowed as if she was about to kiss him, her hair in tangles. Just the sight of her evoked a fragile, wistful tenderness that mingled strangely with his fierce and all-consuming need to win not just her love, but her esteem. To be good enough for the best woman in England.

Out of the blue, in the pulse beat between the pounding sounds came the thought that he would die for her.

Willingly.

With a bittersweet smile he slipped from the bed, drew the counterpane over her shoulder, then pulled on his hose and canions and boots.

Just as he tied the laces of his codpiece, the door burst open. A half dozen torch-bearing soldiers jostled into the chamber.

Propelled by cold instinct alone, Oliver drew his sword from the discarded sheath at the end of the bed.

"Oliver de Lacey," said a gruff, officious-sounding voice.

The torchlight flared and spat pitch. He

recognized the livery of the intruders. It was the white and charcoal gray of Bishop Bonner's men.

Not yet! He was certain he had more time. Richard Speed needed more time.

Oliver heard the bedclothes rustle, and he moved to shield Lark.

"I am Oliver de Lacey, Lord Wimberleigh," he said in his coldest, most vexed-sounding voice. "If you have some business with me, you must wait in the hall below, where I will receive you."

Lark gasped softly. He gestured with his hand behind him and prayed she understood. *Be still.*

The soldiers stayed planted in the bedchamber. "You must come with us," said the leader.

Oliver tried a smile that had worked on meaner faces than this. "I am flattered by the invitation," he said. Then, with the quickness of a lashing whip, he brandished his sword and had the tip pressed into the hollow of the man's throat.

The soldier looked down at the blade. "My lord — "

"I *said*," Oliver repeated, "you and your men will wait below."

The soldier took a shuffling step backward. His men crowded toward the door.

Then, seemingly from out of nowhere, a black-gloved hand delicately took the sword tip and moved it aside.

"There should not be bloodshed so early in the game," said a chillingly familiar voice.

Oliver heard the bedclothes stir as Lark sat up. A black-cloaked shape stepped in front of the soldiers.

Oliver lowered his sword. "Wynter. Fancy meeting you here. You do give nightmares a face."

15

IN the unlikely event that he lived to be a hundred, Oliver would never forget the sound Lark made when she realized they had been betrayed.

It was a sob, but different somehow — as light and airy as the wind, yet heavy with agony. In that moment, before Wynter said another word, she *knew*.

Knew, as Oliver did, that the delicate treasure of their love, the splendor of it, the unutterable bliss they had found at last, was about to be snatched from them.

Someone took the sword from his nerveless fingers. He let it go, for bared steel would not help him now. He turned and jerked shut the bed curtains without letting himself look at Lark. Then he spun back to face Wynter.

"Did they teach you such manners at court?" Oliver asked in his iciest, most hate-filled voice. "To intrude upon a private chamber?"

Wynter kept his face as still and perfect as a graven image. "My lord, you and your *lady* gave up all rights to privacy when you turned traitor."

"Traitor! Where in God's holy name did you get that notion?"

"And heretic," Wynter added.

Oliver was starkly aware that he stood bare chested and defenseless before a party of armed men. There was a time when he would have welcomed the challenge of eluding them. He would have led them on a merry chase through the streets and byways of London, enjoying every perilous minute of it.

But not now. Never again could he run, leaving care in his wake. He had Lark to worry about. Lark and their unborn child.

He narrowed his eyes at Wynter. "By whose authority come you here?"

A cold gleam of triumph flashed in Wynter's eyes. He held out a parchment. Edmund Bonner himself had signed the warrant.

"I'll need to get some things." Oliver knew what awaited him, yet he felt no panic. Indeed, he had expected this, had known the risks of giving Richard a chance to get away. Still, he had not planned on being arrested so quickly. He planned to deny everything, to keep denying it, even in the face of irrefutable proof. For now, he had much to lose by implicating himself.

"You and your men may wait below," he said.

Wynter's gaze flicked to the open window with its broad view of the gardens. Oliver almost laughed. Aye, the old Oliver would have cheerfully fled. The present Oliver realized, with a calm stoicism that was new to him, that he must take a stand.

It came to a war of stares between him and Wynter. As he looked into that beautiful, ascetic face, into those blank, dark eyes, Oliver came to realize that he had finally found a fight he might not win.

And then the impossible happened. Wynter blinked. He said, "We shall wait below." He and his men withdrew.

Oliver stood unmoving. He had compelled Wynter to bow to his will. How? Had he suddenly unearthed some new strength in himself?

The rustle of the bed curtains intruded on the moment. Oliver went to the bed and gathered Lark into his arms.

For long moments neither spoke. She was still warm from sleep; her lips were still full from his kisses; the faint, earthy scent of their loving still clung to them both.

Oliver wanted to forget — or not to care — what the future held, but those days were over. He tangled his fingers into the dark silk of Lark's hair. He kissed her mouth, tasting a hundred years of love and yearning and regret.

"We have been betrayed." His voice was amazingly steady.

"Oliver, I'm afraid for you!"

"Don't be." He forced assurance into his tone.

"Does this mean Richard Speed has been taken?"

"Absolutely not." Oliver knew he might be lying, but he didn't want her to worry. "If they had him, they'd not bother with me."

"Who could have betrayed us?"

He said nothing. What he had done was not so much a betrayal as a calculated diversion. He had known the risks. He was prepared to suffer the consequences.

Lark shuddered and reached for her shift. "Could Natalya have let something slip?"

"No," he said, too quickly. "I told you, Lark, if they knew where Speed was, they'd not be here."

She lifted the wispy lawn garment, and he took it from her.

"Wait," he said. "I'll help you. But first, let me look at you."

She sat unshrinking, staring back at him with bewildered eyes. She did not understand, he realized. Not fully. Not yet.

"My God," he whispered, struggling to keep his voice steady. "You are more beautiful than the moon." And so she was, glowing and full, rounded, her milk-pale breasts tipped dark brown, her belly gently increasing with their child. Her hips, perhaps wider, prepared to accommodate the new life. Her face held a look of wonder, and he touched her cheek.

"I know not how to fashion words for this," he said at last. "If I merely say you are beautiful, you won't understand."

Her smile was bashful. "I shall attempt to endure it."

He brushed his lips over her brow. He, who had always been so glib, could not describe the way he felt at that moment. She *was* beautiful, yet the beauty somehow came from his own heart. His love was a filter, a pane of colored glass held to a candle flame. It did not change what he saw, but how he saw her.

Instead of speaking, he kissed her, holding her with tender ferocity. Then he helped her don her shift and lifted her from the bed. They washed at the basin and finished dressing.

Lark was combing her hair with her fingers when she asked, "What do you suppose will happen?"

Was it possible she did not know? Perhaps in her fragile state she was unconsciously protecting herself from the truth.

He dropped a light kiss on her nose. "I'll be asked a few questions," he said. "Given my status, and that of my father, they will not dare to detain me over long. And of course, I was home with my beautiful, expectant wife. What know I of phantom ships that sail out with the tide in the dead of night?"

"Indeed," she whispered crossing the room, embracing him with a strength he had not known she possessed.

He kissed her one more time, lingeringly, committing to eternal memory the feel of her in his arms, the cadence of her breath and heartbeat, the softness of her lips.

He wondered if she could taste his love and his regret as she returned his kiss. He wondered if she could sense the tears he would not shed, or if she could hear the one word he absolutely refused to utter.

Farewell.

★ ★ ★

"I warn you, friend," Oliver said from his corner of the dim London Tower cell in an area known as the Lieutenant's Lodgings, "I have been six

326

weeks without companionship."

The new inmate shrank back against the opposite wall. "Sir, I am a modest man — "

Somewhere, from the rank depth of despair, Oliver summoned a bark of laughter. "Good Lord, man, it's not *that*, of all things. Your virtue's safe with me." He lifted his hand to shove back a hank of overgrown hair. "I might, however, talk your ear off."

"Talk my — " The newcomer shuffled forward, his feet mussing the straw on the floor. "Rakes and rabble!" The prisoner pushed back his hood. "'Tis you, Oliver!"

"Phineas!"

Snipes leaned back against the wall and sank down beside Oliver. He held out one hand in front of him — the hand on his healthy arm. The fingers were flat and misshapen, running with pus. "I tried to stay firm," Snipes said miserably. "To God, I truly did. And so I held fast un-until they got to my thumb." He could barely move the mangled digit.

"We all have our limits," Oliver said quietly. That, too, was new to him. The peace. The resignation.

The sense that they could not touch his soul.

Of course they couldn't. His soul, his heart, his entire being, belonged to Lark.

Perhaps that was where he got his newfound strength. In the fact that he had already suffered the worst torment they could inflict on him — taking him from Lark.

"How much did you tell them?" he asked Snipes.

Phineas hunched his shoulders, making himself look smaller. Older. Broken, "All that I knew."

A chill rushed over Oliver. "All?"

He nodded. "The safe hold in Shoreditch. My own sweet wife's activities in the Society of Samaritans."

"Damn you, Phineas. Your wife!"

"It was the pain. I could not bear it." His crippled arm stirred. "I failed, years ago, when I was young and strong. All my life I carried this useless appendage as a testament to my own cowardice. I went back to helping prisoners escape. It was a form of penance, but it couldn't last. It were better that I died at their hands than betray innocent people."

"Curse you, Phineas. If I were not so squeamish at the sight of a traitor's blood, I'd finish the job myself."

"And I'd thank you for it, my lord."

The quiet declaration hung between them, echoing off ancient stone walls that bled with moisture.

At last Oliver forced himself to speak. "Go on. You implicated your wife. What else?"

"Why, yourself, of course, my lord, which is why you are here, I presume."

It was not, but Oliver didn't correct him.

"I told them you had helped Richard Speed to escape burning at Smithfield and to flee England. I told them how and when he departed."

Oliver let out the breath he didn't know he had been holding. Thank God for small favors. His instincts had been correct in giving Snipes the wrong information and in changing the ciphered message.

"My lord?" Snipes's voice was thick now with remorse.

"Aye?"

"I do fear that I named the Lady Lark."

Rage and terror boiled up in Oliver, so fast that he could not speak. Finally he choked out, "You snake-bellied recusant. Implicating *women* — " He broke off, crushing his hands together and forcing himself to stay where he was. Killing Phineas in a rage would serve only to make Oliver a part of the madness that held all England in its grip. Phineas would suffer, aye, with the agony of what he had done. Self-hatred was a far greater punishment than any Oliver could inflict.

For now, Lark was safe. He'd had a chance to smuggle urgent letters to his family. They would protect her. He had to believe that.

A new horror struck Oliver. Had Phineas known of the trip to Hatfield, the visit with the Princess Elizabeth? If the queen knew of her half sister's Protestant leanings, she would never approve of the current succession.

Elizabeth had been careful to show no favoritism to either the queen's or the Reformed faith. Queen Mary, willing to give her sister the benefit of the doubt, chose to believe that if she took the throne, Elizabeth would practice the Catholic faith.

If she learned otherwise . . . Oliver remembered Lady Jane Grey and inadvertently touched his neck. His former taste for danger seemed foolish now that he had found Lark. Now that he had so much to lose.

Many long hours later Oliver managed to sleep, after a fashion, but it was not restful. His troubled thoughts dissolved into a black storm of nightmares, and when someone shook him, he came awake cursing.

"Oliver! It's me! Kit!"

He blinked and rubbed his eyes. "Kit? What the devil are you doing here?"

Kit glowered at the stout wooden door with its tiny iron grate. "The same thing you are, my friend."

Oliver aimed a glare at Snipes. "I suppose you named Kit as well."

"My lord," Phineas said in a broken voice, "you do not know what they did. The brands, the irons. I know it will mean little to you at this point, but I am sorry."

"Lark!" Oliver whispered, crushing his hand into a fist and pounding the floor. "Kit, he named Lark!"

Kit swore, then peered at him through the gloom of the cell. "If it's any comfort, Belinda is with her."

"Lark." Oliver formed her glowing image in his mind. "She saved my life, Phineas. You were there that night. You saw, you were a part of that. And now you've betrayed her!" he roared at Snipes. "Were it only her you condemned, it would be a sin past redemption. But she is with child, Phineas, damn your black soul. *With child*."

"Then she can plead her belly," Kit said.

330

"Make the reprieve last for months. I've heard" — he lowered his voice — "the queen is not expected to live out the year."

"Lark doesn't have months." Oliver felt fear pushing like bile up into his throat. "By now it is down to weeks."

Kit made a sound of astonishment, then sat silent for a time. Phineas's weeping filled the chamber. After a time he went still, his breathing the labored cadence of exhausted sleep.

"Why have they not questioned me yet?" Oliver wondered aloud.

"Such things take place in due course. I wonder when they'll question me." Kit rubbed his unkempt hair. "Oliver, it hardly matters now, but I did find out that Spencer planned your marriage months ago."

"What do you mean?"

"As soon as he realized he was dying, he began to look about for a suitable way to secure Lark's future. I think he knew about the Common Recovery right from the start, even arranged for us to 'discover' it."

"You're mad. Why would he choose me, of all men, for Lark?"

"He liked your father. I expect he saw what you were beneath it all."

"Oh? And what is that, pray?"

Kit's cracked lips curved in a smile. "Come now, Oliver. You do love her well. Better than I thought you capable of."

"Is that so?"

"You wanted the world to see you as a frivolous man. Quick to love, for certain, but

331

quicker still to lose interest and move on. Who would have thought that Oliver de Lacey, notorious rakehell, would come to share so deep a love with a woman like Lark?"

Oliver wished he could touch his friend then, enfold him in an embrace and tell him what the many years of their friendship had meant to him. Instead he said, "Kit, I want you to tell me what to do."

"Do?"

"When they question me. I want to know how to keep them from arresting Lark."

Kit thought for a long while. "I cannot be certain, but perhaps there is a way."

"Then tell me! By God, tell me!"

"Oliver, I fear — "

"What?"

"If you do this, it might save Lark but cost you your life."

The words, at first, had little meaning to Oliver. His life. So what was that without Lark, anyway?

"Kit," he said, "tell me exactly what to say."

★ ★ ★

Lark caught Belinda's hands in hers. "I try not to despair, but it comes over me in waves."

"I know," Belinda whispered, bending her blond head so that the sunlight through the office windows touched the golden tresses with fire. "I feel it, too." She looked down at the letters scattered across the table. "As soon as

I learned what had happened to Oliver, I sent word to our parents. But their ship had already left Bristol."

Lark nodded. "Of course, they would be going after Natalya. It was a foolish and dangerous thing for her to do, marrying in secret, leaving England with a fugitive. Yet part of me admires her courage." She took her hands away and mindlessly shredded a bit of ink-blotched parchment. "Imagine, leaving everything you've ever known — family and home — to be with the man you love."

Belinda smiled wistfully. "You or I would have done the same."

Lark shifted on her wooden chair. The baby, growing fast and active these days, pushed a tiny, miraculous appendage against her stomach. She felt such a torrent of love that she nearly cried out with the sharp, sweet pain of it. "Belinda," she said, "I would give anything to be with Oliver now. He was not happy about the baby when I first told him, but when the shock wore off, he shared my joy."

Belinda, tall and golden like her brother, burst into tears. "At least you had that joy to share!" She grabbed one of the myriad, desperate letters they had penned and tore it to bits. "How dare they take my Kit! How dare they take him while I am yet a maid!" Then she could speak no more, for the sobs overwhelmed her.

Lark levered her ungainly form up and knelt on the bench beside the weeping girl. They clung together until Belinda took a long sniff and wiped her face with her sleeve.

"How unforgivably selfish of me," she said, steely once again, her de Lacey pride pushing past despair. "To lament my virginity while Kit and Oliver rot in the Tower."

Lark sat back on her heels. She squared her shoulders. No amount of grief would help them liberate Oliver and Kit. Belinda was near to breaking, had been for days. Trying to pull her out of her melancholy, Lark handed her a silken handkerchief and asked, "How do you do it?"

"Do what?"

"Manage to look beautiful even as you weep?"

Belinda sent her a thin smile. "Having a face some might find comely is no great virtue. It means nothing save perhaps more interest from men than I crave." She stroked Lark's black hair. "In ten years' time, I'll not be so comely. But you, my sister, will still have that look deep in your eyes."

"What look?"

"The one that glows with . . . I'm not sure, but it was one of the first things I noticed about you. You're calm and peaceful, as if you know exactly who you are, where you're going, and what you want."

Lark laughed for the first time in weeks. "I know nothing of the sort. Oliver's love gives me strength," she said, touching the brooch Juliana had given her. She had worn it like a talisman each day since they had taken him. The days had stretched to weeks, now months, and still she had not found a way to see him. Officially he and Kit were 'guests of the Crown' and as such were entitled to decent lodgings and meals.

Yet Lark knew better than to trust the word of officials who answered to Bishop Bonner.

She wished she had told Oliver her true feelings, confessed that she loved him as he was, not as she wanted him to be. She wished she had told him that the way he loved her was enough, more than enough. Instead he had gone to prison believing she still did not trust his love.

"Belinda," she said, "I want you to see something." With shaking hands she opened the coffer on the table. Inside were bottles of ink and sharpened nibs for the quills and styluses. In the very bottom of the coffer lay a well-worn parchment covered in Oliver's scrawling penmanship.

She had read the words until she no longer had to look at the parchment to know what he had written there. The letter was meant for his child, but the tone of it frightened her. He wrote advice and endearments as if he did not expect to live.

In typical forthright fashion, Oliver advised his child to eat his vegetables and avoid picking his teeth at table, to honor his mother, and above all, to enjoy life. That always made Lark smile. It was the simplest of ideas, yet until she had met Oliver, true happiness had eluded her.

At the end of the missive, the tone changed. 'When the breeze caresses your cheeks,' he had written, 'when the waves meet the shores, it shall be my kiss, my touch, ever so gentle upon your brow. I am that near to you, my child. You will never be alone.'

Belinda shook with quiet sobs. Reverently she folded the letter and placed it back in the coffer.

"He knew he was going to be arrested, didn't he?" Lark asked.

"Perhaps. But — " Belinda bit her lip, then took a deep breath. "It might be his illness, too. He doesn't speak of it much, but it plagues him still from time to time."

Lark shivered. "He wanted me to believe the sickness no longer troubled him. If he was falling ill when he wrote this, being in prison could mean — " She dared not finish the thought.

Belinda pounded the table with her fist. "I do not understand how your pleas to see your husband can go ignored." She glared at all the letters. They were copies of copies, sent in a daily barrage to the queen at Hampton Court, to Bishop Bonner in London, to the warden of the Tower, to Dr. Feckenham, dean of St. Paul's. They had written to Princess Elizabeth at Hatfield but had not yet sent the letters. Those were a last resort, for to imply any familiarity with her was mortal danger for them all.

Lark heaved a great sigh. "I receive no answer save 'Wait and see.' I weary of waiting."

She and Belinda stared at the letters to Princess Elizabeth. There were three of them, all in cipher, all small enough to be rolled and tucked into a glove or bauble.

"Dare we?" Belinda whispered.

"We must. I've half a mind to raise an army and storm — " Lark stopped talking when Nance Harbutt poked her head into the office.

The elderly retainer cupped her hands around her mouth. "A caller to see you, my lady."

Lark and Belinda exchanged a glance. As one they picked up their skirts and hurried from the room. Nance shooed them toward the great hall.

They stopped outside the double doors. Belinda straightened Lark's coif. "Perhaps you finally have permission to go to the Tower."

Lark brushed back Belinda's unruly curls. "I pray so."

She pushed the door open, stepped into the room, and gasped. After a moment she found her voice and spoke his hated name.

"Wynter."

Just for a moment, Wynter, whose glib tongue could cut like a knife, stood speechless. His shining onyx eyes focused on Lark's midsection.

She felt the ugly threat like a noxious breeze, and inadvertently her hands folded over her belly. At the same time she thought of the dagger brooch fastened at her shoulder.

With cold, ruthless certainty Lark knew she would kill to protect her child. She imagined unsheathing the dagger, plunging it into Wynter's neck or chest, and felt not even a twinge of distaste.

There was nothing, she realized, as fierce and unforgiving as a mother's love.

At last Wynter smiled and performed a practiced, courtly bow. His ever-present rapier touched the flagstone floor briefly with the movement.

"Ladies," he said, including them both with a nod.

"Do not pretend courtesy with me," Lark stated. "When last you disturbed the peace of my home, you wrongfully arrested my husband. When will he be released?"

"That depends on him. He's a danger — to you as well as to the True Faith."

"Why have I not been allowed to see him?" she demanded. Her voice was that of a stranger. It rang with assurance.

Wynter raised one eyebrow. "So. The mouse has turned into a lioness. I am impressed."

"I," she shot back, "do not care. I want my husband back."

"My lady," Wynter said, "you must come with me."

His words echoed those spoken to Oliver the last morning she had seen him, the morning she had discovered the depth of her love for him. "Am I under arrest?" she asked.

"Certainly not. I am taking you to see your husband."

Belinda, as haughty and beautiful as a foreign princess, glided forward. "She'll need to collect a few belongings."

Only Lark caught the desperate flash in Belinda's eyes and felt the subtle trembling of her hand as it grasped her own.

The letters. Their last hope.

"Call for your belongings, then," Wynter instructed.

"I'll fetch them myself," Belinda said. "'Twill be quicker, and I'm certain you're eager to be on your way."

Some time later, as sorrowful retainers

338

watched from the top of the garden, Wynter stood on the quay with Lark.

"Lark?"

The hesitancy in his tone startled her. She had always been cowed and uncertain in his presence, not the other way around.

"What do you want?"

"Forgive me."

She wanted to laugh and cry and scream with rage. There had been a time when she had wanted to like Wynter, to understand him, to win his regard. But that was long ago. This man had taken her husband from her at the moment she needed him most.

She stared directly into Wynter's handsome, austere face and said, "Tell me, Wynter. Why are you permitting me to see Oliver now? Why not when I first requested it?"

Wynter held himself very still for a moment. His face was as heartbreakingly beautiful as ever. "Because," he said in a soft, kindly voice, "he has been condemned to die."

16

OLIVER stood chained at the wrists, his arms spread-eagle and attached to two wooden beams. He tried to remember when they had removed him from the Lieutenant's Lodgings and conducted him to this cryptlike place in the bowels of London Tower, but the days had blurred in his mind.

A fire roared in a crude, rounded grate. Its purpose was not to keep Oliver warm, of course, but to heat the branding irons.

The radiance of the fire glared off other horrors: the Iron Maiden, designed to crush a man into compliance. The pincers and the strappado and the thumbscrews. He saw other instruments so unique, so new, and so evilly ingenious that he did not even know what they were called.

Yet by now he knew them well. The great hook had held him aloft while they had interrogated him about the mysterious disappearance of Richard Speed. The iron boots, with their interior spikes, had enclosed his legs and feet while they had questioned him about his visits to Hatfield. The glowing brands had rendered him nearly senseless with pain as the interrogators had speculated on his father's sudden voyage abroad.

Exhausted well beyond the ability to sleep, Oliver stared into the heart of the fire. They had

deprived him of rest in order to weaken him, and that — though they knew it not — had been a mistake. It was during these moments that he found his greatest strength.

At some point it had ceased to matter that he was a prisoner, that he had been tortured. He had taught himself to stare into the fire and fly away, far away, like a bird. He could soar beyond their reach, where he was free, truly free, and safe.

They thought, of course, that he was going mad. Perhaps he was, but it was the keen, intelligent insanity of sheer determination. They would not break him.

They tried to get him to admit that Lark was a Samaritan, for the panicked babblings of Phineas Snipes were not conclusive enough for Bonner's men. The mood of London was shifting; outcries against the horrors of Smithfield crescendoed, and the council had to proceed with caution.

Poor, broken Snipes had mewled and pleaded for release from the Tower, but to no avail. A fortnight ago he had managed to hang himself from a rafter. His pitiful death had not even roused Oliver and Kit from sleep. Snipes had gone that quickly, that willingly.

Phineas was a coward, but he was not stupid.

There were some things, Oliver now knew without question, that were worse than dying.

Of late, he had experienced his share of them.

Even so, the torture had the most amazing effect on him. He grew stronger in his will. At first he had tossed out cocky answers, claiming responsibility for every misdeed from the murder of the boy-princes in the reign of Richard III to bringing the sweat upon London.

He had confessed to every crime save those that would incriminate Lark.

The amusement in toying with his captors had quickly palled.

Now he simply waited for the next wave of torment. Perhaps the new session would bring the oblivion of death. He tasted the bitter irony of it. He had always been resigned to dying young. The fact had never concerned him overmuch. Now, though, he had a reason to live. He had Lark.

He knew not whether it was day or night, for the chamber had no windows. His legs gave out once or twice, and he stumbled, but his arms, chained and spread wide, kept him up off the floor. The posture gave him a new appreciation for the agonies suffered by Christ on the cross. But as Oliver slipped deeper and deeper into a dreamlike state, it was not the Lord's face he saw, but Lark's.

Later, with a creak of rusty hinges, the low door with its curved lintel swung open. In marched a troop of bodyguards, stationed like curtain walls around the man they protected.

"Lord Bishop Edmund Bonner," announced one of the soldiers, staring straight ahead.

A black-and-scarlet-robed man stepped forward. Oliver watched in fascination, for this was his first face-to-face encounter with the dread Bishop Bonner.

It was interesting that a man credited with such inhuman cruelty could look so ordinary. Coarse, even, like a workman on the London docks. The florid face and plain brown eyes that studied Oliver, lingering on his bare, lacerated chest, could have belonged to anyone. Bonner might have been a farmer bringing his goods to market, an ironmonger, a seaman, or a lading clerk at Gravesend.

Somehow, the fact that this wholly unremarkable man was responsible for death and torture, for the haze of flesh-scented smoke that hovered over the West End of the City, made him more frightening than the devil himself.

He trundled in a wide circle around Oliver. "I was a prisoner myself. More than once. First at the Marshalsea and then right here in the Tower."

"Feeling nostalgic, are you?" Oliver inquired, quirking an eyebrow.

Bonner completed the circle and stopped in front of him. Almost as an afterthought, he backhanded Oliver hard enough to stir a flurry of stars before his eyes. Oliver merely blinked, refusing to offer even so much as a grunt of protest.

"Faith and constancy proved to be my salvation." Bonner fingered his heavy gold chain of office. The gleaming ornament was attached at each shoulder and draped across his chest, bright against his black-and-blood-red garments.

"My lord," the bishop continued. "I am told you have not yet unburdened yourself of your many heresies. You have not yet comforted your soul against the bosom of the True Faith."

"Ah," Oliver said in a voice rusty from screaming. "Tell me, would this True Faith happen to be the same one that condemns innocent men and women to death?"

The men of Bonner's lifeguard put their heads together to whisper amongst themselves.

"Innocence," Bonner said, "is a matter of opinion. And here, only my opinion counts. I can — "

"You can burn in hell." Oliver's own words startled him. Once, almost a year ago, he had groveled and pleaded for his life. Now here he stood, chained like an animal, beaten but not broken. Not even close to broken.

Lark, he thought, his heart rising on a surge of love. Lark had taught him that a man needed a place to stand, a purpose to drive him.

"That is your final word, my lord?" Bonner asked.

"It is."

Bonner's dark eyes were hooded, as if he concealed some secret knowledge. He sent a nod to the guard by the door.

"You might find," Bonner said, "that you'll change your mind yet."

His silent entourage melted from the room. Only the bishop and the warden remained. Bonner's ham face held a look of expectant relish.

The fire snapped and flared, and a coal rolled out onto the hearth. Hearing a gasp from the doorway, Oliver looked up. His heart seemed to stand still.

"*Lark*," he whispered.

She stood riveted, pale with shock. A voluminous hooded cloak wrapped her, and he had the fleeting, insignificant thought that summer had turned to autumn during his imprisonment.

In that frozen moment he saw himself through her eyes. His upper body lay bare and furrowed by wounds. Chains pulled his sinewed chest and shoulders taut, and his flesh ran with cold sweat. His hair had grown long and lank, his ragged beard was unclipped.

Rousing himself from shock, Oliver yanked at his bonds, feeling the cold burn of the iron manacles, glad of the pain, glad to feel something other than fear for her.

Bonner broke the silence. "Take him down," he ordered.

Keys clanking, the warden came forward. The manacles fell away. It took all of Oliver's strength to remain standing. He swayed, his vision blurring as he watched Bonner and the warden disappear through the door.

The moment the door thudded shut, Lark rushed to Oliver, an anguished cry on her lips. She caught him against her.

She felt sturdy and clean, unbefouled by the corruption of imprisonment.

"Don't try to stand, my love," she said.

As one, they sank to the floor. Oliver felt as if his every joint were on fire, but he ground his teeth together to keep from crying out. Lark

345

untied her cloak and removed it, spreading it out near the fire.

She looked at the burns and lacerations on his chest and back. She seemed to study each individually, and when she saw him watching her, she said, "I feel each one as if it had been inflicted on me." She pressed her lips to his shoulder, which bore the scar of last week's flogging. "I cannot look at all the wounds as a whole yet, for if I do, the pain will be too great."

"Ah, Lark." They huddled close, then, silent, hearts and eyes saying what their voices could not.

In time, he cradled Lark's face between his hands. Was it only last winter that she had saved him from the hangman? "Everything about you is the same, yet not the same," he said.

She gave him a tremulous smile and passed her hand down over her abdomen. "I trow you do not mean the obvious."

He kissed her brow, right at the hairline, and inhaled deeply. She smelled as fresh as gillyflowers in springtime, and he would always think of her this way, warm and clean and new.

"Nay," he said. "When first we met, you were a stubborn, ill-tempered, self-righteous little mort."

She tried to laugh. "So I was. I suppose it was my way of hiding."

"You simply had no trust in yourself." His tone deepened and softened in case Bonner's men had their ears pressed to the door. "I saw

346

you defeat a brigand, save condemned men, and teach the Princess Elizabeth a lesson in humility, all with no notion that you were doing anything extraordinary."

He slid his hands down to cup her shoulders. A thousand times he had held her like this in his dreams.

"Look at you now." He tried to keep the catch from his voice. "Glowing. Self-assured."

"Then that is even more extraordinary," she said. "Never in my life have I been less sure of myself."

He drew her against him and simply held her. It hardly seemed possible that he had once thought holding a woman without bedding her to be a waste of time.

That was before Lark. Back when he had believed love was something to be given out like coppers tossed to the crowd at a pageant.

Now he knew better. Love was too precious a gift to be flung about. Its true value could only be known when it was hardest to give — perhaps to the person who least wanted it.

"Why do you smile?" asked Lark, caressing the line of his jaw.

"I was remembering the first time I tried to make love to you. Being refused was a new experience."

She opened her mouth, looking apologetic, but he stopped her from speaking. "You were right to refuse me. I had to earn my place in your life." Looking into her eyes, he fancied he could see the rain.

She blinked fast. "I found the letter. The one

you wrote to our child."

He blew out his breath. "And?"

"I would hate you if I did not love you so much!"

"Love me? But you said — "

"I was wrong." He heard the bitter edge to her voice. "I thought I was a learned lady. Able to quote scripture as easily as I could spin and weave." Finally she drew a deep breath. "Nothing has prepared me for the way I love you."

From the blackest despair shone the brightest joy. "Say it again, Lark."

"I love you. Does that come as such a surprise?"

"You said you could not. That I was false and shallow. That I failed to love with my whole heart."

"'Tis I who failed," she said. "I wanted you to change. To become solemn and logical and conventional. Now I realize I love you because your heart runs wild. Because you laugh and tease and defy convention. Because you are everything I am not. I do love you, Oliver de Lacey. I do love you with so much of myself that there is none left to ever doubt you again."

He wondered if she had any idea of the value of the gift she had given him. She made all his suffering worthwhile, gave meaning to everything he had ever done, ever been.

"Why did you not tell me about your illness?" she asked.

"What illness?"

"Belinda told me the asthma plagues you still.

You let me believe you had outgrown it, yet you still have attacks."

"You would have worried."

"You had a bad spell the night I told you about the baby, didn't you?"

"Aye."

"You doused yourself with wine and pretended to have gone carousing rather than admit you were ill."

"Aye."

"For pity's sake, *why*?"

He took her hand in his and and stroked it. "That's just it, Lark. Pity. I could live with your contempt more easily than with your pity. There is nothing to be done about my condition. From the time I was a babe, my father consulted physicians and astrologers, healers of all sorts. None of them offered any hope. They consider it a miracle that I survived even this long."

"Oh, Oliver." She held fast to his hand.

"I daresay the greatest help of all was Juliana. She took me out of the sickroom and into the world, gave me the ephedra herb, and in spite of all predictions I thrived." With a pang of bittersweet remembrance, he thought of the rough-and-tumble days of his boyhood at Lynacre. "I even dared to think the disease was cured, for I ceased having attacks around the time I sprouted my first beard. But every once in a while, the illness would besiege me."

"You should have told me. It's too frightening to endure alone."

"Lark, I have looked death in the face. There's nothing fearsome about it, except to be separated

349

from you." They sat still for long moments, listening to the scratching of a rat in the dark and the murmured conversation of the guards outside.

"You know, don't you?" he asked quietly.

"Know what?" Her gaze fled his. She seemed inordinately interested in things about the room: the coals in the grate, the slumping candle in the corner, the walls weeping with moisture, the arched lintel over the three steps leading to a locked door.

"I've been condemned to die."

"You shall get a reprieve," she shot back. "You must — "

"Lark, time is short. Just listen. There can be no reprieve."

"Why not?" The red of anger and fear stained her cheeks.

"Because I refuse to recant."

Her eyes widened, and at last she looked at him again. "You?"

He felt a smile tug at the corners of his mouth. "I surprised even myself. But it's true. To give in to them now would discredit everything we've worked for, fought for. I will not forfeit my honor and the safety of Richard Speed and my sister." And you, he thought, but did not say the words. "I cannot meet Bonner's price, Lark. Not now."

"Would it help to beg you?"

"Sweetheart, you know better than that."

"Oliver." She sat on her heels and regarded him furiously. "I want you to recant. Tell them you'll name the sacraments and believe

350

in transubstantiation and the absolute power of Rome — "

"Stop it!" He flung aside her hand. "Listen to you. *You*, Lark! The woman who told me that the cause of Reformation is worth dying for."

"That was before my beliefs became a peril to your life."

Bitterness chilled him. "Now I understand why they brought you to see me," he said. "Did they instruct you to beg me to recant? Did they tell you the exact words to say, or did you think of them on your own?"

"Oliver, please — "

"Don't 'Oliver, please' me! Think about what you're asking, Lark. Shall I trade my immortal soul in order to spend a few more years on earth?" He caught both her hands then, squeezing hard as if to press his meaning into her flesh.

"I'm dying, Lark. I came close the night you told me about the baby. That night, when the illness seized me, I saw the most extraordinary vision, heard a voice that wasn't a voice. And I had the most uncanny feeling that all I needed to do was reach out, and I would touch the hand of God."

She gaped at him, and he laughed without humor.

"I've never bothered myself with matters of deep faith, but the experience affected me profoundly."

"Why didn't you tell me?"

"It's not easy to speak of."

"If I lose you," she said solemnly, "I shall die, too."

"*No!*" He startled himself with the violence of his reaction. "That would defeat me utterly. You must live on, Lark. And nurture our child and one day tell him about me." He gentled his voice. "I have never been a man of honor, Lark. Never committed to anything save my own amusement. I was shallow and stupidly happy. Until now, my life has been a promise unfulfilled." He smiled. "You once said I loved you because it was easy. What say you now, Lark?"

She waved her hand as if to banish the question. "What of our child, Oliver? A letter is a poor substitute for a father."

He closed his eyes, trying not to see a smiling babe in a cot, a fair-haired child wading in a brook, an earnest youth bent over a book.

"Tell him I died well," Oliver said quietly.

"Nay — "

"Better a dead martyr for a father than a living coward." He didn't want her to break down and cry. Though he hated his own selfish vanity, he feared that if she fell to pieces, he would, too.

Distance, he told himself. Distance would keep despair at bay and allow them to consider pragmatic affairs.

But first, ah, first, he allowed himself a blissful, surreptitious brushing of his lips over her soft hair. Then he put her away from him and stared intently into her face. The small, rounded chin. The wide eyes. The lips that trembled but allowed no sound of despair to pass them.

Her sincerity broke his heart, but he would not let it show. "Lark."

"Yes?"

"I would speak of practical matters."

She mouthed the word *practical* as if it were a foreign phrase.

"You are to put the properties of Eventide and Blackrose and Montfichet into a trust holding. My father will help you with that. Or Kit" — he cleared his throat — "if he survives."

She looked at him with her soul in her eyes, and he couldn't be certain she was listening. He went on. "I want you to leave London. Take Nance with you and go to Lynacre — "

"Stop it!" She put her hands over her ears. "I won't listen to this!"

As gently as he could, he took her hands away, keeping hold of her wrists. The sensation of her heartbeat beneath his fingers was nearly his undoing. He remembered kissing her there, feeling her pulse under his lips. Almost brusquely he released her hands.

"Will you do that, Lark? Will you go to Lynacre?"

"Yes."

"Go soon. Tomorrow. It must be nearly November. The roads will be rivers of mud in the rain, so make certain you travel in dry weather. I think you'd best go by barge at least as far as Wimbledon — "

"Oliver."

" — and do not stay at just any inn along the way. I'll not have you — "

"*Oliver.*"

"For God's sake, what *is* it?"

"Listen to yourself."

"*You're* supposed to be listening. I haven't got all day, you know."

Her cheeks paled another shade. "How can you make a jest at a time like this?" She held herself very stiff and straight. Her face seemed set in marble, white and immobile. "You're so *distant*, Oliver. It's as if you've already gone, and some horrid stranger is sitting here planning my future for me."

"Well, there's not much point in planning *my* future, is there?" he demanded. "Or shall we do that? What will I say tomorrow? Will I stand there with my gaze up to heaven and say, 'Lord, here I am, do You find me good enough in Your eyes?'" He heard the cruel edge to his voice, saw the bewildered hurt on her face. Ashamed, he glanced down.

Her gown had the bodice set high, and her velvet skirts draped her belly, grown huge with her child. His child. Theirs.

As he stared in amazement, something moved.

He must have made a noise, or the look on his face betrayed him, for Lark took his hand, and he could tell from her touch that all anger had drained from her.

She placed his hand on her belly. It was hard and taut. She arranged his fingers so that they splayed out.

"My hands are filthy," he whispered.

"Do you think that matters now?"

It was the *now* that broke down the barrier. That one simple word conveyed, in a single breath, the desperate finality of what was to come.

"Oh, God," he muttered.

She covered his hand with her own. She, too, had felt his wall of reserve crumble. And, bless the girl, she was not falling apart.

"For the first time in my life," he said, "I find myself at a loss for words."

"You don't need to say anything."

He stared at her. "I don't, do I? Not to you."

She smiled, and her lips trembled only a little. "Hold very still," she whispered.

"What?"

"Your hand. Keep it still."

He held his entire being still. A quiet hiss came from the fire. Somewhere, water dripped steadily onto stone.

Beneath Oliver's hand, the baby moved. The wonder of it traveled up his arm and spread all through his body. He was feeling *life*. A life he had helped to create, a life that had grown out of his extraordinary love for this woman.

When he dared to look at Lark's face, he saw her smiling through tears.

"It is a miracle," he said.

"Yes."

"Do you suppose it's a boy or girl?"

"I've never even considered it. Have you?"

"No. I only pray you will be safely delivered."

"I will, Oliver. I promise I will."

"Do not name it for me," he said suddenly. In spite of himself, his mind made a picture of a child with a beautiful round face, wavy dark hair. Blue eyes, like his own.

He took his hand away.

"Why not?" she asked.

He forced a grin. "A girl called Oliver would endure too much teasing."

She, too, smiled, and he loved her for that, loved her for her strength, for not making their last moments harder by flinging herself, weeping, to the floor.

Time was running out. They both knew it, and, oddly, conversation lagged. He wanted to tell her that he loved her, that she was beautiful, that she had given purpose and depth to his life.

But she knew that. He could see it in her eyes.

Nervously she touched his knee through a hole in his hose. "I should have brought needle and thread," she blurted out.

"Sweetheart." He touched her chin. "There's no need." He could see that she was about to shatter, so he took her in his arms and said, "Do you know what I want?"

"What?"

"To dance with my wife."

Her breath caught, and he was afraid she would refuse him. Instead she rose and helped him to his feet. There was no humiliation in leaning on her, just a tenderness that gripped his heart.

"I should have danced with you on our wedding day," she whispered.

"You're dancing with me now," he said, holding one hand at her waist, the fingers of the other linked with hers. With his rusty voice, he hummed a love song. For one magical moment the dank, moldy walls faded away. Oliver felt no pain, only a huge, honest love that filled his chest and heated his blood. The song ended when his voice cracked, and they both stopped and faced each other.

He held her face in his hands then, tracing it with shaking fingers. He wanted to memorize every aspect of her: the softness of her skin beneath his fingers. The shape of her mouth, her nose, her cheekbones. The color of her eyes and the way they always reminded him of the rain.

Like a blind man, he moved his hands over her, gathering sensation into his heart, committing her to eternal memory.

"*I* won't forget," she said, clearly understanding exactly what he was doing. "Oliver, I will never, *ever* forget you."

A shuffling sounded outside the door. Oliver ran his hand over her silky hair.

"They will make you leave soon. I feel as if I should speak some great truth that will make this all come right somehow. But for the life of me, I cannot think of a blessed thing."

The door opened. Neither looked to see who had entered the room. The silence between them spoke volumes.

And then the guards in their splendid livery were leading her away, and a huge roar burst from his throat.

"*Lark!*"

She turned, broke away from her escort, and

Oliver embraced her. With all his heart, he wanted to beg, to recant, to betray all the secrets he knew.

He looked into Lark's face. And it was there that he found his strength. He kissed her lingeringly, imprinting the taste of her on his memory. Then he pulled back. "I do not wonder what heaven is like, my love. I *know*."

He sensed her frantic fear, but she held it in check. "You do?"

"I am that rare, fortunate man who found it on earth. Right here with you in my arms." He kissed the palm of her hand and closed her fist around it. "I have no memento to give you except this."

They held hands even as she backed away toward the door. He gripped her hard enough to hurt, squeezing his eyes shut. Love flowed like a river between them, and the miracle of it lit his soul with fire. Their fingers slid apart at last, and the guards guided her out the door.

Oliver stood alone in the empty silence. Yet he was not alone, for even after she had been torn from him, he still kept the ache where he had gripped her hand.

★ ★ ★

Sensing a presence behind her, Lark jumped up from the writing table and faced the door.

Moving with catlike grace, Wynter entered the room, an office on the main floor of Wimberleigh House.

"You might have asked to be announced," she

358

said coldly. It was a wonder that she had any voice left to speak. Upon arriving home, she had wept, tearing at the bedclothes, screaming with sobs until her voice was hoarse. She and Belinda had sat up all the night through to find a way to save Oliver. Their plan was desperate, and it hinged on a precise timing of events that did not include a visit from Wynter.

"I did ask," Wynter said with his charming, deceitful smile. "I was told you would not receive me."

"You were told correctly. Did you slay my footman where he stood, or did you simply beat him senseless?"

Wynter laughed. "You know me better than that."

She did. There had been a time when Wynter had ruled her, made her feel insignificant and weak, and given her the irresistible urge to seek his favor.

Knowing Oliver had changed that. Even as she formed the thought, she edged around so that her full skirts, made fuller by her huge belly, concealed the letters on the desk. She gritted her teeth in frustration. She had spent the entire morning working out the details of her plan with Belinda. She could not afford to be caught now. Today was the day Oliver would be taken to burn at Smithfield.

"You planned that meeting yesterday, thinking that taking me to see Oliver would cause him to break," she said, her voice poisoned by venom.

Oliver's steadfastness had astonished her. Yesterday she had seen her husband — truly

359

seen him — in a new light. His blithe manner, his nonchalance, were all a calculated act. Deep within him dwelt a steely core of unbreachable honor. He was a champion in the guise of court jester.

His dignity had given her the strength to leave the Tower with composure, not to shame her husband with a display of fruitless wailing and pleading before his captors.

"I want you to come with me," said Wynter.

"Where?"

"To St. James's Palace. And then to watch the execution."

Her heart knocked against her breastbone. The queen was at the palace, having traveled there in recent weeks from Hampton Court. Perhaps Lark could find her. See her. Beg for a reprieve.

"I shall come." The instant Wynter turned away, she snatched her letter and shoved it into her sleeve.

* * *

She had known the palace would be grand. She had known it would be an anthill of activity, crawling with ministers, clerks, pages, nobles, servants. None of them cared that a man was about to be executed. The only man in the world who mattered to her.

But she was unprepared for Wynter's behavior. They arrived almost furtively, accompanied only by a pair of Spanish-speaking guards and stealing like thieves into the palace through the water gate. Wynter had made much of his status at court; now she suspected he had overstated his own importance.

He pulled her along through narrow, poorly lit passageways.

They headed down a half-open gallery and wound their way up a narrow tower staircase, leaving the blank-eyed guards at the foot of the stairs.

At the first landing, an arrow loop invited in the late October gloom, and Lark felt a twinge of unease. "I want to see the palace warden."

For a moment Wynter simply stared at her. And his look, which used to have the power to send her scurrying for cover, only increased her impatience.

"Well?" she prompted.

She saw it then, the flicker of ill will in his face, but he quickly blinked it away. "So you shall, my lady. In due time."

"Now."

Her tone must have startled him, for his eyes narrowed and he took a step back.

Yes, she thought in dark triumph, I have changed. Her will was stronger than his. So was her desperation. Before leaving Wimberleigh House, she had furtively given the letter up her sleeve to Nance, begging the servant to convey it to Belinda.

"Pardon me," she said, brushing past him, starting back down the stairs.

Wynter's hand shot out, clamping like a vise around her upper arm. So remote was the dark tower that no one heard Lark scream.

361

Dressed in a nun's habit, Belinda de Lacey committed several crimes. She lied through her perfect white teeth to get into the Tower of London, she pilfered a warden's keys while pretending to pray in schoolgirl Latin, and she cursed like a tanner's brat when she burst into the straw-strewn cell of the Lieutenant's Lodgings and found no one.

As it had several times in the past, the desperate plan was going awry.

Belinda's fine stream of oaths, delivered with equal fluency in English and Russian, was interrupted by a muffled groan.

"Who's there?" she demanded, peering into the shadows.

The groan sounded again, and she realized it came from behind the door. In her haste, she had flung open the door and thumped her victim almost senseless.

"Are you all right?" She bent and pulled the poor wretch upright. Orange torch glow from without slanted across his bearded face.

"Kit!" she said on a sob. "Dear God!"

He blinked. "Belinda? Jesu, have you taken vows?"

"Not *that* sort, my love." Even as she spoke, she drew another costume from the voluminous folds of her robe. "Here, put this on. Be quick. Where's Oliver?"

"I don't know. They never brought him back here."

She swore again. "Can you walk?"

362

"Sweetheart, for you I would run like the wind."

She felt a surge of affection but spared only a second to kiss him. Later she would do far more than kiss him. "When did they take my brother away?"

Kit dropped the kersey robe over himself and kicked at the hem. "I lost count of the days. Ah, Belinda, how did you get here?"

"I'll tell you later. We — Lark and I — have been trying for months to see you. Each time, we were thwarted. I only wish we could have succeeded before they took Oliver away. What of Dr. Snipes?" she asked.

"Dead."

She squeezed her eyes shut, feeling the sting of rage and futility. "God rest his soul."

"What sort of costume is this?" he asked, shaking out the wide sleeves of his robe.

"A nun's habit, like mine." She held out the wimple and veil. When he shrank back, she whispered, "Be not an infant, Kit Youngblood. I went to some lot of trouble to arrange your escape. For once, the plan seems to be working. This is the only way I'm going to get you out of here."

Ignoring his protests, she slid the veil into place, hiding his hair, drawing the wimple forward to shadow his bearded face.

Several minutes later a drunk stumbled out of a tavern in St. Katherine's Lane and nearly collided with the oddest pair of nuns he had ever seen. They raced toward the river with their robes hiked to their knees, starched wimples

363

flapping, veils flying out behind them.

At the top of the water steps, the nuns stopped running, embraced each other, and kissed. Passionately.

The drunk shuddered and turned away. "Yech," he muttered, spitting into the ditch. "Catholics!"

★ ★ ★

"You're mad," Lark said to Wynter. Yet even as she said it, she knew he was deadly sane. "What possible good can it do for you to keep me here?"

He smiled and looked around the room. The appointments were sparse but adequate, the floor was clean, and coals glowed in a brazier on a tall brass stand by the window. "Don't you know?" he asked. "I'm offering you a chance to save your husband's life."

"Pray you, go on," she said. "Since when have you been granted the power of reprieve — over someone you caused to be arrested in the first place?"

"You'd be surprised at the liberties I've been granted."

"By whom?"

He did not answer. "When is your baby due, Lark?"

The chill of fear scudded over her afresh, but unlike the past, this time she did not let herself become quiescent with terror. "Perhaps a fortnight."

"Interesting," he said, taking a few feline steps

364

forward. "That is when the queen is expecting the heir to the throne."

Now Lark felt not just a chill, but an icy blast of sheer horror. God in heaven. Wynter wanted to steal *her* child and give it to the queen. He *was* mad. By now, everyone knew the queen was dying. News of her illness caused people to gather outside the palace, awaiting the fateful pronouncement. Queen Mary had not even seen her husband in over a year.

Lark crossed to the tower window, tall and narrow with colorless glass that made everything outside appear wavy. Pretending it was the cold air she felt, she moved close to the brazier. Even the red hot coals, glowing like angry eyes, failed to warm her.

She remembered what Princess Elizabeth had said at Hatfield. The queen's desire for a child had become the subject of gossip all over London. Lark had thought the sly hints about stealing another woman's child a cruel jest, but the horrible twist of dread in her gut told her Wynter was not jesting.

"What say you?" he asked, his voice like warm treacle. He was standing directly behind her. "Shall I send word that the traitor de Lacey be spared? I could, you know."

At that moment Lark experienced something so dark and forbidden that she despised herself. Just for a moment she wanted to say yes. Yes, take the child, this little stranger, just give me my husband!

The thought was as fierce and painful as the thrust of a lance. She loved Oliver too much.

And then, as quickly as it had come, the thought subsided. Give up her child? Let it be given, in a lie, to England as an heir?

That was madness.

"Of course," Wynter said in his beautiful voice, "Oliver de Lacey would have to go into hiding. You'd have no need of Blackrose Priory then, would you?"

"Blackrose. It always comes to that, doesn't it, Wynter?"

"It should have been *mine*, Father!" With a lightning motion, he slammed both hands on the table. A storm swirled in his night-dark eyes.

She bit her lip to stifle a gasp. What a strange but telling slip of the tongue. Just for a moment she pitied Wynter, deprived of a father's love, hungering for it.

"Do you want Blackrose?" she asked. "Very well. It is yours." She wondered if, somewhere in the far beyond, Spencer disapproved, but she did not care. Her passion for Oliver guided her now, not rote lessons pounded into her over the years. She wanted to beg Wynter to accept her offer, but she looked at his taut, pale face and knew that was where he wanted her — weak, helpless, promising him anything, just as she had once before.

"You can't even begin to know what I want." He moved as he spoke, coming nearer and nearer. The wind slipped frigid fingers in through the cracks around the window. Lark could see the sky, bleak and clouded with the coming winter. She felt his breath, warm on the back of her neck, and she squeezed her eyes shut, gritting her teeth.

No, no, no . . .

Then his lips were there, barely grazing the skin at the nape of her neck. "It's a long drop to the bottom," he said. He spoke the same words in the same silky whisper as he had *. . . before.*

A wave of desperation hurled her into the past, to another stone-walled chamber with a high window, and Wynter standing, just as he was now, behind her. The dizziness came on like a hive of bees suddenly disturbed. Her palms began to sweat, and she curled her hands into fists.

You want me, Lark. I can see it in your eyes when you look at me.

"I told you no!" she whispered fiercely.

Now, as then, he trailed his finger down the side of her throat. "You never said no, Lark. And you will not say it now. You still think about it, don't you? You still think about that night and how you surrendered to me."

The past came roaring back, and the hideous shame rolled over her. A sob caught in her throat. She swayed toward the window. She could escape that way. She could find a place of oblivion, where she would no longer feel horror at the sin she had committed, would never again weep for Oliver.

"No!" She whirled to face Wynter. Even now she had to deny the truth or she would burn in hell. "You *forced* me!"

He smiled, leaning closer, his sinister scent

of ambergris reminding her of the past. "Nay, Lark. You remember as well as I do. You begged me — "

"I begged you to — to — " She broke off, and the memories battered at her. The fog in her mind parted like heavy curtains, and for the first time she saw what had really happened that night. Finally, after all the years of hiding in shame, she faced the truth. "I begged you to *love me*," she said, feeling nausea push into her throat. "God forgive me, but I did."

"Aye, Lark, and so it shall be again." He reached for her.

The past shattered like a window exploding in a storm. Simply speaking the truth at last set her free. She *had* begged him. She *had* let him take her body, fill her with his vengeful, seductive lust, and she had cried out with the terrible ecstasy of it. She could admit that now, after all this time. Rather than condemning her to the darkness, the truth brought her into the light. He had exerted his power over her; she had succumbed. For Wynter, it had been an act of hatred against his father. Lark had simply been the object of his defiance.

The shame went away, because she had found Oliver, who loved her honestly and unconditionally, would love her even if he knew.

In that moment, facing her tormentor, she was possessed of such a dark, violent loathing that she didn't even seem to know herself anymore.

"You don't frighten me anymore," she told him, her anger burning as hot as the coals in the brazier. "You've lost that hold over me."

"Then you're a fool, little Lark." Even before he finished speaking, he lunged, arms outstretched, ready to snatch and imprison her.

"No!" She took hold of the brazier by its base and swung it in a wide arc. The glowing coals flew at him.

Lark heard his animal bellow of rage and pain. Racing madly, she leaped for the door and wrenched it open. She plunged down the narrow stairs. With fleeting relief, she saw that the guards had departed. The halls and galleries of the palace sped past in a blur.

As she rushed by an open window with a view of the river and marshes, she had only one lucid thought.

Oliver.

She stumbled in her ungainly haste, sinking down on one knee. She had to escape, had to reach Oliver before —

"Stop!" Wynter's hoarse yell rang down the open gallery.

Lark picked up her skirts and ran, a lumbering run, her awkward bulk slowing her down. She was lost in the palace, lost in the gloomy halls and cramped apartments. Her only aim was to get away, to get to Oliver somehow, to stop them form murdering him.

She took every turn and staircase she encountered. She came to a narrow passageway leading to a lightless hole.

One door across the corridor stood ajar.

Footsteps flayed the stone floor behind her.

Swallowing a sob of despair, she slipped

through the door. The room was a chapel, small and elegant as a jewel, with two tapers burning and the host ensconced in a monstrance.

Lark blinked, letting her eyes adjust to the dimness. On a prayer stool in front of the altar, a lone figure knelt.

Lark gasped and pressed her knuckles to her mouth.

The woman turned slowly as if the motion caused her pain. Her face might have been handsome once, but it was white and pinched now, the eyes glassy, the lips bluish.

In her horror, Lark forgot to breathe, to move. Then, somehow recovering, she sank to the floor in the deepest curtsy she could manage.

"Your Majesty!" she said in a tremulous voice.

Queen Mary held out her hand.

17

"**W**HAT do you mean, you lost her?" Bishop Edmund Bonner glared at Wynter. "I thought it was a simple enough task, even for you."

Wynter hitched back his shoulders. Bonner's censure stung worse than the hot coals Lark had flung at him. Wynter knew he looked and smelled abominable. Some of the coals had hit him in the face, raising blisters, one at the corner of his eye. The bitch had almost blinded him. Other coals had singed his hair and bored holes in his garments.

"My lord bishop, the woman is clearly mad. I could not have known how viciously she would attack me."

"You might have at least had a guard or a servant standing by."

"I had to be careful, you know that," Wynter snapped. "I dared only use those two bumbling Spaniards, and she slipped right past them — or else they turned a blind eye."

"You never did quite learn whom to trust, did you, my lord?" Bonner's face was blunt and coarse, totally unforgiving. He, perhaps more than any other man of the realm, had reason to want a Catholic heir to the throne, not the wily, inconstant Elizabeth, who had the audacity to think for herself.

The only man who wanted a Catholic heir

more than Bonner was Wynter himself. The seed had been planted long ago, in the mind of a bewildered boy abandoned by his father. It had been nurtured by the brutal splendor of his childhood, growing with the years spent in the shadow of his beautiful, bitter mother.

Doña Elena had been as remote and cool as an alabaster madonna. She had taught Wynter two things above all else: to serve God and to seek revenge.

By taking Lark's child and giving it to the queen, Wynter could accomplish both. More than that, he would finally win complete control over Lark.

He had always loved her; couldn't she see that? But she had to submit to him. He had been trying for years to master her will, first by appealing to her craving for affection, then by trying to convince her that her worth was measured only by his esteem for her.

Until Oliver de Lacey had come along, Wynter had hopes for success. But the arrant knave had built up Lark's aplomb, had honed a fine edge on her conviction. In more ways than one, she had slipped from Wynter's grasp. Her defiant behavior in the tower room had proved that.

He glared down at a blister rising on the back of his hand. He must bring Lark back to him. He would bend her will to his. His honor depended on it.

Wynter resented Bonner's part in the plan to keep England bound to the True Faith. Presenting the queen with a newborn babe was simply too brilliant an idea to share. Making a beloved sovereign's fondest wish come true was an honor Wynter meant to claim all on his own.

"The woman's a danger to our purposes." Bonner paced, his robes swishing on the Turkey carpets of his opulent apartment. "She must not be found by anyone but you and your servants. Is that understood?"

"Of course, my lord bishop."

"It would be an unmitigated disaster if she were. She is young, with child, and noble. Need I say more?"

"No, my lord bishop."

"When she *is* found," Bonner said, selecting a fat orange from the bowl on the table, "see that she dies in childbirth."

★ ★ ★

Lying in general was a sin, and lying to one's sovereign queen was out of the question.

On her knees in front of Queen Mary, Lark told the truth about her deathbed promise to Spencer and her hasty marriage to Oliver de Lacey.

"De Lacey?" the queen asked, her voice tired and thready. She leaned forward over the swollen mound of her belly. She was not with child; the protuberance was misshapen and unhealthy looking. Weary lines of melancholy scored her sagging cheeks.

She was dying. Lark knew this with chilly certainty.

"The de Laceys of Lynacre." Lark tried not

to seem impatient by casting glances over her shoulder. "His father is the earl of Lynley."

"I know. Stephen de Lacey was last known to have taken to the high seas in pursuit of his daughter and a certain Protestant rebel. Would you know anything about that, my lady?"

Lark's heart sank. Her knees ached from pressing into the stone floor. The distant drumbeat of the procession to Smithfield throbbed into the silence. Rather than panic, she felt cold determination. She would defy the queen of England, if she had to, in order to reach Oliver in time. The dilemma was leaving the palace before Wynter seized her again.

The queen shook her head. "Do not answer that. The truth would condemn you in the eyes of the law. A lie would condemn you in the eyes of God."

Lark expelled her sigh of relief quietly. She felt no awe at meeting her sovereign for the first time. Instead she felt a strange empathy for a woman whose unrelenting dogma had robbed English men and women of their freedom and some of their lives.

The queen's hands were never still; she held a rosary of coral beads wound through her fingers, and she twisted the strand constantly, restlessly. Lark had the sense that some sort of unfinished business haunted Queen Mary.

"Ma'am, are you quite well?" Lark asked at length. "Shall I call for someone?"

"Nay." Mary indicated a glass bell at her side. "Someone will come when I ring. I came here to be alone. To be away from the hovering physicks and hand-wringing women."

Faint shouts drifted in through the unglazed windows. The corners of the queen's mouth turned down. "Do you know why the crowds gather outside the palace gates?"

"No, ma'am."

"Aye, you do, but like the rest of them, you are afraid to tell me so. They're waiting for me to die."

Lark bit her kip and stared at the stone floor. The ancient cracks were filled with brown dust.

"Some of my nobles — I suppose I must no longer call them *my* nobles — have gone to Hatfield already. I wonder how *she* is receiving them." Mary's knuckles shone white and taut as she clenched and unclenched her hands around the rosary beads.

Footsteps approached, ringing in the passageway outside the chapel. Lark froze; then, without asking leave, she stood and backed into the shadow of a stone pillar.

Through small, dark Tudor eyes, Mary watched her. Lark held her breath, wondering if the queen would call out and betray her.

She kept silent. The sound of the footsteps subsided.

"Ma'am, my husband has been condemned to die today," Lark said.

Mary lifted her chin. "I know that. I am ill, but not ignorant."

Daring to further test the queen's forbearance, Lark said, "I beg you for a reprieve."

"Your husband is a confessed heretic."

He had only confessed to keep them from questioning *her*, Lark knew that now.

"I cannot interfere in the sacred work of the church," said Mary. "Surely you understand that."

"Then I weep for England," Lark burst out, furious and uncaring now. "I weep for a country where good men are sent to die and evil ones are advanced at court."

Mary's thin, graying eyebrows lifted. "Who?" she demanded. "If you would cast aspersions on a member of my court, I would know his name."

Just for a moment, Lark hesitated. It was risky. But anger spurred her to blurt out Wynter's name.

Mary absorbed the news with mild interest in her waxen face. "His mother, Elena, was a great favorite of my own mother. Wynter has been a devoted subject — to me and to the True Faith."

"But when does devotion turn to obsession? Would you want an adviser who would steal a baby from its mother's arms?"

Mary seemed to catch fire, bending forward like a thin flame in a stiff breeze. "Why would you accuse him of so pernicious a plot?"

"Because he threatened it." Lark rested her hands on her middle.

"Christ have mercy." Mary leaned back against the prie-dieu. "Such rumors have gone about London since the day I married Philip of Spain." She stared at the guttering candle on the altar. Her face seemed to soften. Lark

376

recognized the look on the queen's face. Poor Mary — sick, abandoned, dying, she still loved her husband.

"Even now, Wynter is searching the palace for me," Lark said.

"Is he?" Mary rang her crystal bell.

Lark nearly screamed in fury and frustration. The queen had merely been toying with her, delaying her. Now she would be seized, given into the care of a madman, and —

"Make haste," the queen said to the bodyguard who appeared in the chapel. "And let no one see you." She lifted her gaze to Lark. "You're to have an escort and an eight-man barge at your disposal to take you to whatever destination you desire."

Lark stared at the queen. The silent message that passed between them was unmistakable. The queen would not put a stop to the execution, but she would not keep Lark from trying.

"Come," she said, holding out her frail arms. "Embrace me."

She felt no more substantial than a wisp of straw, Lark thought as she gently clasped the queen by the shoulders. The smell that clung to her was familiar; Lark knew it from Spencer's last days. It was a feeble, musty perfume. The smell of death.

"Godspeed," Mary whispered so that none but Lark could hear. "And when your babe comes, perhaps you could name him Philip." That painfully wistful voice would haunt Lark all her years.

Shaken by the encounter, she soon found

herself on her way to Smithfield. She prayed she would not be too late.

★ ★ ★

As he was led to the burning grounds at Smithfield, Oliver seemed, even to himself, to be a different man. It was a great irony that once before he had been taken to his execution.

But oh, how changed he was since then. He had been loutish and shameless, pleading for his life. Today some steadfast core held his dignity intact.

Lark had given him that. He wondered if she knew. Her love had transcended care and fear, putting solace and acceptance in its place.

He drew comfort from the fact that the young evangelist Richard Speed was safe and married to Natalya. Lark, too, would be safe in the bosom of the boisterous, loving de Lacey brood.

Life would go on. The Princess Elizabeth would take the throne; Lark would bring forth their child.

He wondered how long she would grieve for him.

A howling wind whipped over the throng of spectators at Smithfield. Oliver looked across the grounds and saw his fate: the hooded executioner and his masked assistant, a pile of kindling and rushes heaped around a blackened stake thrusting up from a pit of sand.

For you, Dickon.

The thought came out of the dim, distant past

and took him by surprise. He had never known Dickon, the brother who had died of the same lung ailment that plagued Oliver. He realized that all his life he had carried a burden of guilt. His brother had died. Oliver had lived on.

He barely heard a droning voice reading the charges, all the outlandish crimes to which Oliver had willingly confessed. He paid no heed to the chanting of prayers, the swish of swinging censers, the low roar of the crowd. He refused his final chance to recant — laughed in the priest's face, in fact.

Many jeered and cursed him, but others cried out for a reprieve. The world was changing. Men and women were learning to take a stand. One day their numbers would be so formidable that not even death could stifle them.

Soldiers took him to the stake and raised his manacled hands high. A thick chain went around his chest. To beat back a sudden welling of horror, Oliver caught the eye of one of the men and winked.

The man looked away and crossed himself. Oliver felt the cold wind streak across his face. He heard a bellowed order, saw two torches touch the kindling at the edge of the sand pit. The crowd was a vast sea of faces and noise, yet he had never been more alone.

In absolute solitude he would make this journey. His destination was the mystery of the ages.

He heard the firewood crackling. The quick little flames were still at the edge of the pit, perhaps six feet away, but creeping closer, eating up the fuel. He wondered if he would be able to stand the pain.

Somewhere in the mob, a child began to cry.

Oliver told himself the agony would be fleeting.

The hiss and crackle of the kindling crescendoed to a roar.

So this was it. The waiting was over. His final journey would begin here, now.

To his surprise, a prayer — wordless and heartfelt — poured through his mind.

Much less to his surprise, he felt like vomiting.

No. You've prepared yourself for this. At least do this. For the sake of your child, die well.

Prepared. He wondered if that were even possible. Horrible pleading words crowded his throat. He became a wild animal, instinctively terrified of the flames taking hold at his feet.

So he would fail after all, opening his mouth to recant and beg them to strangle him instead.

Strength was as simple as summoning an image of Lark. He grew tough, stubborn, more a man than he had ever been. And deep inside him, in a secret, dark place, dwelt a part of him that hungered to know the deepest mystery of all. The final thrill.

A stiff wind snatched at the flames before they engulfed Oliver. With the hot breath of the fire on his face, he closed his eyes and thought again of Lark and the child he would never know.

"Hell and damnation," muttered the executioner.

"Wind's not going to soften today," said his assistant with a nervous stutter.

Oliver opened his eyes and gave the hooded men a censorious look. "I've resigned myself to becoming a martyr. At this rate we could be all afternoon at it."

"Bring me gunpowder," the executioner yelled. His voice was hoarse, his accent common; he was probably a convict offered reprieve in exchange for turning murderer. He seemed a young man, but within the slits of his hood, his eyes appeared ancient.

The crowd cheered at the mention of gunpowder. It was used when fire alone would not suffice, and it added great drama to the spectacle. Avid faces peered through the feeble threads of smoke. People pressed against the rail at the edge of the pit.

"Death to the heretic, Oliver de Lacey!" someone shouted.

"Oh, spare me from the curses of idiots," Oliver yelled back. "Fie, sir, you have the wit of an elf."

"You'll burn in hell," the man bellowed.

"Kiss my breech." Oliver regretted that he could not accompany the words with an appropriate gesture.

"Glory to God in the highest!" called a new voice.

And many people, many more than Oliver had expected, called for a reprieve.

"Burn in hell, Oliver de Lacey," screeched an old crone.

He squinted at her through the wisps of smoke. For a moment her eyes startled him, for they were the same wide, rainy gray as — He shook his head. There was no resemblance.

The unwashed hag, her teeth black and sparse, cursed him again, shaking her fist. "Burn in hell, Oliver de Lacey!"

"Get thee to a barnyard with the other molting geese, old mother," he said, then let his gaze sweep the pressing mob. "What terrible crime did I commit that *this* must be my last vision on earth?"

The crowd roared with laughter.

Oliver could not resist playing to them. "Most martyrs get to see visions of a host of angels. I get a vile, irksome scold. Jesu! Someone bring a shield to hide her face!"

By that time the executioner had set fat bags of gunpowder on the crackling wood. One of the sacks ignited with a hiss.

Oliver gritted his teeth, bracing himself to be torn apart by the explosion.

A fount of yellow smoke billowed upward. The smoke was as thick as a velvet curtain, rising dark and solid before Oliver's eyes. The screeching harridan, and gradually the rest of the crowd, disappeared from view.

Oliver closed his smarting eyes. He had never seen gunpowder produce such thick, sparkless smoke.

Like a last, low blow, the breathlessness started. Ah. So the sickness would kill him after all. Why had he thought he could cheat it? It was almost a comfort to be slain by a familiar enemy rather than a strange one.

He felt himself slipping down and down the narrow black passageway. He had been here before. But that time there had been a pinprick of brightness to light his way back.

Now all was black and infinitely empty.

He used his last strength to whisper a single word: "Lark!"

★ ★ ★

Slipping under the rail, Lark plunged into the bank of smoke. It rose so thick from the bags of powder Belinda had prepared that it was like stepping behind a screen. Her tattered robe, bought from a beggar woman for the price of a silver shilling, caught sparks from the flames.

"Get back, you flea-witted old drab!" a drunkard called.

"That gunpowder's about to blow!" yelled someone else. A low roar of confusion buzzed from the spectators.

Lark could no longer see the crowd. "Kit!" She ignored the hecklers. "Kit, are you there?"

"I'm here." Enshrouded by the yellow fog, he sounded breathless. "I think it worked. Jesu! He's unconscious!" Looking frightening and anonymous in his executioner's mask and hood, Kit had already unchained Oliver.

His slim assistant, similarly hooded, choked out a sob. "He's dead already!"

"*No, Belinda!*" Lark spat, furious with terror. "Hurry. The smoke bombs won't last forever." The three of them took longer than they had planned, for they had not counted on Oliver being immobile. They wrestled him into the most concealing garment they could find — a monk's robes.

Kit and Belinda cast off their black hoods and masks and let the fire burn the garments. "Make way!" Lark screeched, bullying a path in the crowd with her cane. "This clerk is ill! Make way! He needs air!"

Lark prayed that in the confusion no one would see that they crept seemingly out of a cloud. She glanced back over her shoulder. Huge, impenetrable billows of yellow smoke continued to pour from the sacks of false gunpowder. Bless Belinda. She had remembered her formula for sparkless smoke.

Kit carried Oliver in his arms like a child. Or a dead man.

Please let him be all right, Lark thought as they rushed past St. Bartholomew's. Please, please, please.

"It's a bloody miracle!" someone yelled.

Certain they had been found out, Lark prepared to run. She looked back. The smoke had cleared sufficiently to reveal the naked stake.

"The hand of God snatched him up to heaven," someone proclaimed.

"Praise Jesus Christ!"

"Not even leaving his mortal remains for relics!"

"We are blessed this day!"

"It is a miracle!"

People fell to their knees. Oliver was declared a martyr, and many converted on the spot to the Reformed faith. Fearful, bewildered priests waved their hands and exhorted the people to stay calm, trying unsuccessfully to stifle the adulation.

As they left the field and delved into the shadows of the city wall along Fleet Ditch, Lark felt the strangest sensation. A twist deep in her belly. A gush of warmth.

Belinda, agile in her tight black leggings and tunic, put her arms around Lark. "You look terrible."

"It has been a long day," Lark said faintly. Then she remembered her costume. The blackened wax she had put on her teeth tasted foul. The beggar woman's robes held a terrible odor. "Is Oliver all right?"

"He'd better be," said Kit. "This is a lot of trouble to take for a corpse."

They made it to the river and into a waiting lighter-boat. Kit cast off. Belinda and Lark bent over Oliver. His face was smudged with soot. Lark cradled his head between her hands and dusted away some of the blackness. How pale he looked, save around his mouth. His lips were blue.

"Oliver!" she said, grateful for the high gust of wind that blew them downstream, hurrying them out into the crowd of boats, where they could blend in. "Oliver!"

She sprinkled river water on his face. He coughed out stale air, whooped in a deep breath, and blinked up at her.

"Jesus save me!" he said. "I have died and gone to hell!"

Lark frowned and cocked her head.

"Get back, you harpy!" Oliver said, trying to twist away from her, nearly capsizing the boat in the process.

Lark laughed with sheer joy. She spat out the blackened wax and threw back her hood so that her hair spilled free.

The look on his face would linger in her mind forever. "Lark!" His voice was strange — at once strangled and thick and exultant.

"Yes, my love. We're taking you to a safe place."

He grinned at Kit and Belinda. "I take it you two had a part in this."

"Hell and damnation," Kit said, using his rough convict's accent.

"My sister and best friend, executioners?" Blissful wonder shone in Oliver's eyes. "Good show, you two. I had no idea."

"You were cocky enough thinking you *were* going to die," said Belinda, brushing a tear from her eye and pretending it was dust. "If you'd thought you had a chance to escape, you would have been insufferable."

"And you would have given us away," Kit added.

Oliver sat up, put his hand beneath Lark's chin, and kissed her. It was the sweetest, most magical kiss she had ever experienced, for she had never thought to see him alive again. Even when a cramp banded around her midsection, she only smiled.

"I presume you've changed your mind about my taking the easy way out," Oliver said.

She truly did want to tell him — that she

had loved and trusted him right from the start, loved him with forbidden intensity, loved every wonderful, anguished, frustrating moment she spent with him.

But she could not speak. The pain came in earnest now, sweeping her body like a forest fire, doubling her over.

Kit took out a flask and offered it to Oliver. "Claret?"

"Beshrew the wine," Oliver said, staring goggle-eyed at Lark. "The baby's coming."

18

"**I**T'S a girl," Belinda whispered, tiptoeing out of the bedchamber at Hatfield.

"Who's a girl?" Oliver muttered, dragging his hands down his stubbled face. Despite considerable risks, the Princess Elizabeth had given them shelter at an outbuilding on the grounds of Hatfield, even offering the services of her own physician, who quickly deferred to the village midwife. Lark's travail had lasted through the night and most of the next day. Oliver had weathered it in a state of hideous anxiety, pacing and swearing and generally making a nuisance of himself.

"Your *baby*," Belinda said with a weary, happy laugh. "You have a little daughter, Oliver, and an ill-tempered mort she is, so far. Would you like to see her?"

"A daughter." He spoke stupidly, as if he had sand in his mouth.

Belinda took his hand and led him into the darkened chamber. It smelled of herbal ointments and blood, and for a moment he wanted to run away. Lark lay propped against a bank of pillows, a bundle in her arms. She was pale, with damp strands of hair plastered to her brow and cheeks. Her eyes no longer seemed the color of rain but were a light blue gray like the sun-struck sea in high summer.

He sank to his knees beside the bed.

Uncertainty played havoc with his emotions. "Hello, my love."

She looked different in subtle ways — her face suffused with contentment and fatigue, her eyes dreamy and distant as if she dwelt in a place beyond his reach. In sooth she *had* gone away from him, had experienced the miracle of birth, something he could never share.

A terrible worry nagged at Oliver. She had professed her love, but that had been when they were both sure he was done for. Did she really mean it, or had she said so only to give him comfort at the last?

He didn't know. His tormented mind burned with the question he dared not ask. He simply didn't know.

She angled the bundle toward him. "Greet your daughter, Oliver."

With a shaking hand, he moved back the blanket to see a wizened purple-and-red face, the mouth open, emitting a mewling sound.

"*That's* our child?"

"Isn't she beautiful?"

"No!" But he couldn't take his eyes off the elfin face. Infinitely gentle, absolutely terrified, and trying to hide his fear, he half sat on the bed and circled them in his arms.

The child ceased its crying. "More than beautiful. If I had not been up all night going mad with worry, I would think of a better word."

He prayed he had said the right thing. He feared he had not, for Lark simply sat still beside him, gazing down into the face of their child.

Oliver began to sweat, thinking the worst, that she had indeed lied to him about loving him.

The silence lengthened.

He nearly choked on dread.

"I do love you, Oliver," Lark said, looking up at him.

He sent her a crooked smile. "I knew that."

★ ★ ★

The christening took place in a small chapel in an upper chamber of Hatfield.

While Lark stood awaiting Kit and Belinda, who would be the baby's godparents, she stared at the large, wheel-shaped window and contemplated the past several days.

A dark wind blew across England. People whispered that the queen had taken to her bed. Some of her ministers were madly trying to devise a way to keep the Catholic succession in place. A few dared to suggest that the not-yet-widowed king of Spain should wed the Princess Elizabeth. Many more simply abandoned the queen altogether, shamelessly fleeing the Palace of St. James and crowding the roads to Hatfield. It was all a rather pitiful end to Mary's reign.

It did not help that Londoners claimed a miracle had occurred at Smithfield. It did not help that Wynter Merrifield, declared an outlaw and renegade by the queen, had drummed up a band of mercenaries and was scouting the countryside in search of Lark.

But in the bright chamber of Hatfield House, Lark stood above the clamor of favor seekers. It was quiet, peaceful. The huge, round window, set with colored glass in the shape of a Tudor rose, let in streams of jewel-toned sunlight. The baptismal font was a circle of still water in a shallow brass basin.

Oliver stepped into the room, the baby sleeping in his arms. "I did it," he said.

"Did what?" Lark attempted to keep a solemn expression on her face.

"Changed her — you know." His ears reddened. At last the unblushing Oliver de Lacey had been taught to blush — by his daughter. "What a mess she makes for such a little thing."

"Where are Kit and Belinda?"

"They should be along any moment now." Oliver swayed gently back and forth, a habit he had developed from holding his daughter through crying jags each night. "I wonder if Bess will come. I sent word to her. I heard she was out reading in the garden."

Lark pictured the princess seated under her favorite oak tree, ignoring the encroaching hullaballoo.

"She has other things on her mind," Lark reminded him. "Any moment she expects to be told of her sister's death." Lark felt a stirring of anguish. In important ways, Mary's reign had been a disaster. She had lost Calais, England's last foothold in France. Her crusade to restore the monasteries had drained the treasury. She had surrounded herself by hated Spaniards.

But in a quiet moment in a private chapel,

the woman, not the queen, had won Lark's sympathy.

Mary would die alone and unhappy, while Lark had every fulfillment, even those she had never dared to dream of. She had a husband she loved to distraction, a perfect daughter, and the whole, deliriously wonderful de Lacey family.

Shouts and blaring trumpets sounded at the gates.

"More favor seekers, no doubt."

Lark looked down at her hands and noticed that she had clasped them together, the knuckles white. Before her happiness could be complete, she had to conclude one bit of unfinished business.

She had to confess to Oliver, had to tell him the whole truth about the past.

"Oliver?"

He kept his fond gaze on the baby. "Aye, my love? Did you notice how she stares at me? She knows I'm her papa, the one who loves her beyond all — "

"Oliver, I must tell you something."

He must have heard the strain in her tone, for he glanced up. "Yes?"

"It's about — " She broke off. The temptation to look away in shame was great, but she forced herself to hold his gaze. "It is about Wynter."

"Go on," he said with great reluctance.

"That night — "

A muscle leaped in his jaw. "It matters not."

"It does. I should not keep secrets from you."

He made a hissing sound as if he had burned himself. "Then don't."

She nodded, feeling the color drain from her face. "I must tell you everything. Three years ago, when Wynter first came to Blackrose . . ." She paused to take a shuddery breath.

"He *raped* you?"

Lark hesitated. She knew she could continue to lie, knew Oliver would offer sympathy, not censure, if he believed she had been the innocent victim. But she could speak nothing but the truth.

She must tell him the prim little religious maid had been a mask; inside she was as corrupt as any Southwark lightskirt.

"Oliver, he did not force me. I found him fascinating. He was witty, attractive. He made *me* feel attractive. But it was wrong. I sinned. I betrayed Spencer."

"Ah, Lark — "

"Wynter used me, and I allowed it. So long as I was worried Spencer might find out, I was Wynter's prisoner." She searched Oliver's face for censure, for disgust, but saw only sympathy glowing in his eyes. "I — I thought you should know," she finished, feeling exhausted.

"And now I do." He took a step closer, smiled, and kissed her, the baby gently pressed between them. "Do you think, after all we have endured, that it could possibly matter in the least?"

A cry broke from her as she flung her arms around his neck. The healing warmth of his love flowed into her. As she covered his laughing face with kisses, shouts drifted up from the courtyard.

Oliver went to a side panel of the window, hoisted himself to the waist-high embrasure, and looked down.

He emitted a foul curse that brought Lark rushing to his side. Far below, on the stone courtyard, a guard rushed toward the armory. He was bleeding from the arm and shouting orders.

"Oliver!" Cold fear invaded her. "What — "

The door burst open. Like a black flame, Wynter swept into the room. His sword was drawn, and a menacing troop of soldiers guarded his back.

"Sweet Jesu," Lark whispered.

Oliver thrust the baby into her arms and drew his own sword. "You didn't learn your lesson the first time, Wynter," he said. "I warned you to stay away from my wife."

"You can't fight him," Lark protested. She felt vulnerable, defenseless, with the baby in her arms. "There are too many of them!"

Oliver smiled, never taking his eyes off Wynter. "Don't you know I'd fight an army for you, Lark? Don't you know I'd win?"

Wynter lunged. Oliver feinted back against a paneled wall. The point of Wynter's sword stuck into the wood. He jerked it out and thrust again. Shouting in Spanish and English, the mercenaries boiled into the room.

Lark clutched the baby to her breast. She tried to scream, but terror numbed her throat. She cast about for a means to help Oliver. The room had no furniture save the makeshift font and a long seat built beneath the broad window. Her free hand stole up to grip the brooch fastend at her shoulder.

Oliver's blade slashed out, drawing blood from one of the soldiers. Like a pack of dogs they surrounded him, cornered him. He edged back toward the window and leaped up on the ledge.

A commotion erupted at the door. Lark spied Kit and Belinda, both armed to the teeth. Kit's old fashioned longsword scythed down two soldiers at the doorway. Belinda's thin rapier, wielded deftly despite her heavy velvet skirts, stung a Spaniard in the face. He howled, sinking to his knees and clutching his eye.

Despite the imprisonment that had sapped his strength, Oliver fought like a champion. His lithe dance steps seemed regulated by some smooth inner rhythm. He met every slice and thrust of Wynter's sword. He stayed high, with the window at his back. Light from the colored glass bathed him in ruby and emerald. He looked somehow greater than human, godlike, invincible.

Yet all that separated him from thin air was that fragile glass. Wynter forced him back against the window. Lark felt a scream build in her chest. At the impact of Oliver's shoulder and hip, the leaded panes bowed outward with a high-pitched wrenching sound.

Without warning, Wynter ducked beneath Oliver's flashing blade. He landed on the window ledge. Instead of attacking Oliver from his new position, he knocked Lark's coif askew and grabbed her by the hair. He yanked back her head and pressed the edge of his sword to her neck.

Her shrill yelp froze everyone in the room. The touch of Wynter's sword did not hurt, but she knew that with the slightest pressure, he could open her neck.

In the stillness she heard her own heart beating and the kittenish sounds of the baby, getting hungry. She felt the cool smoothness of the dagger in her hand, concealed in the folds of the baby's swaddling. She heard the rasp of the mercenaries panting in exertion and, not so distant now, the clear blaring of a trumpet.

A herald bringing news, she thought.

She wondered if she would live to hear it.

"Drop your swords," Wynter said. He stepped down from the window seat and shoved himself directly behind Lark.

Oliver's blade clattered to the floor. Kit and Belinda obeyed as well.

Rage seared Lark. "You are a hateful, vindictive man, Wynter!"

"Best watch what you say, my dear." His silky whisper warmed her ear. He teased her with the sword tip, caressing her vulnerable neck. "The queen has been brought to bed," he explained. "Some say to give birth to an heir." In that same lilting voice, he said, "Take it, Diego."

One of the soldiers moved forward.

"I'll send you to hell, you mad whoreson," Oliver said in a voice that thrummed with fury.

Lark felt the movement of Wynter's chest against her back as he laughed in triumph. "You *live* in hell, my lord. I put you there. I put you there the night I took Lark's honor, when it was *my* name she cried out, when it was *me* she wanted. You never had a virgin bride, because I took that from you."

The color dropped from Oliver's face. Lark dared not breathe. Oliver had said he did not care, but to hear Wynter proclaim his mastery of her drove the insult deep.

At last Oliver spoke. "You mean less than nothing to her now, Wynter. You destroyed any tenderness she might have had for you."

"*The queen is dead!*" The shout rose from the courtyard. Footsteps echoed in the stairwells.

Lark felt the sword falter against her neck.

"*Long live Queen Elizabeth!*"

The cries gathered strength, echoing across the gardens and through the halls of Hatfield.

Wynter made a wordless sound of disbelief. Lark shoved his sword arm away. With the same movement, she jabbed the dagger at his arm. A ribbon of blood streamed from the wound, and he swore. Like a cornered wildcat, he leaped backward onto the window ledge and crouched low, defensive, snarling, lashing out.

Lark ducked beneath his flashing blade. She sank to the floor, protecting the baby against her chest. Oliver leaped down from the ledge and snatched up his sword. Before Lark could sit upright, Oliver had the tip pressed to Wynter's crotch.

"I always knew you didn't have the balls to

397

fight like a man, you fu — "

"*What in God's name is going on here?*"

Elizabeth stood in the doorway, her face stern, her body rigid as steel.

Wynter's mercenaries melted en masse into a floor-deep obeisance.

"There goes loyalty," Oliver said cheerfully. "Your Majesty" — he seemed to relish the title — "I fear this man had a most pernicious plot in mind."

"I thought as much. My marshal warned me that some unwanted crew of patches had lately arrived."

"*Long live Queen Elizabeth!*" The glad cry rose from all quarters and seemed to shake the very glass in the windows. For a moment Elizabeth closed her eyes, then opened them.

Absently massaging her throat, Lark stared at her. Though only moments a queen, she already had an air of fierce, gorgeous majesty that struck at the heart. The pale face was not gentle; the black Tudor eyes were not kind.

She would make a magnificent queen.

And she did have a heart, for it showed when her gaze fixed on Wynter, who still stood on the window ledge. The beautiful design in the colored glass framed him, setting off his extraordinary male beauty. Just for a moment, Lark saw pity and grief flicker in Elizabeth's eyes.

Would her woman's heart show him mercy, or would she play the monarch?

"Arrest that man," she commanded. Instantly a troop of guards entered the chamber.

Oliver blew out a sigh of relief and sheathed his sword. Lark went to his side and leaned weakly against him.

Wynter's face, with runnels of sweat pouring down it, filled with an eerie sort of ecstasy. "A curse be on your reign, Elizabeth Tudor, you whore's bastard, you devil's get!" The venom in his voice was a poison that froze them all. "May you be as miserable and barren as your sister."

With a vicious sound — laughter or sobbing; Lark could not be certain — Wynter hurled himself at the glass window. His shoulder caused the leaded panes to bow outward. The household guard rushed toward him. Wynter hurled himself again. This time the impact wrenched at leading and casement.

Even as he crashed through the splintering colored glass, he looked darkly beautiful, his face hard and jubilant, his black sleeves fluttering like broken wings.

Lark gave a strangled, horrified cry and buried her face against Oliver's shoulder.

Elizabeth appeared paler than ever, but she refused the arm held out by William Cecil. Her skirts swished busily as she approached Oliver and Lark.

"Madam," said Oliver, "his curses meant nothing! The ravings of a madman, no more. It — "

"Is forgotten. This is a day of joy." She gave a forced smile, and with a start Lark realized that the incident with Wynter *was* forgotten, because the queen had decreed it so.

Elizabeth lowered her voice so no one else could hear. "I hardly know what to do."

Oliver sent her a self-deprecating grin. "No more than I." He whispered, "I suppose I should grovel and seek your favor, but good Lord, Bess, I have all I ever wanted right here in my arms."

"And so you have." The young queen's cheeks took on fresh color, and her voice grew loud and steady. "My lord, this child will need my blessing, for she has an incorrigible rascal for a father."

Epilogue

"WE named her Philippa because Queen Mary wanted it thus," Oliver said to his youngest granddaughter, a carrot-topped cherub in his lap.

"I insisted," Lark said softly. They sat on a long couch in front of the hearth in the great hall of Blackrose Priory, with borzoya dogs slumbering amid the rushes and a little girl gazing up in wonder at her handsome grandfather.

Oliver caught Lark's eye and winked. They had raised a brood of children and grand-children, yet his wink still caused a quiet radiance to glow inside her. King James was on the throne. Oliver, once convinced he was doomed to an early death, had served Queen Elizabeth through all the years of her reign.

Bessie looked up with shining eyes and said, "Grandpapa, you've told me wondrous tales about you and Grandmama. What about *my* mother and father?"

Just for a moment, a cloud shadowed Lark's perfect happiness. Involuntarily she touched the Romanov brooch, the gift from Juliana, encrusted now with new and precious stones to replace the ones Philippa had been forced to sell, one by one.

Oliver seemed to sense her mood, and he slid his arm around her. Love and comfort flowed between them, and Lark sighed with contentment, feeling the fullness of the years they had shared.

"Well?" Bessie demanded, her curls bouncing with impatience.

Oliver chuckled and set the child on the floor, sending her off to play with a gentle swat on the backside. "That, my prying sweet, is another story altogether."

When Bessie was gone, Oliver kissed his wife lustily on the mouth until she was laughing and breathless. "What sort of grandpapa are you," she demanded, "making love to your wife instead of telling stories to Bessie?"

"I'll tell stories when I'm in my dotage." His smile awakened the old magic, and he held her close before adding, "We de Laceys are full of them."

Announcing . . .

Niagara Large Print!

A brand new series of Large Print books
by *American* authors
— on topics of special interest
to *American Large Print readers*!

- **All guaranteed great reads . . .**

  Niagara selections are guaranteed to be of
  special interest or well-reviewed in journals
  respected in American libraries — unlike
  the no-name filler titles that come with
  many standing order plans.

- **Richly appointed editions . . .**

  These deluxe hardcovers will be presented in
  a dual-jacketed format — a traditional dust
  jacket over a full-color laminated hardcover,
  with decorative end pages and top- and
  tail-bands.

- **A Multi-purpose collection —
  a well-rounded, eclectic mix . . .**

Offering a range of high-quality, best-selling titles usually ignored by Large Print publishers, Niagara has everything to delight the widest possible spectrum of Large Print readers. Unlike genre-restricted lines, Niagara is a multi-use collection geared to the walk-in Large Print patron but equally suited to the homebound Large Print reader.

- **Instant book recognition —
  original covers . . .**

Niagara Large Print editions feature original cover art, which will trigger instant recognition by Large Print patrons who've seen the small-print hardcover and paperback versions on display in bookstores and malls.

- **Customer Service and
  the Ulverscroft Guarantee . . .**

We take pride in our customer service — always prompt, professional, and personal. If you have a question about a book or shipment, an editorial suggestion, or any problem we may be able to help solve, just give us a call. If you are ever dissatisfied with any book — for any reason at all — you always have the option of replacement, credit to your account, or a full refund.

FICTION WR

1/96